MW00425031

Murder at
Point Breeze

By

Arthur Cola

Book Six

De Cenza Murder Mysteries

Cover Design by

Connor Christopher Smith

Murder at Point Breeze

Published in 2022 by FeedARead.com Publishing

Copyright © Arthur Cola (Colaianni)

First Edition

A CIP catalogue record for this title is available from the British
Library.

Murder at Point Breeze
By

Arthur Cola

A De Cenza Murder Mystery
Book Six

Book Cover Design by
Connor Christopher Smith

Dedication:

To my wife, Donna, for all her support and love and to our children, (Ron + Tricia, Jana + Chris, Kathy + Mark, Johnny + Elena, Rich and to our grandchildren, Olivia, Arthur, Connor, Riley, Mack+ Kaylee, Meghan and Angelina), who are always there to inspire me.

Curtain holder of Joesph Bonaparte

The Autobiography of Joseph Bonaparte, Original Edition
Courtesy of Mr. Peter Tucci

Table of Contents:

Coins showing Joseph Bonaparte as King of Spain
Courtesy of Mr. Peter Tucci

Chapter One:
Special Delivery

A golden sun peeked out from behind a passing dark cloud which threatened to drop some rain upon the tiny Hamlet of Natural Bridge. They call themselves a hamlet for this tiny dot of population in the otherwise rather well known New York urban centers such as Buffalo, Syracuse and even Albany wasn't even large enough to consider themselves a Village let alone a town. In any case this Hamlet tucked away in upstate New York did have a history and what a history it was for them. The ancestors of most of the families living there had flirted with a King and brother of none other than Napoleon Bonaparte. Unfortunately for them even back in the first quarter of the 19th Century that flirtation did not bring growth but it did bring legend and prestige. The man who brought them such fame was Joseph Bonaparte the older brother of Napoleon who himself was King of the Kingdom of the Two Sicilies when his Emperor Brother made him King of Spain. The high point of his public life came crashing down when his brother finally surrendered for the second time in 1815. Joseph escaped to Switzerland and bought the Chateau Prangins not far from Geneva also on Geneva Lake at the foot of the Alps. His stay in Switzerland was not long lived as his life was constantly in danger from the British and others who sought him. Taking on the name of the Count de Survilliers he fled to America and legend has it that he took with him the Crown Jewels of Spain.

All of this footnote in History was flooding the thoughts of Francois Parrot, who himself was a descendant of note as he was the great great grandson of the cook brought to America by Joseph Bonaparte also bearing the same name which had been handed down through the generations to the eldest male in the family. At twenty-five, he was a dashing figure of a young man who carried himself as if he were a Bonaparte rather than a descendant of Bonaparte's cook. He twisted with a flourish the tiny handlebar mustache of thick black and then pulled at the goatee about his chin also dark as night. His appearance would have made him more at home in Paris or perhaps Montreal so obviously French was he in appearance and mannerisms. Even the dark hair on his head was worn not long but rather short in Bonaparte style though for the famous brothers it was due mainly for the lack of bushy thick hair which was not his case at all. So too, his height of 5'10" would surpass that of his double great grandfather's King and the Emperor as well. In any case, he may have strolled out of the wooden one story Post Office as nobility but his form of dress was anything but regal. He wore tight fitting Levi Jeans, a white tee-shirt under a gray sweatshirt which he wore despite it being late August, for there was a chill in the air. It was also a form of advertising for on it was printed **Bonaparte Boat Launch and Lunch**. He was carrying on the family business which though focused on renting boats also ran a small restaurant where tourists may grab a snack either for the boat ride or dine in or out on the terrace overlooking the lake which bore the name of his ancestor's boss. He stepped out of the Post Office intending to get into his blue 1966 Ford LTD for the drive to Lake Bonaparte some twenty minutes from where he stood. The American flag flapped in the building breeze over his head as a voice called out to him.

"Francois, hold on a minute." Out ran a lovely young woman. Her flashing bright eyes laser focused on the broad shoulders and strong arms of a man who worked outdoors as well as in the kitchen. She was waving a letter tightly held in her hand as she crashed into him.
The keys fell onto the pavement as Francois banged into the car door.

"Sarah, are you all right?" he took her by the arms and gently removed the letter in her shaking hands. Smiling he asked if the letter was for him.

"I'm fine, but I thought you would want to see this as it just came in and since you picked up another Special Delivery letter just now I thought it might be related and important." She rambled on about the significance of receiving Special Delivery Letters in Natural Bridge at all let alone three in one day.

Francois gently pushed to the side the long sandy brown hair from her face. "*Qui mon amie,* I can see your point but you didn't have to chase me down. I am standing right in front of the Post Office." He added a bit of French for he knew it thrilled her when he did so. It was their little flirtation as they had been friends since elementary school days. He looked at her with a question forming as he pulled up his shirt just high enough to reveal a tuft of hair coming up above his belt line. He pulled out the letter from under his belt which had been given to him just minutes prior to the collision.

The revelation did not go unnoticed by Sarah Dupres, who if a family research would have been done would have found out that she was a descendant of a family who fled France during the French Revolution. Many refugees settled in upstate New York and into Quebec province in Canada during those dark years before Napoleon Bonaparte took over the country and most of Europe.

"Well I'm sorry to have bumped into you but I thought it was important." Sarah turned to walk away.

A hand gently took her arm and swung her around. "Sarah Dupres, I am most grateful for the concern. But it's probably just another bill and they are anxious for payment." He bent down and kissed her cheek. "But now I really must get to work. Forgive me. Come by for lunch…on me when your shift ends."

She glanced down at the arm still holding her gently but having slipped down to her wrist. "I think I'll be all right Francois," she picked at his fingers and removed his hand, then grinned. "I'll see you for a late lunch." Off she ran back into the Post Office leaving him with the second letter in hand."

"Hey, wait just a second, Sarah."

She turned with a confused look his way. "What's wrong?"

"Nothing, but you said that there were three Special delivery letters and you only gave me two."

Placing her hands on her hips and taking a stance which said more than the words she spoke, she informed him that he was not the most important resident of Natural Bridge since Joseph Bonaparte. The third letter came at the same time the second one did and from the same

place she informed him while not revealing the name of the person who was to receive it.

"So who is the important person who isn't me?"

"Francois Parrot, really…you know that I cannot tell you that but I can tell you that it was postmarked from Princeton New Jersey just like your second letter."

"Oh then it's probably from the University as well," he replied. "I wonder what's so important that this letter needed to be sent Special Delivery?"

"Perhaps you should read your letters and find out. When I come for lunch, you can tell me all about the important Princeton University invitation to speak to some tourist group about your great-great grandfather. They surely would be thrilled to learn how he helped Joseph Bonaparte come to America by feeding him the best of French cuisine." She laughed at her attempt at humor.

Once again he lifted his shirt and she sighed as he tucked in the letter into his belt totally oblivious to her teetering on swooning. "Why wait for lunch." He quickly pulled out and tore open the first letter and indeed it was from Princeton University. It was a letter of introduction from a Professor Dorothy Witherspoon of the Archeology Department. He knew her well when he was a student there. He purposely took her class to hone his skills as he like so many before him believed in the lost treasure of Joseph Bonaparte. It was worth his time if for no other reason than to get tourists to rent his boats to cross the lake to the caverns and locations which were said to have been the site of Bonaparte's house and that of his mistress Annette Savage.

The latter was not a legend but it did become a folk tale. Annette Savage did stay in America in the New Jersey estate of Point Breeze when Joseph returned to Europe and to his wife and daughters. Her daughter by Joseph, Caroline, eventually married into the Benton family in the City of Bordentown in New Jersey when they returned there. There was no hope of going to Europe with Joseph. They had to remain in America and the Benton family would afford them some prestige and respectability.

Francois leaned against his car, folded the letter and returned it under his belt while keeping his second letter in hand. "Nothing special Sarah, just my Professor introducing some other Professor from Oxford University who's coming here with a group of his students in search of you know what…"

"Oh my God, no kidding, another treasure hunting party; well at least you'll make money off of them."

They laughed as he opened the second letter. "Will you look at this; it's from that Professor guy, an Andrew Pettigrew of Oxford University, very posh and formal."

"He's British, what do you expect. He's probably still gloating for having defeated the brother of your ancestor's boss."

"Let's not get rude, as you said, they'll need to eat, be housed and maybe rent a boat, a good sized one too from the looks of the research party he's bringing with him…six men and two women from what I read here. He wants me to find him a house to rent. He and his group will be here in a few days."

"So now you are in real estate too?"

"Let's not be caddy Sarah, the Professor is just asking for a favor and I do have rental cabins on Birch Island in the middle of the lake."

She smiled devilishly. "And if they're on the island they will have to rent a boat to get around. What a clever boy you are Francois Parrot."

He gave her a wink and a grin as he waved the letter above his head while entering his car. He shouted back to her as he did so. "My *Arriere-gran-pere* may have been a cook but he was no dummy...well except for one thing. He let that damn secretary to Joseph, what's his name...ah qui, Louis Maillard to be the only one who knew of the

Crown Jewels and their true whereabouts. *Se le vie,* such is life as they say across the border and the ocean as well. See you later."

"*Qui*, I mean okay, you said you'd feed me don't forget." Sarah skipped into the Post Office entrance just as the phone rang. She ran, stumbled over the desk chair and crashed to the floor with phone in hand. All of that just to catch the call. "United State Post Office of Natural Bridge, this is Sarah Dupres may I help you?"

The voice on the other end of the line was quite agitated and belonged to a young person whose voice had barely time to change into that of a full grown man. The boy was one of several teens Francois had hired for the summer months to help with the boat and cabin rentals. "Yes, Sarah, it's Jack Shields, you know me. I work for Mr. Parrot at his boat shop. I need to speak with him immediately; he said he was going to Natural Bridge to pick up a letter or something." The teen was quite beside himself as he rambled on.

"Yes, of course, Jack is it? I do remember. Now just calm down what seems to be the problem?"

"Oh God, it's just terrible, I need Mr. Parrot right away." In the background weeping and shouting could be heard. "There's been a horrible accident."

"Dear God, how bad? I mean Mr. Parrot has just left not more than a minute ago. He should be there in ten minutes knowing how he drives. Did you call the police?"

"Police, oh no...I thought Mr. Parrot would want to do that; should I...I mean should I call them, right now?"

14

"Never mind Jack, just take care of... what exactly was the accident? And don't worry I'll call the Sherriff's department, do you need an ambulance too?"

"Ambulance? Oh I think it's a bit late for that; he's not moving at all." Jack went on to explain that he thought that he, Sally Greenberg and Jeff Castignino had found a dead man floating in the lake. Not exactly in the lake but in one of the rental boats stuck on a sand bar just outside of the limestone mouth to the cavern of Joseph Bonaparte. It was so called because for the last hundred plus years many tourists and treasure hunters searched that cave. Rumor had it that Joseph had buried the Crown Jewels of Spain somewhere in it. Over a century later and nothing had ever been found to indicate that burial.

"Listen carefully Jack. First tell Jeff to get some water and have Sally, Jeff and you drink it. Then go back to where this person you found is…I mean you didn't move him did you?"

"Oh no, he's still out there floating…"

"Good, I mean, I see. Okay then after you're hydrated, go back to this person and let no one come near the scene or touch anything until Mr. Parrot and the Sheriff gets there. Do you understand?"

"Yes Miss Dupres, I understand." Sarah could hear Jack shout the orders to Jeff and Sally as she hung up the phone.

"Now listen up guys, here's what we need to do…"

While the three teens were making their way back onto the lake in one of the motorboats, Francois was on North Bonaparte Road and viewing flashing red lights in his rear view mirror. At first, he thought the police could be pulling him aside as he was rushing to get back to his restaurant and boat shop. He wanted to insure that all would be well for the group, with ties to Princeton University, which was coming from Europe. He pulled over cursing that he was going to get a ticket. But he was soon relieved that they were obviously after someone else, as they passed him by without so much as a look his

Murder at Point Breeze

way. But he looked at them and saw that it was a Sheriff's car from the Town of Diana which was the township in which Lake Bonaparte and his establishment were located. As soon as they were out of sight, he sped up all the while wondering where they were going as it seemed they were headed to the lake. He began to panic thinking that it might

be his restaurant which may have been robbed or something like that. Down he pressed on the gas pedal.

While Francois planned his response to the Special Delivery letter as he sped down Bonaparte Road across the pond, as frequent travelers referred to the Atlantic Ocean, night had fallen and dreams were becoming a Nightmare.

By the time the so called clever boy responded to Professor Pettigrew's letter confirming lodging and a boat rental it was already the middle of the night in Europe. The telegram would not be received until the following morning and what a morning it would become.

The waning sun casts a golden glow over the Roman Forum as the pillars of the Temple of Saturn seem to illuminate as in a Biblical scene from the classic movie of "The Ten Commandments" when God is giving Moses His law. Like columns of spinning fiery flames the ruins of the Pagan Temple glows in reddish gold light and casts its shadow over the entire Forum. Through those columns runs a young man, not terribly tall nor was he particularly broad in the shoulder but quite striking nonetheless, with his dark coal-like hair being swirled about by the now zesty breeze, possessing an enduring strength. With hardly a heavy breath his piercing cocoa brown eyes survey the ruins about him and come to rest on a broken column of marble upon which lays a worn brown leather bound Book trimmed in gold. That same gust of wind was bringing relief to what was a rather warm day in Rome in late summer. It also was doing its best to create a bad hair day for the young man was also flipping the yellowing pages within the open Book on the now golden illuminated millennial years old pillar cracked yet standing the test of time.

He pauses to take in the sight and let the building breeze cross his bare chest. It causes the tiny patch of hair in the shape of a cross right over his breast plate to feel a comforting caress. The black hair strands shiver like tips of wheat in the Monks' farm field back behind the Wisconsin Abbey's Latin School where his story and that of the Book he pauses to examine began. Though at the time totally disconnected with what lay before his excited eyes the events which were set in motion as he studied for the priesthood have brought him to this moment in the Eternal City. But it was a particular event which exploded his vocation almost instantaneously. It was his attraction for a certain young lady who he met in that Abbey which changed the course of his vocation. It was over a short period of time as this lovely young woman with the flaming long hair to rival that which was set aglow in the temple ruins would enter his life, in fact not just his, but his best pal's life as well. And what an entrance that was; he could feel his entire body changing each time she was near him. Oh what changes occurred.

His thoughts went back to those early days and how they brought him to this moment and to the Book which lay on the pillar. He quickly pulled the elastic band on his white silk running shorts and peered down into them with a sigh of relief. All was well. What usually happened when she was around was not happening. Letting go of the stretched out elastic band it snapped back onto his abdomen just below his belly button. He jumped from the twinge of discomfort and turned about to insure that no one was witnessing his little examination. The forum was desolate of people save for himself.

Between the sigh of relief and relishing the comfortable feeling of the cooling breeze across his body another gust turned the yellowing pages once again. His eyes immediately saw the notations made in Latin on the edges of the pages now exposed. Luckily he still retained the basics of the language of the Church for was it not that the entire reason which had him sent to the Latin School of St. Benedict in the first place. That is to learn the ancient language in preparation to study at the Apostolic College in Rome once he had the fundamental grasp of it.

He began to translate the handwritten notes but they were not in reference to Church law or theology. In fact the entire Book was about the life and times of the older brother of Napoleon Bonaparte, one called Joseph Bonaparte. Now Joseph was once the King of the Kingdom of the Two Sicilies until his brother, who had become Emperor of France, made him the King of Spain. That of course all fell apart when Napoleon was defeated and Joseph fled Spain eventually

for America. The young man from Chicago smiled as he translated the notes. He was so proud not only that he could do so but also because it was he who broke the code within the pages.

The code breaking verified the truth to a legend surrounding Joseph's years in Switzerland, Italy and America after the fall of Napoleon and his escape from Spain in the second decade of the 19th Century. This pride now swelling in that uncovered chest was not totally the result of the code cracking. Much of it was related to the defeat of others who also sought the Book and the code within it. The fact that he could run through the Forum, examine the Book at all was a small miracle in that one called Niccolo Cavelli almost succeeded in having him killed; not only him but also the love of his life, Susan Marie Liguri, his best pal, Bob Wentz, his own sister, Jan De Cenza and her beau, Alessandro, Count of Pianore, their new friends Swiss Papal Guard Andreas Berne and the love of his life, the Vatican Archivist Dominic Fontana. The fact that any of them were still walking the streets of Rome or anywhere had almost ended on the Isle of Capri.

But that was all behind them now as they possessed the Book titled "Memoires Politque et Militaire Roi Joseph." That autobiography of King Joseph Bonaparte was supposed to change the lives of two hunky men in the service of a rather important man in Naples and throughout Italy. But instead they were betrayed by their boss, Niccolo Cavelli at the same time as they had decided to use the Book themselves and not give its details to him. Cavelli, after quite the escapade on Capri, was ultimately trapped by his own words in Santa Croce Church in Florence, Italy by this young man from Chicago, Ron De Cenza.

Now Niccolo Cavelli was in prison and love was now in bloom for the three couples. Such pairing of course had left out Ron's Watson, his best pal. Bob remained the odd man out as he still was on the road to the priesthood within the Catholic Church. The young man placed his hands on his hips and smiled with satisfaction at their discovery and victory over such a tyrannical beast who would stoop to theft and murder to get his hands on that Book.

As he reached to take hold of the Book, another gust of wind flipped the pages and out floated an engraved card. It was actually an invitation. The young man recognized it immediately and grabbed hold of it as it was lifted off the pages and floated in the air before him. He read it aloud.

"The Families of
Ronald De Cenza and Susan Marie Liguri
Request the honor of your presence at the celebration of their
engagement."

It suddenly dawned on Ron as to why he was in such a hurry as to take a short cut through the Roman Forum almost naked. His special clothes had been sent ahead by his soon to be Best Man, Bob, with the other costumes of the day. He quickly tucked the card into the Book, closed the almost century and a half old Book carefully. With the Book firmly in his grasp he looked up.

There just beyond the Arch of Constantine at the beginning of the Forum was the site for the celebration. The ancient monument to Gladiatorial Combat, Circus performances and persecution of the Christians stood waiting for his arrival. It too was aglow in golden light enhanced by floodlights at the base surrounding its huge circumference. The arches picked up the light as did the now bare brick and mortar, which was once underneath a marble façade. The scene gave off an eerie feeling of stepping back in time. But instead of parades and blaring trumpets announcing the Gladiators he could only hear a band tuning up for the performance that he was to headline with his pals and his gal. The Roman Colosseum was waiting for his arrival and so were the guests.

Holding the Book tightly in his hand as if it was a baton used in running a relay race in the ancient games, off he sped.

Pacing in front of the gate entrance for tourists on the street level was Ron's Watson. Bob was his best friend and soon to be Best Man at Susan and Ron's wedding. His eyes took hold of a young guy streaking, well almost anyway, under the Arch of Constantine. Bob ran to his Sherlock for that is how they referred to each other when they

were on a case such as the one in which the Book on Joseph Bonaparte was discovered along with its legend. He and Ron fancied themselves as Modern Day detectives not unlike Sherlock Holmes and Dr. Watson of literary fame. He intercepted his pal and brought him to a standstill. Given that he outweighed Ron by a good fifty pounds that wasn't too difficult to do.

"Oh my God… look at you. Where the hell have you been? Everyone is waiting for us to kick off the party. Even Professor Pettigrew came from England just for this. Well maybe not just for the engagement; he is dying to see the Book." Bob handed Ron a white cotton terry cloth bath towel he had taken from the Hotel Excelsior where they were staying. "You're sweating like a pig. Dry off, I've got your costume in the bag at the gate."

Ron handed off the Book and began to wipe his face. "So in answer to your question pal, I was taking a shortcut through the Forum when I saw the Book. How the hell did it get into the Forum? Our whole investigation would be impossible if I had not found it just lying there on some broken marble pillar."

"Well don't look at me. I was only in charge of the outfits for the opening number. The Book was your responsibility."

"Aw, don't get that blond head of yours all uppity with me." Ron paused and actually looked at his Watson all dressed up to kill. "Hey, man, you're looking good."

Bob's round cherub-like face became instantly flushed. "Yeah, you really think so?"

"Shit man, the girls will swoon just looking at you…"

20

"The girls!" he shouted. "You know I can't let anything happen."

"So what are you saying Bob; are you now into the guys like Andreas and Dominic? Well that's okay; in any case you're going to sweep them off their feet."
The blushing evaporated and he swung around into his best pal's face. "Now listen to me asshole who I love more than anyone except the Church of course. You know damn well that I meant that priests can't be married or have sexual relations with women or men for that matter."

"Okay, okay, I'm sorry… I just wanted to compliment you and now I've upset you."

"Watson doesn't get upset; he knows how you are." Bob threw his arm around Ron and led him off to the gate and the hanging bag.

"In any case, Susan and Jan were right; that white satin dinner jacket and black statin pants are cool looking."

"Yeah, ain't it the truth… to quote my Lion friend from Oz. This purple silk shirt is cool too and doesn't make me too hot."

When they arrived at the Men's Room turned into a dressing room, they found the guys all in costume and ready to go. They matched Bob in white satin dinner jacket and black satin pants. Each guy however had a different color silk shirt. Andreas had a blue shirt, Dominic a green shirt, Alessandro in a red one. In short order they had Ron in his costume of Gold satin dinner jacket and pants with a white silk shirt.

"Listen guys, I look like that Apollo guy who tried to kill me…"
"Stop it right there buddy boy," began Dominic. "You will slay the crowd and more important Susan will love it."

"Okay Dom, you're the fashion guy so I'll trust you…but really gold everything?"

As the laughter subsided, the music could be heard and then the Professor could be heard at the mike.

"Hi there ladies and gentlemen and all of Rome, we're here to celebrate love and what better way to do that than by having those who are in love entertain you with a very appropriate song. So here they are, "Michelangelo's Bunch."

The spotlight dimmed and soon golden color lights illuminated the stage made up of boards placed over the underground tunnel walls where the animals, Christians and Gladiators once waited to come onto the dirt and sand covered flooring of the Colosseum. In that light the four guys were standing just to stage right and the girls on stage left. The white spots then flashed across them. Jan dressed in a turquoise sequined gown and Susan in white sequins over satin.

Softly at first they began to sing the Lloyd Price song which Ron had gone crazy with on the night when he and Susan were to be engaged. Of course the lyrics were slightly changed from Johnny's gonna get married to Ronnie's gonna get married.

"Ronnie, Ronnie, Ronnie...Ronnie you're too young," the guys sang and then the spot shifted to center stage and up from below the boards rose Ronnie in his gold satin costume.

"But I'm gonna get married," he sang out as he jumped about the stage taking on an energy which had the family and guests in the stone archways clapping along high above them. The seating area was long gone but not the open hallways which led visitors into the Colosseum. And so the song continued..."you're too young..."

Ron responding, "My name she'll carry..."

"You're too young Ronnie, you're so smart..."

"But not smart enough to hide an aching heart," Ron then did a twist type step up to Susan taking her hand and twirling her into his arms continuing to sing, "How come my heart deserts me, burning full of love and desire, how come every time you kiss me, It sets my heart on fire…"

All the while the guys and Jan were singing the background, "Ronnie you're too young."
And then it happened, Ron leaned into Susan and kissed her. They fell to the floor of the stage as the audience went wild and the music blared on as they held onto each other in a passionate embrace.

 Rolling across the boards making up the stage without a care in the world or conscious of their family and friends cheering them on, they came dangerously close to the edge. And then it happened, Ron rolled the wrong way and was falling off the stage as he pushed Susan away just as he fell down into the tunnels of the Colosseum.

Dazed but unhurt he opened those flashing eyes to find himself not in what could accurately be described as the basement of the Colosseum as it were but back in Switzerland where they had once saved the life of King Umberto II, the former King of Italy while solving a murder in The Vatican which took them to Lake Maggiore. He was holding the Book tightly in his grip. As his eyes grew accustomed to the light surrounding him, they focused on two things. The first was that he was back in his satin shorts and nothing else save the Autobiography of Joseph Bonaparte. Secondly, he soon realized that he was in the gardens of a castle of some kind. Hiding behind a row of precisely cut bushes in the French style he looked about the garden. At the far end he could see a grand Chateau also in the French style. Two men were running out of its garden doors as a man on horseback arrived handing the slimmer of the two a scroll and then riding off to warn others of what had happened at Waterloo.

"Your Majesty it's true. Your brother has surrendered to the British. What are we to do?"

The slightly pudgy man dressed in a cutaway coat, silk brocade vest over a non-ruffled shirt paused and fell to his knees weeping. "I knew this would end badly but I still cannot accept it. Napoleon, the only one who truly loved me is no longer Emperor. But he is still my brother; we shall work to get him free."

"Exactly Your Majesty but this is the time when we must be practical, where does that leave you?" The slimmer and taller man placed the metal box he held on the edge of the fountain in the center of the

garden. Placing the scroll into it but not before he lifted out a handful of glimmering jewels. "All you have are these, the Chateau will be lost, all that you see here will be lost if we do not act quickly."
Ron crawled on all fours along the bush line toward the fountain area to better hear the words, though in French he understood them completely.

The kneeling man rose, took a deep breath and placed his hand on the shoulder of the thin man dressed not unlike himself and yet obviously he was the subordinate of the man he called Your Majesty. "They will not harm my brother not now that he has surrendered but as for me, there are those who would see me dead."

Tears rolled down the cheeks of the man holding what could only be described as a treasure chest of precious jewels and coins of silver and gold.

"Ah my dear Louis, you have been steadfastly loyal to me since you entered my service when you were but a lad of thirteen and now you are my secretary and confidant. Through the good and these bad times, and these certainly are the bad times, you still have chosen to stay with me. Do not weep for me but for France and its future, for Spain where I was once their King and for my wife and daughters who must be sent away and be saved."

Ron choked then covered his mouth as if the men in the garden could hear his cough. "My God, that's Joseph Bonaparte of this Book, so then that must be Louis Maillard for that's who was his secretary in America and before that," he whispered aloud as he processed what he was witnessing.

"Why Spain Sire, they hated you since the day your brother made you their King."

"*Qui*, quite true but it was not their fault. My dear brother thought to create a united Europe but the powers of England, Austria and Russia thought otherwise. In any case those jewels which you hold are the Crown Jewels of the Spanish Crown. Let us say they are a gift to me for the bad treatment which I received. Now we must act quickly Louis. There is not a moment to lose."

"*Absolument* Majesty, what shall we do?"

"First, you will stop calling me Majesty. I shall have papers made declaring me to be the Count of Survilliers. Then we shall charter the ship called 'Commerce' for the crossing to see President Madison of the United States. Tell no one except those who will accompany us."
"Majesty…I am sorry Sire, Sir, who will come with us on such a perilous journey to this new land they call America?"

"Ah yes those loyal all these years to us. We'll ask James Carret; he's from America, a place called New York. He will be our interpreter. And we'll need Francois Parrot our cook, God only knows what kind of food exists in that wild land. And finally, let us ask Captain Unzaga from my Spanish protection team. He is good with weapons and can protect us."

"*Qui,* Sir, I shall contact them immediately. Time is of the essence…but what about these Sir?" Maillard held up the jewels.

"Those my dear Louis shall pay for the ship rental, buy us land in the United States, build our house there and provide us with a decent style of living. But we shall not take all of it lest we be found out by the British and they confiscate our treasure. We shall bury part of the jewels here in Switzerland and take the rest with us to America."

"Yes Sire…Sir, shall we choose a spot in the garden or in the cellars of the Chateau?"

"Neither Louis, those who are following me would dig up this garden and remove every brick of the Chateau should they think the jewels are here. No, we shall bury them between Chateau Prangins where we stand and the Chateau Nyon on the way to Geneva. Only you and I shall know where that burial shall take place. There is a road called l'Etraz which ends at the shoreline of Geneva Lake, there we shall find a secure spot amongst the ancient ruins from Roman times."

The scene blurred before Ron's eyes as shouting pierced his ears.

"Ron, come on you're going to be late." Bob shook and shook Ron but his pal kept pushing him away. Stop it; I know where the treasure will be…"

"Holy shit Ron, wake up…"

Ron took a swing at him.

"I'm gonna get married," he then began to sing.

Bob looked to the doorway of the room shaking his head at the three guys gathering for moral support if nothing else. "I think he's dreaming guys. It's like when we were on Capri and he decided to propose to Susan. He won't budge."

Andreas, Alessandro and Dominic ran to the bed and began to pick the whole bed up off the floor and shake it. Then they tilted it until Ron rolled off and hit the marble floor with an area rug covering with a thud and a screech of "Shit!"

Laying spread eagle on the floor in his Jockey shorts the now wide eyed Ron looked up into the four faces bent over him and speechless but in awe that Ron had been singing in his sleep. "What the hell guys…this isn't funny. I think I broke something." He checked down his shorts as the guys suddenly turned their backs on him snickering as he did so.

"Ron De Cenza, if you did it all over yourself again so help me I am not going to help you this time."

"Some best man you are pal. But you needn't worry. I'm okay down there not that it matters to you after all you'll never be using yours except to pee."

In a flash Bob pounced on Ron and they were rolling over the floor as the guys jumped out of the way. "You're such an asshole and this time I mean it with no love behind it." He was on top of Ron now pinning him to the cold marble floor as the other three stood in silence looking down on them.

"So you're all against me is that it? And here I was having such a cool dream and all you guys were in it and the girls too and then we sang and then I kissed Susan and then I was at the Chateau Prangins back in August of 1815 just learning about the treasure when all of you were knocking me on my ass. Why?"

"Well if you'd just listen," Bob began. "His Highness Prince Vittorio Emmanuel is about to leave and we thought we should all be there to say good-bye but you didn't show up, so I came for you and you pushed me away as usual. So the guys came to help rouse you and then this happened."

"Oh my God, shit, help me up… is he gone yet?" Ignoring the Son of the former King of Italy was hardly in his best interest especially after what happened on Brissago, the very island where he stood in Lake Maggiore. But that was over a year ago. Today was to begin a new adventure, actually some would call it a quest.

"Not yet," answered Alessandro, the young Count of Pianore. "Your parents, the parents of Andreas, Susan and her mother and Jan are entertaining him while we came to check up on you. Actually your mother is making the Prince breakfast."

"What, I didn't want my folks to come over here to serve people. They should be served on their vacation." Ron ran from the bureau after taking out clean underpants and to the wardrobe for a pair of pants and long sleeve white shirt. "I'll just hop in the shower, don't leave but don't come in either. No peeking." He laughed. "Seriously, I think I figured out where King Joseph's treasure was buried here in Switzerland."

"Get a grip Ron…okay hurry up and don't be so vain. No one wants to see that little thing of yours anyway." Bob huffed and puffed as being insulted at the thought of seeing his best pal naked knowing full well

that back in high school the male students swam in the nude in Gym Class in Oak Park Illinois. And then there was that time in the Abbey and again in Rome, he thought and then got miffed all over again that Ron would even think that he wanted to see it again.

Dominic snickered. "Well maybe just a little peek…" His effort to add levity worked.

The guys roared in laughter as the water splashed down on Ron. "You're all assholes; that's what you are. So anyway…in the dream," he went on to explain what he had seen at the Chateau Prangins as he shouted through the shower curtains to the guys gathered at the bathroom doorway with their backs toward him. But they were more interested in the part about singing in the Colosseum as "Michelangelo's Bunch."

Andreas of all people decided to actually sing and got the others to join him thus totally ignoring the real purpose of Ron's explanation of what he dreamed. "Hey, what was that song back in Capri that he sang? Okay, I remember, Johnny's Gonna Get Married."

"Right, but we changed the word to Ronnie," noted Alessandro.

"Exactly my dear Count so how about it… Shall we serenade our *amico*?"

Bob wrapped his arms across his chest and refused to sing. "I'm mad at him. All I did was to try and save him from embarrassment with the Prince and he gives me shit for doing it."

28

Dominic, the Vatican research assistant to Professor Pettigrew gave him a joshing poke in the belly over which his arms rested. "Come on Bob, it won't be funny without you…"

"And not nearly as entertaining; you have the best voice of all of us," agreed Andreas who was now the leader of "Michelangelo's Bunch."

Bob caved and hummed the opening notes. Soon they were in harmony and singing the song which Ron had in his dream. They paid the slightest attention to his rendering of that part of the seemingly real event but because they had done so once before on the Isle of Capri where they first learned of the Autobiography of Joseph Bonaparte and the legend of the lost Crown Jewels of Spain.

Andreas jumped into the bathroom forcing the guys to face him and the shower curtain behind which Ron was still retelling the dream as if they were attentively listening. "And a one, and a two…isn't that how that guy on TV in America does it?"

"Oh my God, Lawrence Welk are you serious; this is a rock and roll song by Lloyd Price, jazz it up," Bob was in to the swing of things in no time at all.

As the song rang out in that bathroom, a boy on a bicycle, his dispatch bag hanging over his back, made his way to the Berne Bed and Breakfast on Brissago Island in Lake Maggiore about two hours over the Swiss border from Italy.

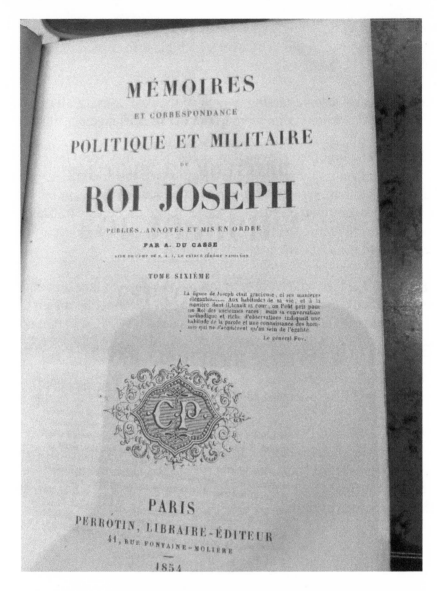

Title Page of the Autobiography of King Joseph Bonaparte
Courtesy of Mr. Peter Tucci

Chapter Two:
Breakfast and Telegrams

Rose De Cenza was in her glory preparing breakfast with the help of Andreas' mother, Julia Berne. She was assuring the girls and Susan's mother, who offered to help, that such a meal was no big deal. Back in Chicago when she prepared the meals for the entire De Cenza Family this gathering would be considered a small crowd at best.

"We just connected two folding tables to the dining room table and let it spill into the living room so that everyone could fit." Rose began to hum a tune. It was "That's Amore'" a favorite of hers especially now that their only son was to be married. Something else added to the joy as well. But she was sworn to secrecy and said nothing of it to Julia as she scrambled the eggs and added a dash of garlic. Into the kitchen walked the Countess of Pianore with Gertrude Liguri.

"Mrs. De Cenza, you must let us help," insisted the Countess.

"Oh no Countess, I am just fine. Ask the girls. Everything is under control, right Julia?"

"Indeed Rose," Julia looked at the faces of the dejected Countess and Mrs. Liguri realizing that they were seeking the company of the women as the men had gathered on the veranda. They had heard enough of the 1946 voting which ousted the Royal family of Italy. "So ladies are the men still talking about that vote."

"I'm afraid so and this being a day after a grand celebration announcing the coming union of our children and please my name is Eva to all of you."

"You mean Ron and Susan of course," Julia clarified.

"I mean no such thing Julia, if I may call you so familiarly. I mean them most assuredly but also your son, Andreas and that charming boy

Dominic from the Vatican. The poor thing is all alone with no family here in Brisaggo."

"I am touched that you recognize their love," the Countess and Julia Berne exchanged an embrace. "Come Eva, you and Gertrude can help us with cutting the bread and then we shall tell the men it will be their turn to cook the noon meal, how does that sound?"

Rose laughed. "It will be a poor meal if my Arthur has anything to do with it."

"Nevertheless, this is 1966 and women are no longer just in the kitchen," replied Eva, the Countess of Pianore in Umbria.

On that point all agreed and turned their attention to talk of weddings. In no time at all Susan and Jan had heard enough of women talk as well and slipped out to seek the guys. They collided with them as they jumped off the last stairs in their rush down. The typically styled Swiss wooden staircase with brightly colored symbols on wooden panels instead of spiraling wood pillars serving as the support for the railings would ordinarily be viewed with a comment on the Swiss decorative arts. However that wasn't going to happen, not on this day of days when all were still basking in the memory of the celebration of the engagements.

"Well it's about time. Our Moms are cooking up a storm and will hardly let the cook do a thing. So move your butts. We're going to set the table on the veranda for them," Jan took a stance with folded arms and Susan pointed to the china cabinet.

On that same veranda the Crown Prince Victor Emanuele III, Augusto Berne, the elder Count of Pianore who was known as Alex to avoid confusion with his son, and just plain ole Arthur De Cenza were sharing the story of the young Count of Pianore, Alessandro. Arthur was so enjoying telling how the shivering lad came to him in the middle of the party of the previous night to ask permission to propose to Jan. He abruptly ended his tale when the young people arrived with plates and silverware in hand and began the task of setting the table.

"Ah, the *ragazzi* are here and I must soon say farewell," began the Prince of Savoy.

While this time of joy on the Isle of Brisaggo in the middle of Lake Maggiore in the Southern Alps took place a slightly smaller gathering was taking place on the Swiss border side of Switzerland and France.

Walking in the Bains des Paquis, a beach along a narrow strip of land jutting out from the main shoreline of the City of Geneva into Lake Geneva were what seemed to be a couple. The two of them were in a deep conversation and oblivious to the sun bathers and swimmers. They had chosen that particular location for their conversation in an effort to appear like nothing more than tourists. Their attempt had failed however in that they were not dressed for the beach but rather for a ride up into the mountains for a cup of Hot Cocoa.

To Carolina Savage Gianetti who spent most of her life in Sorrento in Southern Italy, the August day was not conducive to a swim in her mind at least. The fact that she was even walking anywhere let alone in Switzerland was somewhat miraculous in that she had been shot on the Isle of Capri by the colleague of her lover. Her lover was none other than Niccolo Cavelli who was now in prison along with his so-called assistants Stefano Rinaldi and Apollo Dimitri. They too had been seeking the Book with the code to the legendary tale of Joseph Bonaparte and the treasure he was supposed to have hidden away in Switzerland and in America.

Their effort to succeed was defeated by Ron and his friends with the help of a certain Captain of the Carabinieri, Enrico Verdi and his new wife Sophia but not before Niccolo and his thugs tried to kill them. None of that was important to Carolina as she walked arm in arm with a man in his early forties. He like her was dressed more for a walk down the Corso in Rome or the streets of Paris than one on the beach. He stood a good six inches taller than her slender figure of voluptuous shape easily noticed under the sea blue dress which came just to her knee and flew up now and then revealing a lovely pair of legs to match that almost serene face which had known pampering and untold pleasures which a wealthy man offered her as well as those of the flesh. She could tease a man to distraction and this she did often until that frightful day when a bullet almost ended her life and did end Niccolo Cavelli's privileged life style forever. She gave a fleeting thought to that time as she walked with the American man dressed in a suit coat and tie as if going to the office.

Carolina adjusted her broad rimmed white linen hat as if to conceal any possibility of someone recognizing her. "My dear Signore' Benton, these days of getting to know one another have been most charming but now the time has come to enact a plan of action."

"*Signorina*, there is no need to be so formal, Charles if you please. After all we are *cugini,* cousins related through the Savage family blood line. And as to this plan may I say that I have already sent a telegram to my contact in the Lake Bonaparte region of upstate New York. Antoine Murat will keep me abreast of the visitors which your men have been following here and when they arrive at the Town of Natural Bridge just outside the Lake Bonaparte region."

"Si cousin, that is all well and good; but let us not lose our focus on the prize. Everything must be planned to perfection. Luigi and Pietro should be returning soon and then we shall be off to America and hopefully untold wealth."

"And my family shall be revenged in the process. We have been ignored in history despite our family having salvaged Annette Savage's reputation as the mistress of Joseph Bonaparte. But that was a hundred and fifty years ago; now we must look to the present and what will bring us comfort in the future."

"Well stated cousin and now tell me what you told this Antoine Murat person."

They stood at the tip of the narrow strip of land and looked out over Lake Geneva. Charles relayed the information that Antoine had for years been researching the legend that on the estate of Joseph Bonaparte in what is now called Lake Bonaparte was buried treasure. He went on to point out that in his day he named it Lake Diana after the Goddess of the hunt. For a hundred years people have combed the region and the natural caverns to seek the so called treasure of Bonaparte and soon the lake got his name. Not so much as a coin or bauble was ever found even when the house he built was torn down. So too had been the fate of Joseph's Point Breeze Estate near Bordentown New Jersey where he first built a house so grand that it rivaled the White House of the Presidents in Washington D.C. in beauty. He as a Benton family member has been part of that history since Joseph Bonaparte arrived in Philadelphia and bought the land on the New Jersey side of the Delaware River in 1815.

Between the Benton family records in Bordentown New Jersey and the findings of Antoine Murat in Lake Bonaparte New York they had come up with a reasonable approach to finding the treasure of Bonaparte. Nonetheless Carolina placed her bets on the American Ron De Cenza. To this end she had been having him and his friends followed from Italy into Switzerland to the Isola of Brisaggo. Only then did she feel it safe to call back her accomplices Luigi Tonelli and Pietro Giuliano as they could be recognized by Ron and his friends because of the shoot out on Capri. Carolina too could be easily recognized by them since it was the young Count of Pianore, Alessandro who rescued her from being murdered by her lover's accomplice, Stefano Rinaldi, as he tried to get the secret to the Book on Joseph Bonaparte.

It was agreed that Charles would be the one who would have to keep tabs on Ron and company while they remained in Europe as he was totally unknown to them. Carolina would leave with Luigi and Pietro on a flight the next day which would take them to New York City.

Now that Cavelli was gone, they pledged themselves to protect her. The plan was created based on the information supplied by Luigi and Pietro by phone that afternoon. They had learned of the Prince of Savoy being on the Island of Brisaggo. All they had to do was chum up with members of his retinue' to learn that the Prince was returning to Geneva and not accompanying the Americans to Prangins. Charles Benton would make sure that he would be at the Chateau Prangins when they were and hopefully also staying at the same inn. It wouldn't be too difficult to find out where a party of seven would be staying given the size of the town near which the Chateau was located.

When Pietro and Luigi arrived at the Hotel Royal in Geneva Switzerland, Charles bade *adieu* to Carolina and set off in his Volkswagen up the Rue de Lausanne which was the only street on which he had to travel in order to reach the Chateau Prangins. It would prove to be an interesting if not a lovely ride up the coastline of Lake Geneva.

Coming from the opposite direction to Benton in his Volkswagen was a diesel fueled mini-bus. It chugged its way toward Prangins from the Lake Maggiore area on the Swiss side of the lake. This time however it was not filled with seven but eight passengers. Professor Andrew Pettigrew was now part of the team and once again they traveled under the guise of a research party attached to Oxford University in the United Kingdom. Now Pettigrew was once a victim rescued by Ron and his friends and later took them to Ireland in search of the Chalice of St. Malachy once again under the guise of a research team. On both occasions, they were involved in solving a murder while also protecting the former Royal Family of Italy.

This adventure however was thought to be quite passive in comparison in that the evil players in the Murder on Capri case were in prison. They felt confident that they could follow the clues in the biography of Joseph Bonaparte without worry. The professor thought this would be an easy research effort because of the arrests and convictions. He, Pettigrew, had connections with University people around the world, so well-known was he in the Historical Research world.

 At the moment none of that was important. What was the topic of conversation was the room assignments and where to stop for lunch. The room assignments were easily done. Jan and Susan, Andreas and Dominic, Ron and Bob and now since they were eight, Alessandro and the Professor were roommates. Alessandro was rather down in the dumps for a brief time. He actually was going to miss being the third guy in the room and witness the bantering of Ron and Bob about who should sleep where. They were like an old married guy couple if there ever was one without the sex of course. And as for the thought of Susan and Ron sharing a room now that they were engaged; well just perish the thought. If he got to make out with her now and then on the trip he'd consider himself lucky. And don't even think about getting to second base and yet he had hope. And then there was the actual gay guy couple. They were always discreet but they got to share a bed, shower together and were the envy of Ron but not of Susan who felt they should wait until they got married. After all it was only less than a year away. That year would be like an eternity to a guy, especially one who was newly out of the seminary and celibate most of his post pubescent life; but she didn't budge on the topic even though he was now twenty-one and a legal man and she twenty and a legal woman for two years.

And so it was onto a late lunch. Alessandro was driving as usual while Jan served as navigator with map in hand. She called out that a restaurant was coming up called Café les Aberiaux.

"It should be pretty and it's very French sounding which is cute."
"Cute?" Alessandro glanced over to her.

Jan fiddled with the map getting all flustered. "Anyway, it's right near the lake."

Bob was the one who put things in perspective as food was of no interest to Ron on most occasions. And as for the others, no one had a chance to pipe in with a suggestion. "We are not after pretty. I'm starving and it should have good food."

Andreas decided to have a bit of fun with his new pal. "So you're saying that the breakfast our Moms made was not filling?"

Bob got flustered but didn't relent. "No, I'm not saying that…but that was at eight in the morning and it is now three in the afternoon."

"Okay, okay I think Andreas gets it. Jan how far is that place?" Ron poked Bob in the ribs. "We need to feed this guy or he'll fade away."

"Asshole," Bob leaned into Ron and whispered not so sweet nothings.

"Alessandro, there's the exit, turn here…" Jan yelled out.

Everything and everyone went flying about the mini-bus as the young Count turned on a dime and sped down the off ramp. On the positive side everyone virtually ended up on the lap of their sweetheart except for the Professor who landed on top of Bob. On the negative side the map was now in Alessandro's face and he was driving blindly so he slammed on the brakes and jerked the bus to a stop just as a Volkswagen came across from the other exit.

"*Mama Mia*, did I hit something?" shouted the young Count as the others were in various modes of yelling "stop the bus."

Luckily he had not hit anything but the bumper of the bus was mighty close to that of the Volkswagen. The shaken driver jumped out of his car, stopped to view the almost collision just as Alessandro jumped out of the bus followed quickly by everyone else all talking at once.

"*Mi dispiacere, Signore'*, I am so sorry for this," a contrite Alessandro offered.

"You Italians, you drive like maniacs… that was Italian you were speaking wasn't it?"

The Professor decided to take things in hand as he and the man were about the same size and close in age around forty. "Now excuse me Sir, my friend here has offered an apology and though this could have been a disaster, it was fortunately not so. In any case this has nothing whatsoever to do with his nation of origin. The map you see was in his face and he had to stop quickly which he did, Thank God. In any case I am British and a subject of Her Majesty the Queen. And these fine young people are Italians to be sure and this one is Swiss where you happen to be and finally these four are Americans. So you see; you have insulted the entire United Nations as it were."

The driver fumbled for words at first but decided on focusing on the Americans. "Americans, why am I glad to meet some of my countrymen over here and women too, sorry Ladies. I think I was just flustered and upset. You know what they say about one's life flashing before one's eyes near the moment of a catastrophic event. Please accept my apologies. I am Charles Benton of Bordentown New Jersey." He held out his hand for someone to take hold of it.

Bob took it, "Bordentown, why that's where we going in a couple of days. What a coincidence."

Ron almost had a meltdown but Susan calmed him with a stroke of her hand on his reddened cheek. "Just say nothing Ronnie; let it go. He doesn't know us from a hole in the ground."

Softly he replied that Bob could have spilled the beans of why they were going to a place like Bordentown instead of Philly or New York which would be more obvious for tourists. In the end he too took the hand of Charles Benton. "Sir, let us make this mishap up to you. We were just going for a bite to eat as my Mom would say. Would you please join us?"

"Well I don't want to impose, but…" Charles played his role well not letting on to his interest as to why they would be going to Bordentown.

"I am a bit hungry; haven't had but a glass of juice since this morning. I was just too excited about getting to Chateau Prangins. I heard tell that its gardens were magnificent."

"Now that's just what I was saying when all of this happened," Bob chimed in again and once again Ron was not happy about it.

Oblivious, he took Benton to meet each of his friends formally. "So you're into gardening; you know back when Napoleon was exiled, his brother Joseph actually bought that place and he loved gardening more than being a King…"

Ron gave one of his soul penetrating stares at his best pal and his eyes bulged out as if to attack Bob. In his mind much too much information was being dropped randomly but more importantly with a sense of knowledge that an ordinary tourist wouldn't have. Graciously he took the hand of Benton and shaking it again pulled the man closer to him.

"You'll have to forgive my pal for the history lesson. He just learned all about that guy when we toured the place."

"Not at all Mr. De Cenza, I found the story to be most interesting; for as I said I am on my way there after touring Geneva to have a look."

"Is that so, and please Mr. De Cenza is my father, do call me Ron."

With a slight turn of the head he gave a wink and a nod to Susan to catch up with him. "So what brings you to Switzerland?" The time had come to pump him for information. For indeed the likelihood of meeting someone from Bordentown New Jersey just outside of Geneva Switzerland was just too coincidental in his mind.

Bob however felt that he was the one breaking the ice and making nice talk. He wasn't about to be put in his role as sidekick and decided to take control of the moment. He would be the one to change a nasty moment into a welcoming one as he made the introductions. Andreas helped him out as the only Swiss national. He welcomed Benton officially to his country. Charles was quite taken with his appearance and six foot two stature and doubly so when he found out that he was a Swiss Papal Guard in the Vatican. Dominic wasn't quite sure if that impression was because he was on their team or not but decided to watch him for indications.

Jan still focusing on Benton's remark of not haven eaten, flipped open the map still in her hand. She pointed out that the restaurant was just down the road near the Lake. "It should be nice this time of year. Not too hot like it was in Italy."

"So Miss De Cenza you are coming from Italy then, touring the continent, I take it?" Charles Benton was now plotting the course of these people who almost crashed into him.

"Oh, I wish that was true, but the British guy is actually our professor and we are part of his research team."

"Is that so and what possible research is there for you in little Bordentown, New Jersey?"

Now Ron started to worry about his sister as well. When she began to explain that it was just a quick stop on the way to a big lake in upstate New York, he really began to worry despite her shrouding the trip as part of the American experience for their Italian and Swiss friends and yet she had already told the proverbial tall, dark and handsome stranger that they were part of a research team. Despite Benton's age being more than twice that of Jan, Alessandro was not too pleased with the flirtation as he saw it. Ron however had a decision to be made and quickly. It was time to either squash the entire conversation or embellish it into a believable one; at least in his mind. There was no alternative.

Ron began to spin his tale to gage Benton's response. He decided on weaving truth with a bit of fiction and let this Bordentown New Jersey guy sift one from the other if he could. And he would do so on the veranda of the Café les Aberiaux overlooking Lake Geneva.

They were directed to an elevated veranda overlooking docks with small pleasure boats and the vast lake where the border of France could be seen opposite them. The late afternoon sunlight bounced off the smooth water creating a mirage effect of the French shoreline. The view finally began to wash away the trauma of the almost collision with an American who just happened to be from Bordentown New Jersey. The guys immediately pushed together two tables each with a festive Umbrella of red and white, the colors of the Swiss Flag. Their group of now nine would easily fit around them. When Heidi herself came to present the menus it was as if they were going back into the movies of the Golden Age of Hollywood. She was costumed in a short skirt with a white apron flared out with the help of what would be called petticoats in past decades. The sleeves were trimmed in timeless heart shapes, the Swiss Cross, and mountain peaks so familiar in the Alps. She was a blond and had her hair parted in the center and braided into two pigtails one with a red bow at the end of it and the other with a white one. To say this was done to impress the tourists would be an understatement. In any case the menus were received graciously and the chatter went from car crash and Bordentown to Shirley Temple as Heidi in one of her famous old movies that Jan and Ron had seen on late night TV with their father sitting on the floor of their living room eating from a big bowl of popcorn.

Jan became homesick and they had just left their parents. "I think we should have brought Mom and Dad with us. Mom would have loved seeing this and the castles too."

Ron just smiled not wanting to burst her bubble. He knew, as did she if she had bothered to think about it, that the parents of everyone were planning a little trip of their own before they returned to America. The parents of Alessandro were escorting them to Florence to view the David which of course Jan thought was second in looks to the young Count of Pianore as well as Santa Croce Church. The church was where they found the clue in the empty tomb of Joseph Bonaparte which led them to Prangins in the first place. From there they would be taken to their province of Umbria and stay in Alessandro's family's 12th Century Castle for a couple of days before heading back to Rome for some sightseeing and their return flight. That part was their Dad's dream, to see an actual functioning castle that was not a ruin and get to stay within its walls to boot. In fact Ron was a bit jealous about that Castle part too. He said nothing but Susan did.

"But Jan, they are actually going to stay in a real castle with actual nobility," she turned and shot a grin at Alessandro.

The young Count shivered in embarrassment. He didn't like the title to be thrown about let alone the castle which was his home until it was made into a hotel by his parents to raise funds to keep the vineyards and farm going with a profit so that he could be educated at the

42

University of Bologna. Now they had a modest Villa on a hill overlooking the Medieval Town of Pianore.

Bob brought the entire scenario to a close with the announcement that all the dishes offered on the menu came with French Fries. "How cool is that, and here we sit and we can see France right over there." Ron jumped on the change of focus. "So Andreas, what should we get at a real Swiss restaurant?"

Andreas began to read off the menu list, explaining what each actually was as the names were in French and Italian but they all had French Fries. It boiled down to the hamburger plate to keep it familiar and the Spiedini di pollo which is an Italian version of chicken sausage on a stick. However only Benton ended up with a hamburger; the others stuck with Italian as that's what they were now use to in their adventures in Italy and the Swiss Canton of Ticino.

Benton found himself seated next to Alessandro and Dominic though he had tried to squeeze in between Bob and Jan as they seemed the most open to talk about the research project destinations. He was thwarted by Dominic who wanted to keep a close eye on him and there was no way that the young Count wanted him next to Jan. His efforts to sit himself between the chatters may have been thwarted but finding himself seated across the table from them couldn't have been better planned and Ron could see the gleam in his eye as he began to bring the conversation back from food to New Jersey. He did so with a tantalizing bit of truth as he produced a pamphlet from what could be called a hiking jacket with many pockets. But that gleam was toward the Professor as Ron soon learned.

"Professor Pettigrew," Benton unfolded the pamphlet. "I see that the Chateau Prangins was once the home of Joseph Bonaparte, Napoleon's older brother. That's why I am so interested in seeing it."

Pettigrew shot a side glance to Ron looking for a sign on how to address the statement. He got none save a slight grin which did mean something. He then went on to scan the faces of his so called Research Team. Everyone could feel his dilemma in the dead silence which continued. The Professor needed to be rescued. He was overthinking a simple statement which any visitor to Prangins would know and obviously it was touted in the brochure as well.

Benton could feel this discomfort level of the Professor and see the blank stares from the others. So he added a bit more to the pot of consternation. "Now you're probably wondering why I would be so interested in Prangins being the home to Joseph Bonaparte and the answer is quite simple. After he left the Chateau, he came to Bordentown New Jersey, bought land and created a lovely estate called Point Breeze. The people were thrilled to have a King living in their midst and his home became the go to place for High Society events. "Isn't that why you're coming to Bordentown for your research Professor?"

The Professor nodded and cracked a smile, again glanced around the table. "That is indeed mostly accurate Mr. Benton…excuse me Charles. But let Ron here elaborate a bit from the student perspective."

Ron expelled a breath hardly taken as the baton was handed to him. He knew his grin delivered a message to string Benton along. He baited the hook further and began what he hoped would be a tantalizing story to hook Benton on the real reason he came all the way to Europe and specifically Geneva Switzerland to check out Chateau Prangins. He squeezed Susan's hand and then stood. Walking around the table ala the fictitious Perry Mason in a courtroom scene he began his presentation as it were.

"Charles and I only call you so familiarly with your permission for my mother always taught me to call elders by their formal name. Anyway, I don't think you truly know who you've met here at that intersection which almost was a disaster. Professor Andrew Pettigrew of Oxford University is more than our teacher on an expedition. For instance, about two years ago now he discovered the lost Fountain designed by Carlo Fontana, who just happens to also be an ancestor of Dominic Fontana seated right across from you. And guess what, it was right in the Piazza San Pietro in Rome. But that's not all; his research uncovered other lost Renaissance works of art as well. And just last year he did this same type of research and discovered the lost Chalice of St. Malachy known as the Holy Grail of Ireland." Ron paused and placed his hands on the shoulders of the Professor.

"It's an honor for us, his students to help him uncover what he hopes to be proof that Joseph Bonaparte did meet with President Madison at that time of his American residence. If this could be proven; it would discount the current view and alter history Books."

His delivery of credentials was temporarily halted as the food appeared on trays brought by Heidi and some bus boys. "Ah, the food has arrived. Shall we talk and eat if you don't mind?" Ron returned to his seat, stooped over and gave Susan a peck on the cheek and sat with a sense of accomplishment that not one word about Spain or the Crown Jewels had been uttered.

"Not at all this has been most edifying to be sure." He covered up his displeasure of being called an elder at just over forty-two years of age. "Professor, I meant no disrespect of your efforts. It's just that you will not be the first to lead such research at Point Breeze which as you surely know was torn down by subsequent owners after Joseph Bonaparte. They never found anything but some pottery and china pieces."

The white wine was poured for those with the chicken dish and a red wine for Benton with the beef hamburger. That is except for Ron who had a Coke with lots of ice and Alessandro who was the driver who decided to have a Mineral Water with ice which was really an out of the box choice for an Italian. Europeans rarely used ice in their beverages and if they did it would never meet the standards of Ron who filled his glass to the top with the frozen water cubes.

"My, aren't these chips…what you call fries so crispy and tasty. Now my dear Charles, don't fret so. I know this expedition may be challenging. But as Ron has pointed out all too flatteringly, I might add," he diverted his glance from Benton, "and thank you Ron for the accolades which you and all here deserve more than I. At the same time we did have some success in the past two years in finding that which was thought nonexistent." Pettigrew smiled with a confidence that he had done what Ron intended.

By the time the dessert of "Tarte Au Citron Meringuee" or what Bob called Key Lime Pie was served, there was excited chatter as to where the Research Team was now headed. Benton was impressed to learn that after Prangins the team was going to Geneva to meet with the Crown Prince of Italy in exile. That reference enabled the conversation to switch from Point Breeze which was what Ron had desired should too much information be dropped.

As for the Research Team and the Professor, they learned that Benton was due to leave for America shortly after his Prangins visit. At that moment in time, it seemed to Ron that the New Jersey man knew nothing about the Book let alone the clues within it about the missing Crown Jewels of Spain supposedly taken by Joseph Bonaparte. He glanced at the satchel hanging on Bob's back knowing that within it was the Book which had brought them to Prangins and wondering if this guy from New Jersey was just playing dumb or if he really didn't know about the Book.

The only reason to let that tidbit of a Royal visit drop was to explain why they were going northwest from Prangins to Geneva. Only Ron had a clear understanding from the code in the Book as to what they were truly looking for and that it wouldn't be found at the Chateau Prangins which they now had to visit if for no other reason than to reveal nothing further to Benton as to their true destination. In true European style by the time lunch ended some two hours later, there was not much they could do than to check into their hotel. It was then that they found out that Benton was also going to the Hotel Barcarolle not far from the Chateau.

The blue beast as Jan was now referring to the diesel mini-bus chugged along the lakeside road toward Prangins castle and the Hotel which actually appeared before the Chateau. Pettigrew had no choice but to register with his team of research assistants at the hotel. He turned to Benton and suggested that they meet in the morning and go to the chateau together. The American tourist who was certainly anything but readily agreed. This observation about Benton being more than what he presented was touched upon by Ron. He then laid out what everyone would have to do as the eight crammed into Pettigrew's room. They thought that they were isolated from eavesdropping as each pair had one of the rooms on the second floor thus leaving none for Benton should he be inclined to keep an eye on them. The newly engaged young man from Chicago placed the autobiography so hardly fought after on the desk. He flipped open the Book to where he had placed the century and a half Laurentian Library card last used by Caroline Bonaparte Savage, daughter of Annette Savage who was the mistress to King Joseph during his years in America.

Andreas and Alessandro then pulled out the desk as far to the center of the room as they could so that everyone could encircle it. The fading light of the bright day seemed to form a ray of light on the revealed page with the Latin notations which Ron had realized was a code to reveal the meaning of the text concerning the life of King Joseph Bonaparte whose one time Chateau, now a museum, was not ten minutes away from where they stood. The excitement was building without a word being said as they looked at those pages now aglow in golden light as if the secret of the age was about to become known.

That spell was broken as Bob interjected a few choice words. "Okay Sherlock, enough of the drama; let's get to the meat and potatoes of what's on those pages. Watson knows that you just didn't arbitrarily open to those pages." He used their special Sir Arthur Conan Doyle character names as it always brought on a smile and focus as well.

Ron shot out what his father would call a "shit ass grin" to his best pal, his sidekick, his brother from another mother. He released holding the hand of Susan because that would definitely result in an inappropriate kind of focus. And he needed to be zeroed in on the task at hand.

"Watson is right, we need to get to this next step of the puzzle or should I say treasure hunt professor?"

Pettigrew returned a shrug for he didn't know what the code cracked by Ron pointed to but he did know that they were definitely on a treasure hunt. In typical Oxford style he pointed out that a puzzle was most assuredly being solved in that for years the legend that King Joseph took with him into exile the Crown Jewels of Spain was well known. In fact for the last hundred years trying to search for those jewels had treasure hunters combing the caves of upstate New York around Lake Bonaparte as the original mansion of Joseph Bonaparte near Bordentown New Jersey had long ago burned down and the second one he built was destroyed by Hamilton Beckett who was the son of the British envoy Henry Beckett who was stationed in Philadelphia. He pointed out that even decades later, the animosity against all things Bonaparte was still alive and well in that family. He ended by noting that what he just had shared was commonly known amongst historians and archeologists.

"All of that is about to change, isn't it Ron?"

The eyebrows twitched up and down and the cocoa brown eyes sparkled in the golden rays filtering into the room. "That was quite the history lesson Professor. I don't know if I can live up to that lead in but here goes."

As Ron began to point to the Latin words on the edges of the pages a thin black wire was being lowered from the edge of the balcony of Room 322 just above the room where the team of investigators stood. At the other end of that microphone wire was Charles Benton who was sitting on his balcony with a headset over his ears listening to Ron's explanation.

"See this, it reads 'Roman ruins' in Latin but on the page of the autobiography it talks about Prangins Chateau. It would seem to be meaningless and not related at all because the world has known for years thanks to the letters of his secretary, Louis Maillard, about the Chateau. Now Louis became the secretary of Joseph Bonaparte when he got older but he was in his service as it was called since he was thirteen years old. Nothing sexual, just like a house boy I would think until he became educated thanks to Joseph and became his right hand

48

man to the very end of his life. Anyway, everything we know about Prangins being bought by Joseph Bonaparte is verified in this autobiography and those letters of Maillard. Only Joseph and Louis knew what took place at the Prangins Chateau as they settled there only to have to flee as the British were after the former King of Spain when his brother Napoleon finally surrendered."

As Ron was reviewing what was known about Prangins Chateau a pesky renegade dark cloud was being whipped across the sky ablaze with gold and pink light of the waning sun. The brisk wind which was stirred up took hold of the black wire and banged it against the stone side of the hotel under the balcony above. The result was a loud static sound which pierced Benton's ears. He pulled off the earphones and poked his ears which had become clogged as if he were on a plane which hit turbulence and experienced a change in cabin pressure.

"Shit, what the hell…"

The backs of Bob and Dominic were closest to the open balcony door of Room 222. That gust of wind swept through those doors, along with the expletive. "Hey Dominic, did you hear what I think I just heard?

"Not really, just the wind blowing; shall I close the doors?" Dominic turned to do just that as the thin wire was disappearing above the extension of the balcony above them. He pulled Bob next to him and motioned to Ron with a finger to his lips to be silent. "Bob, you said that you thought you heard something. And I'm telling you that I just saw something hanging over there in the corner and now it's gone. I think it was a wire."

"Get a grip Dominic; this isn't an Alfred Hitchcock movie. See over there it's just the electric wires on the pole."

The entire group was now lined up across the balcony door threshold. Ron stood at the desk not joining them. He closed the Book and slipped it into Bob's new messenger bag as his old faithful satchel was stolen on the Isle of Capri and when recovered could not be saved.

"Okay guys, come on back in and close the doors."

The team scattered as best they could and took a seat on the edges of the two beds in the room. "Ronnie, what' going on? Where's the Book?"

"Oh the Book is right here Sis, in Bob's new satchel." He patted the highly polished brown leather bag. "And as for what's going on it appears that Bob and Dom know more about that. Let them tell you and I'll finish with what I know."

Bob began with explaining how he felt a strong gust of wind on his back when the dark cloud passed by. He added that wasn't all for with the wind came some choice words from someone who was upset about something. "Then Dominic said that he saw something…"

"Right, but Bob thinks I've seen too many Hitchcock movies. But I swear I saw a thin black wire in the corner of the balcony hanging from above. But it's gone and Bob thinks it was those electric wires on the pole." Dominic pointed to the telephone pole outside the balcony window.

Professor Pettigrew tried to put it all into perspective stating that it had been a long day, that they met a stranger who seemed to be interested in Prangins Chateau as well and with the breaking of the code by Ron it certainly seemed like a mystery movie. "I think that we should go to dinner and get a good night's sleep. Tomorrow night we have to be at the airport for our flight to New York City."

Bob was all for the dinner suggestion. The others went along with him except for Ron. He just stood there with the satchel in hand.

Susan walked up to him and kissed him on the cheek. "Okay, so you're not hungry? I don't think so. What's the issue?"

"Oh nothing, just a thought that I had…"

"Ronnie, spill it or I will kiss you right in front of everyone and on the lips too."

"That won't work anymore Susan." He took her into his arms and planted a kiss on her lips while squeezing her tightly. Jan sighed. The guys hooted and hollered and Ron got their attention. "Now that I have your attention, may I suggest that we do go to dinner as the Professor suggested. But first let me share something with all of you. Dominic has said that he thought he saw a wire at the corner of our balcony which is no longer there. Bob said that he heard someone swearing, I did too but couldn't tell if it was profanity or just surprise. But it got me thinking about that Benton guy we almost crashed into earlier today."

Ron in Sherlock mode went on to inquire if they recalled the battery operated tape player that Andreas used to play the Volare' song on the Isle of Capri. He reminded them that it was used to create a romantic environment for the proposal he made to Susan and Andreas made to Dominic. Unfortunately he pointed out the device was destroyed when Apollo and Stefano tried to kill them in the Blue Grotto.

"Sherlock, *per favore'*, I am starving; get to the point."

"Sure Watson sorry about the background story and all." H released the embrace of Susan. "You all surely remember that beautiful day turned to terror for a brief time in the Blue Grotto. So here's the point. That player was in a black leather case like a small suitcase when Andreas brought it to the Grotto. He just left the case there when Captain Verdi needed it for his police forensics people to examine."

"You're getting long winded again."

"Okay, okay, I hear that stomach of yours growling, everyone does. Well this afternoon when we checked into this hotel along with that Benton guy, he was carrying a case just like the one Andreas had on Capri."

"Oh my God Ronnie," Jan knew her brother well. "So you think that just because he has a black case similar to the one Andreas had, that he was carrying a tape recorder or…"

"Or some kind of listening device…yes I do."

"And you think so because of what he carried into this hotel?" asked an incredulous Professor.

"I know what you're thinking but it's just too coincidental that this guy from America happens to be interested in exactly the same things we are. In any case he's way too friendly with…"

"Andreas?" interjected Dominic.

"Hmmm, I was going to say Professor Pettigrew. In any case, let's go to dinner and then we'll see what our friend up above us does."

"Above us, how do you know that?"

"Elementary my dear Watson, I looked at his registration card while he checked in as I was taking a closer look at that black case of his. It was just too square looking for a suitcase."

Across the pond on the shores of Lake Bonaparte in upstate New York in a colonial style small frame single story house a restless Francois Parrot tossed and turned as it was in the middle of the night given the time difference. His mind was still churning over the events of that afternoon when the dead body of a man was found in one of his boats. At that very moment in one of his cabins on Birch Island, the only one not to be rented by the Professor from England, a single light could be seen through the open window. Antoine Murat was reading a telegram which informed him that his colleague would arrive in New York City the following day. He was to report to him at Princeton University in two days with his report on Bonaparte's Cave.

He crumpled up the telegram and thought better of it and smoothed it out on the arm of the plush chair. "Two days, what an asshole; does he think that I can find a treasure lost for over a century when no one has been able to?"

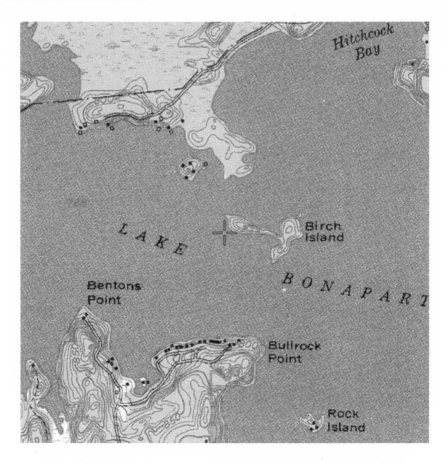

Map of Lake Bonaparte New York State with Birch Island

Chapter Three:
Murder on Lake Bonaparte

The events of the previous day still flashed in the mind of Francois Parrot after a troublesome night of sleep. Tossing his shorts into the hamper he jumped into the shower. Still he saw in his mind's eye his Ford LTD speeding after the squad cars which had their sirens blaring. He knew they were heading out toward his Bonaparte Launch and Lunch establishment on the shores of the lake. He rubbed his smooth body for he had very little body hair with the towel. Looking out the tiny window he could see Birch Island and knew that he had to get those cabins ready for the visitors from overseas. Within that view he could also see where he had parked the car outside of his property line as the police had already cordoned off the actual dock area, though they left the restaurant open for business. Despite that allowance he knew that anyone who could see the events at the dock would be questioned and that would impact his business. The reality however was that only the three teens actually saw anything and that was only a body of a man in one of the rental boats floating near the mouth of one of the caverns. He began to piece together what happened on that previous afternoon as he pulled up his Jockey shorts. He began to relive that afternoon.

Francois made his way down the gravel path to his dock and the yellow ribbon stating that the area was a crime scene. Approaching one of the Deputies, he identified himself and was admitted to see the Sherriff.

"Ah, Francois, it seems that your helpers here have had quite the fright out on the lake. Perhaps you should have a word with them; you know to calm them down."

The three teens stood huddled together at the land's end of the pier. As soon as they saw Parrot they made a bee line for him and all began to speak at once about what they found out on the lake as they were checking in the boat rentals. He tried to address each of them but could not understand any of them as one drowned out the other.

"Now let's just step up to the boat hut and have a Coke shall we?" He glanced at Sherriff Fontaine for approval.

Having received the nod, he led the three to the rental shed and sat them outside on a wooden bench while he walked casually to the cooler and opened it. Pulling out three Cokes and popping off their caps, he handed the cold bottle to each of them. "Here you go; take a sip and then Jack how about you telling me exactly what happened." The teen gulped down the drink as if he were taking a shot of whiskey to bolster his resolve. He shivered though not from the cold though he wore only a pair of denim jeans cut off shorts and a Bonaparte Launch and Lunch tee shirt. Then he began to tell his story of how they were conducting the inventory of the boats rented and returned. All were accounted for except for one which was past due the time for check-in.

"Number 16…the boat was number 16. We are good about knowing the numbers and the boats."

"Of course Jack; just go on with what happened next."

"Sure Mr. Parrot, we looked out over the lake and saw nothing so Jeff here brought down the binoculars from the hook over there on the shed…"

"That's right, right there on the hook," added the still shocked Jeff. "I couldn't find anything so we thought we had best go out on the lake and look around in case the guy got grounded on a rock or something as he was obviously not from around here."

Sherriff Fontaine was standing at a discreet distance so that he might be able to hear and yet not be noticeable and frighten the teens. Parrot remembered that he took out his notepad and jotted down the number of the boat and description of the guy which came next.

"So tell me Jack why would you say that he wasn't from around here?"

"That's easy, because he said so. He was from Princeton he said…"

"That's right Mr. Parrot, the University all fancy and Ivy league type. Not dressed for a boat outing that's for sure," added Sally. "And he was so gorgeous with that blond hair and piercing blue eyes and broad shoulders…"

"Is that so, good looking was he and from the University was it; so did he say why he needed a boat.

All three took another gulp of Coke and breathed out heavily. "Well he had a brief case with him…"

"Yes not a big one but one with a strap which he had over his shoulder and across his chest. It was brown." Jeff added with apology for the interruption of Sally.

"So then he was dressed like for a business trip then?"

"Oh not quite that fancy Mr. Parrot; but not like us with jeans and a tee shirt or even with fishing gear which he had none. He wore pants like you have on not jeans, a blue shirt with collar and buttons down it and a windbreaker jacket which was dark blue and gave a cool contrast with his eyes…"

"Navy blue sir, yes it was definitely Navy blue. And he was an older guy, even older than you," Jeff added, again interrupting Sally.

"Oh was he now, so how much older?"

Jack was back to answering, "I'd say at least five years older like maybe fortyish even, wouldn't you say Sally, Jeff?"

Murder at Point Breeze

The two agreed with Jack's assessment of age and the Sherriff jotted it down on his pad, while Francois tried not to smile at being called an old man at thirty.

"And that's about it sir, except when we went out to look for him. We found number sixteen stuck on a sand bar near what people call the Bonaparte Cave on the other side of the lake. He was slumped over and not moving. We knew right away that he was dead."

"So you called to him and touched him to see if he might have fallen asleep or had an attack of some kind?"

"I did call out to him at first," began Jeff. "But then we saw it…"

"Oh Mr. Parrot, we knew right away that he was not sleeping."

Jack wrapped his arm around Sally trying to console her. But she would have none of it. She scooted to the end of the bench. "Thanks but I'm okay."

She then looked at Jeff on the other side of Jack. It was obvious that he and she had a thing going. Francois saw the teen crush thing as well and sought to bring them back into focus on what they encountered. He did so by addressing their observation that the man was not just sleeping because they saw "it." He asked what they saw.

All three answered, "The arrow."

"Arrow, are you saying that this man had an arrow in him?"

"Yes sir," began Jack taking back his role as narrator. "It was sticking out of his back," he twisted Jeff around, lifted up his tee shirt so that he could show the location which was on the upper back near what the kids called the wing bone. "You see just to the left of the bone not in the bone."

"Someone was a pretty good shot to hit that mark," observed Jeff, as he lowered his shirt glancing at Sally to see if she was looking at him.

58

"Yes, I would agree. Is there anything else the Sherriff or I should know?"

"Just one more thing," Sally added. "The leather bag, it was not around his neck like it was when he rented the boat."

Francois was remembering how he looked over the heads of the teens who were seated facing him. The Sherriff gave a thumbs-up and motioned to send them to him. He pointed to his watch and then to the sky so as to say that they needed to get to the body and get it off the lake before dark.

"Well that was just fine. You are helping a lot with this unfortunate accident…"

"But Sir, this was no accident." Jack was firm in his view. "This was a murder plain and simple. There was no bow and the bag was gone so someone had to have taken it."

"I stand corrected young man. But let's get back to Sherriff Fontaine. I think we need to get back out on that lake and go to the crime scene."

No sooner had he said the words than he saw Sarah being stopped at the yellow crime scene ribbon. He called to the Sherriff and she was then allowed to come to him. "Thanks Sherriff, I think she can call the parents for us. I hope that you don't need them to go back out on the lake and see that again."

"I understand your concern Francois but they are the only ones who can tell us if anything was touched and changed since they found him. I'm afraid once we get the parents approval I need to get them out there."

"Okay then but I need to be with them, they're quite upset."

"I get it. Of course you may come as well. Perhaps you might even know him."

"Well they think he's from Princeton University so that's a possibility but I doubt it. In any case, the kids would have taken his info from his license and put it in the log Book for rentals." Francois turned to Sarah. "Would you mind taking the young people to call their parents and then bring them back with the log Book?"

She looked at the Sherriff. "Is that okay with you?"

"Certainly, I'm sure they'll feel more comfortable with you than Deputy O'Malley. But make sure they don't talk about the details of the crime just get the parental permission and the basics that an accident has taken place out on the lake." Sherriff Fontaine could easily be a grandfather to any of the three teens and felt sorry for them to have to be a part of such a crime investigation. He smiled at the three teens off in the distance and waved to them. "You kids just go with Miss Dupres and call your parents. Then we'll go out on the boat."

The three were not too pleased with being called kids, but Sarah told them that's how the Sherriff talked about anyone younger than him. They managed to suppress a chuckle at the thought of her or Mr. Parrot being called a kid at their age.

"So tell me Francois, why would someone rent one of your boats for just a couple of hours and end up dead? He obviously wasn't going fishing." The Sherriff followed Parrot down the pier to a white fiberglass speed boat.

"I haven't got a clue Sherriff... I think this one will fit all of us just fine," he then returned to the question. "But I bet the answer to your question is in that missing bag the kids saw around his neck when he checked out the boat but not when they found his body."

"My God, don't tell me that he's some kind of thief and had stolen goods in that bag."

60

"Maybe who knows but that's jumping the gun or should I say arrow in this case. The kids never said how that bag looked. Was it thin and just holding papers or stretched out as if a bulkier item was in it?"

"Papers, hmmm or maybe a map as in a treasure map; I hope that it's a simple theft of jewels. What I don't need is another treasure hunter roaming the lake and its caves."

"Don't knock it Sherriff. Those so called treasure hunters keep our little town going and certainly my business as well. In fact I am expecting a rather distinguished group of Treasure Hunters here in a day or two; all the way from Oxford University."

"A Brit; oh my God, this is about King Joseph Bonaparte and his lost crown. Those Brits still have it in for all things Bonaparte."

Francois laughed at the scene he was imagining as he slapped the Sherriff on his back gently. He pointed out once again that he was a descendant of the cook of the Bonaparte king and never had a crown been included in the speculation of exactly what Joseph had taken from Spain when he fled. Only two people would know exactly what was taken he pointed out. One was his secretary and confidant, Louis Maillard and the other the Vatican diplomat who legend said was the go between in selling the jewels. When Joseph needed money to build his mansion at Point Breeze New Jersey or when he needed funds to buy the land around what the locals now call Lake Bonaparte, it was to Giovanni Battiste Sartori that Louis was sent to visit in Philadelphia.

"So you see I just don't think that there was a crown in that missing leather bag of the dead man, whoever he is. And another point should be noted while we are talking about Crowns and such. In all the royal paintings of Joseph Bonaparte as King of Spain or of Naples and Sicily for that matter, he is never shown wearing a crown but he is shown wearing a lot of gem studded gold chains and medals and those would be more easily hidden don't you think Sherriff?"

"Oh Francois, I didn't mean a literal crown; all this talk of Kings, jewels and now murder has my head spinning."

"Here comes Sarah with the kids, perhaps we'll learn something about this poor man when we get to him."

With Deputy O'Malley at the wheel they settled on their seats with Sarah and Sally being on one and Francois with the two boys, Jeff and Jack on the rear seat. The Sherriff parked himself on the swivel seat next to O'Malley so that he could face the others. And yet he didn't mean to cause discomfort by his seeming to watch the teens' reaction as they sped around Birch Island and approached the sand bar outside of the cavern entrance on which boat Number 16 was still stuck.

"O'Malley, don't get too close lest we also get stuck out here," ordered the Sherriff. "That's it just coast us near the boat so that we, I mean you and Francois can jump into it."

Turning to Jeff and Jack, he asked them to drop the anchor. The two sixteen year olds did as directed and looked over to the slumped body just a few feet away. It was as they had seen it earlier except for one thing and it was Sally who brought that change to everyone's attention as she leaned on the edge of the boat railing to view the grizzly site. She pointed out that the man had been wearing a cap, the kind worn on the golf course or maybe in Ireland like one sees in a movie. She was remembering the movie "The Quiet Man" in which John Wayne tosses such his cap over the stone wall and chases Maureen O'Hara kissing her passionately as the rain pelted them. She had seen it on late night TV the Friday just past.

Glancing at Jeff as she recounted the scene of the movie, she smiled. Jack confirmed the cap. "Sally's right. He was wearing a cap when he rented the boat and when we found him like that. But why would someone take it off after he was dead. I would think that it would have fallen off when the strap was pulled over his head when whoever was taking the leather bag."

"Or maybe, the boat just shifted a bit or the wind came along; let's not conjecture about that now." The Sherriff then directed O'Malley to jump into Number 16 while he radioed to see if the police boat was on the way with the Medical Examiner. "Francois, would you mind helping him out?"

It was the great great grandson of Bonaparte's cook who did the jumping first. He was familiar with the type of metal fishing boat with the tiny motor on the rear so that visitors might explore the caverns which opened onto the lake. He held out his hand and pulled O'Malley over to him. Luckily like Francois, the Deputy was tall and thin thus he didn't rock the boat much but was almost able to step into it with his long legs.

"Don't touch a thing; just tell me what you see."

"Yes Sherriff," replied O'Malley. "Sally was right sir, there is a cap lying on the floor of the boat just under the guy's head. I'd say the boat got some water in it as it's wet and there is a little water on the bottom."

Francois stooped down to get a look at the dead man's face. It was clean shaven, and his eyes were closed. "Sherriff, do all people die with their eyes closed?"

"Actually, most die with them open, why do you ask?"

"Because this poor man's eyes are closed; wouldn't you find that strange given that he was shot in the back with this arrow...hey wait a minute. Sherriff this is no ordinary arrow like in archery class."

"Could it be from a Tribal bow? There are still members of Tribal Nations living in this area and they are allowed to hunt with bow and arrow."

The three teens were leaning further over and Jeff pulled on Sally so as not to have her fall overboard. Jack yelled out. "Mr. Parrot, that is not a tribal arrow at all take a good look at it. My great grandmother was a Mohawk so I know for sure that it's not from that tribe. In fact it's not from a long bow at all."

"Jack is right Sherriff this arrow is much shorter and sleek in style. I've seen something like this before when I was at Princeton University. Does anyone have a camera with them? I can send a photo to Professor Dorothy Witherspoon. She'll be able to tell us from what type of weapon this came."

While Sally pulled out an instamatic camera from her purse, the Police Boat pulled up next to them. On board were the Medical Examiner and his assistant with her own camera equipment.

The sun shone in the eyes of Francois bringing him back to the new day. He turned from the window overlooking the pier at the end of which he could see that the Sherriff had returned and was making his way up to his house next to the restaurant. His thoughts had now returned to the new day and the realization that he hadn't as yet contacted Professor Witherspoon regarding the arrow found in the dead man's back. He walked across the narrow hallway and into his office lined with knotty pine wood panels. Picking up the phone, he looked up at a copy of a painting of Joseph Bonaparte as King of Spain. "Nice jewelry Your Majesty; now if we can only find out if it ever really got here that would be quite the discovery."

While that morning phone call was being made across the Atlantic the evening sun was lighting up the sky with a painter's brush of colors bouncing off white fluffy clouds hanging over Geneva Lake. The rather pretty scene was lost on Bob who was quite disgruntled and complaining that dinner to him didn't mean a bag of chips and a bottle of Coke from the hotel gift shop.

"I don't know why we can't just drive through a McDonald's or something on our way. And by the way, where the hell are we going?" Bob crunched down on a couple of chips so hard that crumbs spilled all over his sweatshirt across which was written, Switzerland with the Swiss flag consisting of a white cross which looked more like a plus sign in a math problem on a field of red.

"Really pal, McDonald's, look at your own sweatshirt. We are in Switzerland not Chicago, there are no McDonald's over here. I don't think they are in Europe as yet."

Dominic leaned over the seat and interrupted the little feud at the rear of the mini-bus. He pointed out that there was indeed one and it was in Rome across from the ancient Pantheon which contained the bones of the Christian martyrs as well as the Kings of Italy.

"I stand corrected. We'll drive to it as soon as we figure out what Joseph Bonaparte wanted his daughter to know. How's that pal?" Ron patted Bob's belly, "Everything all right in there?"

"Jerk."

Alessandro, as usual, was at the wheel of the mini bus suddenly pulled over which was no easy task on the Route de Lausanne which ran alongside the famous Lake Geneva on his left. Opposite was a hilly area on his right. On top of the hill were ancient Roman pillars and ruins of their empire. The group looked out the windows wondering why they were stopping in the middle of nowhere or so it seemed. The young Count of Pianore leaned over to the glove compartment in front of Jan. He smiled at her, gave her a quick peck on the cheek and reached into it.

"So sorry that Italy is so far away for a treat for you but here's a bit of America." Alessandro tossed a package of Twinkies to Bob who squealed with delight. "You and Ron talk so much about these that when I saw them in the gift shop I couldn't resist."

"Are you kidding me? If it wasn't for these, the cartons of milk or bottles of Coke Ron would have starved during our first year at college." Bob tore open the package while offering his thanks. He even offered one of the two Twinkies to Ron who actually took it. Ron was laughing, "And don't forget about the cherry pie. It was the only decent thing worth eating in that cafeteria." In seconds it was devoured.

"How does your brother stay so thin and eat that crap."

"Susan, it's the mystery of the ages."

The Coke bottles were emptied, the bag of chips and pretzels were consumed and the Twinkies were but a sugary memory. Ron pushed open the side window and poked his head outside. "Good job Alessandro, we're here."

The young Count glanced at Jan and turned to look to the back seat. "Here; where's here?"

"Okay, I am so sorry for being so mysterious and rushing out of the hotel but if Dominic was right about seeing that wire hanging down from Benton's room, I knew that we had to postpone Prangins until tomorrow and get here quickly."

"So again, I ask where's here?"

"Right, here ah really up there on that hill are the ruins of an ancient Roman town which is now called the Nyon Roman Museum. The Professor was kind enough to place a call to its curator who will give us shall I say a private tour."

"And this is important to us why?"

"Watson, would I lead all of you astray? It's important because written on this page in the autobiography by the hand of Joseph Bonaparte or maybe Louis Maillard, I can't be sure right now but in any case," Ron lifted up the Book. "The word *Romana* is written meaning Roman. Then right here Prangins Chateau is crossed off and Nyon is written on the edge of the page. These ruins are just outside of the town of Nyon. Here is where Joseph and Louis buried the clue for the treasure he left in Switzerland. This of course was after he took, what most historians will tell, the Crown Jewels originally buried in Prangins Chateau with him to America.

Everyone began to shout at once with excitement as they thought the legend of where the Crown Jewels were hidden had been solved. That is until Andreas paused amidst the cheering and asked the question of all questions given the situation in which they found themselves.

"Hold on, *un momento,* if we have found the Crown Jewels then why are we going to America?"

Ron returned the Book into Bob's new satchel. "Listen up everyone, my dream and these words just say that something was placed here. Until we find that something we don't know what we have. Secondly, it is a historical fact that Joseph Bonaparte brought jewels to America so it's unlikely that we'll find all the Crown jewels. Having said that, we need to go for the gold so to speak and dig where this notation tells us. That would be in the shadow of the Roman pillars holding the crossbeam. Right now the sun is setting and casting shadows off those pillars right there above us. So, Alessandro, follow that road which is *Rue Maupertuis* to *Rue Vieux-Marche'* there the Professor's curator friend will meet us for the tour."

With the sound of crunching gears, Alessandro got the bus moving as directed up the hill. It was not far and Ron had a lot to explain to his companions. And explain he did as he pointed out that while the tour was being given he would go search for the clue or whatever by the pillars. Andreas pointed out correctly that doing it alone would be foolish and also require digging and that shovels and a strong back would help. Without saying it directly Ron realized that he was not exactly built to dig a ditch or maybe several of them without help. And yet they could not all go digging as that would alert the curator as to their real purpose for the evening visit before leaving for America the next day. It was decided that the Professor's job would be to keep the curator engaged with questions about the ruins and history behind them. Only Ron and Bob would go on the hunt for the jewels or whatever remained if anything. Andreas was disappointed that he could not assist but he being the only Swiss national was needed to assist with the language barrier issues. All the others would act as tourists. The plan was set.

Picking up digging tools at the excavation shed of the museum wasn't a problem. Ron and Bob made their way with pick and shovel in hand toward the pillars now being illuminated on the edge of the rocky hill. They glowed like the ones in Ron's dream, the waning sun setting them afire in golden red light as it set across the calm lake waters shimmering as if covered in the gems of Bonaparte. Ron paced out the shadow knowing that he would have to match the dimensions given by Joseph Bonaparte in his notations in the metric system.

"Oh shit, Ron can you convert the measurements?"

"I think so…let's see 39 inches to a metric yard. That means…"

"Amici, the sun will set before you get that figured out."

"*Gesu Cristo*s be praised, I don't think Ron can do it fast enough Andreas." Bob was in a panic and then relieved when he saw Andreas walking toward them.

"I get it. Dominic and the Professor can handle the language problem. Show me the notes Ron."

Ron laid out the Book on the top of the broken third pillar next to the ones still holding their burden of stone and marble. "You do realize that I could do this."

"No doubt in my mind *amico;* nevertheless it would just be faster with one doing it who uses those measurements in his life."

"*Molto grazie amico,*"Ron patted Andreas on the back and handed him the pick. He and Bob would shovel out the loosened rock and dirt.

"*Prego*, you're welcome," and with that Andreas paced off the measurement from the pillar's shadow and split the ground as Sherlock and Watson began to shovel out the dirt and stones. "Now keep working and make noise. There is another reason that I followed you. We are not alone here by the pillars."

Bob began to fidget and panic. "Oh my God, not like back on Capri when those thugs wanted to kill us.

"Keep shoveling Bob," Ron pounded on stones with his shovel to keep the noise level up.

"Is he right, are their more than one?"

Andreas hadn't a clue as to how many might be following them. He just noticed a car not unlike the one they almost hit earlier in the day with their dinner guest Charles Benton. He suspected that Dominic's wiretap guy was the person in the car. Everyone was so excited about the Twinkie story that no one noticed that also alongside the road another car pulled off he went on to explain. Ron felt that if it was Benton then he was alone. It was decided to keep digging based on the dimensions of the shadow of the pillars caused by a setting sun. What they thought might be a long dig turned out to be only about three feet after a flat stone was discovered about a foot or so down. A clinking sound followed as Bob jabbed his shovel down. It was not the sound of an excited Bob which they heard but a gasp of some sort off in the distance wafting its way over them.

"Make no sound," Ron meant it for Bob but didn't single him out. "I'm going to open the box in the hole. And whatever is in there I'll pretend it's empty and swear and stuff like that."

Bob and Andreas both nodded understanding as Ron knelt down to brush the loose soil from the box and tilting it to reveal a latch but no lock. He pried open the lid, grabbed his flashlight hanging on his belt and shined it in the hole. "Oh shit," he shouted.

At the same time Bob and Andreas let out a few expletives only for them it was real for they hadn't caught a glimpse of anything let alone a box full of jewels. Ron threw himself onto the ground and pounded it all the while shouting that all their work was in vain, that the legend was false. In his tantrum no one, least of all the one behind a pile of rocks and vegetation some twenty feet away from them, saw that he had slipped something into his hiking jacket pocket. Bob played along by trying to console his pal. Andreas pulled out the metal box and threw it on the ground. He then began to shovel in the dirt with such force as to fling it everywhere but in the hole all the while cursing up a storm.

In a short time with some of the hole being refilled, the three simply sat with their backs against the base of the pillars and Ron flipping the lid up and down making sure it clanked as he did so. They didn't have to create the drama for long. The chatter of many voices could be heard coming their way. The curator was ending the tour with the view of Lake Geneva from the pillars at sunset. Their kicking of gravel and conversation drowned out another voice softly spoken in the rock formation.

"Son of a Bitch, she'll be so upset." Benton ran off down the hill to his car and sped off back toward Prangins Chateau.

The Professor and the Curator had flashlights and luckily they did for Jan just about hit the edge of the hole had not Alessandro caught her. The beams of light settled on the three at the pillars. Ron had just finished placing the metal box into Bob's satchel with the Book inside it. He thought that was most appropriate. They surrounded the three with the Curator wondering aloud why they seemed so distraught and not enjoying the view.

The lies came pouring forth one after the other. First it was how Bob fell into the pothole which seemed believable as Jan had almost done the same. Next it was that Andreas was upset with Dominic over the cost of the engagement party but didn't want to say anything. And finally it was their sadness over having to leave for home on the morrow. All of it was played to the hilt and except for the Curator all knew that it was but a scene from a melodrama being played out. It wasn't until they were all ensconced back in their mini-bus and on the way back to the hotel that Ron could actually reveal the entire truth of what happened at the Roman Pillars of Nyon. It began with Andreas having heard someone lurking near where the digging took place. In the coming darkness however it was impossible to know from where the gasp originated. Nevertheless if Dominic was correct about the hanging wire, then Benton had to be a suspect. Finally, Ron opened the chest pocket of his jacket and pulled out a frayed purple colored silk sack. He held it up and apologized to all his friends, his sister and the Professor for the deception.

"You see I did find something in that metal container. We couldn't say anything for fear that we were being watched so we acted out that scene of disappointment. All we have is this pouch but something with weight is in it."

Eyes brightened that all was not lost. Ron pulled open the top of the pouch. He cautioned everyone not to get their hopes up as it was obviously not a sack of gems. Whatever was in it was flat and it crunched. He gently pulled out a page of something and delicately opened it as it was wrapped around a silver coin. He handed over the coin to the Professor. Pettigrew recognized it as the image of Joseph Bonaparte on one side and the Bonaparte Coat of Arms on the other side.

"This is a coin minted when Joseph was the King of Spain." Pettigrew pointed to the writing on the edge of the coin stating that it was a *"Rey Jose"* or translated as a crown of King Joseph.

Bob got all excited that they had indeed found a crown of sorts.

"Cool your jets Watson, there is more. This is a letter of sorts. It is written in Latin not Spanish or French as one would expect. I think Joseph or whoever wrote this had a sense of humor. It congratulates the person finding the coin for that is all the treasure which will be found. 'When you find this' it goes on to say, 'we will be safely in a place of the United States called Philadelphia.' It is signed in French, *Roi Joseph.* And that appears to be all folks."

"Not quite," added Professor Andrew Pettigrew. "The coin proves that there was something of worth and the note says it's the only treasure one would find here. Thus it alludes to a treasure to be found and that would be in the United States."

Amidst wild cheering, Ron observed that there is surely a treasure and it's the Book they almost got killed discovering; "and it's right there in a metal box in Bob's satchel. The game is afoot *amici.*"

Joseph Bonaparte in America

Chapter Four:
The Secret of Point Breeze

Two of the three couples stood at the same door of Room 224. Jan
snuggled into the arms of Alessandro as they leaned against the door
while Ron and Susan walked back and forth, up and down the hallway
of the second floor arm in arm. When they reached the end of the
hallway which opened up onto a small balcony they just stood there
looking out onto the sparkling lights along the lakefront below them
and across the lake itself announcing that France lay in the distance.

"It's just all too beautiful and to think Ronnie, we're going home from
all of this after almost two years tomorrow." Susan held Ron's arm
tightly. "Will you miss all of this?"

Ron was never the one who could be accused of being a romantic. An
exception was the attempt to create just such a scene which lay before
them in the Blue Grotto of Capri. Even then he needed the help of
Dominic and Andreas to almost pull it off. But then it wasn't his fault
that Stefano and Apollo attacked them just after the proposal of
marriage. His thoughts may have been on that moment as he peered
through the French doors. And there one would be wrong. He simply
swung open the doors and carried Susan in his arms through the
threshold as if it was their wedding night. "I love you Susan, I hope
that you know that."

"Ronnie what's gotten into you? I said yes remember."

He lowered her to the wooden floor and looked down into her emerald
green eyes twinkling like the myriad of lights below them. "I'll never
forget that moment, ever but…"

"But what?"

"Listen carefully because in the next few days you may forget that I
said that I love you and will never forget that moment in the Blue

Grotto when you said yes. The 'but' is that what was discovered in the metal box in the Nyon ruins was not just a coin and a sarcastic letter. It was for the one who possessed the Book a clue in finding the Crown Jewels of Spain minus the crown of course as Bob pointed out. Our time here in Europe may be ending but the adventure continues back home. Remember I said the Game is Afoot."

"Honey child," she turned on her southern charm accent. "I know what that means after all this time and I'll be right there with you at Lake Bonaparte or that place they call Bordentown in New Jersey."

This time her 'honey child' didn't get him all flustered. He simply grabbed hold of her and twirled around until they fell onto a chase lounge, she crashing on top of him. He pulled her close to his face and kissed her as if it might be their last kiss ever. He could feel the rising of his problem whenever she was so close to him but this time he didn't care but she did. She had glanced up and saw a figure through the balcony door windows. Instantly she jumped off him and adjusted her white cotton blouse to hang just so over the waistband of her red Capri pants. She had deliberately worn the colors of Switzerland to honor Andreas on their last day in his homeland. Tomorrow it would be all about the red, white and blue.

"What the…"

"Ronnie, there's someone looking at us through the window. I can't tell who because the glare of the light just gives a shadowy effect but it's someone all right."

Erection or not, up he jumped from the lounge chair and placed himself between Susan and the doors. Shielding his eyes with one hand and pulling down on his pants with the other, he let out a shout that brought everyone out of their rooms and since all the rooms on the second floor were occupied by his friends and the Professor that meant everyone he knew.

"For shit's sake, Bob get your ass out here right now. You scared Susan half to death."

Timidly Bob pushed on the door so that it swung open and stepped onto the balcony with the metal box clutched in his arms. "I'm so sorry Susan. I didn't mean to frighten you but it's getting late and I felt that we all need to get a good rest after all the Game is Afoot, like Ron said."

Susan gently pushed Ron to the side and pranced up to Bob. She stroked his cheek and smiled. "You sweet thing always worried about everyone else and no one to worry about you. Well, you just come with me and we'll get all those folks in the hallway back in their rooms. You're right of course; we need to get some rest," she leaned into him and whispered, "especially if that Benton guy was the one in the ruins with you and Ronnie." She then turned to face a steaming Ron. "Come on sweetie, it's time for night-night."

Ron stomped off the balcony and followed them. As they passed Andreas and Dominic, Susan kissed them on the cheek and told them that they needed their rest. She did the same to the Professor and Alessandro who were next in line. The next room was number 222 which belonged to Ron and Bob. "Well boys, I must leave you both, right here. Now you just go to bed like good little boys and we'll do that game afoot thing tomorrow." She gave a peck to Bob and then Ron on the cheek and waved to Jan standing in front of Room 224 with a big smile on her face. In seconds the hallway was empty and quiet returned to the second floor except for Room 222.

"Why you asshole, what the hell were you thinking to appear like that after what happened in the ruins?"

"I'm the asshole, you're the one who is an asshole not me. I was all alone with God only knows who shirking about this hotel and another thing, I had the duty to protect the Book and the pouch with its letter and coin."

"Christ Bob, we were just down the hall. Give me that box and go to sleep." Ron made a move to take the box from his pal. "Well give it to me. I'll sleep with it under my pillow to make sure it's safe."

Bob walked to the table between their beds. "You don't have to sleep on it Ron, just keep it here between us."

"Well okay, but I wanted to read a few pages in the Book anyway."

"What you should be reading is the back of that letter in the pouch…"

The words had hardly left Bob's lips than Ron flipped open the lid and pulled out the pouch. "What are you saying?" He flattened the letter on the table top and began to read it. "It says just what I said it said all sarcastic and inferring that there is a treasure."

"Flip it over asshole." Bob plopped himself on the bed and fluffed up his pillow.

"Holy shit, there's a date and some faded writing. Oh my God this was placed after Joseph went to America. It must have been placed there when Louis, his secretary was sent back to retrieve the jewels from Prangins castle. It was Maillard who left this box as some kind of joke."

There was no response. Bob had faded away into a sound sleep. Ron pulled the covers over him smiling as he remembered the first time he saw his pal in those blue PJ's with little clouds and fluffy sheep. "Dumb ass, you still are wearing them like a five year old." Replacing the letter into the pouch, he then took out the Book for a little night reading. He turned to the pages about the Point Breeze estate. It was his intent to figure out the timeline of when Louis Maillard was sent back to Prangins to retrieve the jewels and why he left that coin and note in the Roman ruins. He was wishing that Andreas was with him so that he could fluently read the French and translate rather than rely on his first year of college French but then he did have the Latin notations so that would help.

Down at the end of the hall the Papal Guard he needed was wrapping his arms around the expression of his love. "Dom, do you think that we'll like America?"

Dominic looked into his sky blue eyes while brushing the blond hair off his brow. "What's brought this on Andreas." He kissed that brow. "I mean what's not to like? It's America and we're going to New York City first and we'll see Broadway and the Statue of Liberty and the Empire State Building and 'Little Italy' so that part should make me feel at home and you too. Ron promised to give us the grand tour before…"

"That's my point Dom; before we go on some wild goose chase as they say in America, searching for some long lost whatever which may bring on dangers like on Capri."

"Am I hearing that my Papal Guard is afraid?"

"Not for me," he stroked Dominic's cheek, "for you and the others. I can handle thugs. I am after all a soldier. But I don't know if I can handle being a foreigner whose English is broken and who Americans will point to as out of place."

"Out of place, one look at you all soldier-like and their hearts will melt just like mine did. You're just worried about going to a strange land where those chicks and dicks had best keep their hands off you."

"Chicks and dicks?"

"American slang, I'm learning to fit in."

"Oh so you're having the same thoughts about fitting in; but let me set you straight…well not in that way so stop smiling. The slang is chicks for girls and dudes for boys. True dudes have dicks but that's crass to say openly." They began to laugh and snuggled under the covers.

Next door Professor Pettigrew was seated at the desk jotting down the events of the day in his diary as the faint sound of Church bells wafted through the open window. It was, after a rather exciting evening of finding a Bonaparte clue, a heavenly sound of peacefulness where it not for the young Count of Pianore who was pacing the floor behind him.

"Alessandro, why don't you get some rest? The bells are announcing the eleven in the evening hour."

"Huh... *si,* sleep sure thing but I can't." He leaned over the desk and peeked at the diary. "I suppose you're writing about me in that thing too."

"Well it is a diary Alessandro, so yes everyone is in my reflection of what happened today."

The young Count fell onto the edge of the bed and leaned backwards stretching his arms behind his head and thus emphasizing a well-developed chest and arms. "So I suppose you'll say that 'then there was Alessandro who was with me as we toured the Roman Museum in Nyon' am I right on that point?"

"Of course you'll be a part of the tour narrative but not only that..."

"Then what else Professor," Alessandro jumped up off the bed and adjusted his loose fitting sleep shorts, then placed his hands on his hips. "There is nothing else to say because I did nothing. I wasn't there to help Andreas search for the one who spied on Ron and Bob digging. I, who my love, my dream girl thinks to be like the David which Michelangelo carved from marble... but in real life he was a warrior king. And what am I? I walk around a museum and do nothing."

Pettigrew quietly rose from his chair and faced the self-defacing young man. He placed his hands on the broad shoulders of Alessandro secretly wishing that he had such a body rather than his slender frame on which clothes just hung. He shook it off for he was becoming like the young man who was no more than five or six years younger than he and whose spirit he was trying to bolster. He suddenly felt much older.

"Now look at me young sir. You are a fine looking chap who Jan De Cenza admires greatly; anyone can see that if they only open their eyes. You are the David to her to be sure but even King David had days when he played music and sang psalms. He wasn't always ready for battle. Who would have thought that Ron and Bob might be in danger?"

"Andreas did…"

"Absolutely correct but that's not the point. You are the one who saved that Carolina Gianetti woman on that balcony on Capri from certain death. You are the one who helped Ron save the Royal family. You are the one who chased after the murderer in Mellifont. Do you understand what I'm trying to say? You are the warrior when one is needed and you are the singer of songs so to speak when that role is needed. By being with us, you protected Jan and Susan, Dominic and me just in case something went wrong in that museum."

"Thank you Professor," Alessandro embraced him and kissed him in the Italian fashion on each cheek. "I think I get it." He jumped into bed, pulled up the sheet and entered slumber before Pettigrew could suggest that he call him Andrew.

Back to the desk he went, tightened the cord around his silk robe and entered his reflection on what just happened into his diary never knowing that in the other rooms such fears were being expressed except for that in Room 224 where the girls were lodged. They had taken their showers, dressed themselves in cotton pajamas with a button down top and talked about how the boys would feel seeing them in their pj's. Jan made it quite clear that there would be no way that Alessandro would see her in what she called a child's pajamas. She saw herself in a satin number with lace trim like the new Mrs. Sophia Verdi wore on her honeymoon on Capri with the police Captain. What love they have for each other she would say, wondering if one day such a love would be hers.

The moon was full outside their window and she thought of her mother's favorite song, "That's Amore'." She opened the balcony doors and leaned onto the wooden railing singing its verses. In no time at all Susan joined her and entered at the chorus. "When the moon hits your eye, like a big pizza pie that's amore'."

When the song ended they went to their beds and wondered aloud if there really was a treasure at all given that what was found was nothing but a coin and a sarcastic letter.

Right next door however in Room 222, Ron had no doubt that he was on the road to proving the Legend of Joseph Bonaparte to be true. Sentence by sentence, word by word he managed to decipher the meaning of what was printed on the page and what correlated with it written on the margins. His cocoa brown eyes widened like those of a cow as he made one of those connections. He wished that he could have shared that find with his pal in the next bed but he was off to Never Never Land in his blue cloud pj's with Peter Pan. He mumbled to himself about flying as well but on a plane on the morrow going back home and dozed off.

As the Church bells chimed the Midnight hour he found himself back in history and on the Point Breeze estate of Joseph Bonaparte in New Jersey. But in this dream he wasn't interacting with anyone, he was an observer.

The morning sun was warming up an early Fall day as Joseph tended his gardens probably for the last time as the growing season was ending. Those gardens had become the envy of the east coast which attracted many visitors. The former king of Spain looked like one of his gardeners which actually pleased him. He often said that he preferred working in his gardens than running a government of a nation. Behind the mansion of Point Breeze one could hear the rushing waters of Crosswicks Creek as it flowed down to meet the Delaware River. All of this sereneness was not to last as his secretary came rushing out of the mansion waving in his hand a letter.

"Your Majesty, a letter has just been delivered and the courier awaits an immediate response."

"Louis, you're forgetting again. I am the Comte de Survilliers."

"Yes, of course sire…sir I am just excited as this comes from the Capitol of the United States, a place called Washington in the District of Columbia."

"Does it now, well we must have a look, mustn't we? But let's walk Louis lest we be overheard. And stop waving that damn thing around like a flag." Joseph looked around seeking fellow gardeners. Three of them were working between where they stood and the mansion. So he chose to enter the wooded area and take a set of granite stone steps down to Crosswicks Creek. There he felt safe enough to speak of communications from the American government.

Louis shoved the letter under his cutaway coat and into his vest. Unlike Joseph who was pudgy and shorter, the secretary was leaner, much younger and a bit taller yet it was Joseph who was in better shape for the hike.

As they descended the stone steps Joseph questioned Louis about the courier. It turned out that he was an American and spoke no French.

"Luckily Monsieur Carret was in the mansion at the time for my English is still not very good."

"So then we now have four people who know of this communication from the American government, Qui?"

"This is true if one counts the courier himself."

"And you do not think this man from Washington would not mention to all he meets that he was in the home of the Comte de Survilliers?"

"I see your point. What shall we do?"

"Do, we shall walk to that dock down the creek bed and enter the tunnel which leads to the house. You did bring the gate key so that we may enter via the tunnel?"

"Sire…I mean sir, you surely know that I always carry the keys to the secret room and the tunnel gates whenever I am in the mansion."

"I do Louis, of course, I was being overly cautious." Joseph held out his hand to receive the key in question.

Up on the bluff looking down at the two men was one of the gardeners and another man in riding attire. The gardener had excused himself to relieve nature's call. Not typically a worker in the fields as his hands were hardly calloused he also understood French. However he feigned ignorance of the language in the company of fellow workers. As for the man in the riding attire he was speaking English to the gardener with an accent not typically heard in New Jersey.

Louis lighted the candle in the lantern and led the way into the tunnel while Joseph locked the gate behind them. "Now then Louis, we can speak more freely."

They entered the secret room behind the Bookshelves of Joseph's famous library which contained thousands of Books. By that time the King felt that the courier was truly not a spy of some sort. Confidence reigned that the American courier would not come to haunt him months later.

Louis went about lighting candles in the secret room as Joseph seated himself at a lone desk in the center of the room. The key to that flip down desk was always in the possession of the King. He inserted the key and gave it a twist, then lowered the writing platform. He then laid the letter on the green velvet pad and leaned over it motioning for Louis to hold the candle closer as there were no windows in the hidden room.

"Louis, I can't imagine that we should be summoned to an audience with President Madison as we were told that it would be impossible to arrange for such a meeting years ago when we first arrived in this land."

"Qui Majesty…Sir, I remember clearly how we were stopped in Philadelphia and told to turn around."

"We should have Carret here to insure that we are reading this English correctly."

"Quite true, as an American he certainly could tell us exactly what this says; but I think I can manage, Sir."

Louis Maillard bent over to examine the letter. He pointed out that it was not from the Executive Mansion of the President or the White House as the common people referred to it. Rather it had the Coat of Arms of what Americans call the Seal of the Department of State at the heading. At the bottom the signature, he noted, was that of a James Monroe. "His title, Sir, is that of Secretary of State."

"Ah, of course the Foreign Minister of the United States, *bon*, and now what does this Monroe have to say Louis?"

"Majesty, he wants to meet with you. It says that events in France may make your stay here difficult."

"We have heard of no such events. Could he mean that the return of the Bourbon Dynasty is, once again about to fall? Does he mention that quite dull King Louis XVIII?"

"No Sire, just 'events' in France."

"We shall respond immediately. Louis, take pen and paper."

As the response was being penned one of the two men up on the bluff was making his way down to the small pier at the tunnel entrance. He found it locked and quickly returned to his colleague. But now the British sympathizer knew of a secret entrance into the Bonaparte Mansion. They began to plot how to make use of it. Ron found himself trying to identify the man at the tunnel gate as he stood there dressed only in his sleep shorts and shivering in the dampness of the brick subterranean passageway. Feeling like Scrooge in the Dickens' novel of "A Christmas Carol" who had just viewed the past, he got back to the secret room just in time to view Joseph signing the letter. All the while he was thinking that he would like to be wearing a nightshirt with a robe as in the novel.

"There, now get Carret, have him write an English version and send both copies to this Mr. Monroe. We shall hope to meet with him at his convenience in Philadelphia."

Louis placed the letter into a portfolio. "Sir, shall I bring James Carret here to insure secrecy of this matter?"

"*Qui*, that is a good thought. Now let us put out the candles lest we have a fire."

Louis extinguished the candles as the King pushed open the moveable Bookshelf which let in natural sunlight. He entered his grand Library said to rival that of the Library of Congress knowing that his presence would not be known there as the staff thought him to be working in the garden. Louis pushed the Bookshelf back against the wall. Ron just made it through as he did so. He found himself next to a large window draped in damask curtains which were held back by porcelain tie backs with flower prints. He clearly saw one of the gardeners walking out of the forested area inside which was the bluff overlooking Crosswicks Creek. It was with the courier, he was sure of it since about his neck was the leather pouch and he wore riding clothes. Ron was in a panic, he began to shout that he knew who was plotting to destroy the fortune of Joseph Bonaparte. Running in circles and waving at Joseph and Louis to no avail as he was but a shadow, no more like the Invisible Man for not even his shadow could be seen on what was a fall day in 1820.

"Ron, what's the matter? Hey, come on wake up…" Bob pushed up and down on the mattress shaking his pal.

The disoriented Ron popped open his eyes and saw those baby blue ones of his best buddy hovering over him. "What the hell, what's the matter with you. You scared me half to death." He pushed himself into a sitting up position with lightning speed thinking another disaster had befallen their little group getting ready to depart for America. Sweat was beaded on his brow on what was a cool morning in Prangins Switzerland.

"You were shouting in your sleep. I think that you had a nightmare or something." Bob jumped backwards tripping on Ron's slippers and falling onto his bed. "Sorry that I was worried about you."

The immediate response was a pillow crashing into his face. "Stop being a Diva. I was just shocked that's all." Ron jumped out of the bed and went to the balcony doors. He slid them open and a gust of that cool morning breeze gushed into the room. He shivered just like he did in the dream as he followed King Joseph and his secretary into that secret tunnel. He ran his fingers through his bushy charcoal briquette colored hair and shook it off.

"You're shivering, maybe if you'd put some clothes on that scrawny body of yours…"

"Asshole, it's the cold wind that's all," Ron turned with what his father called a 'shit ass grin' on his face lit up like a light bulb. "We can't all be a modest Father Bob in pj's with clouds and sheep and buttoned to the top like you were in a cloister. Anyway pretty soon pal, Susan will be seeing a lot more than just this," he puffed out his chest, twirled and took a bow. "Jealous…"

"Asshole, no I'm not jealous. I happen to be a good friend but I'm not too sure of that these days."

"Oh Christ Bob," Ron walked to the dresser and pulled out clean underwear. "Why would you say something like that? You're going to be my Best Man." He turned holding in his hands what was his usual underwear choice of Jockey briefs and a v-neck undershirt. No more of those sexy Italian silk briefs.

Squeezing the thrown pillow in his arms, his best pal looked like one of those sheep on his pj's the lost one like in the Scripture story.

"I know but still think about it Ron, after we get home and you finish decoding that Book we'll find whether or not there is a Bonaparte treasure in no time flat and then it's over. You walk down the aisle and I go back to the seminary in Mundelein Illinois."

"Whoa pal this is way too heavy to talk about right now like this. Let me shower and shave and get dressed then we'll have a nice talk, just you and me not the other guys."

"Whatever, I'll call the Professor and tell him that we'll be late for breakfast."

As the heart to heart was about to take place in that hotel room overlooking Geneva Lake in Switzerland, across the pond at another lake called Bonaparte in upstate New York the investigation had continued. On the previous day the body was taken from boat Number 16 and brought to the morgue at the hospital in the Town of Diana on the other end Lake Bonaparte from where it was found. It would remain there until the English Professor and his research team arrived. Two days later Sherriff Fontaine was sitting with Francois back at the Bonaparte Launch and Lunch dock reviewing the case.

"Professor Witherspoon of Princeton had alerted Professor Pettigrew who had just arrived in New York City with his team as what to expect upon arriving at Lake Bonaparte," Francois was saying when Sarah came running down to them with another Special Delivery envelope. "Francois, it's from New York City."

He ran to her but she stopped in her tracks and held back the envelope. "Oh, it's not for you; it's for the Sherriff."

"What, I'm the one who met with Witherspoon. She said she'd do a bit of research with the photo and get back to me."

"Sorry, Francois but this must be delivered to Sherriff Fontaine." And with that she walked causally down to the surprised Sherriff and handed him the legal size white envelope with a return address of New York Bureau of Investigations.

Beginning to tear the edge of the envelope quite carefully he observed that he couldn't imagine why someone in New York City would be interested in a body found on Lake Bonaparte. "Let's see here, Dear Sherriff Fontaine, this communication has been sent to introduce to you Detective Lieutenant Brandon Malone who will be leading the investigation in conjunction with Professor Andrew Pettigrew of Oxford University and his team due to arrive within a few days. Due to the international ramifications of the murder Lt. Malone will be accompanied by Captain Enrico Verdi of the Italian Carabinieri and Interpol as the finger prints and photo of the body have now been recognized as that of Apollo Dimitri who is an escaped prisoner from Italy. Please afford him your utmost cooperation. And it ends with the signature of the State Commissioner of Police."

"Sherriff, what could possibly be so important about this dead man?"

"That Sarah is what we need to find out as there was nothing on him to identify him and obviously he was in disguise given the hair dye job. He obviously did something to his hair after those teens saw him."

"And you mentioned a Professor Pettigrew, that's the guy who made the reservations for his research team through Professor Witherspoon. She told me that he would be an expert in historic artifacts and the arrow which was the murder weapon which was not recently made but from a very old Crossbow."

"Francois, where the hell would one find a Crossbow up here in Lake Bonaparte?"

While that question was being addressed for it certainly could not be answered, up on the arm of the Statue of Liberty was a group of what seemed to be excited tourists. They were standing on the outside balcony surrounding the torch being held up by Lady Liberty. They had other thoughts on what the Professor had recently told them about a Detective Lieutenant Malone. Ron was particularly, if not upset with the prospect of having him at his heels, certainly concerned in that he was the Police Detective who almost threw him in jail over the murder at the World's Fair some two years prior.

"But that's another tale for another day. So look over there guys, that's the Empire State Building towering up over the skyline." Except for Susan, Bob and Ron it was the others first time going up the Statue which Andreas remarked was so much larger than the one in Arona Italy of St. Charles Borromeo onto which Ron had climbed out onto as he tried to escape would be terrorists.

"I thought you were a goner for sure when that Argentinian guy tried to catch you out there hanging on a rope."

"No shit, it was like that old Alfred Hitchcock movie when the hero and villain were climbing out on this statue's arm right down there over this railing. So cool for a movie but not too much when I was up on the arm of the Colosso statue and it wasn't nearly this big."

The Italians and Swiss guy were just thrilled to be sightseeing, and not chasing after terrorists and murderers. That feeling of excitement would be short lived. When they got out of the elevator at the gift shop level there stood waiting for them was the Professor and with him was the newly promoted Detective Lieutenant Brandon Malone. Ron and Bob stayed at the back of the group as the introductions were made trying in vain to be inconspicuous.

"Now here are two more that I know quite well," Malone pulled them into a hug. "These two and Susan helped me catch more than a thief at the World's Fair. My God how you have changed in those two years."

"Thanks and you look different too; congrats on the promotion." Ron smiled relieved that Malone was remembering the positive aspects of those days during the New York City World Fair.

"Right, Lieutenant, that's cool." Bob was genuine in his remarks. "You do look different. More rounded out and…"

Malone laughed. "And more like you my friend, a bit too much in the belly. But enough of this, we must be off, a boat is waiting to take us off this island and back to Manhattan. There waits for us someone else who I am told that you know quite well." Off Bob and Ron walked with Malone's arms around their shoulders.

"Professor, what is going on?" Jan was getting upset. She along with the others thought they could see a Broadway show before going on the treasure hunt after all that happened in Italy and Switzerland. Pettigrew had to explain that unfortunately a glitch had come along to hamper their research and it had to do with someone that all of them except for him knew from their holiday on Capri.

"Oh, you mean the holiday which turned into a nightmare in the Mediterranean." Susan was none too happy about the change in plans. Pettigrew on his part pointed out that she and Ron as well as Andreas and Dominic got engaged despite the murder and attempted theft. Susan smiled agreement and noted how romantic it was before their dance was abruptly interrupted. The still single Professor was at a loss for words. So he changed the focus from Capri to Lake Bonaparte by informing them that he was told that it was a lovely place set in the mountains and surrounded by caverns to explore.

By the time they disembarked off the Police Boat at the tip of Manhattan the talk was about upstate New York and its mountains, Lake Region and caves to explore. The latter never thought of by Malone as having anything to do with treasure. In any case all of such talk abruptly ended, as they saw standing on the dock two people who the so called research assistants and the Professor knew quite well. There stood Captain Enrico Verdi and his wife, Sophia Verdi. Sophia waved wildly as the girls jumped off the plank and ran to her open arms.

"Oh Sophia, this would be so wonderful for you and now…" Susan threw her arms around the Captain's wife.

"Do not say so my dear; this is just a short delay to the second honeymoon…"

"Oh, I'd say it was the first honeymoon after what happened on Capri ruined the first one; move over Susan and let me have a hug." Jan and Sophia embraced.

While that reunion took place the guys were making a dash for Captain Verdi who greeted each of them in the Italian style of a hug and kiss and each cheek. "*Amici,* this treasure hunt of which your Professor spoke has turned nasty I hear." Verdi stopped in front of the Professor, hesitant in greeting him in the Italian manner.

The Professor however was not about to be given just a hand shake, British or not, this Captain was the man who helped to save his life when the girls, Bob and Ron found him wounded in the Piazza San Pietro back in Rome. He pulled the Captain into an embrace and waited for the kiss of friendship which did come along with a hearty laugh.

"So Professor, we Italians have rubbed off on you, *Si?*"

"I shall be ever grateful to you and these young people who admire you so and with good reason. But you are on your second honeymoon and we should let you get to it; but after we go to Mulberry Street for a scrumptious dinner to celebrate your arrival." Pettigrew turned to the guys surrounding them. "What do you say gentlemen? Shall we take the Captain and Signora Verdi to Little Italy?"

The guys were all for it. Ron was looking forward to sharing with him his findings in the Bonaparte Book, which he helped to save on Capri. How much to share was his only issue. Malone however had other news to share and it burst Ron's bubble. He along with all the others was looking forward to a quest for the Bonaparte Treasure. He squeezed his way between the Captain and the Professor, the latter graciously ceding his place to the Detective.

"Captain Verdi, *mi piacere,*" he began in Italian with a greeting of being a pleasure to meet him. "I am Detective Lieutenant Brandon Malone of the New York Bureau of Investigation."

"It is also my pleasure to meet you," Verdi responded in English. "The letter explained that you would be leading me to the scene of the crime as well as to…" he stopped his reply and looked towards his wife and the young people encircling them.

Ron couldn't stand it any longer. There was more to Verdi's presence than just the Bonaparte treasure or even his second honeymoon. That was obvious. "Captain, Detective please share with us what you mean about a crime scene." He was in Sherlock mode.

Malone took the lead and informed them of a murder on Lake Bonaparte and that the victim may be someone they might know. Their trip to Lake Bonaparte would entail more than just researching and exploring caves. They would be taken to identify the body.

Chapter Five:
The Dead End

Two days later a slightly better equipped mini-bus rambled down the Lake shore road toward the Bonaparte Launch and Lunch which which had been allowed to remain open. Only this time a uniform officer was driving the vehicle not Alessandro, who was quite miffed at having his job taken away. In a separate unmarked car ahead of them rode Malone, Verdi, Sophia and the Professor. They were to pick up Francois Parrot and then meet the Sherriff at the hospital morgue. Susan, Ron and Bob would be used to identify the body as they had come into close contact with him on the Isle of Capri, if he was indeed who they thought he was.

The three teens who had found the body were busy renting out the rowboats with outboard motors and helping tourists into and out of the returning boats. It was near the end of the summer rush just before the start of school. The mini-bus and car pulled up in front of the Restaurant located higher up on a ridge. It was rather unobtrusive and typically simple in country style and nautical accents. Large windows were at the front and rear to afford a view of the lake in the rear and the forest in the front with its leaves already changing colors. Francois stood with Sarah on the wooden porch-like structure leading into the restaurant. He offered the entire group lunch to which Bob offered profuse thanks. Lt. Malone felt that they had time to feed the troops as it were before meeting the Sherriff but he would have him radioed to inform him that they would arrive a bit later than expected.

They were led onto a wooden veranda which had a staircase at the far end which one could take down to the pier and rental hut. As soon as they were settled up those stairs came running the three teens. They had already heard as had everyone in the hamlet of Natural Bridge and in between that a famous Oxford Professor was coming with his team to find Bonaparte's jewels. One look at Andreas, Dominic and Alessandro and Sally had loss her heart to another, which one would be decided later at Jeff's expense. Jack however was pleased with the soon to be outcome.

"Let it go, Jeff; look at them all muscled up and Italian and everything…but they're old and we're young with lots of fish in the sea as my Dad would say." Jack's delight would be when Sally realized that Dominic and Andreas had a thing for each other. Had she looked beyond their looks, she could have seen that immediately. Even if they were younger they'd have no interest in her. And as for the guy called Alessandro, he had his eyes on a pretty little brunette girl who he wouldn't mind asking to homecoming, even if he had to fight off the big dude who held her hand. Jeff ignored Jack's observations as his eyes were drawn to the red haired girl with the boobs to die for but whose sparkling green eyes could make a guy quiver with desire and Jeff was a teen not unlike what Ron was when he first met Susan and did a lot more than quiver with desire much to his embarrassment. Luckily Jeff was more in control of his nether regions.

The teen crushes just beginning to bloom and soon to crash aside they were introduced. They offered to answer questions about the victim they found in the boat at the cavern. The girls immediately took Sally under their wings as they were amused with her blushing upon just glancing at Alessandro and even Ron. Had the former would-be priest known that he garnered only an afterthought glance blush, he probably would have been insulted but thankfully he did not. In any case his mind was not on teen crushes but on what Jack was telling him about the cavern where the body was found.

While crossing the Atlantic on the plane, he and Andreas had ample time to go over the pages which dealt with Joseph Bonaparte's acquisition of the upstate New York property and the house he built there. It was clear that as with the Point Breeze estate he used secret tunnels once again. But unlike the New Jersey location, the tunnels of Lake Bonaparte had been explored over and over again as had many of the caves surrounding the lake. Between those translations and the Latin notes in the margins of the pages Ron had formed a theory that Joseph used misguidance and legend. He kept people off the track of finding his hidden treasure if there was any in the first place. Even that he had managed to cloud in legend and rumor even in his day. His autobiography only added to those rumors except for the copy which Ron and his friends possessed which had been notated with the truth for his daughter by his mistress Annette Savage. And all of that was centered in New Jersey not the State of New York.

Despite his feeling that Lake Bonaparte would provide no useful information, he thought he'd play it safe and planned to meet Jack the next morning. It was time that he went into the cave which Apollo had singled out as a potential hiding place for the jewels of Bonaparte. After all, whatever he was searching for got him killed, of that Ron was certain. The question also on his mind was who broke him out of prison and sponsored his way to America. His first thought was that Carolina Gianetti would have the resources to do so but then she had been shot, was at odds with Stefano and Apollo who had become rogue and out to kill her as well as her lover the powerful Niccolo Cavelli who was also in prison in Naples. With Cavelli in prison, his influence and financial abilities were virtually nonexistent and as for Gianetti, she was wounded and last heard to be recuperating slowly. The only other candidate who would know of Apollo would be Lorenzo Medino the partner of Stefano who found the Book in the first place and who Stefano killed to save Apollo. He had hit a dead end. The frustration of getting nowhere did result in a conclusion which he shared with his friends on the way to the Morgue. He felt assured that this visit to identify the body of Apollo and finding his murderer was not connected to the quest they were on regarding the information in the autobiography. The connection was that Apollo was obsessed with the legend of the jewels in that very Book. If he could find someone to back him and get him out of prison, then he would be in a position to search for the treasure with the little information that his lover Stefano had before the Book was found by Ron in the room of the murder victim Lorenzo Medino back on Capri.

Ron sat in this semi-meditative state mulling over the murder at the mouth of Bonaparte's cave. His friends, including Susan to whom he was now engaged and who would have preferred to be working on wedding plans, were proposing their own theories. How did Apollo, if the dead man they were about to see was indeed him, get out of jail and make his way to America. They seemed to be in agreement that somehow Niccolo Cavelli, whom they helped to trap in a wild confession at the empty tomb of Joseph Bonaparte in Florence, was somehow behind the escape. He had the connections to create forged papers, for Apollo or anyone. Such passports and papers would have been needed to make his way across an ocean. He certainly would have the influence to pull it off despite his imprisonment or so they thought.

While these deliberations continued on who did what, two events were unfolding. At the JFK Airport in New York City, Carolina Gianetti had just disembarked with Luigi and Pietro from the First Class Cabin area. Greeting them at the customs area exit was a hired driver who had a car waiting to take them to Princeton University to meet with Charles Benton newly arrived from Switzerland. The second event, which would impact Ron and his friends as well as Carolina and her thugs, was taking place at Princeton University. There Professor Dorothy Witherspoon had just visited the College Museum and was heading for the office of the Dean of the History Department to speak with Professor Richard Stockton about a murder on Lake Bonaparte with which her friend from Oxford University was involved.

As the forest on one side and Lake Bonaparte on the other side, which is what Ron was seeing as he looked out the rear side window of the mini-bus, presented a lovely pastoral scene, he nodded his disagreement with his friends' expressed theories. It wasn't done in a manner which anyone would have noticed. In fact no one was paying the slightest attention to him. Bob, in particular, knew that when his best pal entered such a state of contemplation that it was best to let him be and then get the results later. Officer O'Malley, now at the wheel of the bus, much to the displeasure of Alessandro, Count of Pianore who was the usual driver of the band of sleuths, drove into the hospital driveway. Ron's sister Jan was consoling her melancholy boyfriend with a rational explanation that he being from Italy wouldn't know the best way to get to the hospital. The remaining engaged couple Andreas and Dominic were in the thick of the discussion as to who could have the power, money and connections to get Apollo to upstate New York. Dominic had been Professor Pettigrew's research assistant for several years. He clearly understood the cost behind such an enterprise as seeking out historic treasure. Wasn't that what the Crown Jewels of

Spain long lost actually were? As the bus came to a halt with a slight jerk, Dominic grabbed hold of the Papal Guard's arm.

"Andreas, you and I will have to go identify the body with Ron. You're a soldier, look for something."

"Dom, whoever this man is, he was shot with an arrow. The Vatican Guards may carry a lance but bows and arrows are not part of our training. In any case from what the Professor was saying earlier, even the arrow was unique and not from a bow like Robin Hood would have used."

A smile crossed his partner's face. "Really, Robin Hood, now you use a character from English literature as a reference? *Andiamo*, let's go, the Professor is at the door motioning to us."

The van had stopped in front of a modest three story brick building with a canopy over its entrance supported by white painted colonial style pillars, under which O'Malley had driven. Sherriff Fontaine was standing at the entrance doors with the Lieutenant Brandon Malone of New York City Police Investigation Bureau, Captain Verdi and Sophia Verdi. O'Malley pulled a lever to the right of the steering wheel and opened the door outside of which Pettigrew stood.

"Ladies and Gentlemen, we have arrived at the Town of Diana Hospital. Needless to say, given the appearance and location of this medical facility they have probably had little to do with an international conspiracy and theft of historic artifacts. You will afford the authorities every courtesy and not present your theories of which I heard many expressed on this ride here…" Pettigrew continued to ramble on as he led them off the bus.

Ron was now tuned into what was going on. He pulled on Bob's arm and into his lap off which he immediately jumped. "Will you listen to the Professor? He's talking to us like we're those teens back at the boat launch. I just turned twenty-one, I'm a man who is about to get married for shit's sake."

"Cool your jets Ron, he's British and well... you know he's all formal and stuff like that."

"Well perhaps he should take a lesson from that Beatles singing group just arrived from his homeland to invade us. They seem rather relaxed and with it."

"And you are now the lover of pop music? I'd say you'd be more into what the Professor's probably likes, a bit of Verdi, Vivaldi and a touch of Mozart."

"And don't forget Rossini's William Tell Overutre, Hi Ho and away." With a slight jab to Bob's shoulder he was off like the Lone Ranger character from an old TV show. Bob was complaining about the non-existent pain as they ran to the front of the bus and out the door to join the others lined up on the asphalt driveway like Papal Guards on duty or in this case the Queen's Guards at Buckingham Palace since it was the Professor lining them up. Watching the spectacle Malone smiled and leaned into the Sherriff.

"If you don't mind Sherriff, I think I should speak with these young people. Those two, Ron De Cenza and Bob Wentz I know from a previous case."

"Do tell Detective, those nice lads were in trouble with the law?"

"Not in the way you are thinking; and the red hair girl, Susan Liguri, she was with them too. I came to know her quite well too when the culprit we were chasing was killed."

"So then these young people know of murder. What they are about to see won't be such a shock."

Captain Verdi added that death is shocking despite having been exposed to violence. He then related how they actually helped to save lives and Renaissance artifacts in Italy over a year ago and again on the Isle of Capri just a few months ago.

"Let us just say that they fancy themselves as some kind of Sherlock and Watson team with Susan as a third sleuth who has eyes for that one with the dark hair and big brown eyes. But alas the De Cenza lad was in training to become a priest, too bad for her," Malone observed. The Sherriff smiled broadly as he pointed out to Susan holding onto Ron's arm, pulling him down and whispering something in his ear. "I don't think that lad as you call him is becoming a priest anytime soon. Take a look at her ring finger on her left hand. I see a diamond on it if I'm not mistaken."

"And I thought that I was the detective. Sherriff, that is quite the development. Good lad, to catch such a lovely young lady or maybe it was the reverse... in any case I hope it doesn't impact his detecting ability; he has a knack for it." Malone invited Verdi to walk with him as he was familiar with all of them.

 They came up to the Professor, shook his hand and then Malone addressed the seven. He explained that St. Mary's Hospital was serving a small rural community and therefore its morgue and viewing area was not what might be expected in New York City or even Rome Italy. "In other words, you will be in the morgue itself where the victim will be presented directly to you. Now should any of you feel that this would be uncomfortable you may stay in the Hospital Lobby. I really only need those who had come in close contact with the deceased." He looked directly at Ron and Bob.

"Yes, Sir, I'll be fine. I think all of us will be able to be there. You haven't been around us for two years and a lot has happened since then."

"Fine Mr. De Cenza, then shall we enter," Malone invited Verdi to bring his wife and the others to follow him, and the Sherriff.

They walked through the sparsely appointed lobby with about eight chairs and through a corridor past the ER room. Then entering through swinging double doors they found themselves in the main morgue facility with its office to their right. On the wall opposite of them was a series of stainless steel doors, four in number, behind which was a

98

cooling cubicle from which a sliding stretcher of sorts pulled out. On that platform a body would lay. Sherriff Fontaine led them to the door with a number three attached to it. He glanced at the girls in particular as the Medical Examiner unlatched the door and slowly opened it. He was relieved to see that the M.E. had covered the body in a white sheet to provide some dignity to the remains.

"Now then, Doctor Goldberg will pull out the tray and uncover the remains. I believe that Andreas Berne, Bob Wentz and Ron De Cenza were the two closest to the victim when you were on Capri and of course Captain Verdi who arrested him; that is if this is indeed who we think it is. Please come forward and stand next to the doctor."

The three being in place, the Doctor then unveiled the body pulling the sheet to his waist so that he might turn the body and show the penetration area made by the arrow. "Young men do you recognize this man? You will note that he had dyed his hair which we attempted to remove to verify that it was not his natural color, which is a vibrant blond as you may see."

"Yes Sir, he was a light hair man like me; this is the man who I saw Captain Verdi of the Carabieneri arrest on Capri." Andreas turned to Bob.

"Yes Sir, this is one of the two men who stole my satchel at the Green Grotto on Capri." Bob looked at an uncharacteristically distracted Ron and gave him a poke. He then nodded that it was his turn.

"Right, thanks Bob," he returned his eyes from the metal table on which laid the murder weapon or at least part of it. "Yes Sir, I fought with this man on the rocky hills of Capri not more than four months ago. His name is Apollo Dimitri. His partner was Stefano Rinaldi who attacked Susan." He looked over the body into Susan's emerald green eyes and smiled.

"That's accurate. I too saw him fight my…well my fiance' Ron. He thought he was like the god come down from Olympus of the same name. Poor thing made all the wrong choices to bring attention to him."

"Thank you for identifying the victim," began Malone, "And now if Professor Andrew Pettigrew and Dominic Fontana would come forward."

Doctor Goldberg turned the body to reveal the wound on Apollo's back. He then directed the Captain and them to a table used to prepare a body received in death. On that metal table lying on a white cloth was the arrow. "This is the arrow which was taken out of the victim's back. It is unlike anything I have ever seen. As you may note it is about twelve inches long with a wooden shaft and actual feathers not at all like those used with hunting Crossbows of today which use copper or aluminum arrows or bolts as hunters call them. I thought that given your background in Medieval and Renaissance History it might mean something to you. We know it didn't come from a regular archery bow or even a Tribal weapon."

Pettigrew agreed that it was not from a long bow. He identified it was coming from a Crossbow. Dominic agreed and recalled the time when he and the Professor were excavating in the Vatican subterranean levels when they found a long forgotten sealed tunnel which connected to the Castel San Angelo. Besides the art pieces they found within it, there was also a variety of weapons including a crossbow.

"Professor, look at the shaft and feathers."

"The arrow's shortness indicates that it most assuredly came from a crossbow."

"Right, and the condition of the feather and wood, I would say clearly demonstrates that this is not a modern weapon made in a medieval fashion for a movie or hunting or something of that nature. It is aged perhaps centuries old."

Back at the coolers, the others watched and listened intently.

Andreas poked Ron in the ribs. "That's my guy; all full of knowledge and a stallion in looks as well."

"Shhh, the Detective will hear you."

"Oh I see, but he's just so loveable when he's into his history stuff."

"Okay then so you're proud of him," then Ron thought of what he had said. Was it because it was about another guy? He tried to cover his tracks. "I get it but this is a morgue."

"Sorry, I got carried away." The Papal Guard offered a sheepish smile of embarrassment.

Back at the table the Professor was speaking to the love of Andreas' life.

"I concur with you Dominic and I know who could possibly identify its precise age and she's a colleague who teaches at Princeton University and with whom I have contacted about this matter." The Professor looked across the table into the eyes of Malone, Verdi and the Sherriff. "I suggest that we be allowed to bring this arrow with us to Bordentown New Jersey where we are to conduct an excavation in a few days. We can stop at Princeton University where Professor Dorothy Witherspoon could test it for age and probably the type of Crossbow from which it was shot."

Malone agreed with the Professor. The arrow was wrapped and placed into a container for transport with him to New Jersey which was out of his jurisdiction but he would contact the local authorities for cooperation as it was still a New York state case. "We may have to call in the FBI Sherriff given that we are crossing state lines."

"Let's just cross that bridge when we come to it, shall we. In any case I will handle things here while you continue the investigation in New Jersey if there is a connection at all."

It was decided that they would leave in two days which would afford
the Professor and his team a chance to explore the cave outside of
which the body of Apollo was found. Ron however had other plans
and those he would discuss once they were settled in their cabins on
Birch Island. Francois had four small cabins on the island and each
one had access to a motor boat to tour the lake. Given the presence of
the Captain and his wife, one of those would now be assigned to them.
Another was already rented to a man identified as Antoine Murat. As
soon as Ron heard that name a spark ignited in his brain. He would let
it fester for a bit. That meant that all the guys would be crammed into
one cabin and the girls in the remaining one.

Francois was escorting the guys to their cabin while Sarah had come
over from town to help settle in the girls and now the newlyweds as
well. The four cabins were set in a line on higher ground which
overlooked a small cove with a narrow sandy beach and small dock to
which the boats could be tied. Each Cabin had a number and a name
Francois pointed out. "Murat is in Cabin Three or the Savage named
after Joseph's mistress Annette Savage. The Captain and Mrs. Verdi
will be in Cabin One which we call the Maillard after Joseph's
secretary, Louis. My friend Sarah will take Miss Liguri and Miss De
Cenza to Cabin Two, the Parrot, who of course was my ancestor also
named Francois and the cook for King Joseph. Finally, we come to
Cabin Four called the Bonaparte naturally after King Joseph not
Napoleon his brother."

Upon entering it became crystal clear that six guys in a two bedroom
rustic cabin would be a bit much to handle. The cabins were family
style meaning that there was a full size bed in one bedroom for the
parents and then a children's room which in this case had a twin bed
and bunk beds. Thus it could sleep three. That would mean that one of
the guys would have to sleep on the floor or what some might call a
sofa which was more like a wooden bench with cushions. Obviously
Andreas and Dominic would be assigned the double bed room given
that they were in a relationship and wouldn't mind sleeping in the
same bed. At least that's what Francois thought but they did not. They
suggested drawing names to see who got the double bed and who got
the bench. Francois helped to solve part of the problem by inviting the

Professor to use the guest room in his house. The invitation was readily accepted as the Jet lag was still a bother for him more so than the others.

Francois stood at the door with the Professor's suitcase and pointed to the vibrant orange and red sky at the horizon across the lake. They needed to leave before it became too dark to take the boat and thus there would be two who would need a place to sleep.
As soon as they departed, Bob and Alessandro made a bee line for the room with the double bed. "I call dibs," shouted Bob.

"What is this dibs?" Alessandro tried to push Bob out of the doorway in a playful manner so as not to hurt him.

"Ah shit, I can't fight you over this but can't you understand that I'm a big guy and need a…well a bed that supports me better than a kid's bunk bed."

"But I am bigger than you Bob, *no capis*co. I do not understand."

While they sorted out what Bob meant about size, Dominic also called dibs but not in those words. He would go and take a shower while Ron and Andreas poured over the Book's pages dealing with what Ron had dreamt back in Switzerland about a secret tunnel at Point Breeze and the letter from James Monroe to Joseph Bonaparte. They found the passage about the Library and its moveable Bookcase. In the margins, written in Latin, was the name of Monroe, and that of another man, who Ron was certain must have been the courier or the gardener as the word "traitor" was written over a name and that name was Stanley Stonegate.

"Now look here Andreas, see this? I think it means that somehow this guy learned about the secret tunnel and maybe the location of the Crown Jewels. But why did Bonaparte label him a traitor? There's something missing here."

"Well obviously, this guy betrayed the secret of Joseph and his secret room."

"True, but I think he did more than just that; I think he's connected to the meeting between James Monroe and Joseph Bonaparte in Philadelphia in January of 1820. Don't you see it works out perfectly? Bonaparte was off the estate. See here, it talks about the New Year's Eve gala he hosted for the Community of Bordentown. He placed his works of art on display as part of that party, like a gallery showing at a museum which his house certainly was."

"I am beginning to understand what you're getting at Ron. Look here; there is a list of the paintings and one of them is that of his brother Napoleon crossing the Alps by Jacques-Louis David and look at this, he had a Da Vinci and a Rubens too. But what does that mean to us and his treasure?"

At the door of the bedroom with the double bed, Bob suddenly gave Alessandro a shove. "Hey look over there. What's Ron doing with Andreas?"

The young Count glanced over stating the obvious which was that they were huddled over the autobiography. "…and from the looks of it they may have found something interesting."

"Not without Watson," Bob stomped off toward them just as Dominic wrapped in a towel stepped out of the bathroom and right into him.

"Get dressed; your boyfriend thinks that he can replace Watson."

"Slow down Bob no one can replace you as Watson to Ron's Sherlock… Forget that; someone's at that window." Dominic slowly walked toward a rather large window, with no curtain and wide open. He gave a hand sign to Alessandro still standing at the bedroom door to follow him while his other hand was holding up the towel.

Without a word they approached the open window from each side of it. Bob watched them acting like Mountain lions stalking their prey and ready to pounce. "Now what?" He ran between them and leaned out the window, then fell right back into the room and into them. "Oh shit, I am so sorry guys. There was someone there. I could see a shadowy figure going around the cabin next door." Leaning against the window sill, he took a deep breath. "Well what are we waiting for let's go get him." He grabbed hold of the bare shoulders of Dominic and thought better of it and pulled on Alessandro to follow him. "Sorry Dom, but I don't think a future priest should be touching a naked guy. You're not insulted or anything are you?"

"No Father Bob, I wouldn't want to tempt you in any way," he laughed as he jabbed Alessandro who got the message and forced out a laugh as well.

His words however floated into air. Bob was already running across the room and picking up a poker at the stone fireplace on the way to the front door. Just as he placed his hand on the doorknob two sweet voices like birds singing in the trees could be heard with a loud knock on the knotty pine door.

"Yoo hoo is anyone home," sang out the melodious voices.

Bob swung open the door; Dominic screamed and ran behind Alessandro, his towel dropping from the collision. The heads of Ron and Andreas popped up from the pages of the Book with Andreas giving out a shout. "O Christ, he has a bare ass." He jumped up knocking over the chair which crashed down onto the oak boards of the floor and ran to Dominic to form a shield with Alessandro.

"Oh Jesus have mercy, it's only you two."

"And what do you mean by that?" Susan was in Bob's face and he was sweating to beat the band.

"Nothing Susan, it's just that we saw a guy at our window and given the murder and all…"

"Ronnie, what's going on in here? And you," Jan pointed to Dominic peeking out between the shoulders of Alessandro and Andreas, "get yourself dressed we just had a scare."

"Oh my God," Ron now jumped up and ran to Susan taking her into his arms. "What happened? Are you okay?"

Alessandro tried to go to Jan but Andreas held him back to preserve the dignity of his boyfriend.

"Well I see that I am chopped liver, whatever. So you saw him too Bob?" She pulled Bob in front of her actually much to his relief as he found himself between a naked guy hiding behind two of his friends and a hugging couple about to make out as far as he was concerned. The rejected Watson had to admit that it was Dominic who saw the figure at the window. He just went over so that he could prove him wrong. "It was just shadows created by the setting sun, I thought. But I was wrong. I did see something turning the corner of the cabin next door."

"Man or beast?" asked Jan just as the howl of a dog or perhaps a wolf could be heard. She closed the door and began to give a series of orders, the first of which was to have the guys back up to the bedroom and allow Dominic to find some clothes.

Dominic still crouched behind the two Michelangelo like statues of muscle and strength followed her order immediately. "That's a good idea Andreas. Just back up and I'll slip into the bedroom." The research assistant to Professor Pettigrew had restored the towel as his loin cloth and sheepishly began his backward walk with the Papal Guard and young Count doing the same in front of him.

Next she shoved a blanket depicting Lake Bonaparte in the weave into Bob's hands and went to Susan and her brother still lip locked. She pulled on the blanket Susan held which was now between them, fortunately for Ron as his reaction to Susan when she was in such a hold would have been like with Dominic a bit disconcerting to say the least.

"Shit Sis, what gives?"

106

"What gives Ronnie De Cenza is that Susan and I were coming over to invite you all to sit on the dock and watch the final rays of sunset. Then maybe look at the stars as it's a clear night. We had thought of inviting the Captain and Sophia as well but we think they were otherwise occupied, as there were no lights visible," she winked. "And then we saw that shadow of a guy but tried to act nonchalant which is why we sang our greeting to you. Then this Watson of yours scared the… you know what out of us when he swung open the door. That's when we saw a naked guy and couldn't help but to wonder what that was all about and then you finally noticed that we were here at all so engrossed were you in that damn Book…"

"Oh Sis, Mom would be upset with you using the 'D' word."

Alessandro saved the day as he finally was able to leave Dominic and Andreas and ran to Jan sweeping her up into his arms and kissing her on the lips. "Where is this guy, I will thrash him for you."

"Sweet honey, but if there is to be any thrashing it will have to wait, at least until we find the guy."

That interlude allowed Ron to step in with a plan just as Dominic reappeared in jeans and a Capri tee shirt with Andreas at his side. He proposed that they follow the original plan of the girls. They will go out to the dock and watch the sunset. If the lights were on in the Captain's cabin they would invite them more for his weapon just in case the shadow of a man was real and he was the murderer. They would have to walk past the cabin next door and somehow Bob, since he didn't have a partner to hold hands with, would slip away and give a peek in its window to see if someone was actually in there. His Watson was not thrilled to do so alone but said that he would do it for his friends even if it meant the end of his life by some mass murderer.

"For shit's sake Bob, get a grip and stop being such a Diva. If there was such a murderer at that window wouldn't he have had plenty of opportunity to do away with the three of you who stood at it? Still you're right. You shouldn't go alone. Sherlock should be with his Watson to stake out the cabin."

The plan was set with the change that Susan would walk with Andreas and Dominic. Bob and Ron would follow Jan and Alessandro and slip away, circle the cabin and return to them as they reached the other side of it. Like a "B" crime drama movie they crept out of their own cabin just in case someone was about. There was no one. So they strolled like a parade in front of the cabin toward the path leading to the dock. Each cabin had a small front porch with an overhang so that one could sit on it even in the rain. Each had a couple of rocking chairs as well. On one of those on the porch of the Savage cabin in front of which they were now walking, there sat a man around the Professor's age, forty plus years. He was dressed in Bermuda shorts and a button down plaid shirt which hung loosely over his waist. He was in the process of lighting his pipe as the sleuthing parade passed.

"*Bonsoir mes amis*, oh do forgive me for practicing my French. Good evening my friends, you too are taking advantage of the lovely evening with the painter's sky." He rose from his rocking chair and leaned over the log railing fixing his, what appeared to be dark, eyes on Ron and Bob for all the wrong reasons. "But do be careful for I hear that they have not as yet caught the murderer."
Now he had their attention and he knew it as they stood frozen right below his gaze. Ron could feel that sense of triumph as the slightest smile beneath his goatee and mustache could be noticed from the last of the reflection of sunlight. With their plan vanishing before his eyes, Ron swung into action.

"Oh my word Bobby, did you hear that," Ron grabbed hold of Bob's arm as his Watson tried to pull it away unsuccessfully. "Stop fighting me and play along," he whispered in Bob's ear.

The baby blues widened with understanding. "Dear God," he ran to the others insisting that the girls be protected as some damsels in distress. "Just play along," he whispered as he hugged each of them. The guys immediately created a circle around the girls all the while keeping their eyes on this French speaking man on the porch.

Ron left the circle and walked just below where the man grasped the railing. The porch level was elevated about two feet above the walking path which ran in front of all the cabins. On a small table next to the rocking chair he noticed a tin of pipe tobacco and a notepad. On one of the end pine rods making up the back of the chair hung a beret not unlike the cap they saw at the morgue which Francois Parrot originally saw in the boat where the dead man was found.

"Sir, you've given us quite the fright. We have only just arrived and have heard nothing about a murder."

"Indeed, and Mr. Parrot having been with the Sherriff when the body was taken off one of his boats on the very day that I arrived certainly would know all the details. But then he probably didn't want to frighten all of you coming for a holiday…you are here for a vacation, aren't you? But I am being too intrusive. My name is Antoine Murat and I am here seeking solitude as I write an article for the magazine called the New Yorker. You perhaps heard of it as students which I presume that you are."

"So that's the reason for the notepad even in the approaching darkness."

"Very observant Mister…?"

"Oh sorry about that, my name is Ron De Cenza, this is my partner in crime Bob Wentz. That dark hair girl is my sister, Jan and the lovely red head is her friend Susan Liguri. The three handsome dudes are from Italy and Switzerland, Andreas Berne, Dominic Fontana and Alessandro the Count of Pianore from Umbria in Italy."

Murat was obviously impressed especially by the titled Alessandro or at least that's what he tried to convey. He used that title to share his story which in turn allowed Ron to share some truth about their presence in such an isolated area rather than touring New York City. He explained that his article for the magazine was about Joseph Bonaparte and his life on Lake Bonaparte where he had built a home. Instant excitement had to be suppressed else to give away too much information. So the others let Ron continue the conversation. This he did just as Bob suddenly realized, upon hearing the Bonaparte name that the Book was still on the table in their cabin unprotected; so he interrupted.

"Excuse me I need to make a quick run back to our cabin. Be right back, nature calls." Bob ran off and Ron continued.

"What a coincidence Mr. Murat, for we too are here because of Joseph Bonaparte.

 Ron explained that some of them were indeed students, him, Bob, his sister and Susan; the others are already accomplished men. "Andreas is a Papal Guard in the Vatican, Dominic is a graduate student who works for a Professor at Oxford University and Alessandro is working on his Master's Degree at the University of Bologna. We are all part of a research team with our Professor who is working on the Life of Joseph Bonaparte; now isn't that something." The young man from Chicago was beginning to think that perhaps the events of the day had not brought them to a dead end.

Princeton University Library

Chapter Six:
The Crossbow

Their day which was filled with identifying a body, decoding the autobiography, which Bob was now placing in his satchel and hanging it about his neck, was finally ending albeit with meeting this writer of magazine articles. However several hours away on the Campus of Princeton University in New Jersey Professor Dorothy Witherspoon had walked into the Office of Professor Richard Stockton. In her hand she held a telegram from Professor Andrew Pettigrew requesting her help in identifying an arrow from a Crossbow which was found in a murder victim on Lake Bonaparte in upstate New York.

"Oh Richard, I'm glad that you are still here…," she stopped in her tracks and brushed the long brunette hair away from her face. "Oh dear me, I am so sorry to have interrupted you but I literally ran across campus to get to you…I shall come back at another time."

Stockton rose from the chair behind a small conference table in the corner of the office where he was huddled with another man looking over a pile of papers and a map spread across the table. Behind him she could see his family crest with the motto *"Omnia Deo Pendent"* (All depends on God) emblazoned on it. She understood his pride in his ancestor of the same name who signed the Declaration of Independence as had her family member at that time.

"Nonsense Dorothy," he folded up the map as the other man shuffled the other sheets of paper together in a stack. "I was just working on a project with a colleague. May I introduce you to Mr. Charles Benton of Bordentown New Jersey? Mr. Benton, this is Professor Dorothy Witherspoon of the Archeology department."

"My pleasure Professor; I have heard of your excavations to seek evidence of Tribal people prior to Colonial settlement right here in New Jersey as well as in the State of Virginia for their Jamestown Settlement Museum."

"You are too kind but as I said I can talk with Richard at a more convenient time." She placed the telegram in the pocket of her lab coat. "Benton, now you wouldn't happen to be related to that family who married into the Savage family amidst all that Joseph Bonaparte philandering?"

"Yes Professor, I cannot deny that affiliation much to my embarrassment. But then aren't you a descendant from an illustrious signer of the Declaration of Independence?" he chose to change the subject.

She returned a smile of humility. "You know your history Mr. Benton. Yes, the Reverend John Witherspoon was a Presbyterian minister, a signer of the Declaration and President of the College of New Jersey which was the predecessor of Princeton. The fact that he also owned slaves is a blotch on our family history. In spite of that fact his contribution to the Declaration and the new government of the United States both under the Articles of Confederation and the Constitution is noteworthy especially in placing a timetable for the end of slave trade and importation in the new Constitution.

Stockton had other things on his mind other than a history lesson. He was after all the Head of the History Department. He brought their focus back to the murder and insisted that given her state of urgency that he would be happy to answer whatever question she might have. He was correct about her state of urgency as she quickly agreed to stay. She went on to tell Stockton that there had been a murder and that she was being asked to help with the identification of the murder weapon.

"A murder good heavens Dorothy do sit down and tell us what happened." He gave a quick glance at Benton still occupying himself with the papers he was collecting.

She tucked in her tweed tight fitting skirt over which she wore a brown blouse and the white lab coat.

Benton felt compelled to say something all the while knowing that he had spied on Ron and Bob as they dug in the ground at the Roman Ruins of Nyon in Switzerland and would have attacked were it not for the intervention of Andreas. "Surely whoever asked you for help cannot expect an archeologist to know about murder weapons in this day and age."

She explained that in this particular case she could help and so could Professor Stockton given that the weapon was a Crossbow's arrow. Stockton remained confused over their ability to help even as he glanced at Benton wondering where he had been since his arrival back in the United States. He retorted with the argument that a Crossbow could be a hunting weapon in their time or a military weapon going back to ancient Greece and certainly in the Middle Ages. They were fully developed for use in Europe in wars and even earlier in ancient China.

"Yes of course Richard, you would know all of that, but in this case I recognized something in the photo…"

Richard jumped out of his seat. Benton had to tug on his sport coat to get him back down. "Photo, you hadn't mentioned a picture." She was apologetic and explained that it had arrived by special delivery just that afternoon. Pulling the photo out of the lab coat pocket she presented it to Stockton as Benton looked on without saying a word. "As you can see Richard, there is something familiar about this arrow so I went to our Medieval Display section in the College Museum. Two things struck me at the same time. First the crossbow in our display always faced to the right; that is the crossbeam would be to the right of the viewer. But today it was facing to the left. Secondly, one of the two bolts or arrows as we call them in our ignorance was missing."

Stockton fell into silence but Benton could not. "Professor Witherspoon, are you implying that someone stole the bolt…arrow or whatever it's called and used it with a crossbow from modern times?"

"I am implying nothing other than one of the display arrows is missing. But we shall know for certain in the next day or two at most. My colleague from Oxford University will be here with his research team and the actual arrow which killed some man by the name of Apollo Dimitri."

Both Stockton and Benton went into a coughing fit. Dorothy ran to Stockton's private bathroom adjoining the office at the far left corner. She found a stack of paper cups and poured some water into two of them. Her absence was long enough for both men to calm down before they took a sip of the water she brought to them.

Stockton began to question Witherspoon about how such a theft could even happen from their museum and as to when the last time anyone was in that display gallery. She couldn't answer with total accuracy but she did observe that it was the 1960's and that their students were more interested in protesting war than visiting a shrine to war. She pointed out that only his students and some of hers would schedule a visit to the gallery if they needed to do so as part of a class. He reluctantly agreed with her assessment.

Benton dwelt on the theft part and thought that the police should be summoned. The two Professors disagreed in that they were not certain that the missing arrow was from the Princeton museum display. Dorothy pointed out that issue would be resolved when Pettigrew arrived with the killing arrow. Stockton agreed to seal the museum until her colleague arrived and if all things matched then the police would be called. He had no idea that Detective Malone of the NYPD and Captain Verdi of Interpol would be accompanying the research group.

By the time this decision was made the same sun setting in upstate New York was doing the same thing in Princeton New Jersey. Stockton called security to have the Weaponry Gallery sealed off in the museum.

Back at Lake Bonaparte Professor Pettigrew was placing the metal container holding the arrow on the mantel of the fireplace in the home of Francois Parrot. He thought that Detective Malone or the Sherriff should have kept it with them but they felt that he was the expert and it would be safe for the night with him. Francois for his part was bringing out a pot of tea with what the British called biscuits and he called petite pastries. The rugged stones making up the hearth ran up the entire wall to the ceiling, within it a fire burned though the evening was not particularly cool. Francois thought it would create a more comfortable setting to discuss the events of the day and what would take place in the morning. He placed the tray on a small smoothly finished table not at all like the cabin furnishings which were quite rustic in appearance. Flanking the table were two plush arm chairs also made by hand but not rustic more of a Colonial finish. Pettigrew remarked on the beauty of the furnishings. Francois pointed out that they were Amish pieces from a local colony in Pennsylvania. Looking down on them was the head of an eight point buck, his eyes aglow from the fire below. Whether it presented a scene from a horror movie or one of romance would depend on one's point of view. And since Francois was interested in Sarah Dupres and vice versa and the Professor though unattached at the moment was easily seduced by the lure of women as was done to him in Dublin Ireland not more than a year and a half ago, it would be safe to say that it was a comfortable setting created for conversation and rest after a grizzly day of seeing the dead man.

Francois and Pettigrew may have been enjoying tea and crumpets on the mainland but back on Birch Island blankets had been spread out at the end of the dock. The sun was now gone and a canopy of stars wrapped around the Lake. The charade of Bob and Ron being a pair continued as Murat had been invited to join them on the dock to star watch. They made sure that Murat sat next to Ron with Susan on his other side. What had been planned to be a romantic evening of star gazing and not a word about the Book or the murder turned out to be more play acting that is until a familiar voice broke the uncomfortable silence which had fallen on the group.

"Jan, Susan is that you on the dock." Sophia Verdi couldn't help but notice the flaming hair of Susan all lighted up in moonlight and reflections of light off the smooth lake water. For Susan it was a

Godsend as Murat's hand had a way to creep up near her leg and had Ron seen it, the entire act would have been shot to hell.

She jumped to her feet and ran toward the newlyweds, pulling on Jan to go with her. "Yes Sophia, it's us, we're all here to look at the stars." "Good evening Captain, the guys are over there if you know…you need some male company. I think you'll want to meet the new guy we met from the Savage Cabin."

"*Signorinas,* you are too kind." He gave a forlorn gaze at Sophia who returned a broad smile. The rapture of loving embraces and joining of their bodies was rapidly becoming a ghostly memory as he looked toward the end of the dock. The young men, his *ragazzi* as he called them seemed engaged with one who he didn't recognize. Like the First Honeymoon, it would appear that murder would cast a cloud over the newlyweds love once again.

"Yes, Enrico, you go talk with the boys and I will catch up with the girls like we're back in school, no?" Sophia took hold of the girls and they walked up onto the grassy knoll to some benches on the pathway. The guys were up and standing at attention as the Captain approached. "*Ragazzi*, relax, this is just us meeting to talk about the events of the day and enjoy that sky though in truth it would be far better with Sophia on my arm rather than any of you, do not be insulted. I mean no harm." Verdi glanced at Bob and Ron who appeared to be acting strangely given that they were holding hands a sure sign of something else in his Italian culture. All the head jerks and eye twitching couldn't end his confusion until they introduced him to Antoine Murat. Within seconds he understood the issue was an act from a play. The suave would-be Frenchman talked of the Joseph Bonaparte article and not a word about the murder until Ron tossed it into the conversation.

"Captain Verdi may we introduce you to Antoine Murat; he was here when the body of Apollo was discovered." His big brown eyes became even larger as he raised his eyebrows with the hope that the police Captain of the Italian Carabinieri might take the hint that he thought this man to be a person of interest.

Verdi did take the hint and began reviewing the case with the young men who helped him take down an assassination attempt back in Italy when Professor Pettigrew was brutally attacked on the Tiber River in Rome. "As I said, it is a shame that on such a lovely evening we should have to speak about murder and by such an unusual method," he turned to face Murat who being about his same height and build looked directly into his dark eyes with a gaze which would send shudders down the spine of most men. Murat however returned the gaze with detachment. He didn't seem connected to anything which the Captain brought up in his summary of the visit to the morgue or the actual finding of the body on the lake.

Ron standing next to the Captain was a receptor of Murat's gaze as well but for him, he saw an attempt to cover up something but what that was would be the challenge to find out. "Captain, when Bob and I were in High School we had to take an Archery class for Physical Education credits, but it wasn't anything like what we saw today." He continued his laser like stare into Murat's eyes. "Mr. Murat, do you know anything about bows and arrows and such? I mean did you go to school here in the States or in France?"

"I am most complimented that you thought my use of French was so good that I would appear to be a Frenchman. But then most of us in Quebec province in Canada still have our loyalties to the motherland like you Americans do with Britain."
"Ah, is that so?" Ron addressed his words to the Captain. "Mr. Murat is French Canadian; that is kind of like me being an Italian-American and Bob here being a German-American and then there is Andreas who is Swiss and Dominic and Alessandro who are simply Italian as from Italy like you are."

Verdi smiled for the first time and patted Ron on the shoulder, the good one which hadn't been wounded in a shooting incident back in the day when he was studying Latin in the Abbey in Wisconsin with Bob. It was there that he first met Susan and the rest as they say is history. "Thank you Ron for the heritage lesson." Holding onto Ron like a long lost brother, he continued. "Mr. Murat, so you have come to America from Canada to work, is that correct? For you said that you are working for the Magazine called the New Yorker which I presume by the name is created here in this State of New York."

Murat leaned against a piling pole and looked out over the lake to the shore beyond them twinkling with lights of vacationers' cottages and Country Homes. It was as if he were trying to escape from this interrogation as he felt it to be. In the end, he knew that he would have to speak. He explained that he indeed worked in the United States, in fact a branch of his family came from a small town in New Jersey called Bordentown. "However, I usually work in New York City but given the subject of Joseph Bonaparte and his life up here I thought it would be more inspirational to come to the source to write."

Once the town of Bordentown was mentioned all was lost to Ron who was about to jump out of his skin. If he knew about Joseph Bonaparte's life in upstate New York, he certainly knew that he lived in the very town where his relatives lived. And just maybe he was the person at the window listening to he and Andreas translate and decode the pages of the autobiography. Then again perhaps it wasn't sinister but a journalistic enterprise to learn more about the guy he was writing about. Then again why wouldn't he just ask if we knew anything about King Joseph? His mind was flooded with theories but none took root. The Captain could feel the tension building in Ron's shoulders and his best pal could see it in his eyes as the others were lost in a world of confusion still focusing on whether or not this Murat guy had archery lessons in school. In that regard they were on the same track as the Captain.

"Mr. Murat that is a beautiful site to be sure and I wish that I could be enjoying it with my new wife but we all have jobs to do. You must write this article on a Bonaparte in the States and I must seek a murderer and evidence to solve a crime." Not once did he allude to the lost treasure of Joseph Bonaparte. "So then, if you are or were a student of Archery you might be able to help in identifying the murder weapon."

"But you Sir are from Italy aren't you? Why is a murder here in upstate New York of interest to the Italian police?" Murat again avoided the topic of archery.

"Ah, so now you turn the tables and question me and I shall answer you forthrightly. You may not be aware that the victim is an Italian who escaped from prison and made his way to the United States. I came here to bring him back dead or alive. Regrettably it will be dead. So now I have answered your question would you do the courtesy of doing the same for me?"

"Of course Captain," Murat had no choice but to answer for a background check would reveal the information in time anyway. "I attended Princeton University and received my journalism degree almost ten years ago. While there I was on the fencing and archery teams."

The connection to the crime was made as far as Ron was concerned. The Captain however had to proceed more cautiously. Ten years was a long time to be removed from the sport if he didn't continue involvement after his graduation. He decided that the hour was getting late. "Tomorrow is another day; we shall meet again in the morning." It may have been too late for continuing the discussion for Captain Verdi but for Carolina Savage Gianetti the setting sun only meant that she had to rush to the University from the Washington Inn. There she, Luigi and Pietro had been dropped off. A certain Professor was waiting for a meeting that very night no matter how late the hour. It would take place. Despite the near fatal shooting on Capri which almost ended her life, she maintained a new energy to pursue the search for the Crown Jewels of Spain. Her lover now in prison ignited within her more than desire for pleasure and comfort. She felt empowered to carry on his work to become a powerful and respected patron of the Arts and Education.

Despite the howling of Luigi and Pietro about the lousy food on the plane and that they were hungry, she kept to her schedule to meet with the Professor and then they would eat, she told them. She picked up the phone and called for a cab. The hired driver which the Professor, with whom she was to meet, had hired was finished for the night. As soon as she hung up, the phone rang.

"*Pronto*, oh, I mean Hello." The operator verified that she was Carolina Gianetti and connected the call.

"This is Professor Richard Stockton. I believe we are to meet this evening. I am checking to see if we are still planning to do so, given the hour."

She affirmed that the meeting was still to take place and asked about the location. Stockton decided to have the meeting in the museum where he was headed to insure that it was sealed until his colleague Witherspoon met with her Oxford friend to verify if the missing arrow was indeed the one found in the body of a man on Lake Bonaparte. He however did not share the information about the missing arrow or the murder with her. Twenty minutes later the cab drove down Nassau St. and stopped in front of a large stone building in front of the Chapel. Pietro jumped out of the cab and opened the door for Carolina. Luigi came around from the other side and ran to the main doors of the Library building which housed the Historic Weaponry Gallery. They were locked given the hour as the Chapel chimes sounded 9:00 p.m. Luigi pounded on the door. A few seconds later, Stockton appeared behind the glass paneled doors and opened them.

"*Signorina* Gianetti, welcome to Princeton University; and who are these gentlemen?"

"These are my, shall I say, assistants, Luigi and Pietro. Since the unfortunate events on Capri we are all that remains to carry on the work of Niccolo Cavelli."

"Yes, his imprisonment was most unfortunate. But now you carry on his work. Please follow me; gentlemen I don't think we'll need your services we are quite alone here except for another colleague in this enterprise."

Despite such an assurance, Pietro and Luigi continued to follow them as they made their way to the second floor wing facing Rivers Way where the gallery was located. Upon entering Carolina was shocked to see Charles Benton standing at the crossbow display. Her composure began to wilt and it wasn't just from jet lag. She began to realize that Benton had played her in the same manner that she tried with Stockton and obviously failed. She was using Benton who had inside information about the search for the Bonaparte treasure and not telling Stockton who was sponsoring the search. Benton obviously was using her to get the information Cavelli had acquired before his fall from grace. At that moment in time in the Gallery all three of them knew what game had been played.

Carolina chose to make the first move ignorant of the murder. "Charles, how good to see you again." She embraced him as Luigi and Pietro flanked him. She kissed him on each cheek in the Italian fashion and squeezed him into her bosom which he adored from afar. He was but a peon in her connections with no hope of ever expressing his desire to have her in a manner more than that of a treasure hunter. She released him with a slight shove into Pietro who grabbed hold of his arms. Luigi quickly placed himself between them and Carolina who was now facing Stockton. He backed up into Charles being held and nonchalantly grabbed between the quivering man's legs until he got hold of his testicles and then he squeezed lightly at first and then harder. Charles moaned but tried to say nothing as Pietro whispered in his ear to remain silent. Luigi took a step forward and released his grasp. The sigh of relief from Benton was the sign for Carolina to confront Stockton who stood frozen as she walked up to him and stroked his bearded cheek.

"Richard, I need you to take off your clothes…"

"What, this is a University Museum and…"

"And you are head of the History Department; yes, I am well aware of that. You are also a handsome man shall I say in his forties? It doesn't matter Niccolo was in his fifties and I found him to be most able to satisfy me."

122

"Miss Gianetti, please, this meeting is to set up a plan to seek out the Bonaparte Treasure. I have no interest in you in a sexual manner."

"Perhaps, my men are of more interest to you; they are most handsome no?" There was on Capri a beautiful man, two actually, one dark like the caverns before sunlight and one as bright and light as the Blue Grotto as the sun explodes its light through its water. Such beauty was to be wasted on other men though they pretended to seek my attention but it was just a ploy to kill my Niccolo. In the end they failed and are in prison but not before the dark one shot me but that was a mistake; he meant it for my Niccolo."

"Miss Gianetti, I grieve for your loss and yes your assistants are very good looking. But Benton here and I were only working together for your best interest I assure you. And now we have a murder on our hands."

She continued unbuttoning his shirt. "Murder you say and how does this affect our enterprise?"

"Will you please stop what you are doing Miss Gianetti and let me explain? I cannot think straight and I think Benton is going to collapse."

Carolina waved her hand, Pietro released Benton and he slid down to the oak floor boards. "*Va bene*, it's okay, I think you have gotten my message. Our arrangement can be pleasant or not; it's your choice. I must be able to trust you or … but let us not think of that part. Now how does this murder impact our project?"

"*Grazie*, thank you," he began to button his shirt, "at the moment I don't know which is why we are meeting in this Gallery," Stockton glanced over to Benton sitting on the floor trying to gain back his composure and dignity. "Charles, let me help you to stand." He still didn't realize that Benton had been working with Carolina in Switzerland and had he been successful it would have been he who was getting the short end of the stick as far as finding the treasure was concerned.

Benton slapped back the helping hand. "I can get up myself thank you very much."

"You needn't be so flippant. I was just trying to be empathetic with your state of distress." Stockton walked up to the display area and pointed to the crossbow. "There my dear Carolina is what very well may be our downfall come tomorrow. Someone has moved that crossbow and one of the bolts or what most people call arrows is missing."

"And what does a historic display have to do with Bonaparte's estate of Point Breeze?"

"Miss Gianetti, it's not about the estate; it's about whoever killed this Apollo Dimitri person up at Lake Bonaparte…"

Carolina let out a scream of shock and stumbled into Luigi who took hold of her to steady her.

"Carolina, it's just Apollo who tried to kill your beloved Niccolo Cavelli; he deserved what he got if you ask me."

She pushed him away. "I did not ask you. I am just shocked that the world has lost such a beautiful man who shone like the sun and had a…shall I say a way with which to please both men and women."

"Then you know this person. Miss Gianetti they will find out that you know him and that may indeed impact our project at Point Breeze."

"Then my dear Professor Stockton they shall not find out." Carolina Gianetti was back in control dabbing her eyes heavy with mascara now running down her cheeks. "Who knows that I am in the United States? No one that's who; I shall leave tonight for this place called Bordentown and you will loan me your car to do so. Also my men are too conspicuous, I need to get them a change of clothes to look more like tourists; is there such a place in Princeton? And one more thing; again I ask what has this crossbow have to do with us or the murder of that lovely man who made the world a sexy place?"

"Let me begin with what I have been told by my colleague Professor Witherspoon. Your friend Apollo was found in a boat in Lake Bonaparte with an arrow in his back…"

Carolina let out a gasp of horror; her men just smiled at each other.

He continued. "If that arrow is indeed the one missing from this display then it would mean that someone from our University may have taken this crossbow and used it as a murder weapon."

"Or perhaps it could just mean someone broke into this museum and stole it…"

"But then they came back to replace the crossbow? It just doesn't make sense."

"*Capisco*, I understand. But then that would only leave you or Charles here who would know of our project." She ran up to Benton. "You, I trusted you and you betrayed me." She slapped his face. "You were in Europe and could have contacted Apollo to use him to find and keep the treasure all for you."

Holding his hand to his face glowing red with her handprint Benton managed to get out a few words carefully chosen so as not to antagonize her any more than she already was. "I regret that you think so Carolina however, I have no knowledge of such a person as Apollo Dimitri."

She spun around and got back into Stockton's face with Benton standing next to her. "If Charles is telling the truth then that would mean only you would have the knowledge and opportunity to get into this museum, take the crossbow, travel to this Lake Bonaparte place, kill Apollo and return here. You run this Museum and can come and go at any hour."

Stockton was sheet white in the face. He certainly knew that he was working with Benton who he now began to realize was working with Gianetti who was colluding with Benton and him separately. In his mind he could see the police coming in the morning accusing him. He had to think of other scenarios. At the same time he understood that the police would figure out the probability of Carolina committing the murder was remote unless she hired someone in the States before she arrived thus giving her the alibi of being on a plane when the murder took place. That left Benton and he was with him in his office when Witherspoon came in to ask for help. Still Benton could be seen as having the time to commit murder in upstate New York and get down to New Jersey in time to meet with him? All of this raced through Stockton's mind as she confronted him along with the realization that a simple wave of her hand to her men and he would be in the same mess that Benton was, holding his privates and trying to breath normally or worse. A plan quickly formed in his threatened brain.

"Miss Gianetti, it's getting late. We must act quickly and be ready for what will take place tomorrow. I agree with you. Go to Bordentown and remain as a tourist, the Bonaparte estate of Point Breeze is owned by the Divine Word Missionary Order. Perhaps you could go to them and ask about going on a retreat. It would give you a reason to walk about the estate. Benton should go with you as your boyfriend perhaps? In any case keep those two assistants of yours out of sight. Those priests and brothers would be scared out of their wits just to look at them. I have no choice but to remain here and face that Professor from Oxford and the police. Finally, there is no doubt in my mind that the arrow they are bringing will be the missing one from this display. I will become the prime suspect but no one will know about you or Benton."

Throughout Stockton's proposal Benton remained silent not only because of the pain but out of necessity. He knew full well that the Oxford Professor and his research team all knew of him in that they almost crashed into him in Switzerland, had dinner with him and almost caught him spying on them. He dared not mention that for even Carolina didn't know of that encounter.

Carolina looked at Benton. "The plan sounds reasonable. And you Charles can you be a man to escort such a person as me? Stand up straight, stop holding yourself. Act like a man in love."

The Princeton Chapel chimes announced the eleven evening hour as they left the museum to enact their plan. On Birch Island there were no chimes just a ticking wall clock in the Cabin called Bonaparte where Ron was now stomach down on the upper bunk studying the Book which had brought on such terror on Capri and now on Lake Bonaparte. Bob was on the lower bunk and Alessandro in the twin bed on the other side of the small bedroom. Both of them were sound asleep.

Andreas and Dominic ended up with the parent bedroom with the double bed. They lay in it face to face, eyes wide open with yearning.

"Go to sleep Andreas. There will be no Hanky-Panky as Ron calls the love making. It's one thing for the guys to accept our love but it's quite another to hear us making love, so we shall not."

"Did anyone ever tell you that you have a heart of gold which is so full of understanding and compassion? *Bona Serra cara mia*," He placed a light kiss on the brow of Dominic and rolled over.

"Good night my love," Dominic crossed his arms on his bare chest and smiled with contentment.

In the cabin with the honeymooners, Captain and Mrs. Verdi, there was no such worry. The Captain was standing at the doorway of the cabin looking out across the lake wearing only those Italian style briefs which emphasized the positive of the male anatomy. Sophia stepped out of the bathroom in a negligee of white satin and lace which left little to the imagination. She sweetly called out, "Enrico."

He turned with a heart already beating the blood to his friend between his legs. Just the sound of her voice made the desire build within him. Murder or not, this night would be filled with passion and love as he picked her up into his arms and placed her on the bed while caressing her with kisses. From her navel up through the valley between the girls and onto her neck he traveled slowly until he reached those tender lips pink and receptive as his manhood entered her and the two became one.

Back on the top bunk Ron was distracted but not from his arms being around Susan for she and his sister were fast asleep in their own cabin. He was torn between finding the results of that meeting of Joseph Bonaparte with James Monroe then Secretary of State to President James Madison and trying to figure out what the trajectory of an arrow could be in order to hit a man in a boat so precisely in the back. And then the shooter had to have a route of escape while carrying a cumbersome crossbow. Perhaps in his dreams the puzzle could be solved.

The Desk of Joseph Bonaparte
Courtesy of Mr. Peter Tucci

Chapter Seven:
The Meeting and The Plot

A string quartet played quietly as guests at Point Breeze roamed the grand house of Joseph Bonaparte. His guests included the grand families of New Jersey and the common folk of Bordentown who were excited to be invited to such a Gala to bring in the new year of 1820. The former King already had a reputation for attracting the rich and famous as well as gardeners and farmers to his palatial house second only to the White House of the President of the United States some would say. Thus there was bedecked with emerald jewels surrounded with diamonds a Lady from the Court of the Romanovs in Russia. She was said to be with her husband on a trade mission but no one saw hide or hair of such a man. She walked with many men dazzled by her regal appearance in the new Republic. Joseph always with an eye for a lovely lady could not help but notice her. She stopped in front of the Painting of Napoleon Crossing the Alps set up on an easel in a place of honor. Joseph always remembered his brother Napoleon with affection. To all it seemed that she was admiring the heroic scene and great campaign of crossing that mountain range to reach Italy as did Hannibal during the days of the Roman Empire. He however was successful in a way that Hannibal never was.

Though it was Joseph's intent to speak with the lovely Russian lady, he was surrounded by admirers coming from distant places like Philadelphia and New York, Washington D.C. and Trenton New Jersey. Each of them had news about recent events happening in France. This directly impacted the news in the letter from James Monroe, the Secretary of State. He had sent off a reply to that letter in which plans were set to meet in Philadelphia on January 2. Luckily the weather conditions seemed favorable for travel on New Year's Day to the City of Brotherly Love where he hoped to receive some favorable news from the Government of President Madison through Monroe. Watching this Gala event was Ron De Cenza standing amidst the glamour of high society and common folk in his white boxer sleeping shorts and nothing else. He felt the chill of the last day of December but didn't shiver. The Christmas decorations of pine boughs still decorated the portals around the home and the Nativity Scene of hand carved statues still adorned the Mantel of the fireplace in the Reception Room where the exhibit of much of Joseph's art was on display. The fairly new tradition of the Christmas Tree in one's home had come to America with the Germans. Both Napoleon and Joseph had dealings with the various German states during their time as Emperor and King of Spain. Joseph liked the idea of the candlelit tree and used it in his home at Point Breeze from those first years when it was built. One of those 1819 Christmas trees still stood in the Library on that New Year's Eve.

Stewards walked amongst the guests serving wine and small pastries. For some reason the spirit of Ron observing the event wanted to taste one of them but as a shadow of history could not take hold of one. So he followed the Russian lady at first as she was attracting quite the gathering about her. Amazed that the lady was speaking French rather than Russian which he still understood, he marveled at how many of those admiring her could converse with her. But then French was a diplomatic language in the Courts of Europe. She had moved on from the Alps painting and now stood before a Marble bust of Napoleon Bonaparte sitting atop a marble pedestal. Leaning against the pillar was a wreath of holly and ivy. Rather than talking about Napoleon she spoke about its sculptor, Antonio Canova. As the evening drew to a close and the midnight hour was about to bring in the New Year, the lady was again seen but this time it was in the Library. She was speaking with someone who Ron recognized from an earlier page in the autobiography.

It was the gardener who he had seen speaking with the Courier with the letter from James Monroe. Why would such a non-royal person get the attention of someone as regal as the Lady from Russia whose name was never mentioned? Even so, everyone seemed to recognize her simply by the Brooch worn upon the upper right breast area of her gown. A gilded eagle with turned head over which floated a Crown dominated the piece. Ron having tired of listening to Joseph's plan for the spring planting and the gardens had roamed around the Point Breeze Mansion and into the Library.

The revelry of midnight had subsided and the guests were leaving. Joseph was alone with his mistress Annette Savage and ascending the staircase to his room. Ron being who he was had no interest in watching their love making which led him to explore the mansion. That brought him to the Library once again. Once he entered it was no longer New Year's Eve but obviously another day. Joseph was dressed in a navy blue cutaway coat with a gold and brown silk brocade vest. A white silk scarf wrapped around his neck the ends of which were tucked into the white shirt under the vest. He was speaking with Louis Maillard, his secretary and Captain Unzaga of his Spanish Ordinance and security who entered exile with him years before.

"*Mon Dieu*, why hasn't this tree been taken away. Christmas was over a week ago and it's all dried out. It has become a fire hazard."

"I shall see to it immediately, Sire...I mean Sir." The Captain left to find the gardener to clear away the tree.

"Now then Louis, about the Jewels; I think that we should take a gem or two to that Papal Envoy while we're in Philadelphia. The project in New York needs some cash flow."

"Yes Sire...good grief I mean Sir, I shall never get use to this American term."

"Louis if you cannot master such a simple term just use *Monsieur*, it will feel more comfortable for you."

"Thank you, *Monsieur*...ah yes this is quite easy. And shall we open the panel?"
"*Qui*, there should still be some loose gems left to sell before we have to return to the cache' brought from Spain."

Ron was jumping out of his skin as he anticipated seeing the hidden location of the Crown Jewels.

Louis pulled forward the Bookcase as Joseph lighted a candle while keeping it away from the dried out Christmas tree. He had hoped that it would last until the Feast of the Epiphany or Three Kings on Jan. 6th but he wasn't to be home anyway so it really didn't matter.

Once inside the secret room, the former King unlocked the desk and took out a small wooden box. He decided to bring the entire box of gems as there weren't many left and funds were needed for the spring planting as well as the property development at Lake Diana in the State of New York. At the last moment he decided that they would leave by the secret tunnel as the Captain was to return to remove the tree and may see them come out of the wall. Ron followed them out of the room and through the tunnel to Crosswicks Creek. They locked the gate of the tunnel and walked up the granite stairs and across the green to the Main House. The carriage was waiting and they were off without Captain Unzaga as King Joseph felt that his presence might frighten the Secretary of State. Only Louis and the interpreter James Carret would go with him. Ron was torn as to jump onto the coach or stay at the Mansion. When he saw the Russian lady approaching dressed as a kitchen maid he decided to remain at the house and watch. There was no doubt that it was the Russian lady. Her hair was too clean and well styled and her bosom was epic in proportion and unforgettable.

The Lady approached the British spy disguised as the gardener, Stanley Stonegate. It wouldn't be unusual for a maid to talk with a gardener on the way to the kitchen area.

"Sir, all is ready. I shall enter the house to clean. At each fireplace I shall pull out a burning log and let its flame take hold of a curtain or tablecloth. Can you enter the tunnel?"

"Yes, there should be no problem as our helper who came as the courier is already at the tunnel entrance and should have the lock open by now."

The next thing Ron realized was that he was back in the Library. The Captain was running down the hall shouting that a fire has broken out on the fourth floor. He ran into the Library and picked up the marble bust of Napoleon and handed it through the window to staff who were trying to save the works of art throughout the house. People came running across the lawn still without snow and shouting get water which was fruitless as the fire was spreading too fast. So they entered the blazing house to save what they could for their neighbor the King. Inside the tunnel Stonegate and the courier were running into the secret room just as the final Books were pulled off the shelves by Captain Unzaga revealing a latch which opened the wall behind the Bookcase. He pulled on it as Ron shouted that Stonegate was in the Secret Room but of course no one could hear him.

Unzaga rushed into the secret room taking the two men by surprise as they rifled through the Secretary desk's drawers which weren't locked. They turned as the Captain shouted for them to identify themselves. They said nothing as they walked backwards closer to the tunnel entrance. Once reaching it they fled down the tunnel. Unzaga chased them and tackled the courier. They rolled about the tunnel until Stonegate realizing what had happened turned back. He picked up a brick from a broken piece of the tunnel wall and smashed it into the head of Captain Unzaga. The two arsonists shouting "down with Bonaparte" ran out of the tunnel and down to the banks of Crosswicks Creek until Ron could no longer see them.

Crawling along the mud floor of the tunnel toward the secret room the mortally wounded Captain Unzaga moved no more. At that moment the tunnel began to collapse. The bricks of the tunnel walls split and cascaded down followed by earth and rock entombing Unzaga. Ron found himself outside of the collapsed tunnel watching the mansion fire now so wide spread that the showplace home could not be saved. Scattered across the lawn were furniture pieces including the desk from the secret room, paintings and artifacts worth a fortune in their own right. The people of Bordentown began to take them home for safe keeping as it was January and storms would be brewing. Ron watched with appreciation and no attempts to stop what some might have called pillaging. He was aware from the Book's notes that these were returned to Joseph later when he returned to find his Point Breeze estate in ruins.

All Ron could do was watch the mansion collapse in flames amid shouts of neighbors directing where the artifacts should be taken. A carriage rolled onto the estate where the smoldering ruins still glowed as streams of smoke spiraled into the air. Joseph had been sent a message in Trenton where he had gone for the business part of his clandestine trip. The visit to Trenton was to arrange for a communication to Natural Bridge New York requesting access to water for his newly planned estate. The trip took place after his meeting with the Secretary of State in Philadelphia. That mission to James Monroe didn't seem to matter anymore. The political chaos in France was rearing its head again thanks to a group called the "ultras."

This group of political activists sought to destroy French Revolutionary ideas as well as laws which had King Louis XVIII trying to balance the French government between the extreme groups trying to control France. Joseph was warned that he was in danger once again. And yet Joseph had pointed out another possibility, should the Bourbon dynasty fall again, the Bonapartists may get the upper hand. It was evident as he peered out of the carriage window that Monroe was right about his being in danger. The smoldering ruin of his mansion lay before his gaze. He slumped back into a sullen state of mourning but it was short lived.

He lifted his head bowed is despair and looked at his secretary. "Louis, move our things to the stables. We shall rebuild but not on this spot. It shall remain empty as a tribute to what was once here."

Ron stirred and tossed and turned as he mumbled while half asleep. "He never gave a thought that the destruction may have been deliberately caused by those who sought revenge on the Bonaparte family."

His eyes popped open and he leaned over the edge of the bunk. Calling to Bob and then across the room to Alessandro he announced that he could solve the murder at Point Breeze.

"Murder, what murder; the Beckett family tore down the second mansion and the first one burned down." Bob was baffled and

Alessandro was not quite sure what was going on, so it appeared that he too was confused.

Jumping down from the top bunk he shook off the chill of the morning and got into Bob's face. "Get everyone together the Game is afoot."

"I know, you said that before…"

"I did indeed but this time it's a new game, two games actually. We shall find the treasure of Bonaparte and solve the murder, well maybe not solve but prove that there was a murder and that the First Mansion was deliberately destroyed by a British sympathizer who did not want a Bonaparte back in power and a Russian who sought to avenge the invasion of Russia by Napoleon."

"Alessandro, I think that he just had another nightmare, but one in which he was awake. Is that possible?"

"Come on Bob, get out of those baby pj's and let's get hopping. Times a-wasting…"

"Asshole, you're nuts just like the real Sherlock."

"Ah, there is no real Sherlock; he's a character in a book. But thanks for the thought." Ron grabbed a towel off the hook and clean underwear from the top drawer of the dresser. "God I love this." He ran across the cabin to the other bedroom and pounded on the door. "Hey love birds, get your asses out of bed; the game is afoot again."

Dominic let out a yelp and rolled out of the bed onto the floor. Andreas jumped off the bed as a soldier being called to revelry but the only thing at attention was his friend between his legs. "What the hell Dom, I think our skinny ass friend has gone mad." He grabbed the sheet and covered his nakedness. He wrapped it around to appear as a toga and went to the door. He opened it just a crack and there his *amico* stood arms crossed over his bare chest and in his shorts. "*Bon Giorno amico*, what's up?"

136

Ron winked and then shoved his way into the room of two gay guys in his underwear, well sleeping shorts, same thing really, which he would never do under most conditions. But this wasn't just another morning in a murder investigation and he was busting to tell everyone about his vision.

Dom peeked up over the edge of the bed from his position on the floor. "Ron is everything all right. I mean I'm naked and so is Andreas."

"I can't see a thing; anyway we all have the same parts; who cares about that anyway. Don't you get it? We need to get off this island and get down to Princeton pronto. There is no treasure up here of that I'm pretty sure. Poor Francois, I hope this doesn't kill his business." He sat for a second or two on the bed.

Andreas froze at the door which now had Bob and Alessandro standing in the threshold. In the meantime Dom was motioning to them with his finger going in a circular motion at his temple at the side of his head.

"He's *potso...*"

"Come on Dom, I'm not crazy. I just read this page in the Book and then it all connected as to why Joseph or maybe it was Louis; that I don't know as yet but I will get there." He swung his skinny almost hairless legs around to where Dominic sat on the floor. The Italian scooted away from him. "Anyway, one of them wrote 'traitor' over the name of the gardener at Point Breeze and then a Cross with RIP, Requiesce in pace or Rest in Peace by the name of Captain Unzaga, you know the military guy who went into exile with King Joseph. That means the guy died. Don't you get it? He was murdered by those who set the mansion, the first one, on fire."

Andreas came to his senses and it clicked. "Shit man, you're a genius! Listen guys he's right on with all he is saying. I helped him with the translation from the French."

Bob looked peeved as he noted that to be true, "and it kicked Watson out from the process."

Ron jumped off the bed and leapt into the doorway embracing Bob. "Never Watson; you're my pal, I'll always need you." Off Ron ran to the bathroom shouting, "I got first dibs on the shower, no peeking," and then laughing his ass off as he slammed the door shut.

A glistening drop of water spilled over from Bob's eye and trickled down his cheek.

"I think that I'm still dreaming. I need an espresso and fast." Alessandro turned to go to the kitchen.

"Wait for us, but I think we need something stronger than coffee." Dominic pulled up his underpants, a silky Italian style brief and then his jeans. "Come on Count, let's find something to drink." He draped his arm over Alessandro and pulled him along. "Can this really be Ron De Cenza or has something taken over his mind?"

Andreas dropped the toga sheet and realized that Bob was still there in the doorway. He grabbed the sheet back to cover his nether regions. "Bob, I'm getting dressed now; you do understand that right? You're going to see my bare ass."

"Huh, oh sure it's a nice ass. See you in the kitchen." Confused and bewildered Bob followed the others to the kitchen.

Andreas kicked the door shut. "*Madonna mia*, I think whatever has infected Ron is contagious."

No sooner had the four guys gathered around the table with their coffee laced with a dash of brandy than a loud banging jolted them. It was the girls and this time their voices were not like the morning song of melodious birds singing in the trees.

"Hey you guys are you up yet?" shouted Susan.

"Come on, Alessandro, open the door," called out Jan all freshly dressed and showered and ready for the new day in a lovely outfit of navy Capri slacks with an overhanging yellow cotton blouse which she knew Alessandro liked.

"Oh shit, look at me *amici,* I cannot let Jan see me this way." Alessandro ran to the bathroom and pounded on the door.

Ron could be heard singing, "She loves me, yeah, yeah, yeah."

Alessandro opened the door and poked his head through, "Ron, your sister is at the door with Susan. I can't let her see me this way. Can I come in and clean up?"

"Oh sure amico," Ron pulled the shower curtain and jumped out of the stall as it was a stand-up shower with no bathtub. "Your turn, I'll just dry off in the bedroom and get dressed." He wrapped the towel about his waist and flung the door wide open. "Don't forget to brush your teeth or you can't kiss my sister," he laughed. "But no tongue…" Just as he slammed the door shut they could hear, "she loves me yeah, yeah, yeah."

The three at the table watched in disbelief.

"Oh Christ, he's singing the Beatles and he doesn't even like them,"

Bob gulped down the now heavily laced coffee. "You guys get cleaned up. I will handle the girls as I have on regular pj's."

Dominic just had to say it. "You will let them see you in those?"

"Not funny, *amico,* or should I just let them come in and see you not all prettied up?"

"Oh no please, I'm sorry; let us get properly dressed and washed."
"That's better, go get clean clothes. I'll handle them."

Off the two ran to the bedroom as Bob strolled to the door. He opened
it a crack and then in a flash squeezed out and found that he was facing
the girls who had jumped back to avoid him colliding with them. "It's
kind of early for you to be pounding on the door isn't it?"

"What? It's nine in the morning and Francois and the Professor are
already with the Captain and Sophia planning the day."
Jan suddenly realized that Bob was in his pajamas, those blue ones
with the clouds and little sheep jumping around. "Will you look at how
cute Bobby looks in those," she pinched Bob's cheek like her Cookie
Grandma did whenever she saw her or Ron.

"Well honey child, I do declare that you are the cutest thing since
peach blossoms bloomed on the trees in Georgia." Susan followed suit
and pinched his cheeks.

"Now cut that out; it's not funny. You know we're five guys with one
bathroom, it's not that easy to get everyone ready."

The girls became all serious and sat themselves down on the rocking
chairs. "We're not being funny Bob; those are cute pj's but Jan and I
understand the situation. I wonder how Ronnie would look wearing
something like that?"

"Now Susan you just stop it. You're talking about my brother. So Bob,
we're all packed and ready to go. Why don't you go use the shower in
our cabin?"

The day was saved and Bob went to tell the guys to move along while
he ran to the girls' cabin to get showered, shaving was not necessary
on a daily basis for him. He was a pretty hairless guy. He never said a
word about Ron's condition of being *potso*. As he ran toward the kids'
bedroom to collect his clothes, he could hear Alessandro singing in the
bathroom.

"Oh solo mio…"

"Oh my God another one is singing. It is contagious." He stopped at the door of what they called the parents' bedroom. He could hear Dominic and Andreas giggling and carrying on; at least in his mind they were. Running into the bedroom he found Ron pulling over an "I Love New York" printed over a large red heart tee shirt over his head.

"Really Ron, you're going to wear that today."

"What's the matter with it; I just bought it when we were in New York City. It's clean."

"The matter is that we are going to one of the most prestigious Universities in the country to meet with highfalutin Professors not one of those knock off shops on Canal Street."

"Oh, then should I wear this one," he picked up a tee shirt from his suitcase with the Statue of Liberty imprinted on it in full color. "Nah, I'll save that for later."

"You are such a dork. I'm going to the girls' cabin to get cleaned up and dressed…"

"And you are full of shit pal. You are not going to their cabin; what if they're in you know their unmentionables. In any case it takes girls longer to get ready so just cut the crap and wait your turn."

"And you're such the expert? You just got to kiss Susan in the Blue Grotto and then we almost got killed in the process so I don't think you're an expert on sex."

"Who said anything about sex; I just meant that they need privacy; you're such an asshole when you get like this…" he closed his suitcase and placed it on the floor. "And I have you know pal that I'm over that thing that happened to me. I'm just a normal reacting guy now that we're engaged."

"Yeah sure; well you had better zip up your dick is hanging out." Out he ran crashing into Alessandro on the way to the back door.

Stumbling down the stairs, he rammed into the Weber grill sitting on the stone patio. The crash gave him pause. He looked back for surely Ron would be giving chase like so many times in the past when they went at each other with such aggravation and something else which he refused to acknowledge. Ron didn't come out that screen door. He picked up his clothes scattered about the patio and noticed that Murat was standing at his back door instead of the front door. He was looking to his left and then to his right. He thought that to be odd. He would have to go to the dock located in front of the cabins to get a boat so that he could get back to the mainland if his plan was to avoid the Captain.

Murat noticed Bob picking up his clothes but particularly what he was wearing and couldn't help but to smile. "Is that you Mr. Wentz?" He strolled over to him, not too fast so as appearing in a rush.

Pretending that he hadn't noticed him Bob identified himself; and with clothes bundled in his arms walked over to him. "Hi there Sir, yes it's me all right. I was just going over to the girls' cabin…"

The eyebrows lifted up on Murat's brow. "*Monsieur*, I had no idea that you were shall I say such a romantic and in the morning too."

"Oh my word… oh no… it's not like that at all. You don't understand, I am going to become a priest and well it's just not what I would do and you see the girls aren't there anyway. They're sitting on the front porch of our cabin waiting for the guys to get ready."

"That is too bad for you but such a blessing for the Church to be sure. My friend you are all red in the face have I embarrassed you?"

"Not really, maybe a little; the real reason is that I am still mad at Sherlock, my so called pal.

"Sherlock? I do not recall such a name among those who were with us last night."

Bob found himself explaining the nick name given to Ron and how it was given to him because he would get these crazy ideas about a case and then twisted his thoughts into actually solving it. Murat pumped him for further details of what he meant by cases and soon Bob was sharing the stories of their crime solving escapades in Rome, Ireland and even New York City. "And just this last spring on the Isle of Capri in Italy we caught a guy. Niccolo Cavelli was his name. He tried to kill that very guy who got killed here on Lake Bonaparte. Some coincidence wouldn't you say?"

"Indeed, but such a young man to be so astute to be called such a name as the famous literary character of Sherlock Holmes whom I would presume is who you meant. Does that then make you two like some say about Holmes and Doctor Watson?"

Bob crossed himself and assured him that wasn't the case while pointing out that he is mistaking them for Andreas and Dominic.

"I see but you can understand how I thought incorrectly of course what I did given how upset you are."

"Sure, I guess but even good friends fight; anyway that's what this is all about now that I think of it. I am hurt that Ron who we call Sherlock was working with Andreas and not me who is his Watson because of that damn Book…" he cut himself off but too late. Murat had just learned about the Book being in their possession.

Murat, seeing how distraught Bob had become, decided not to push for more information. It was enough to know that the Book with all the secrets, as he thought it contained, was right in the cabin next door to him. The issue became how to get hold of it and bring it to the one who sent him to Lake Bonaparte while he went off to Switzerland in search of treasure. Having found out that Benton had failed at retrieving the secret at the Roman ruins in Nyon, all was thought to be lost again. But now the Book was right in that cabin next door. He would be the savior of their quest if he could get his hands on it.

"Well my friend I see that you are in bare feet; perhaps you should go on to get dressed but you may feel free to use my cabin if you wish. After all you are becoming a priest," he made the sign of the Cross, "and being in a girls' cabin may not be appropriate, even in their absence."

It worked. Bob got a sudden surge of Catholic guilt and the idea of placing himself in the occasion of sin. He accepted the invitation and ran for the back door of Murat's cabin, disappearing within it as Ron stepped out of the back door of the guys' cabin. Standing right behind him was Alessandro wrapped in a towel.

"Shit, he's not here. Where the hell did he go? You might as well go and get dressed. You can't search for him like that."

Alessandro left and Ron stepped down the stairs and onto the patio. Seeing the tumbled over grill, he picked it up as Murat walked up to him.

"*Bon jour, Monsieur* De Cenza."

"And good day to you as well but it's Ron; Mr. De Cenza is my Dad."

Murat smiled. "And here I thought your name was Sherlock." He tugged lightly on his goatee.

"Really, so you saw my pal Bob around here then did you?"

"Yes he just left to get dressed. He said that he was going to the girls' cabin…"

Ron needn't hear anymore off he ran toward their cabin, "Thanks, see you later with the Captain." He had the sense to remind Murat of Verdi's intent to speak with all of them as he muttered, "shit Bob why the hell do you have to be so whatever. I need Andreas to translate the French."

While that was happening on the backside of the cabin, Andreas and Dominic stood on the front porch totally ignorant of the tantrum. They were talking with the girls and sharing that Alessandro was almost ready. They added that they had no idea where Bob or Ron had gone off to.

The warming sun of the late summer morning wasn't even noticed by them nor was the lake coming alive as people began to get out onto it with their boats. Water Skiers could already be seen skimming across the water still rather smooth before the motors kicked up the waves over which the skiers would try to jump.

All was quiet behind the cabin as Murat pulled open the screen door and poked his head through. No one could be seen or heard. He entered and scanned the kitchen area as he stepped into the great room which wasn't really that big but cozy with its rustic furnishings and stone fireplace now cold.

His eyes quickly took in the mantel, a Bookcase on the far wall with a desk next to it. Seeing nothing to attract his attention as the Bookcase didn't have Books on it but knickknacks, he stood not more than twelve feet from the dining table where Andreas and Ron had been working on the clues within the autobiography. It was littered with loose sheets of paper and a noteBook, the kind that one would use when taking an essay exam in college. There was however no Book, at least visible from where he stood. Thinking that it might be lying under some of the papers he approached the table.

A loud voice stopped him in his tracks as his heart began to beat so fast in fear that he thought it would leap from his chest.

"Hey you, what the hell are you doing in our cabin?" Alessandro had stepped out of the bedroom tucking his Capri Tee Shirt into his cut-off jeans shorts and then pulling it back out to hang loosely over them. Murat spun around. "*Mon Dieu*, you gave me a fright young man, Alessandro isn't it?" He held his hands over his heart with a dramatic flair.

"Oh, it's you Mr. Murat, I didn't realize it from the backside of you. I mean not your behind…oh this English can still be a problem for me. I mean I didn't recognize you. Still what brings you to our cabin, the Captain said that he will meet with us at Mr. Parrot's restaurant later."

"Indeed he did," Murat was thinking fast on his feet while trying to control a slight trembling in them and his legs. "I do apologize for just walking in but your friend the one they call Sherlock, he was distraught and looking for another of your friends, the Watson, Bob. I told him that I had seen him and that he said he was going to the Girls' cabin to get dressed. And then he ran off before I could say another word."

Alessandro eyed the papers on the table especially the notebook. He made a bee line for it and began to gather them. Spotting Bob's satchel on the seat of one of the chairs he stuffed the papers and notebook into it. Murat watched his every move and Alessandro noted it.

"That Professor Pettigrew, he keeps us pretty busy even on a holiday. We're his research assistants you know and have to keep notes and organize the findings on our projects. That's what all of this is," he closed the messenger bag's flap and snapped the strap shut. The Book was already in the satchel but he made no mention of it.

"I see but what does a Professor from Oxford University in Britain think he'll find here on this lake?"

The young Count of Pianore smiled broadly. "Now come on Mr. Murat that's just too easy a question, the treasure of Joseph Bonaparte of course, just like everyone else who comes to Lake Bonaparte and probably you too."

Murat began to cough and choke.

"Shall I get you a glass of water?"

"That would be so kind of you. I must say that I am embarrassed that you found me out. Everyone in these parts knows of the lost treasure

146

147 | Arthur Cola

of Bonaparte and I just had to come and see for myself." He accepted the glass of water and took a sip all the while eyeing the satchel Alessandro left on the table.

His lingering glance did not go unnoticed. It was interrupted when a head popped in from the front door.

"Alessandro there you are; your girlfriend is wondering if you got lost." Andreas noticed Murat. "Excuse me; I didn't know that we had company."

While the explanation of why Murat was there took place, Ron was at the back door of the girls' cabin and pounding on it. "Hey, Bob what the hell are you doing in there?" He tried the doorknob and it was locked. "For shit's sake, now where did he go?"

Deciding to try the front door, Ron stomped down the few stairs to the grass just as Bob was coming out of Murat's cabin. "Hey, jerk off was that you yelling like a banshee to wake up the dead?"

Ron was in a growing rage as he ran up to Bob and took him by the scruff of his neck. "Who are you calling a…wait a minute; what the hell are you doing in Murat's cabin?"

Bob pushed his best pal away. "Mr. Murat offered me his cabin to keep me from an occasion of sin so that's why I'm here. What pray tell are you doing here; shouldn't you be with Andreas?"

"What! Are you really that jealous?"

"I'm not jealous asshole, I just want to be included and not always the odd man out."

Ron placed his hands on Bob's shoulders and looked him in his baby blue eyes all tearing up and emotional. "Now get this for once and for all. I need to work with Andreas because he knows French. Do you know French? No you do not so don't even say a word. Secondly, you're my Watson, get that through your thick skull," he tapped the side of Bob's head. "And another thing why the hell would you use a total strangers' bathroom what if he has a disease or something?"

"A disease, now you're worried about my health. His cabin is spotless and the bathroom was too so I don't think you need to worry…"

"Really, what else did you see?"

Now they were huddled in low tones and back on the case. Bob admitted to taking a peek into the bedroom and the suitcase was open on the bed. It appeared to him that he was packing to leave as the dresser drawers were also open. Other than that there was nothing unusual except for the letter on top of the dresser.

"Letter, you saw his mail?"

"Not really, it was addressed to Antoine Murat but the address was in Bordentown New Jersey."

"Bordentown, that's the city where we are going to; that is if the Detective doesn't keep us here?"

"Shit Ron, you're right; so what's that mean?"

"It means Watson that this is some weird coincidence that we just happen to meet a guy from Bordentown or that whatever was in the letter told him to come up here but why? That's the question.

"Well maybe he murdered poor Apollo to get information about the treasure."

"Holy shit, you're a genius Watson," Ron hugged his pal and then pushed him away. "I'm still pissed at you so…"

"So get over it, the game is afoot as you say and we're all made up and stuff."

"Oh, okay then," he slapped Bob on the back. "Now let's get back into that cabin. You keep a watch out here and I'll go inside and take a peek at that letter."

"Oh my God Ron you can't do that; tampering with someone's mail is a Federal offense."

"I'm not tampering; I am just taking a peek inside." Ron headed for the back door and then stopped. "Hey, wait a second here. Murat told me that you were going to the girls' cabin; that's why I was shouting for you over there. So he lied to me."

"And why would he do that?"

"Good question and I think that I have the answer." Ron sat on the steps of Murat's cabin. "He needed to keep us apart so that he could do something because he didn't stay with you did he? No and then he went off after I met up with him."

"He probably went to the mainland. Aren't we all supposed to go there?" Bob plopped himself down next to Ron on the steps. The question didn't need an answer for just as it was uttered Alessandro and Murat walked around the corner from the side of the cabin.

"There you are," the Captain and Mrs. Verdi are with the others at the dock waiting to go to the mainland." Alessandro paused to assess the situation as he saw it. "So are you two good now or what?"

"Huh, does the whole world need to know that we had an argument? Ron looked at Murat. "We're just hunky dory; Bob just got dressed in your cabin Mr. Murat after you told me that he was going to the girls' cabin."

"Qui, I did tell you that and then you ran off before I could finish my sentence which was that I offered him my bathroom so that he would not be tempted by seeing the girls' private things."

Bob jumped up and went to Murat. "Yes, that's what you said all right and thanks. You keep a neat and tidy bathroom sir." He turned his head and gave it a jerk.

Ron got the message. He too jumped up off the steps and apologized for the confusion as he called it. With one of his shit ass grins he poked Bob in the gut and told Murat that his Watson was a sensitive guy but everything was just fine now. "So shouldn't we get ourselves to the dock before Captain Verdi thinks we flew the coop?"

Alessandro had no clue as to what Ron meant by "flew the coop" but he had a more pressing matter to address as they walked to the guys' cabin so that Bob could drop off his pj's. He pulled on the strap hanging around his neck and pulled up the satchel. "And another thing Watson, you shouldn't be leaving this thing lying about. Anyone could have come by and walked off with it."

While the morning sun reflected off the bright blue water of Lake Bonaparte and life was perking up in upstate New York, down on the banks of the Delaware River in New Jersey the little City of Bordentown was greeting a new visitor.

The black Cadillac sedan pulled over on Park Street just after the intersection with Prince Street. From that position one could just see the waterway and a series of vacation cabins surrounding the Bordentown Municipal Boat Ramp. Charles Benton turned toward the raven hair beauty sitting next to him on the passenger side.

"We just passed Prince Street Carolina so that means this road will end just ahead. That river ahead is actually Crosswicks Creek to the right would be the Delaware River into which it flows. But we want the Creek because that's where the Point Breeze Estate was located."

"Why Charles, you're just a wealth of knowledge about this place." She patted his smooth cheek.

He flinched slightly as just the touch of her hand so tenderly sent a shiver through him. Yet he was able to compose himself while remembering the pain that her thugs caused him back at the University meeting. He informed her that he was after all part of the Benton Family into which the daughter of Annette Savage, Carolina's ancestor and mistress to Joseph Bonaparte, married.

"I am well aware of your credentials or we should not be sitting here especially after your failure in Switzerland."

Rather than try to explain that it wasn't his fault and that some young people from America and Italy thwarted his efforts by trickery, he opened the car door and jumped out of the car. Leaning back into it, he invited Carolina to step out of the car and survey the area with him. She did so but stayed on her side of the vehicle.

"So over there is Crosswicks Creek?" She pointed to the just visible creek. "I think we should have brought Luigi and Pietro with us instead of dropping them off at the Inn. They could have rowed the boat."

"Yes they certainly have the strength to do so. Alas they are not here," he was delighted to point out, "so look over there to the right. That is the boat ramp where I suggest we rent a boat and go onto the Point Breeze Estate from the Creekside given that it is now owned by the Divine Word Missionaries and is a seminary."

"Charles, are you really suggesting that we enter the grounds in a clandestine manner when all we have to do is enter the grounds, go see the priest in charge and tell them that we are planning a retreat as Stockton suggested…let us say for a tour group and would like his help."

He leaned over the hood of the car. "You are the clever one aren't you?" After what happened at the University to him it was a bold move to be sure. "However, if we need to get into the forested area without a bunch of priests or brothers accompanying us, we'll need to get on to the grounds from the creek because that's where the Bonaparte Mansion stood."

"You make a good point. Let us get to that boat rental place and arrange for something and then go to the good Missionaries who may be sitting on a fortune and not knowing it. In any case getting on the grounds will be of little help without that Book now in the possession of those so called research assistants of that cute Professor." She reentered the car knowing full well that she had struck a nerve.

Benton was not thrilled with the description rendered for Pettigrew but he wisely kept silent and got behind the wheel. The focus would now be on exploring the grounds with the hope that once they possessed the Book, it would be easier to locate the actual foundations of the original mansion and second mansion.

The work of Captain Enrico Verdi of the Italian Carabinieri and agent of Interpol was actually concluded with the identification of the body of Apollo Dimitri in the morgue of the Diana Town hospital in upstate New York. He had found the escaped prisoner and arrangements were made to return the body to Italy. His wife, Sophia, was thrilled that they might actually be able to have a second honeymoon. However the murder investigation was ongoing in that the weapon being an arrow from a crossbow and the person who fired it were still unknown. Thus he was directed to assist Detective Lt. Brandon Malone with the investigation into the murder of Apollo. The honeymoon would have to wait but Jan and Susan assured her that they would help ease the disappointment in whatever way they could except that neither of them had ever visited Princeton or the City of Bordentown in New Jersey. But they did know Philadelphia and had high hopes of showing her the Liberty Bell if they could arrange for a side trip.

In any case it had become necessary for them to travel to Princeton University where Professor Pettigrew had a connection with the archeology Professor Dorothy Witherspoon. She on her part had a colleague who was Chair of the History Department who might be able to identify the arrow's historic period and thus narrow down as to where such a crossbow might be found for use as a murder weapon. The Department Chair, Professor Richard Stockton, of course already knew that someone had tampered with the Medieval History display.

Malone had left Antione Murat with the Sherriff. He may have been a person of interest but there was no connection between him and Apollo, the murder victim found. He would be allowed to continue his work as he had presented; that is to research the life of Joseph Bonaparte at his Lake Bonaparte home near Natural Bridge New York. He was free to roam the area. However as soon as Malone and his entourage were gone he checked out of the Parrot Cabin.

"Mr. Parrot, I must say that this stay has been quite the experience unlike any in my memory." He stood at the Boat Rental hut.

"Mr. Murat, that is an understatement to be sure. I am so sorry that you are leaving us so soon." He glanced over to Sarah who was speaking with the teens who had discovered the body and were tying up the boat Murat used to the dock. "You say that you are going to Natural Bridge next and that's where Sarah lives. Shall I ask her to direct you to an Inn or library where you might conduct some research?"

"Oh that won't be necessary. You mentioned that she worked at the Post Office; if I need directions and any introductions, I'll just go to seek her out."

"Well then, it's *Au revoir* as they say up from where you are from; you did say French Canada, no?"

"Indeed, I did, but now I must be off and eventually get back to New York City to finish the article."

"Good luck and do treat us kindly in the article."

"Most assuredly, you have all been most hospitable despite all that took place." Walking off toward the parking lot, he turned and waved as he headed for a gray, almost silver, Chrysler which Parrot thought to be a rather expensive car for a magazine reporter. Once off on Bonaparte Rd. instead of going toward the hamlet of Natural Bridge, he went south but it wasn't toward New York City. The signage he followed along the highway he had reached read, "Princeton."

Chapter Eight:
Princeton Investigation

While Murat made his way toward the University, the mini-bus with Alessandro back at the wheel made its way onto the campus of Princeton University. He was following Malone with Captain Verdi in the passenger seat of the unmarked squad car and the Professor in the rear seat. Mrs. Verdi was invited to sit with Jan and Susan in the mini-bus instead of Malone's car. It would be a long ride which would be consumed with discussing the details of the murder investigation. In the rear seat behind the women were Ron, Bob and Andreas who spent the entire ride pouring over the notes made at Lake Bonaparte from the autobiography Book. This time Ron made sure not to overlook his pal.

As for Dominic he assumed the role of navigator with map in hand. It was about one in the afternoon when Alessandro drove onto Nassau Street toward the library. Bob was already complaining that they had missed lunch. Ron ignored his pal's plea for food for the game was afoot and now he realized that the murder on Lake Bonaparte may actually have a connection with what they were about to embark upon once they got to Bordentown.

"You see guys, at first I thought that Apollo's death was disconnected to what we were doing. The whole treasure hunting world always has thought that the lost treasure of Bonaparte was somewhere around the Lake Bonaparte caverns. Whoever helped Apollo escape from prison and get to America obviously thought it to be somewhere in the caves too. Why else would he have been found at the mouth of that cave, near which once stood King Joseph's house with its secret tunnel? And another thing, his murder would indicate that whoever killed him thought so too."

"So why are we coming to Princeton?" asked the famished Bob.

"Elementary my dear Watson; we are here to help Malone and the Captain find the murderer. Once that person is found we would be in a better position to prove the Natural Bridge theory wrong. And it is

154

wrong because we have the Book which obviously they never had or they would have gone to Bordentown New Jersey instead of Natural Bridge in upstate New York."

Light bulbs illuminated simultaneously in the minds of everyone in the van except for Sophia who was clueless to the contents of the Book. It had caused her husband and her to have no honeymoon on Capri. Now they were caught up in yet another murder investigation. The girls were given the eye from Ron to not share too much with Sophia. In his Sherlock mind what he had just presented was but a theory and it needed to be proven which of course could not be done until they got to Bordentown and the Point Breeze estate.

Susan nodded and simply explained that Apollo may have been onto something about the legend of Bonaparte's treasure. He was wrong according to Ron and after all Sherlock mode or not, the love of her life was not infallible or was he?

And to make sure that point was well taken by Sophia, Jan added that her brother thought that he's a big know it all when it comes to puzzles and stuff like that but he's not always right.

"You see Sophia, Apollo was working on the common held theory that Bonaparte hid his treasure at his New York house after what happened to his mansion at Point Breeze."

"*Capisco*, I understand Susan but Ron speaks of a secret tunnel. Is that not where this Apollo was found?"

The wife of Captain Verdi had hit upon the very word which was the secret of the Book which Andreas and he had worked on in the cabin. The secret tunnel was indeed the key to the mystery of the Bonaparte treasure. Joseph Bonaparte was always living in fear for his life even when he came to America and what Ron had seen in his dream was a verification of that fact. Thus he built tunnels. Some were to simply be an easy way to move unobserved from his home to his daughter's house on the Point Breeze estate. He after all had children from Annette Savage and the one surviving daughter, Catherine Charlotte, was to be kept away from his legal daughter (Zenaide) and her husband (Lucien Charles Bonaparte) to avoid a public scandal. Annette's daughter felt strongly that it was her right to receive the recognition which the daughter of Joseph and his wife Julie Clary (who never came to America) received.

However, there were other tunnels built as escape or secret entries given his relationship with Annette Savage. Even the second house built after the fire of 1820 destroyed the first mansion had tunnels. These were essential especially as the power struggle in France grew and threatened the Bourbon Family and the reign of Louis XVIII. Bonaparte haters abounded in France and England and well did Joseph know of that reality.

Andreas leaned into Ron. "Can it be possible, but did I not hear the Signora Verdi talk of the tunnels?"

"She did but hopefully it was about the one in New York where Apollo was killed."

The jerk of the mini-bus brought an abrupt end to the conversation as Alessandro announced that they had arrived at the University's library building. Captain Verdi and Detective Malone were already standing on its steps with Professor Pettigrew waiting for them. He knew quite well that his authority was limited as they stood in New Jersey. As for the Captain, he only had credentials to find the escaped prisoner from Italy. Thus he was there as a guest of Malone.

Malone took the container holding the arrow which killed Apollo from the hands of Pettigrew. Sophia made her way directly to the Captain and kissed his cheek while whispering something about tunnels and secrets of Bonaparte into his ear. He nodded and cast his gaze onto Ron just running up to the steps with the others behind him. The small platoon of so called research assistants, academia people and policemen crowded the gray granite stone patio in front of the arched entryway. It was quite the sight as Malone tried to quiet them down and explain what was to take place.

He began with Bob's rather vocal insistence that lunch should be a priority. "Ladies and Gentlemen, before we go to lunch, which seems to be an urgent issue with some of you, I must remind you that we are guests of the University. We are here to seek only verification that the murder weapon was indeed a crossbow and that said bow did or did not come from what Professor Pettigrew describes as the Special Collections Display in this library. Once that is established by the expert, Professor Richard Stockton, we shall then determine if this arrow," he held up the box, "is from this particular crossbow and display. Do I make myself quite clear?"

Agreement was being offered by nods and comments such as "sure thing", "of course" and a simple "yes" Detective Malone went on to say that it would be Professor Pettigrew who would handle the introductions and presentation of the arrow. He was the one with the connection to Professor Witherspoon who offered to connect them with Stockton.

Except for Pettigrew no one in the formidable entourage had ever visited Princeton University. The library building like the stone patio on which they walked was made of gray stone. Pettigrew was pointing out to the young people in awe of its size for a library that is was built in 1948 but in the Gothic revival style of the Medieval period. It even had a tower reminding one of those in Britain such as in Oxford, York and even London. He led them under the arches which covered the entrance doors and into the lobby. The gigantic cathedral like windows trimmed in Gothic stone carvings made the interior bright with natural light. Though the university was not in formal session as yet, students were scattered about. Most were being given a tour of the campus on which they would soon be studying. Ron's eyes grew even wider as he took in the sight and sighed that such a place would be studying in heaven.

His attention was soon drawn to the staircase rather than the elevators as Pettigrew guided them up the stairs to the second floor where the particular Special Collections display they sought was located. Standing outside of the Office of the Librarian were Professors Dorothy Witherspoon and Richard Stockton waiting for the entourage.

As soon as she spotted Pettigrew leading the group in British casual consisting of sleek pants, not jeans like the young males, long sleeve dress shirt in white of course and a cap minus its usual umbrella companion she bolted from Stockton. She ran to Pettigrew throwing her arms around his neck and patting his five day Five o'clock shadow of a beard.

"Andrew, you look so…" she whispered into his ear, "so rugged and enticing I might add."

His immediate blushing in crimson was well taken by everyone else watching the spectacle.

"Well now Ronnie, doesn't this remind you of what happened in Dublin?"

"Shush Susan, she'll hear you. And no, it's not like that at all. Can't you see that she really likes him?"

Given the situation, Stockton took it upon himself to welcome the group. He walked up to Malone and the Captain, and guided them away from the embracing couple oblivious to all around them. Only when Professor Stockton welcomed the group to Princeton did it finally sink in that they were quite abandoned to do their thing in front of everyone.

"Andrew, it's so…so wonderful to see you again." She ran her fingers through his bushy brownish hair.

"I only wish we could be together under better conditions…" he kissed her lightly on the lips. "Maybe later we might have a visit?"

"Just name the time," her comments abruptly ended when she heard Stockton welcoming the others and invited them to follow him to the Special Collections Room. "Oh my word, Andrew the arrow, your colleagues, they've all been watching us."

The British in him immediately took hold. He gave her a smile of regret, brushed the hair from his face and pulled on his pants to let some air in around his rising issue. She fluffed out her lab coat, adjusted the collar and pulled out a tissue from its pocket dabbing his lips to remove the lipstick smear. Hand in hand they rushed to catch up with the others.

When they came to a screeching halt inside the gallery Malone was placing the metal container on a small table which had been set up in front of the display case with the Crossbow. Pettigrew slipped to the side and made his way up to the Detective who gave him a grin. He then continued with his presentation of the container by lifting off the cover and exposing the arrow. There was complete silence as the lid was removed.

"And there it is Professors," began Malone. "This is what was in the back of the victim on Lake Bonaparte."

Witherspoon and Stockton leaned over the container to get a closer look. Stockton didn't utter a word but Witherspoon let out a gasp.

"Richard, there is no doubt about it; this is the arrow from the display." She turned to point to the Crossbow in the display case and let out a yelp of sorts as if shocked. "Detective Malone, Captain Verdi, I can assure you that this is the missing arrow from the display. Come closer and look at its twin."

Everyone crammed in closer to look at the twin arrow and the Crossbow. Once again Dorothy gasped. "Richard, the Crossbow is back in its proper setting. I thought you had the gallery secured." There was a sudden wave of chatter as everyone began to speak at once. They focused on the fact that the murder arrow was indeed a match to the one on display and that someone got access to the display to remove it.

Ron moved next to the Captain with a question. "Captain, something is rotten in Denmark or in this case Princeton."

Verdi squeezed Ron's shoulder and nodded in agreement. Luckily it was his good shoulder. "Say nothing right now."

As Ron affirmed the request, Stockton was telling Malone and Dorothy that they shouldn't be concerned about the display representation of the Crossbow. "You see I placed it back into its normal setting so that it wouldn't fall off the board and get damaged."

The detective was at a loss for words for a moment but Stockton's colleague was not. "Richard that means you touched it…"

"Exactly correct Professor Witherspoon," began Captain Verdi as he stepped forward and ended her comment. "It means that your fingerprints are now on the weapon Sir and may have damaged any others made by whoever may have used this bow. In any case detective Malone wouldn't you agree that the fact that the Crossbow was moved would indicate that it was used with its own bolt or arrow as the case may be?"

"I agree Captain Verdi." Malone turned to Stockton trying to hide his perturbed feelings quite unsuccessfully as everyone saw his frustration. "Sir, you will need to verify that this arrow is from this display and one more thing."

"Of course what can I do to help?"

"Is there a way to determine if this bow was recently shot?"

"Certainly, that's easily done. This bow is hundreds of years old as is its string. There would be newly frayed slices on the string used to pull back on the device."

Malone was visibly relieved and felt certain that they at least had the murder weapon. The next issue would be who could fire a Crossbow from the Middle Ages. "Professors Stockton and Witherspoon given the type of work you do would either of you ever had the opportunity to use a Crossbow?"

Pettigrew was upset that Dorothy would be questioned as if she was a suspect. She, however, felt quite all right with the question. She was an archeologist and would unearth all types of artifacts, some of which were weapons. However she pointed out that her current focus was on Native Americans along the east coast of America and thus she would have no chance of finding a Crossbow. She did inform Malone and Verdi that she was one of those who procured the Crossbow in question as it was a rare set which included its original arrows.

"And who were the others Professor Witherspoon?"

"Why that would be Professor Stockton of course Detective. You do remember the discovery don't you Richard? It was about five years ago when we were just teachers and came across them at a dig in the south of France. It was a joint effort between Princeton and Oxford and that's how I met Andrew who was part of their team."

While Andrew smiled at the memory and Jan and Susan sighed at the romantic aspect of it, the beads on Stockton's brow were becoming more pronounced. He tried to explain that it was just an excavation sponsored by a benefactor interested in Medieval History. "We call it a dig but in reality it wasn't one at all. We actually found them in a cellar of an old monastery fortress once associated with the Popes in exile in Avignon France back in the 14th Century."

"Still it was terribly exciting to break through that wall and find it wasn't it Richard? I remember how you demonstrated it to the students who were so terribly excited to have actually found something. And it did help us to move up the ladder here at Princeton."

Stockton admitted that it did help with his becoming Chair of the History Department. He also feigned only a slight memory of trying to show how it worked as it was terribly frail when it was found.

"Certainly our students were excited and remembered such a clumsy attempt to demonstrate a four hundred year old bow. They imagined a Hollywood image rather than what it actually was. But then you are working with these young people who probably could relate to them."

The seven to whom he referred cast glances of contempt but kept quiet for the moment. Ron however had enough of the "I am after all a Princeton Professor" attitude. His face became flushed and Bob noticed it first. He knew what would come next and before he could stop it, Ron erupted. It wasn't like "Vesuvius" covering Pompeii in ash but it did spurt out a cloud of ashen litanies of what the young people he identified as ones who would be giggling over an archeological find had actually accomplished in the last two and half years. But instead of directing his comments to Stockton directly he addressed them to Professor Pettigrew and he did so using his first name which he had never done previously. That too was to demonstrate familiarity with a well-known academic in Stockton's field.

"Andrew, perhaps your colleagues are unaware of how we saved Michelangelo's Pieta, or how we discovered and saved a Renaissance work of art by Carlo Fontana and Michelangelo himself, or the 11th Century Chalice of St. Malachy in Ireland not to mention the...." Ron cut himself off lest he give himself away on how far he, Bob and Andreas had gotten in translating the autobiography of Joseph Bonaparte and his decoding of the former King's notes in the Book which had brought about death and revelation.

However, his Watson had become empowered by the litany and he dropped the bomb of the Book being found on Capri and how valued it was. "And that's just the tip of the iceberg isn't it Ron. Why this whole murder investigation revolves around a Book we found and of others who tried to steal it just a few days ago in Switzerland but failed. We have it and we know a lot about..."

Ron was about to have a meltdown even though he knew his pal meant well. All six of his friends knew that as well but felt helpless until Jan and Susan swung into action.

"Oh Bobby, you're just so cute when you get all worked up about nothing, isn't that right Jan?" Susan pinched Bob's cheeks hard and he suddenly understood why.

Jan tugged on Bob's arm and tried to change the subject by actually drawing attention to the Book in the satchel but not indicating that it was there. "My brother is right isn't he Bobby? We have gone through a lot with Professor Pettigrew and even before we knew him and through it all this satchel was always there holding those precious things we discovered. You know Madam, Gentlemen, Bob here is going to become a priest but he's in love none the less; only it's with this little leather bag in which the fate of Italy was once held. Did you know that when the election of 1946 took place in Italy to decide if the King should remain King of Italy, that…"

Alessandro caught the eye of Ron who was back in control. Something had to be done to shut up not only Bob but his sister as well. The young Count wrapped his arms around Jan and planted on kiss on her red lips thus silencing her spilling the beans about King Umberto II to which they had pledged silence.

"My sister, I suppose does get excited about little things like your students did Professor Stockton over a Crossbow. In the end they are all just museum pieces which wouldn't change a thing would they, Sir?"

During the litany Stockton had stood virtually mesmerized as to the breath of what Dorothy's colleague from Oxford, who he now realized was more than just a colleague, and seven young people had accomplished. His eyes began to twitch as he tried to focus on the satchel. He looked at the Captain, the Detective and then to Dorothy. She was still holding the arm of Pettigrew seeking some kind of reaction of shock or understanding. Then he zeroed in back on Ron and into those cocoa brown cow-like eyes. He wondered if more than Italian election results over two decades old were contained within that satchel. Even more importantly he asked himself what was found in Switzerland which might be in it. He knew that Benton failed to find something as did Carolina. Could these so called assistants really have something which he wanted so desperately?

The bells of the chapel tower located behind the library began to ring out the two in the afternoon hour as Stockton spoke while shaking the hand of Pettigrew. "Sir, I had no idea that your team was so accomplished. My students obviously couldn't hold a candle to them. Might we all have dinner this evening and talk about our work and how it does make a difference?"

Ron caught the remark meant as a dig to him and smiled. He knew that he had gotten to Stockton.

Malone however still had a murder investigation to conduct and stepped back into the conversation ignorant of most of what Ron and Bob had presented. He was however well aware of how they helped him solve a murder in New York City during its World's Fair some three years ago.

"This has been quite enlightening Professors, Ladies and Gentlemen but we must continue with the reason as to why we are here. We have the murder weapon at least we are fairly certain that we do. It needs to be sealed in the display. No one must come in contact with it until we are able to send it off to forensics who will try to discover someone other than Professor Stockton who may have had contact with it." He was not pleased that it was touched. "I think that's all that we can do for now. Perhaps we should feed these young people though as I see our friend here looks faint." He smiled and wrapped his arm around Bob. "How does that sound to you?"

"Thank the Lord for you Detective. You are a man of good sense."

"Why thank you Mr. Wentz. Perhaps Professor Witherspoon might direct us to a restaurant."

"I would be pleased Detective. There is a staple of our students and faculty alike just down Nassau Street. The Pancake House has a variety of foods obviously breakfast dishes being its specialty. But trust me they are so good even for lunch." She smiled at Bob. "I will call them and make a reservation as we're quite the group."

"Do accept my apologies but I cannot join you as I have acceptance letters to create."

Malone took Stockton's hand and shook it. "That's all right Sir, we'll talk again in the morning if not sooner. Where might we find you?"

The detective presented his question as a matter of fact and not threatening. However it was apparent at least to Ron that Stockton did not feel that way. He hesitated and glanced at the doorway leading to the main staircase before he answered. The others began to file out of the gallery and toward that staircase as Malone and the Captain remained waiting for Stockton's answer and Ron stood at that doorway toward which Stockton glanced to observe and hear the answer.

The minute seemed much longer than it was. Stockton replied that he would be in his office until 5:00 p.m. and then he'd probably get some take out and go home as the day had been quite the ordeal for him what with the break-in for the Crossbow and murder report. Verdi and Malone expressed their appreciation of the shock of it all. They went out of their way, Ron thought, to assure him that everything that was being done was just routine. Their words seemed to serve their purpose. Stockton offered them his card with his phone number.

"Just call me should you need me today and I will direct you to my home."

Malone slipped the card into his jacket pocket and strode off with Verdi who was pointing out that the Crossbow being taken, verified as being replaced in the wrong way and then being placed again in its proper display fashion was indicative of the break-in being an inside job. Malone glanced back to Stockton standing in a frozen state before the display case. Neither of them noticed Ron in the shadows of a bathroom door opposite them peering out into the gallery.

No sooner had the police joined the others outside than footsteps could be heard running across the oak panels of flooring. The sound came closer and closer to that bathroom door and Ron could now see that it was a man who shouted at Stockton as he ran past him.

"I've been holding it since I left Lake Bonaparte Richard, talk to you in a minute."

Murder at Point Breeze

Ron jumped back and entered the last stall away from the urinals and
stood crouched on the toilet seat.

The sound of the door swinging open and making a thud as it banged
against the wall startled Stockton still processing the man's words.
Stockton headed for the bathroom. In seconds there was a sound of
relief as the flustered Professor entered the bathroom.

"What the hell are you doing here Antoine?"

In the stall Ron held his mouth as the name was mentioned.

Antoine Murat shook the last drop off and began to zip up. "Really,
you couldn't let a guy relieve himself."

"Fuck you, like you've never held a conversation in a men's room
before."

"What are you implying Richard?" Murat turned. His face was red
with rising anger not embarrassment.

The Professor had hit a delicate spot and backed off. "Nothing at all,
it's just that you were supposed to go to Bordentown not here to the
University. Carolina is already there with Benton. Time is of the
essence now that the police are here interviewing everyone about the
Crossbow."

Murat stood at the sink washing his hands. The splashing water
distorted some of his words as he spoke into the mirror while watching
Stockton behind him nervously wringing his hands. "Just calm down
Richard, I will get to Bordentown and your slut of a friend." He turned
to face the Professor. "I thought that it was essential to let you know
firsthand what happened on Lake Bonaparte."

"Are you mad to call her that? She has those two thugs with her. They
could break you and me in two with hardly exerting effort."

His still damp hand patted Stockton's cheek. "Calm yourself Richard; she isn't anywhere near here. So do you want to know what happened on Lake Bonaparte or not, time's a wasting." He slowly moved his hand down to Stockton's belt. "So when's the last time you had any? That's why you're so nervous." He pulled on the belt and peered down smiling. "This view you think is inviting but alas you have the wrong equipment, so sad for me."

Pushing Murat away, Stockton insisted that his private life was none of his business and that there was a fortune out there to be found. "Or have you forgotten Antoine?"

"I forget nothing Professor that's why I came to tell you in person, but it seems the police arrived first. Apollo Dimitri is dead."

"I know that and it was from the arrow of a Crossbow, the one from our gallery display right out there. They know it was moved and replaced incorrectly in the display and then fixed again in its correct format."

"So you slipped up did you?"

"I don't know what you're talking about." Stockton began to pace. "You need to get out of here before someone sees you. Go meet Carolina and Benton they're at the Bordentown Inn. I won't be able to go right now; the police will probably want to see me again now that my fingerprints are on the Crossbow."

Murat exploded and shoved Stockton into the side panel of the first stall next to the urinals. The crash vibrated the entire row of stalls as Ron steadied himself on the rim of the toilet. "So you did slip up; what an asshole you are and you supposedly being such a brilliant Professor."

"Get your hands off of me right now." In a most unusual stance for him he pushed Murat off and took a swing, missing him. "Of course I had to move the Crossbow back to protect you, Carolina and Benton. It was obvious that one of you probably took the weapon."

"Nice try Professor but a little slow." Murat came back at him and spoke within inches from his face. Stockton could feel the hair of his goatee against his face. "Now you need to listen up and take it all in before I really lose my temper and fuck you up right here in more ways than one."

Stockton's backbone stiffened. "I thought that I had the wrong equipment or is that all part of your charade here?"

Murat grabbed hold of the lapels of Stockton's tweed sport coat and swung him around. "Who are you calling queer?"

Stockton rammed his hands up through Murat's arms forcing him to back off. "I'm not calling anyone gay; I am just making an observation from what you said to me. So are we done here? Might we deal with why you came here and trust me it will not be for sex."

Antoine Murat began to smile. He brushed down Stockton's hair and stepped back. "So you've guessed it. I use sex to get what I want no matter who the other person is. That's how I found out about the treasure from this Apollo dude before he died. Shit was he a beautiful dude; almost made me wish that I was on his team."

"So you are a gigolo then? Whatever you are, I don't care if you get results."

Ignoring him Murat thought aloud. "Only felt that way one other time and it was up at Lake Bonaparte just the day I found that poor guy dead in the boat. There was this group of young guys and girls with some kind of Professor like you who came to search for Bonaparte's treasure, only he was a Brit. There was this tall blond guy, I think he was a soldier from how they talked."

Ron was gagging in the stall using all his strength to stifle it.

"I don't get you Antoine but like I said, I do not care if you had sex with that Apollo guy or that soldier."

He moved into Stockton again. "And like I said, I am not queer. I just flirted with this Apollo guy because it was obvious that he liked guys."

"Okay, okay, I think I understand but you're in denial. In any case what did you learn about the Bonaparte treasure?"

"Just the same old stuff that everyone thinks; he was going to show me the cave in which the treasure was supposed to be hidden. But when I got there, he was dead in the boat. I saw the arrow in his back and jumped into the boat. He was wearing a small leather bag hanging on a strap across his chest. I checked him out; he was dead, poor guy. Anyway, I took off the bag and got away quick because a boat was coming." Murat pulled on the unnoticed strap across his chest and brought around a small purse-like bag. "This is it."

Stockton became ecstatic exclaiming how he had found the clue to the treasure of Joseph Bonaparte. He took hold of Murat and hugged him after almost wanting to punch him out. He effused about being rich men as he took hold of the bag and opened it. First he took out a map of sorts indicating various caverns around Lake Bonaparte. Handing it over to Murat he took out a letter. He skimmed across its two pages as his eyes began to grow wide. He waved the letter in front of Murat's face.

"Do you know who wrote this letter which is more like a set of instructions on what to do with Charles Benton at Lake Bonaparte? "Cool it Stockton, of course I know Benton. He works for you like I do."

"Exactly, but I don't mean him. We'll deal with him later. The writer of this letter is Carolina Gianetti."

"Fuck me, I know; it's that Italian woman you mentioned going to Bordentown with that dumb wad Benton. So what, we all work for you."

"So you might think but this is a set of instructions for this Apollo guy to find the treasure before we do obviously. There is no mention of you or me. She's working on her own while also working with us to find the treasure." Stockton folded the letter and carefully placed it back into the envelope. He slipped it into the breast pocket of his sport coat and patted it. "When you get to Bordentown you shall make no mention of this to either Carolina or Benton is that clear."

"Okay if that's how you want it but I think she's just playing the odds and covering all her bases to get rich just like you. You sent me to Lake Bonaparte to check out the legend of Bonaparte didn't you? And I'll lay odds that you didn't tell this Carolina or Benton for that matter about my little exploration in upstate New York."

Stockton placed his arm over Murat's shoulder and patted it. "You are quite the clever one Antoine aren't you?" he then swung himself around to face him.

"What the fuck, stop this cozy shit..."

"Oh Antoine, I am not being as you say cozy with you. I want you to look into my eyes and know how important this trip to Bordentown is for both of us and our future life as wealthy men."

"I get it but can you give me some personal space while you do it?"

The Professor stepped back two paces. "There now are we all better? Now listen to me carefully. I don't care who you have to fuck or who you have to deceive, the goal is to find that treasure before Carolina does so that we don't have to split it three ways. You fancy yourself as some kind of French lover; then prove it. In her ecstasy let her tell you what she knows."

Murat actually took his words as compliments as a broad grin crossed his face. His manliness no longer in question he readily accepted the assignment to seduce Carolina. "No problem Richard, once she gets a taste of this, she'll fall for me hard." He grabbed between his legs to emphasize his point. Quickly releasing his package he turned for the door. "I'll get right on this; see you in Bordentown."

Stockton had to inform him that with the police investigation his departure from the University would be delayed. He wouldn't want to arouse any suspicion on the part of Detective Malone or Captain Verdi he explained. Murat returned a shrug while telling him that it was too bad that he wouldn't be seeing him in action. "But not to worry as I'll be getting everything under control by the time you do get down to Bordentown.

"And speaking of a little city, you should know that there is nothing up at Lake Bonaparte. That I did find out from that dead guy, Apollo. So it appears that there is definitely something at some place called Point Breeze."

Stockton exploded with excitement and tossing aside the fact that Murat and Carolina Savage Gianetti were planning their own treasure hunt without him. "And you wait until now to tell me this? Point Breeze is the name of the estate which Joseph Bonaparte built when he escaped to America and it's in Bordentown."

"Calm down Professor, there's more to that part of the story. I actually met some British Professor who's like you. He and his assistants appear to be seeking the same thing as us. And what's more, I befriended the kid they call Watson but it's the one who is called Sherlock who's got the inside information about what's in that Book…"

"The Book; are you telling me that there actually is a Book which details where the treasure of Joseph Bonaparte may be?" He ran to Murat with outstretched arms as if to hug him.

Murat thrust up his arm to hold him off from such an act of endearment. "Not so fast Professor; you aren't rich enough to have me; at least not yet. See you in Bordentown." He turned and slammed the door shut, as he yelled out, "I'm leaving right now for that town." Stockton stood like a statue in a museum just staring at the bathroom door. "You bastard just wait until I get down there."

Ron could hardly keep his balance on the toilet bowl rim as he reacted to hearing what had just transpired. The opening and then the thud of a closing door allowed him to risk jumping off the bowl and peeking out the stall door. The bathroom was empty and the lights had been turned off. Only the natural light from a small window illuminated the men's room. He quietly crept up to the door and peeked out. He could see Stockton running across the oak paneled flooring toward the Exit doors. Closing the door, he leaned against it and wiped his brow as he began to piece together what appeared to be not a double cross but a triple cross plan gone badly. He now knew that Carolina Gianetti was alive and well and in the United States in a town called Bordentown in the State of New Jersey. It being the town where they were scheduled to conduct their excavation on the once grand estate of Joseph Bonaparte, called Point Breeze.

Chapter Nine:
The Pancake House

When all was silent outside that bathroom door and the afternoon sun was all that illuminated the Princeton University Library Gallery, Ron slipped out and chose not to run so as to create a sound and slowly walked towards the exit. He stopped briefly at the display of the Crossbow. A thought exploded in his head, one which might solve the murder of Apollo Dimitri. At the same time it may counter anything Carolina was plotting to find the lost Crown Jewels before he and his pals could. He pulled out his handkerchief from his pants' pocket and placed it over the crossbow. Then looking about as if eyes hidden from sight were watching his act of thievery he slipped the Crossbow off the display panel and then ran to the exit with it under his arm. Virtually flying down the ornate staircase and then out the main doors he found himself without transportation standing on the granite plaza in the warm afternoon sunlight.

He looked about wondering how he would get to the Princeton Inn now that everyone went to lunch. "The Pancake House," he shouted out and then covered his mouth with his free hand. As it was only a couple of blocks away on the very street where he stood he decided to walk rather conspicuously with the crossbow still tucked under his arm and worried that his tampering with evidence would get him into a lot of trouble. He knew full well that it would indeed get him in hot water with Detective Malone and Captain Verdi. Stepping onto the street level sidewalk he shuddered as if a cool breeze swept across his back yet realizing that it was a rather warm day. Glancing upwards to the gallery windows he felt as if someone was watching him steal the Crossbow. The glare of the sun off the windows made it impossible to tell if anyone was there. That was unfortunate for if he could see through those windows he would have seen Professor Richard Stockton looking out his office window, noticing Ron briskly walking away from the library building.

"What the hell! That's the De Cenza punk and with the Crossbow."
Stockton grabbed for the phone to call security but then slammed it
down. "Calm yourself Richard. This could work in your favor." He
spoke aloud as if to expect an answer or advice.

Running down the same staircase as had Ron, Stockton decided to
catch Ron in the act so to speak right in public view and accuse him of
theft of an historic artifact. He couldn't have gotten too far on foot and
by the direction he was going he knew that it wasn't to the Inn. *"So
this punk they call Sherlock thinks that he can pull a fast one on me
does he."* He picked up his pace and began to run at full throttle as
Ron was now at least a couple of blocks ahead of him. As his pace
quickened so did his thoughts as to why he would have taken the
Crossbow. In his mind that act for whatever reason would play right
into his hands. Just then he realized where Ron was going.

The Pancake House sign hung out over the sidewalk. *"Shit, he's going
to find his friends, probably that one they call Watson or whatever."*
Ron pulled on the door of the restaurant after waving to his friends
sitting at a long table along the windows lining the front of it.

Bob was first to see what Ron was carrying and jumped out of his seat
and running for the door as his best pal entered. Behind him where
gathered all the others including the Detective Lieutenant who at the
last minute decided a bit of lunch sounded like a good idea. He and
Professor Pettigrew had been discussing what would take place next in
the investigation. The Professor and his crew were focused on leaving
for Bordentown in the morning and had not noticed Ron's entrance.
The hustle from the table and the chattering of shocked young people
brought their conversation to an abrupt end.

Bob stood in front of Ron who was barely through the door. "What in
God's name are you holding? Oh God no, please don't tell us that…"

"Will you all just stop it and let me explain. Go back to the table and
just keep looking out the window."

"Now you've really done it Ron," Bob was beyond hysterical as were Susan and his sister Jan both of whom pleaded that he turn around and return it at once.

As for the guys, they couldn't get a word in edgewise as the Professor and Detective were pushing their way through them. The restaurant guests were now all tuned into the fuss at the front door. In a loud booming voice, Malone gave orders that everyone go back to their seats while assuring the people in the Pancake House that all was fine just excitement in seeing their friend. He and Pettigrew stood in front of Ron with Bob at his side as parents would who were about to scold a young child. Only this child had just turned twenty-one, was engaged and about to be married not to mention that he was a major crime solver. So they waited for Ron to speak first.

"Oh, Detective Malone, am I glad to see you." He glanced out the window behind him and turned back to face his eagerly awaiting friends who thought Ron had dug himself into a hole from which he would not be getting out.

"And I might say that we, all your friends and the Professor here are interested in hearing why you are carrying around a Crossbow, which looks quite familiar to me."

Ron was getting antsy as he again looked out the window behind him. "Well it should, it's the one from the gallery display. Now don't get all excited. I can explain but first just look out this window. In a few seconds someone we all just met will appear and… oh here he comes. Please just trust me."

Everyone began to speak at once as Stockton appeared framed in the window and peering inside. Stockton made right for the door and stormed in. Seeing Malone with Ron at his side, he confronted him.

"Detective, this person just made off with the very Crossbow you need to help solve the Lake Bonaparte Murder." He pointed his right index finger in Ron's face. "I demand that you take action immediately."

Malone took hold of the hand with the pointed finger and began to shake it. "Well now what a surprise to see you so soon Professor Stockton. Now what seems to be the problem?"

"The problem, I just told you what this young man did."

"So you did," the police Lieutenant smiled and turned to Ron. In a calm yet authoritative voice he spoke to him. "Now Mr. De Cenza, it seems that this Professor, not the one you work for," he was driving Stockton mad with what could be considered an avoidance of what Ron did and he was well aware of it.

"This is ridiculous Detective. This Ron De Cenza person is in possession of a prized museum artifact and as if that isn't significant enough, it also is part of a murder investigation."

"So then you are verifying that it is the weapon from the display in the library gallery."

"Of course, just look at it. You can see that it is an aged piece." Stockton's frustration level was building.

"Thank you for your verification." Malone looked into Ron's eyes; they sparkled with mischief and he was well aware of it. "Now Ron, you have a bit of explaining to do, I'd say to the Professor and to me and all of your friends as well. Now then shall we begin at the beginning?"

"A very good place to start, I'd say," Bob chimed in praying all the while that what his pal had done was a part of a wonderful Sherlock type of scheme.

"Indeed, so Ron shall we begin?"

"Sure, but I think everyone should just take a seat even Professor Stockton; it may take a while to explain."

"Good idea, now then Professor Stockton why don't you take a seat next to Professor Pettigrew? Here, take my seat. I'll remain standing with Ron, just in case he tries to get away."

Stockton did as was suggested with a comment to Pettigrew. "That student of yours is a menace I tell you, a menace to the peace of our University town."

Andrew Pettigrew smiled. "On one point I must agree; Ron De Cenza has a knack for turning things topsy-turvy before a solution is found. I've only known the lad for a couple of years but in that time he has saved my life, and helped solve a murder in Italy and Ireland and discovered an Irish Historical artifact and Italian Renaissance treasures. For such a young person he is quite accomplished. His story should be most interesting."

"Story indeed, he's a thief as well." Stockton pushed back in the wooden chair until its wooden legs screeched on the tile floor.

With his back to the rest of the restaurant and Malone standing beside him, Ron began to tell his tale. "All of you guys left me alone because my pal there was so hungry and had to get lunch or fade away to nothing and that's how this all began." He pointed to Bob and grinned; it was his famous half-ass smile as his father called it.

Susan pulled on Jan's arm and whispered her hope that this time Ron hadn't gone too far. Jan patted her hand while she took hold of Alessandro's hand at the same time with a worried grip. This didn't go unnoticed by Andreas who cast a look of worry toward Dominic.

Stockton interrupted the scene. "What does lunch have to do with any of this; it's a case of theft pure and simple."

"Never simple my dear Professor Stockton and certainly not pure," Ron responded in Sherlock mode as he placed the crossbow its main shaft wrapped in his hanky on the table in front of the two professors. He looked into Stockton's dark eyes. "But like I said, it began with everyone going to lunch. I however went to the men's room where it all began with a rendezvous."

"Oh my God Ron, not like that time at the United Nations in New York City; not with the girls here."

Susan knew exactly what that reference was all about. She smiled as she remembered that shortly after that event in the men's room, Ron told her that she drove him crazy and that's when love began to bloom.

"Hold your water Bob; it's not that kind of meeting."

"Thank the Lord for that, okay; go on then."

"Thanks Pal. So as I was saying I was in the bathroom when who should enter but that Antoine Murat guy we met up at Lake Bonaparte and right behind him was none other than the Professor, this one." Ron placed his hand on Stockton's shoulder.

"How dare you. Get your hand off me. Really Detective is this necessary?"

"I'm afraid that it is as now we have another person in the picture and he seems to be connected with you Sir. Continue Ron; by the way why weren't you seen by these two men?"

"Right, getting to that; I was in the stall when this Murat fellow stormed in to take a… I mean relieve himself. He wasn't too happy that the Professor bothered him as he did so. When that call of nature was over, they began to talk about what happened at Lake Bonaparte. Murat seemed to be the one who knew Apollo Dimitri the guy who got killed in an intimate way and yet both accused each other of having taken the Crossbow to upstate New York and use it on poor Apollo."

At that point Stockton was getting fidgety. Ron continued to unveil what he had heard regarding not only who may have taken the Crossbow to kill Apollo but also how it was related to the Treasure of Joseph Bonaparte. After all he had a home on the lake back in the early 19th Century where over the years many had come to find the lost Crown Jewels of Spain. Then Ron dropped the proverbial other shoe and brought in the name of Carolina Savage Gianetti. He reminded everyone that she had been shot on the Isle of Capri the previous year and was thought to be incapacitated. Now Malone had two people who he didn't know existed and possibly related to the crime of murder. Ron pointed out that Captain Verdi would be able to fill him in on the details about Carolina but as for Murat, he was already gone from Princeton and that's why he took the Crossbow.

"Detective you now have three primary suspects in the murder of Apollo. For if what I heard in that bathroom has any truth to it; then Murat could have killed him. He had ample opportunity to do so and is connected with Princeton and could get the Crossbow and arrow from the display. Then we have Carolina Gianetti. She could have hired Murat to do so or Stockton for that matter but I think she is working independently for herself as far as the jewels are concerned. And yet she always had an eye for Apollo even though he wasn't playing on her team, if you get my meaning. He was kind of like this Murat guy who seems to use sex with male or female to get what he wants. And then of course we have the Professor himself," Ron leaned into Stockton's face. "You Sir had ample opportunity as well to go upstate with the Crossbow from your Historical display use it to kill Apollo and get back before any of us arrived."

Stockton jumped from his chair. "This is an outrage. I am a Professor at Princeton University seeking a historical find, valuable of course but not criminal."

Malone stepped between him and Ron. "Now let's not get all steamed up gentlemen. Professor, take your seat. Ron step back and just tell us the story."

"Well that's it Detective, I took the Crossbow to bring to you but didn't have a ride to the Inn so I remembered the team was here so I came here with it and found you here as well. If Professor Stockton has any connection to the murder he has already damaged finger prints which may be on it and may want to cause further damage to it so that a connection could not be made. And as he can get into the museum anytime, I thought it prudent to bring it to you for safe keeping until forensics can check it out."

"It seems young man that you have created quite the kettle of fish with this story. Professor, you should make no plans to leave Princeton until we have a chat. As for you Ron, under the circumstances, I shall ignore the tampering with evidence law as you have brought a much needed light on what happened up at Lake Bonaparte. As for these Carolina Gianetti and Antoine Murat persons, I shall have an APB issued and gather them for questioning."

Ron pulled on Malone's sleeve and asked him to step away from the others. He agreed but before doing so instructed Andreas, since he was a soldier and could handle weapons, to secure the Crossbow and cover it with napkins allowing no one to touch it. The Papal Guard went into immediate action, pulled the table away from the group and stood in front of it after having covered it. Dominic just smiled at him as his friends did. They were told by him to remove themselves from the area of the Crossbow.

"Now Ron, what seems to be the problem?"

"Just this Sir, if you put out an APB then the police will be disrupting our work in Bordentown. We may still lose them once they get wind of what you know. Carolina has no idea that we know she is alive and Murat doesn't know that I know he is off to Bordentown. Let our group continue our research and excavation at Point Breeze. That activity will surely lead Carolina and Murat to get involved in some manner, probably not a good one. To protect us let Captain Verdi come with us; after all it's still an international incident isn't it? And one more thing Sir, there is a guy named Charles Benton and I bet he's involved in this treasure hunt and maybe the murder as well in some fashion. So what do you think about letting us continue onto Bordentown this afternoon before any chance of Stockton getting hold of any of them."

Before Malone had a chance to respond Stockton bolted off his chair and made for the kitchen and rear door of the restaurant. Andreas was hot on his trail as was Alessandro. Through the swinging doors they ran as the guests and kitchen staff alike shouted and ran from them as pots went crashing to the floor. Stockton grabbed a pan and threw it at Andreas and Alessandro. It hit the stove but not them and it gave enough time for Alessandro to tackle Stockton to the floor just as Malone ran in with Ron and the others behind him. The young Count of Pianore was sitting on the back of Stockton as Andreas tied his hands above his head with a cotton dish towel.

"It seems Professor Stockton that you shall be my guest for questioning." He turned to Ron. "You and the others are free to continue your expedition and research in all matters; do I make myself clear young man?"

"Yes Sir, crystal clear." Ron called to his friends to gather around him.

"We're off to Bordentown right now, every minute is time lost in finding Carolina and Murat not to mention what we came to find in the first place."

Taking hold of Susan's hand and grabbing Bob's arm he gave a tug and pulled them toward the entrance doors. His pal protested saying that he hadn't even touched his Apple pie. While Ron's sister and Dominic stood at the table not quite knowing what they should do as Andreas and Alessandro were helping Malone. They lifted up Professor Stockton from the floor and sat him on a chair. All the while Stockton protested the manhandling and threatened legal action.

Malone was apologizing to the guests in the Pancake House explaining that there had been a misunderstanding but all was well now. He had already ordered the manager to phone the local police and request a squad car to be sent. The sirens could be heard when he agreed to let the Oxford Professor take his team to Bordentown.

Pettigrew was dumbfounded looking at the scene before him. Here was an esteemed colleague though newly met bound and yelling at everyone around him like a lunatic out of control. He stood frozen at his chair first looking at Jan and Dominic and then to the swinging doors of the kitchen beyond which would be Andreas and the Young Count of Pianore and then to the entrance doors of the restaurant where Ron was explaining to Bob and Susan the need to get going immediately.

Malone leaned over and got into Stockton's face. "It would go much better for all concerned if you would just quiet down and let me do my job. Once at the police station you may call your lawyer."

The Detective then dismissed Andreas and Alessandro telling them that the uniforms would be at the restaurant soon. Finally he had to say something to the statue. He stood at the winging doors, "Professor Pettigrew, you may leave now with your team; everything will be okay. I shall keep you posted through Captain Verdi who will go to Bordentown with you. I will join you later as soon as this mess is taken care of."

"You are most kind Detective." Pettigrew found that he could actually move, thanked Malone and scurried toward Ron. Andreas bolted out of the kitchen and took the hand of Dominic as Alessandro did the same to Jan and followed. As the Squad car pulled up Pettigrew and his team exited. Malone who was removing the dish towel and attempting to replace it with handcuffs suddenly screamed in pain as a kick in the groin doubled him over. His long suit coat covered arm with the handcuff dangling from it swung upwards and then came crashing down on Malone's head as he pushed him aside and fled out the back door. The few remaining customers and staff were in a panic when the screams were heard and ran to the main doors as two Uniform officers tried to enter. The ensuing chaos and confusion allowed Stockton ample time to make it to the Princeton Campus proper which he knew like the back of his hand. Knowing that he couldn't possibly go back to his office, he headed for the staff parking lot.

Oblivious to what was taking place at the Pancake House, Alessandro drove the blue mini-bus up to the Princeton Inn. Ron pulled open the door and jumped out when he saw Captain Verdi pacing back and forth.

"Captain Verdi, we were just coming to see you."

"Ah, *Buon Giorno* Ron, call the others out of the bus. I have some news for all of you."

In short order the team had created a people arc in front of the Captain. "*Molto grazie ragazzi, signorinas e Professore universitario*, I have just learned that I was to accompany you to the City of Bordentown. The Signora is packing and we shall be ready to go with you momentarily. It appears that with the arrest of Professor Stockton that the Detective Malone shall be occupied here…"

As Verdi explained what his duties would be his wife Sophia appeared at the doors of the Inn. Behind her were two bell boys laden with suitcases. She called out to him. "Enrico, if you please there has been an incident as the Detective Malone called it."

The Captain stopped in his tracks and ran to her.

"This doesn't look good Ronnie," a concerned Susan softly spoke.

"She's a new wife, maybe it's about the bill or something like that."

"Really, the bill; we just got a Professor at Princeton University arrested and you think she's worried about the bill. Where is that Sherlock mind of yours today?"

He cuddled her in his arms, "Obviously not here at the Princeton Inn. I'm already thinking about what needs to be done at Bordentown once we get there. Remind me that we had best arrange for reservations." Ron turned to Bob and suggested that he go into the lobby while the newlyweds had their chat and find rooms for all of them, the Captain and his wife as well."

"Of course Sherlock, now I am also the sidekick servant and with no apple pie to sustain me."

Will you stop with the persecution thing? Okay, if you find it too difficult to do on an almost empty stomach, I'll go do it. Take care of Susan." Off Ron stomped toward the Lobby, with a smile to Sophia Verdi as he passed.

Susan called out to him. "I don't need to be watched over. This almost Mrs. Sherlock can handle herself quite well thank you very much."

Ron stopped and ran back to her and planted a fervent kiss on her lips as the others oohed and ahhed at the public display of affection so unlike their Sherlock friend. "I know that," he added concluding the embrace and punching Bob in the shoulder. "See what you've done and all over making reservations so that you might have a bed tonight and maybe even dinner."

"Asshole, I didn't do anything." He called out as Ron made a bee line for the door. "You're always taking me for granted."

Ron stopped in midstride and turned with a reddening face. "You try to talk to him Susan; when he gets this way I can't handle it."

Sophia had returned the smile to Ron. However the look on her face was anything but pleasant. The message that she had for her husband was more than a concern about a billing issue. "Enrico, the Detective Malone just called. The Professor Stockton has just escaped police custody. I fear that our young friends are in danger once again."

Verdi wrapped his arms around his wife and looked over her shoulder to Ron standing at the lobby desk waving his arms about as if trying to push away news he didn't want to hear. "*Cara mia*, it will be fine. Did Malone say anything else?"

"Only that you should go with our friends to Bordentown and that he would join you once they get things under control here." She pushed herself away from him grudgingly. "Now you must tell everyone to leave at once before that man can get to them. We shall follow them down to this Bordentown place, Si?"

184

"Si, yes of course," Verdi walked slowly to the team now hovering over Bob like protective mother geese. "*Por favore,* excuse me but I have some news."

When Ron returned from getting the reservations arranged, the others were already loading back onto the mini-bus which was more like a large van.

Verdi quickly told him what had happened. "So Ron, you see that leaving now is most important. The *Professore* Stockton, he would not know of your departure and that works in your favor. Sophia and I will follow as soon as I can arrange for a car."

"You don't have to do that Captain; we can squeeze you into the van."

"You are most kind, but did you not see the amount of luggage the Signora has for this second honeymoon as she calls it? It is best that we follow. Now get going and call the Detective Malone through the Princeton Police Department to let him know of your arrival and place for sleeping."

"Speaking of sleeping for tonight; I made reservations for you and the Signora at the Crosswicks Inn. You will be staying with all of us well almost all of us. There weren't enough rooms for everyone so Bob and I will be staying in another location as is Professor Pettigrew."
"No, no not at all; you must all stay together. Sophia and I will seek another place."

"You don't understand, capisco…there is nowhere else. The Bordentown Inn is filled as well. I made a quick call to the Abbey in Wisconsin and talked with Abbot Lawrence. It's a long story but the short version is that Bob and I began our seminary days in that Abbey studying Latin. Anyway, he is making arrangements with the Head of the Divine Word Seminary in Bordentown to house Bob and me. So you see it's all taken care of. And as for Professor Pettigrew, he got the last room at the Bordentown Inn. We'll be together except to sleep so it's *va bene,* okay."

Verdi was most appreciative and bade him farewell with an embrace and a kiss on each cheek, as did Sophia.

She adding that he should take good care of his love and his *amico* who seems hurt about something. Ron rolled his eyes when she referred to his friend Bob but assured her that he would watch over both of them and all the others as well. As the Captain wrapped his arm around his new wife watching Ron entering the van, a cab pulled up and out stepped Professor Dorothy Witherspoon.

Divine Word Sign at Point Breeze Estate
Courtesy of Nancy Faherty, drgreenway.org

Chapter Ten:
Spinning the Tale

The blue mini-bus was soon rambling out of the University town now abuzz with the news of one of the Professors being involved in a murder. The riders in the van however had their thoughts fixed on Bordentown as they entered the Garden State Parkway and headed down to the historic town where the brother of Napoleon, one King Joseph Bonaparte who called himself the Comte de Survilliers to avoid recognition when he sneaked into America back in 1815.

 Riding alongside the Delaware River and passing one quaint Colonial town after another Ron was enjoying giving a history lesson to everyone. However it's when he got to Carolina Savage Gianetti and explained her connection to the Bonaparte family, chatter about her actually being alive and out to seek her inheritance as it were really got into high gear. If she could prove that she was a descendant of Annette Savage the mistress to Joseph who bore him children then it was quite possible that the lost Crown Jewels of Spain could be hers to inherit or so thought everyone except Ron.

It was his opinion that the jewels belonged to the Royal Family of Spain, if anyone, and not any Bonaparte descendant from nephews who remained in America or offspring of Annette's surviving daughter back in the 1800's. Professor Pettigrew as he snuggled with Professor Dorothy Witherspoon, who had joined the entourage just minutes beforehand, was inclined to agree with Ron's premise save for one exception. He felt that as King, Joseph had a right to the jewels and if that was proven to be true then his descendants would indeed have a claim to them should they be found.

Ron grinned one of his famous smiles and noted that the jewels would be found for they had the Book with the clues and secondly, that any remaining jewels should they be the actual Crown jewels would indeed be property of the State perhaps not the personal property of the Monarch. However he felt the jewels were not necessarily the State Crown Jewels and thus did belong to the Royal Family of Spain. The

King is representative of the nation despite them living in exile at the moment. That being temporary due to the Generalissimo Franco keeping Spain a Monarchy but ruling in place of the King for the time being.

"In any case we need to find the jewels before we can determine who they really belong to and before we do that there is one other, well really two other little issues which we need to resolve. First, we now know that Carolina Gianetti is alive and well and in America. And if you recall she had a thing for Apollo back when we were on Capri…"

"But Apollo had a thing for Stefano Rinaldi didn't he?"

"Ah yes, that's true Dominic, but he had a way with women as well kind of like our friend from Lake Bonaparte Antoine Murat, who by the way is part of what we have to face in Bordentown."

In the back seat Dorothy Witherspoon whispered into Pettigrew's ear. "Andrew what on earth are they talking about? Who is this Murat? Is he not a descendant of the Bordentown Murat family who are related to the Bonaparte family?"

"It is most disconcerting to be sure Dorothy but I'll try to explain how we know him from our time at Lake Bonaparte with him."

Ron continued his history lesson mix with the case of the murder of Apollo which possibly could have had a woman scorned motive.

"Obviously Carolina couldn't do it herself as she was in Europe or on a plane coming to America but we do know that she had dealings with Professor Stockton who had a relationship with Antoine Murat both of whom had ample opportunity to seek out Apollo and shoot him with the arrow from that Crossbow."

"And let's not forget about another American so called friend we met in Switzerland in a car crash that almost happened, one Charles Benton. He surely was the one in the Roman ruins of Nyon who followed us there to find the treasure." Bob was quite proud of himself to be back in Watson mode to Ron's Sherlock after his little melt down and that being all over an Apple Pie not eaten.

"Quite right Watson; now listen up all of you…" Ron paused and shot out a grin to his buddy; they were back in sync once again.

Jan dropped the map and leaned over the back of the front seat to hear the next bit of observation or deduction or whatever her brother did to come up with his ideas. "You my dear Count keep your eyes on the road." The two Professors, Papal Guard and Pettigrew's assistant, Dominic, leaned forward resting their chins on the back of the middle seat.

While all of this was taking place in Princeton and on US Route 1, in the city of Bordentown, Carolina Gianetti and Charles Benton entered the grounds of the Divine Word Seminary built on the Point Breeze estate grounds of Joseph Bonaparte. Their order purchased the acreage along Crosswicks Creek leading into the Delaware River back in 1941. The tan brick sign stating "Divine Word Missionaries" indicated to go past the wrought iron gate loosely hanging on a brick and stone pillar which obviously was part of the main gate back in the early 19th Century when Point Breeze was created by Joseph Bonaparte. Charles was driving the black Cadillac which he had rented back in New York City before Carolina arrived with Luigi and Pietro. He was delighted that Carolina had assigned them the chore of renting a boat at the launch area on the banks of Crosswicks Creek. They were to row it into what would be the Point Breeze estate grounds noting anything which indicated the ruins of the Bonaparte house. Their presence was intimidating to Benton.

A gravel road appeared just past the signage and old gate. Turning left onto it he paused once again, this time to take note of a building just inside and alongside the road they traveled. "Carolina, I thought that you said the Bonaparte House burned down back in 1820."

Her look of contempt could not be exaggerated more as she glared at him in his ignorance. "*Gesu*, Charles can you really be so ignorant as to think that the King of Spain would live in something like that even in exile?"

His meek glance at her to avoid her eyes said it all. He slowly drove up the road as she tried to explain that the Mansion Joseph Bonaparte built both of them were spectacular buildings and quite huge in terms of early American houses in a nation just forty years old at the time.

She had done her homework on the history of Point Breeze. "That building is probably just an outer one where servants lived. Now do sit up straight and man up in front of these priests. We are supposed to be a couple and look at you all frumpy and stooped over. Who would think that you are my man? Now stop the car for just a moment."
The jerky stop bounced her forward into the dashboard. She handled it quite well and opened her purse to take out a small brush. "Now look at me, your hair is a nice color, chestnut I'd say so let's see if I can do something with it." She began to create a part and brush the hair back. "Well that will have to do for now. Now as for that tie, it's rather gaudy but will have to do." She straightened the tie and pulled it tighter around his neck. "*Va be*ne, get going the Reverend Father is expecting us."

To their right across an expansive grassy area stood what appeared to be a small mountain range. Huge rocks rose from the ground and surrounded a large pool like basin. It was not a natural formation however as there were no other signs on the property of such rocks. These were brought on the land to create the scene. Benton incorrectly attributed the creation to Bonaparte and once again was put in his place. But this time she did so with another desired reaction. Leaning over into him she caressed his inner thigh as she told him that she will teach him all about the history of Point Breeze and how the American Millionaire Harris Hammond had the rock creation constructed.

"Oh Carolina, this is holy ground do you think this is a wise thing to do?" he began to breath heavier and in gasps as her hand traveled up the thigh.

"Ah, now let's go," she abruptly stopped, swung open the door and jumped out of the car. She adjusted her dress pulling the bodice down slightly.

Benton didn't move. She leaned into the car. "Charles, let's go." She smiled. "Oh I see, and do I see what I needed to see. You are a man. Get out of the car and let the world know that you have such a woman as me."

Slowly he squeezed out from behind the steering wheel; his manhood bumping into it as he did so. He stood stoically waiting and then tried to close his suit coat to conceal the problem as he saw it and which was amusing Carolina. His predicament actually put her in a pleasant frame of mind for the first time since they left Princeton. She pranced around the car to him and slipped her hand under his arm.

"Now then, let's go see this priest." With a tug and a smoldering smile she guided him to the entrance of a rather bleak looking rectangular building with no ornamentation. Made of gray stone it simply didn't announce what normally one would expect upon entering a Catholic seminary. The entrance hall inside reflected the functionality of the building and was barren except for the four wooden arm chairs which lined the wall and a table at the far end at which sat a young man. Behind him off to the right was the only work of art visible. On a wooden pedestal stood a painted statue of the Virgin Mary holding up the Christ Child.

"Good afternoon and welcome to Divine Word."

Standing in front of the table, Carolina released Benton's arm and leaned over the table so that her cleavage would appear beneath the gaze of the handsome young man at least fifteen years younger than her. "My name is Carolina Savage Gianetti and what would be your name?"

"Mine, well…" the sweat began to form on the young man's brow. He probably had never been so close to such a voluptuous woman in his young life. "I mean my name is David Chan. I'm the greeter for today."

"David, what a lovely name; like that of the warrior king of Israel who Michelangelo made famous. Tell me David are you like that statue depicting courage, strong will and manliness?"

Benton had had enough of the teasing and pulled her back from the table. "Young man please tell Father Garcia that the Signorina Gianetti and Signore' Benton are here for their appointment."

The young man jumped out of his chair, asked them to have a seat while he checked to see if the Superior General was back in his office. Then he ran down a side corridor. Benton wasted no time in telling Carolina that they were at the Religious institution on the pretense of arranging for a couples' retreat and tour the grounds not to have an orgy.

"Oh Charles you are no fun at all. I am well aware of why we have come but I needed a little distraction shall I say? And don't get so pushy; if it wasn't for your failure in Switzerland we would possess what those so called research assistants found and be a step ahead of them."

Benton chose to ignore the insult and continued. "Distraction, we are here to find a precious treasure before that British Professor gets here." She brushed her smooth hand across his cheek. "Now you just worry about finding the Book and get what they know from their research. I will take care of Professor Pettigrew."

"And what about Professor Richard Stockton our partner in this enterprise?" he shouted in a whispering tone.

"**Managia**, you frustrate me so…Stockton is only valuable if he can help us retrieve the Book otherwise he is expendable."

"So you say but he probably killed that guy on Lake Bonaparte. You more than anyone should know that you're dealing with more than a school teacher given how you were almost killed on Capri over that Book."

"*Va Bene*, okay, okay, I get your point. I won't try to make that boy or the priest break their vows. Now are you satisfied?"

Before Benton could answer a timid voice pierced their conversation. "Father Garcia is ready for you. Please follow me." He didn't move an inch closer to them but turned asking them to follow him.

Carolina couldn't resist and broke her promise to keep quiet. "David, will you be the one who gives us the tour of the grounds?"

Never losing a step, David replied that would depend on the rotation and quickly added that if a guide was needed there would be two conducting the tour. Coming to a stop, he knocked on the door and opened it. Benton held Carolina's arm as if to escort her into the office. Father Garcia was just ending a phone call and returned the receiver onto the cradle.

He rose upon seeing them. "Good afternoon and welcome to the Society of the Divine Word. I do apologize for the phone use but it was the Abbot of St. Benedict's in Wisconsin and a friend since our seminarian days. Now then enough of that; do take a seat." He looked at David frozen in the doorway. "Brother David, perhaps our guests are hungry." He walked around his desk and stood in front of it. "Have you had lunch?"

Benton replied before Carolina could say a word. "Thank you Father, but we've eaten."

"Ah, very good so then Brother David could bring you some lemonade perhaps?"

Carolina jumped in, "that would be lovely Father. It's quite warm today don't you think?"

With a wave of Father Garcia's hand and a nod of his head, David got the message and left to fetch the drinks. "There now, David will bring us some refreshment and we can talk about your 'Couples' Retreat' which you mentioned over the phone. Shall we move to the table; it's by the window and the air conditioner in my office is not working properly so it will be more comfortable."

On the way to the table, Father Garcia picked up his appointment Book. As Carolina and Benton took a seat across from him, he opened the window and stood there for a moment before speaking. "No matter how often I look out this window I cannot help but to see history come alive before my eyes." He turned toward them but remained standing at the window pointing to a rather peeked looking tree just beyond the back road behind the office. "Can you see that tree just there the one that looks like it's at death's door? Well it has plenty of life within it let me tell you. It was planted by Joseph Bonaparte in 1816. Now that's a couple of lifetimes ago."

Carolina and Benton made their way to the window to get a better look and try to show interest despite having none whatsoever. The priest continued his reflection. "For over a hundred and fifty years it keeps re-blooming and sprouting new growth albeit at the top. When you spoke of this retreat idea this tree came to mind. I believe that love at times seems to wither and even die. That's why like this tree or a garden it needs care. Such a retreat may help to rekindle love and keep the passion of it brightly shining. But I am speaking too long, do have a seat and let us discuss this idea of yours which intrigues me so."

"Father, you are so eloquent about love. I didn't expect that from…" Benton hesitated and Garcia answered.

"From a celibate priest, that's what you're thinking I'm sure." Father Garcia laughed. "Well our Lord blessed love at the wedding feast of Cana. It is our privilege to foster love and help to keep that fire burning."

Carolina liked where the conversation was headed. She offered her agreement with the view of the priest more to get the talking part done and the touring part started and yet the idea of love burning with passion did excite her especially when David walked in with the lemonade. For her it was all about the passion part of love. She touched David's hand as he handed her the glass of lemonade and smiled sweetly. She was thinking of another who was so good looking as to be named after the Sun God. Through her mind's eye she was seeing Apollo up on the rocks over the Green Lagoon on Capri. His nude body shimmering in the sun as if he had just came down from Olympus. Suddenly she began to weep, just a trickle down her cheek but smudging her mascara nonetheless. Despite his love for another, she was realizing that the beautiful sight she beheld would be no more; now that someone killed him. And she knew why. The murderer sought what she and Benton were seeking and like them that someone would do anything to get the lost Bonaparte treasure even kill.

The priest noticed the change in her demeanor. "My dear child, have you lost someone you loved?"

She quickly wiped away the tear drop. "Oh Father, trust me he loved another but still I will miss him. So when might we tour the grounds? I have so much to plan as far as what activity should be done where."

"Of course I understand completely. Now let's see," he opened the appointment Book. "You were planning this retreat for what weekend?"

"The Columbus Day weekend around October Twelfth, as some might have an extra day off work," she responded.

"Excellent choice, that's about six weeks away. The colors of the trees will be lovely at that time of year and enhance the experience." He marked the Book. "There we are all reserved. And now shall we have a look around our grounds? You know it has quite the history. Napoleon's brother built two houses on this land. The first one burned down shortly after New Year's Day in 1820 and the second one was torn down by the new owner the British Consul at the time by the name of Henry Becket…that was around 1850. He actually tore down the second mansion and replaced it with an Italianate Villa. The very one on the main road of our grounds, Some say that he still held a grudge against the Bonaparte family. Now I can't support that view but there is talk even to this day." He laughed as if he was sharing a bit of gossip and paused in thought. "Now as I say this, I am remembering something which has intrigued me since we took over Point Breeze. Why you may have heard about it as well because all of Bordentown holds the legend to be true."

Carolina played ignorant and prodded him to share the story as they left the office, passed David back at the table in the Hall and moved toward the Main Doors. "This is all very intriguing as you say. We have just arrived in America so I am not acquainted with the Bonaparte tale."

"Is that so?" The priest may be past middle age now but when he had been assigned to Point Breeze back in 1941 he was around thirty years old. It was shortly after his order purchased it. He looked confused for a moment as he took the arm of Benton. "But didn't you say that your name was Charles Benton?"

"Why yes Father, I did. And I know what you're going to say. Let me see if I can get it right. Annette Savage who was the mistress of Joseph Bonaparte when he settled here in Bordentown eventually married Zebulon Benton to gain respectability for her daughters by him after Joseph left, because of illness, for Europe."

"Mr. Benton, you do know the story then. Your family has been a part of Bonaparte history in these parts for over a hundred a fifty years. This is all so exciting to have a Benton back here on Point Breeze land."

"You flatter me, but I have spent little time here and travel for business extensively. The famous descendant near you right now is the *Signorina* Gianetti. She is part of the Savage family on her mother's side."

Carolina was not too pleased with Benton's revelation of her heritage as she felt he was sharing too much information which may come to haunt them should they have a setback in their plan to get information from the Bonaparte Biography from Pettigrew's team. She played the humble role regarding the affiliation by attaching such a story to all families who have legends surrounding their family name. "It's nothing more than your George Washington and the Cherry Tree story."

The priest let out a belly laugh. "Oh my dear Miss Gianetti, please do not promote such a notion in these parts where we have many buildings which claim that Washington slept within their walls."

Together they laughed as she agreed to remain silent on the subject. "And now Father where shall we start the tour?"

"I think we should begin at another rather famous tree on the grounds. It's an Osage-Orange which was planted by Lewis and Clark upon their return from the Expedition exploring the land purchased from Napoleon by Thomas Jefferson, the Third President of these United States. Of course it's not an orange tree at all and is usually called a 'horse apple' or its Latin name of *Maclura pomifera.*"

"Another Bonaparte story; how very interesting."

"Quite so, just follow me along this path. After the tree we shall take a brisk walk down to the Gardener's House. You probably saw it as you drove onto the property. And here's another note in history the designer and builder was a Michel Bouvier who was the great great great Grandfather of our former First Lady, Jackie Kennedy."

"Oh I will be thrilled to enter such a home. Mrs. Kennedy has such style and elegance; it must be a beautiful home."

Father Garcia had to offer his regrets about actually visiting the house. "Though the outside has been resided with material to appear as stone similar to what George Washington did at his home of Mount Vernon, the interior is still a work in progress and unsafe."

Carolina and Benton feigned disappointment but leapt onto another place on the grounds which they would like to see. They began to talk about Crosswicks Creek and their desire to visit the forest leading down to it. Father Garcia was all too happy to show them the carriage path through the forest where once the famous of the United States and the citizens of Bordentown would ride to the artificial lake and over bridges to Crosswicks Creek. It was a risky request as Pietro and Luigi might be searching the area from their boat rented from the City's launch site.

What they didn't know was that there was another person exploring the woods and Creek area. Antoine Murat had arrived in Bordentown still steaming mad over the heated encounter in the Library men's room. After he checked into the Bordentown Inn he also had rented a boat and made his way onto the former estate via Crosswicks Creek. Shortly thereafter arriving in the small City was Professor Richard Stockton on the run from the Princeton Police.

Crosswicks Creek Home, Historic Colonial Dining Room
Courtesy of Steve Lederman and Bonnie Goldman

Chapter Eleven:
Crosswicks Creek

The blue mini bus chugged along US Rte. 1 filled with chatter about what would happen to Professor Richard Stockton. Totally unaware that Stockton had evaded Malone and the Princeton police their focus was now on finding Murat. After the bathroom encounter between Stockton and Murat, which Ron overheard, it was clear in his mind that finding Murat in their cabin on Birch Island was not an innocent visit. In fact the entire meeting of him was planned as he had already met Apollo before he was kille. That much he knew from what he heard in the bathroom at Princeton. It was as clear as the nose on Bob's face Ron was saying to them that he either knew about the existence of the Book or discovered it as being real when he met Apollo.

His pal of course protested the singling out of his nose when Dominic had a larger Roman nose. Instead of being offended the research assistant to Pettigrew took a pose emphasizing his Roman attribute and insisting that he indeed looked like Caesar. Andreas leaned into him and kissed it. Susan thought it was a romantic gesture. The others were giggling and acting like Junior High School kids as they began to sing the rhyme of Dominic and Andreas sitting in a tree K I S S I N G. The two Professors were right in there with them welcoming the relief from the tension of what took place at the Pancake House. As the nonsense ensued a thought popped into Ron's mind. Stockton had Carolina's letter and he didn't have the specifics in it but he did know that the Professor kept it while telling Murat to make no mention of it to Carolina when they met up. He would have to inform Malone and Verdi.

It was short lived however as Jan distracted from her navigation duties glanced at the Triple A map Booklet and flipped the page. "Oh my God Alessandro there's the exit we need to take, Route 29 to Interstate 295 to get to Bordentown."

Luckily Alessandro had the van in the right lane as he quickly turned onto the ramp with only the slightest throwing of people on top of each other. "*Mi dispiacere*, I mean sorry about that but we're okay now and there's the river. At least it wasn't as bad as what happened in Switzerland."

He was quite correct. They did not almost hit another car and the Delaware River was to their right and if he kept it there and followed it they would drive right into the City of Bordentown. With the city only a few minutes down the road the next decision to be made was where to go first. Should they drive directly to the Divine Word Seminary so that Professors Pettigrew and Witherspoon could announce their arrival or should they go to their lodging, get settled and then go see the Superior General? The women decided that freshening up first would be the better choice and that brought about the next little issue.

When arrangements were originally made they were only a group of eight. Professor Pettigrew chose a quaint Colonial Bed and Breakfast called the Crosswicks Inn. It was an historical site dating back to Colonial times in America. The history Department at Oxford Booked four rooms for him and his team. Because of the events which took place on Lake Bonaparte and in Princeton their group increased by four people, Detective Malone, Captain and Mrs. Verdi and just a short while ago, Professor Dorothy Witherspoon. That meant three more rooms were needed unless Witherspoon and Pettigrew who were obviously an item chose to keep up appearances and not share a room. Ron in his usual style immediately saw the developing problem as soon as the Princeton Professor exited the cab. At the front desk of the Princeton Inn he made several calls until the problem was rectified and everyone had a room in which to sleep. Without consulting Bob he gave up their room at the Crosswicks Inn and switched the reservation to Captain and Mrs. Verdi when they arrived later in the day. He felt that since it was their honeymoon a taste of America in a lovely Colonial House would be quite nice for them.

As he thought this he became quite proud of the act as one of romanticism which most would agree he lacked. He was confident that Bob would agree. That confidence would be shaken a bit later. When

202

Malone arrived, he could try for a room at the Bordentown Inn downtown just down the street from the Clara Barton Schoolhouse, yet another historical center for the little city. He had been assured that a room should become available in a day or two. Not realizing tourist season was still in high gear Ron ultimately found another place for him and Bob. That place was the Seminary of Divine Word Missionaries and Detective Malone if no vacancies opened at either Inn he could stay there as well.

When Carolina and Benton arrived in Father Garcia's office earlier, he was on the phone with a friend he had told them. Indeed he was but that friend was Abbot Lawrence of the Benedictine Abbey in Wisconsin where Ron and Bob had studied Latin when they first entered the Seminary. That was the beginning of their crime solving adventures and where Ron first met Susan and began to fall in love. The Abbot was asking Father Garcia to provide rooms for Ron and Bob during their time in Bordentown as they would be conducting an excavation on the Point Breeze grounds and such a location would be most convenient.

Ron had it all arranged and figured out. He presented his lodging plan to his friends and the Professors. Everyone was most grateful that he taken on the responsibility of insuring accommodations for everyone except, that is for his Watson. Bob voiced his concern that they would be back in the Abbey environment again. Would that mean they would have to follow certain rules like the Grand Silence and no talking at meals and speaking of meals would they have to eat with the seminarians. After two years of studying in Italy with their fabulous cuisine going back to milk and homemade bread as the only thing to look forward to was not too attractive.

Except for Ron and Susan no one really understood as to what Bob was referring. Only the three had actually lived on the Abbey grounds and only Bob and Ron had to follow the Rules of St. Benedict which were rather austere for the young college boys at the time of their entrance into the Latin School. So Ron let his pal rant and get it off his chest before he settled the issue by assuring him that there would be no strict rules. They would actually be staying in the retreat wing of the building and not with the Seminarians, Brothers and Priests in residence. The news flash worked and peace had returned to the bus as it left Interstate 295 and was already down east Chestnut St. There the Crosswicks Inn was located. A small vintage sign hung out from a pole alongside a driveway. It simply had hunter green lettering painted on a shield like wooden base which read, **The Crosswicks Inn**.

Alessandro, the young Count of Pianore from Umbria Italy had found the Inn with almost no impeding issues. Much of that was due to Jan's narration of the Triple "A" map he assured everyone. She shot him a De Cenza grin so familiar to all of them but usually coming from Ron. Then hanging out the side window she waved at the middle aged couple standing on the front porch of the 18th Century stone building which they had converted into a Bed and Breakfast by adding an extension to the back of the house which contained the bedrooms for guests. As they piled out of the vehicle, the man and woman walked to the wooden gate set on iron posts which were older than the nation itself. Professors Pettigrew and Witherspoon as the titular leaders of the expedition of Bonaparte's Point Breeze estate made the introductions to Innkeepers Bonnie and Steve Lieberman.

Bonnie, a slight woman with graying hair effused hospitality as she introduced them to an authentic Colonial American garden part of which they had to walk through to enter the house. Walking into a home built over two hundred and fifty years ago for the Americans in the group was quite an experience. Sure they had walked into Palazzos which were four and five hundred years old, Churches which were over a thousand years old in Ireland and Italy and of course strolled through the ancient Roman Forum and Colosseum. But for the Americans, this was a home in their own country before it was a nation. It was like entering a page of United States history and the Innkeepers made sure that they had the full experience on entering a historical age. Bonnie suggested that they leave their luggage on the front porch so that they may take in the fullness of what the house had to offer and enjoy some refreshments made to welcome them. Bob of course continued to wear his new satchel holding their prize possession of the Autobiography of Joseph Bonaparte. He was rarely without its leather strap about him.

The first thing that the guys noticed, especially Andreas and Alessandro who were both over six feet tall was the low doorways and once inside the ceiling as well. Even the overall size of the rooms were cozy and intimate as compared to what a modern home would have in their day. Steve, a trim and fit man and more the size of an American in Colonial times used himself to emphasize how the home was built for much smaller people a couple of centuries ago. He spoke of about George Washington who being well over six feet tall was consider a giant of a man compared to his Vice-President, John Adams who was the average height of an early American male which was about 5 ft. 6 inches tall.

Turning from the entrance foyer, Bonnie led them into the kitchen fully restored as in Colonial days, including a stone hearth which opened on both sides. The group filled the room completely. As they took in the original dark stained wooden beams supporting the ceiling and walls their eyes were drawn to rows of rolling pins of every size and shape lining the walls. Bonnie was a collector and some of them were over four hundred years old. But it was the paintings in the dining room which really got to Ron in particular. While the others were taking turns seating at an original dining room period set, just to say they may have sat on something Washington might have used Ron was examining a painting with Steve at his side. He was explaining that the landscape was an original work of art depicting Point Breeze as it looked when Joseph Bonaparte created the estate. It did not emphasize the Mansion but rather areas around it including something which Ron felt he had seen before. It was an elaborate staircase obviously made of stone but only the platform to which a carriage would pull up with brick fencing surrounding it and a couple of the steps was visible.

I find this most intriguing Steve," Ron pointed to the stairs in the painting. "I mean why would an artist focus on a staircase in the middle of what obviously is the edge of a forest area and is this pond thing still at Point Breeze?

"Good questions Ron; let me begin by addressing the art itself. Charles Lawrence is the painter. He was known for landscapes thus he wanted to capture what Joseph Bonaparte wanted to present to his visitors. King Joseph desired an idyllic pastoral scene where one could roam, be inspired and be cut off from the pressures of the turbulent world which of course he had firsthand experience with given what had happened to him after the fall of his brother Napoleon. Secondly, that water is an artificially created lake on which visitors may ice skate in the winter as they were doing when the 1820 fire destroyed the first mansion and boat on in the summer."

"I think King Joseph was ahead of his time what with the idea to give people a place to escape from the cares of the world. In my world we call that a retreat."

"Interesting observation young man; he was not loved by the common folk of Bordentown and the high and mighty of early American society solely because they were impressed to have a king living in their midst. He gave them a sense of beauty, a feeling of repose and enlightenment. I think hospitality too in a new nation still rough around the edges. But let us take a closer look at this area." Steve traced his finger in a circle around the area where the staircase was located in the painting. "You have a good eye Ron; most people wouldn't have even noticed the stairs. After guests had a carriage ride around the grounds and along the lake they could choose to disembark at the stairs by the forest and take them down to Crosswicks Creek to enjoy the natural beauty of the area and stroll along its banks. It would be cooler down the bluff to the creek as well. When Professor Pettigrew takes you to Point Breeze tomorrow look for the granite stairs which remain. It used to bring visitors to a small dock where they could use rowboats and canoes. It was what I'd call a resort today, something for everybody. In any case you'll be able to see what remains of it on the hillside leading down to the creek when you begin you own exploration of the estate."

I'm very excited about being a part of the excavation project or hadn't you noticed?"

Steve smiled, "I wish you luck. Maybe you'll find a trinket of two from those days when a king entertained the common folk."

An announcement from Bonnie ended their conversation and everyone else trying out the chairs and bench surrounding the dining table. She informed her guests that it was almost four o'clock and that she would serve tea and refreshments. She suggested that they now bring in their luggage and freshen up in their rooms. There was a mad dash to the porch to retrieve their suitcases except of course for Bob and Ron. Steve apologized to them for not having a larger Inn so that they could all be together and then invited them to come for breakfast in the morning and dinner should they choose to dine at the Inn just like their friends. Bob was thrilled with the invitation.

Tea time was being observed at the Crosswicks Inn on Chestnut Street in what had become a residential neighborhood over the last hundred years. At the same time coming down those very granite stone steps which Ron had seen in the painting were Carolina and Benton. Father Garcia had been called away and for some reason David after delivering the message had chosen not to be their guide.

"Charles, stop walking ahead of me, what if I trip or something."

Benton turned and walked back the three feet and took Carolina's hand. "Well I don't know why we had to explore the woods right now; couldn't you have left that to your body guards or whatever they are?"

"Why Charles, do a detect jealousy in your voice? Well you're right about one thing," she pulled him closer to her as she jumped over an exposed tree root. "And that thing coming out of the dirt is an example. I simply am not dressed to take a hike in the woods." She pulled up her skirt and examined her hose. "See this, they are torn to shreds from the brush and these pumps…I will have to throw them in the trash when we get back to the Inn. I need to go shopping for some practical hiking clothing immediately." She suddenly stopped. "Charles look at this, are those stones really a series of stairs?"

Charles told her to stay where she was while he took a closer look. "These are definitely steps and not just stones jutting out from the hillside. They are smooth and cut." He took her hand and led her down two of the steps.

"I wonder if these lead anywhere. Oh Charles what if they do and what if we can get to the lost jewels before Stockton or Murat get here?"

"Let's not get ahead of ourselves Carolina. I don't think Joseph Bonaparte built a staircase which led to his secret treasure. If you take a look through the trees down there, you'll see water, probably a river or babbling brook of some kind along which we can spread a blanket, if we had one, and drink wine and munch on cheese if we had those too." Benton laughed at his own attempt at humor. "It's definitely not the Delaware River, too small. In any case this staircase if it is indeed one, has been here for a hundred and fifty years, do you really think we are the first persons to discover their existence?"

Carolina accused Benton of being a black cloud which cast its shadow over their discovery. The water they viewed was indeed a babbling brook, it was Crosswicks Creek which flowed into the Delaware River near which Luigi and Pietro had rented a rowboat. Her body guards were tying their boat to a fallen tree hanging over the creek. Luigi jumped from the bow of the boat onto the not too soggy bank of the creek. Nevertheless his black Italian leather shoes would never be the same. No one could accuse these two obviously tall, dark and handsome Continental men to be fishermen. Maybe they could get away with passing for tourists from Europe given that they were dressed in Florentine Italian leather pants and jacket which were not meant for hiking in a forest or rowing a boat. Luigi grabbed hold of Pietro's hand and pulled him to shore.

"The Signore's lover, she is quite the demanding woman." Pietro found his brown Italian leather shoes sinking in some mud with him in them. Quickly he scurried up the embankment to firmer land. "She could not wait for us to do this when we had hiking supplies and digging equipment?" Now he took Luigi's hand and pulled him up the slope.

"So you still remain loyal to the Signore' Cavelli?" Luigi placed his hand on his counterpart's shoulder and shook his head as if in disbelief.

"Si, and you do not? He found me in the slums of Naples, gave me clothes as you see of quality and brought me to parties to meet women who swooned over me when just a short while before they would not even cast an eye of sorrow for my plight."

"*Vero* Pietro, true but we must be practical now. Cavelli is in prison and the Signorina Carolina Gianetti is about to become a rich woman. It's not that I am not grateful. I may not have such a heartbreaking story as you but life was tough working in the vineyards of Tuscany where Niccolo Cavelli once visited during a festival in *Monterosso al Mare* one of the Cinque Terra villages on the sea. I was working in a vineyard up in the hills at that time and had come down to the village with other workers to bring the wine for the judging during the festival. It was a good red wine, I think as it did win a ribbon." Luigi gestured for him to hold back as he had to relieve himself. "Ah all this water around me…" he jumped over some protruding rocks. "Come along."

As they walked along the embankment, Luigi continued his story. "Look at me Pietro; do you think that I am handsome?"

"What the fuck, I don't know. The women they like you so I guess so."

"Calm yourself I am not after your manhood. It's that I was just thinking. The Signore' he surrounded himself with beautiful things like Carolina, you, me and before the betrayal Apollo and Stefano. Oh that Apollo, he was like a god come down from Olympus when I first met him at that festival. His golden hair and smooth body for he wore his shirt open to catch the sea breeze was a sight from ancient times. One look and the women swooned and left their vending stalls. The men became envious and wished they were in his shoes. He saw me hammering the spigot into the barrel to draw out the wine. He walked up with a woman on each arm. There was no Stefano back then. His crystal eyes looked down on me as the women giggled. And when he spoke, asking for a taste of the nectar of the gods I was stunned. He asked if I liked what I saw. Naturally, I thought he meant the gorgeous brunettes on each arm but he didn't. He meant himself."

"Come on Luigi everyone knew that Apollo liked men and that Cavelli knew that to be true but that his beauty attracted beautiful women.

That's how he got Carolina who had eyes for Apollo well really any handsome man, even me."

"So then you are saying that you are handsome Pietro?" Luigi laughed.

"Go on, did Apollo make a move on you?" He made the Sign of the Cross over himself and kissed the fingers before lifting them up to the heavens as he knew they were talking about a man once their colleague before the betrayal and now murdered just a few days ago.

The question didn't get an answer. They both stopped speaking as they heard the cracking of branches. They gestured to each other to listen and move upwards on the increasingly steep side of the bluff. Grouching down they silently waited to hear more and what they heard was a woman's voice. It was not sweet and melodious but harsh.

"I can't do this. We'll have to turn back. What will that priest think we've been up to when he sees me like this, just look at these stockings all torn and shredded? Turn around I'll have to take them off."

Benton slowly turned while she did what she felt she had to do to not shock the priest. As he did so he thought he saw a head popping up over a mound of dirt and rocks. "Is someone there," he called out.

Another head rose above the ground level. "Is that you Signorina Carolina?"

Two arms wrapped themselves around Benton as he tried to see what he thought he saw. "Charles, someone just called me by name."

"Just stay behind me and let me do the talking. You there, I am Charles Benton. How do you know the woman behind me?"

Luigi gave a tap to Pietro's arm. "I told you that it was her and that buffoon who pretends to be her boyfriend. She should have chosen one of us; it would have been more believable."

He climbed over the rocks to address Benton. "It's me Luigi and Pietro is with me as you directed. We just docked a boat down by the river and have been searching the area when we heard your voices."

Carolina jumped out from behind Benton. "It's my boys Charles." She ran to them shouting, "We are saved." Saved from what Benton hadn't a clue as they were just in the woods bordering the Point Breeze estate grounds. She ran to the burly men and threw her arms around each of their necks one by one and kissed them on each cheek. "You found us, you dear boys. And do you have good news for me?"

Neither of them had an inkling as to what the good news she referred to was. They were told to rent a boat and find a way onto the Point Breeze grounds from the Crosswicks Creek side which they had done. Of course they knew of the legend of Bonaparte's jewels being hidden and his autobiography Book as that's what their imprisoned boss ended up in jail over. What they didn't know was that where they stood was near the site of both of Joseph Bonaparte's houses.

The confused men did share how they rented the boat, and rowed upstream against the current and the time it took them to do so. All the while they were questioning in their minds why they had done so in the first place. Carolina realizing their quandary decided to share with them more of what she and Benton had tried to do in Switzerland. She emphasized Benton's failure to get hold of the items found in the Roman ruins and the Book which forced her to stay connected with Professor Richard Stockton. They were familiar with the names of Ron De Cenza and Bob Wentz as they were involved in the shootout in the Piazza Umberto I on Capri where Carolina was shot by the boyfriend of the dead man Apollo. They walked through the woods as she explained her relationship with Stockton and how she intended to get the lost jewels before he did and thus cut him out. The problem as she saw it was that all of them were known to everyone on Professor Pettigrew's excavation team except for the Oxford Professor as he had not been on Capri when the Book was discovered. She stopped walking and stood on a brick arch over a dried up gully hardly visible because of the brush growth.

"It's because of that knowledge of all of you that I must take the opportunity to seek out this Professor Pettigrew and get the information we need in ways that only I can do." She smiled and stroked the cheek of Charles and then spoke to him directly. "Charles, you must stay out of sight when the excavation search begins. Luigi and Pietro your Italian accent is a problem but there are many people of Italian ancestry in this part of the United States called New Jersey. Perhaps if you could disguise yourselves by growing the beard and cutting your hair very short…maybe wear sunglasses and get some American clothes you won't be easily recognized by the De Cenza boy. I shall tell the good Father that I hired you to build booths for the Couples Retreat which he thinks Charles and I are holding on these grounds. What you will be doing is watching every move of Pettigrew's research people as they excavate."

"That's all well and good for the three of you but what about me?" a frustrated Charles asked.

"Why I think that your role is obvious. When Stockton arrives you must do what he says and then give us the information you are able to get out of him." She again stroked his cheek with the soft fingertips of her hand ending with a tussle of his neatly combed hair.

Then it was all back to business. The rental boat would be left and picked up later to return as they would have to go into town and get the supplies they needed to feign the building of vender booths for the Couples Retreat. Afterwards they would wait for Stockton at the Inn. They had no idea that he was now the prime suspect in the murder of Apollo Dimitri.

They also had no idea that they were actually standing on top of what was once part of a bridge. It was one of several which were built over streams and gullies during the time of Joseph Bonaparte. It enabled his guests on the carriage rides to go through the forested areas near the creek on one side and the artificial lake on the other side.

Directly under that brick arch foundation for the original bridge, a man pressed himself against one of the foundation's stone base. He too was not dressed for a hike in the woods. Rather with his tweed suit and cap to match, he appeared more like someone from Britain or Ireland rather than French Canada. In fact he would have been better suited to be having tea with Pettigrew's team at the Crosswicks Inn. Instead he was sweating in the wool suit and pulling branches poking his rump away without making noise.

Antoine Murat found himself quietly listening to the woman who hired him and Benton to get the Book. Like Benton, he too had failed to get it though he had come so close standing in that cabin on Birch Island in Lake Bonaparte. He pulled a white linen handkerchief from the jacket's breast pocket and patted his brow. It wasn't the heat that was causing him to sweat. After all, he was in the gully, near a creek and under brick structures which made it a cooler place to be than on top of the arch.

No his cause of distress was in the making of a decision as to make himself known to Carolina who he just heard would cut he and Stockton out of the treasure's wealth. Should he pretend that he was still in her employ or keep silent and tell Stockton what he had heard? He pressed closer and closer to the brick wall as if to become one with it and not be detected. His hands clutched the rough surface of the century and a half aged bricks loosening one of them. He pushed it back trying to keep it from falling and making a noise which those above him might hear. And that's when it happened.

A red fox literally scurried across Murat's shoes pausing in fear at first and then snarling. The sound of several familiar voices could be heard at the creek's bank where Luigi and Pietro had moored their boat. The voices, well one of them actually was rather agitated and loud. Murat shocked by the appearance of the fox frozen in front of him and at the same time connecting those voices first heard in upstate New York gasped. He tried to muffle the sound by holding up his arm to his mouth shoving the tweed suitcoat sleeve into it. His efforts partially worked. The fox also heard noises and ran off.

The four standing in ignorance of his presence above him were distracted by the voices.

"What the hell…Carolina I know those voices."

"I think all of us know those voices Charles," she replied. "The girl's voice, I remember it faintly from when I was in the hospital on Capri after being shot."

"And the *ragazzi*, those young men, they are the ones who fought with us and got the Signore' arrested," added Luigi.

"Quiet everyone," demanded Benton. "You don't understand; if it's who I think it is then we'll have a lot of questions to answer as to why we are here at Point Breeze when I saw them all in Switzerland just a few days ago."

"Charles is right. We must get out of this place and back to the priest. The boat as planned will be fetched later."

They began to walk toward the edge of the woods. Murat sighed with relief as the agitated voice became clearer.

"Oh Susan, let's go for a boat ride, you said. It will be relaxing after the day we've had, you assured her." Bob got into Ron's face as he was trying to tie the rope on an overhanging tree. "So now what; and why did I have to come? It was supposed to be your time alone I thought."

Ron ignored his ranting and helped Susan get out of the canoe.

"Oh Bob, we needed your strong arms to help paddle," she patted his reddened cheeks and then jumped into Ron's open arms. "So tell us Ron, why did we paddle all this way when we could have driven here?"

214

"Yeah, good question." Bob walked away from them and tripped over a branch falling onto another boat. "Shit, I think I broke something."

Susan taking one arm and Ron the other lifted him to his feet. "You didn't break anything or you'd be screaming your head off but you did find another boat, a rowboat in fact like back on Capri." Ron jumped into the boat to search it. He found a plaque with the Bordentown Boat Launch name and boat number on it. "So look here, this must have been rented from that boat launch we passed."

"So what, some other dumb people wanted to take a boat trip; but why I wouldn't hazard a guess."

"Really Watson and where are those so called dumb people now?"

Ron followed a set of footprints along the bank and came across another boat. "Look at this; it's from that same Boat launch place but not tied next to the other one."

"So what does that mean?"

"Elementary my dear Watson, it means that this set of footprints did not come with those sets of footprints which are larger by the way. In fact see how they go off in different directions?"

"Oh Ronnie, you are too much when you get like this." Susan leaned over to peer into the second boat. "Well will you look at this." She picked off a piece of black leather from the oarlock.

"Susan, don't touch it…" It was too late. She held it in her hand. "Well at least we know whoever rowed this boat wore leather clothes of some kind." He wrapped his arm around her. "Okay, let's follow the footprints. Susan and I will follow the larger prints, Bob you follow the other ones."

"Alone, no way; I'll stay right here, thank you very much."

"So you'd rather stay here at the water alone and wait for someone to return and do God only knows what to you rather than figure out if it's just a couple having a romantic interlude or something."

"It's the 'or something' that worries me."

Ron got the message as Susan tugged on his arm and whispered that Watson was right. "Oh...come on Bob, we'll be better off together. Anyway they all seem to lead to those stone stairs up the bluff."

As they made their way up those granite steps, Carolina, Benton and her protectors had already reached the grassy knoll already cordoned off for the excavation dig which was to begin the next day. They made their way toward the main building. Murat climbed out of the gully under the bridge's arch and stood on top of it. He had the feeling that he was now caught between a rock and a hard place. He looked at the brick absentmindedly being held; the very one he had loosened and threatened the fox with earlier. As a weapon he certainly felt that it couldn't compete with Carolina's guys so he decided to take his chances with the young people he met on Birch Island. He walked back towards the staircase ruin with the brick in his hand.

The Bonaparte Bridge at Point Breeze

Chapter Twelve:
On The Lamb

The late afternoon August sun was still quite warm as the Blue Mini Bus screeched to a halt on the gravel road leading to the main seminary building. The cordoned off area on the grassy area bordering the woods could be seen as Jan De Cenza hung out the window and pointed to a group of people coming out of the woods.

"Oh my God, Alessandro, what if that creep Stockton got here first? Where's my brother?

The young Count of Pianore jumped out of the van and ran to the passenger side. He held out his hands to the distraught young woman and begged that she just get out of the van and go with him to confront whoever was coming out of the woods. "Maybe it's just a family of a seminarian or missionary." He took her hands and kissed each of them tenderly. "Come on, just take a breath..." he paused and then little by little he took hold of her arms and literally pulled her out of the window and into his arms. "There's no way that Stockton could have beaten us here. Malone said he escaped custody after we were already on our way here."

"Well maybe he has accomplices. I mean he is a Professor with all kinds of connections."

"We're talking about theft and murder here Jan. I don't think Stockton is part of a crime syndicate or the mafia. He's after the Bonaparte treasure plain and simple."

"Simple, are you *potso*...crazy? She thumped the side of his bushy black hair and then kissed his right temple where she had done so. "Exactly and we have a dead guy, jerk that he was which says he is capable of anything. What if he found out that Ronnie overheard him in the bathroom with that Murat guy we met in the Cabins on Birch Island. What if these people were sent here to get that Book?"

He twisted around to take a look at the three men and one woman now picking up their pace towards the gray stone building seemingly oblivious to them standing on the roadway. "The Book, of course; it's all about the Book and Bob has it in that damn satchel of his…"

"Which is with Ronnie and Susan on that stupid canoe; as if Ronnie knows anything about paddling such a thing."

"Okay, so he wanted to do something romantic and paddle up the creek…"

"Really romantic, my brother…Bob was with he and Susan. How mushy could it get?"

"*Capisc*o, I understand. Your brother then is in Sherlock mode and Watson is needed to bounce ideas off as he seeks to discover something, but what is that something?"

"God only knows but you had best put me down. See those two hunky guys? Well they just broke away from the others and are headed our way. I told you Andreas and Dominic should come with us."

He gently lowered her from his arms. As her feet touched the gravel road, he suddenly pulled open the door of the van, took hold of Jan and lifted her up again but this time back into it. "*Gesu,* help us; those two they are familiar to me and to you I'm sure. Look over my shoulder but say nothing."

"Lord, help us for sure; it can't be they're in jail aren't they?"

"Not if they are Niccolo Cavelli's bodyguards. They did nothing wrong but protect their boss."

Alessandro ran to the driver's side, jumped in and started the engine just as Luigi and Pietro picked up their pace to a run.

"I think that they saw us but maybe they didn't recognize us." He didn't want to appear as if they were running away from them so he slowly shifted into first gear.

The two so called 'hunky guys' picked up their pace but it wasn't toward them; they veered off running at full throttle toward something behind the van toward the main entrance by the old mansion once owned by the Hammond family who built the swimming pool and rock formation on the other side of the estate but visible from where they were driving. In fact a car was now visible; a dark sedan slowly made its way onto the grass and stopped at a huge tree, the very one which Father Garcia said that Lewis and Clark planted after their exploration of the Louisiana Purchase. Out from it jumped a man dressed rather formally for a hike on the grounds. Clearly he was wearing dark brown pants and a sport coat, not a wind breaker and his shoes were brown leather not hiking boots or gym shoes. His disheveled brown hair was being tossed about in the stiff breeze which had developed as evening approached.

Alessandro stopped the van and watched what was taking place with Jan on his arm leaning out the driver's side window to get a good look. They couldn't see the man's face. But he was about five ten and filled out but not pudgy like Bob. Jan thought him to be quite older than they as well; "Perhaps he's a bit older than Professor Pettigrew," she observed. "Wait a minute; this guy isn't going to those rock formations at all. Look he's trying to catch up with that man and woman running toward the main entrance of the seminary."

"And those two Cavelli thugs are trying to stop him." Alessandro stopped the van again. "Perhaps we should see what happens as they seem to have no interest in us." He was getting somewhat distracted himself as Jan hung more of herself out of the window leaving her posterior at his eye level just past the steering wheel. "Jan, get back in here before you fall out or worse."

Jan slid back inside and immediately saw that face like Michelangelo's David back in Florence contorted with an effort to control his thoughts given her proximity to him. She patted his cheek as she plunked down on the passenger seat. "Holy cow, you're not getting like my brother, when Susan is too near him are you?"

Alessandro forced out a grin. "Not quite that bad but still you are so *bella* and so near me."

"Ok big boy, let's get out of this van or drive fast to those doors. In either case, we need to cut off that guy from those two."

"Which two would that be; the man and woman, for clearly he is heading their way or the two big guys coming after him?"

Jan was now wishing that Dominic and Andreas were with them. "We need to split up. I will go toward the man and woman and you go to those two dudes and stop them."

"Absolutely not," insisted Alessandro. "You shall not go alone. We must choose which ones to confront together."

"Time is of the essence here sweetie, but okay we'll both go and talk to the dudes and see what happens when the man reaches that couple."

"You call me 'sweetie' what is this sweetie term?"

"What, this isn't the time for all of that; just follow me." Jan jumped out of the van and ran toward Luigi and Pietro. Alessandro was at her heels and quickly passed her just enough to be a barrier between the dudes and her.

Stockton knew who they were as he paused briefly watching them go after Luigi and Pietro. They had met at Princeton University earlier before all hell broke loose. He resumed his sprint and caught up with Carolina and Benton. They briefly exchanged a few words and Stockton was off toward the woods.

None of them realized that on the stone stairs leading down to Crosswicks Creek a meeting was taking place. Ron wasn't quite sure how he should greet the man who in the bathroom with Stockton was planning on finding the Bonaparte treasure and cutting their other partners out of the equation. So he started the conversation quite simply.

"Mr. Murat, we meet again…"

"Is that you Ron and Susan, you are looking so lovely in that red, white and blue ensemble." He walked up to Bob and patted him on the back. "So Bob, did you ever get that shower?" He feigned laughter but Bob was having none of it. "Well now I suppose you are all wondering what I am doing walking down these steps dressed like I was going to the library for research rather than a hike in the woods."

"Now on that point we can all agree Sir, what are you doing walking down these steps?"

"Now Ron," he approached and placed his hand on Ron's shoulder, not the good one as it turns out but the one that had been injured when he was shot some two years prior while a seminarian in the Abbey. To that day, the shoulder was tender and sensitive to a squeeze. Ron twisted his way out of the hold though it wasn't a strong one and grimaced with a twinge of pain. "I'm sorry lad, did I hurt you?"

Before Ron could reply, Bob stepped into his face. "Listen Mr. Murat, you'd feel a lot worse if you were shot like my buddy was when he was saving a life, mine included."

"Why lads, I had no idea that I was in the company of a hero…"

"Cut the crap Mr. Murat," began Ron who pulled Bob away and virtually placed him in Susan's grasp. "I'm no hero, just happened to be in the right place at the wrong time. But let's just drop the shoulder thing and get back to your question and ours as well. What are we all doing in these woods?"

222

He looked Murat up and down studying the dirt on his clothes and mud on his dress shoes. Then he saw the brick sticking out of his jacket pocket. "So are we collecting souvenirs from the creek, Sir?"

"Oh this isn't just any brick young man but I think you know that already don't you?"

Ron returned one of his famous half ass grins.

"I thought as much. But for the sake of our little conversation and your friends may I enlighten you. Look around you what do you see. Not much to be sure just a lot of brush, trees and the creek of course. Let's not be concerned with the rowboats and I presume that's your canoe as I came in that one over there and someone else came in the one right next to your canoe. In any case let's focus on the obvious, these stone stairs, which obviously were once part of a grand staircase leading down to the creek. On these very steps Joseph Bonaparte would descend to a small pier which was located right where those old pilings are sticking out of the water. He and his guests would stroll along the banks of the creek, row in the boats he provided and rumor has it, enter a secret tunnel. You do know who Joseph Bonaparte was, don't you; after all you were also at Lake Bonaparte searching for the same thing that the poor man who was killed sought." He sat himself down on the stair behind him. "Do have a seat and let's have a chat."

"Okay, we're seated and you have our attention. So what's the story about the brick?"

"Ah, the brick," he took it out of his pocket. "It's just a brick, Ron, like many others you'll find strewn about this forest, only this one was part of a bridge's foundation and it came loose while I stood next to it just a short while ago."

Ron couldn't help but to give a side-glance at Bob and Susan. He was well aware of the bridges Bonaparte had built as part of his carriage paths.

Was it the one which might be concealing one of the secret tunnels which he worried that Murat may have stumbled across by accident.

Or was it? What did he see on that dining table in the cabin on Birch Island? Could he have seen some of the work that he and Andreas was translating from the biography which spoke of the secret tunnels and the Bonaparte jewels? His mind was swirling with possibilities all of which he couldn't let be known so as to allow Murat to divulge what he knew in his story telling. At the same time he had heard the bathroom conversation between Murat and Stockton. He didn't want to let that be known, not yet at least. So he prodded Murat.

"So then you were standing under the bridge it would seem. But why would you be standing under a bridge rather than on top of it? Could it be that on top of what remained of the bridge there stood other people? And if so, did they even know of your presence as you were of theirs?"

With a twist of his little handlebar mustache he gave a wink at Bob and Susan. "Bright lad, this friend of yours," he scooted down a step to sit right next to Ron, who did not enjoy the close proximity, not after what he heard in that bathroom at the Princeton Library. "Now then where was I? Ah yes, I was about to tell you about those people who stood on top of the bridge."

A loud "Son of a Bitch" scream abruptly ended his thought. "Shit, that's the voice of Professor Stockton. He must not find me here, at least not with all three of you. If you help me, I will help you," he whispered.

"The issue here Mr. Murat is far more serious than Stockton finding us here with you. He is an escaped suspect who was arrested for the murder of Apollo Dimitri up on Lake Bonaparte. It all happened after our visit with him. We just got the word of his escape ourselves."

"Then you realize that what I am saying is true. There is no telling what he'll do if he thinks I am sharing our knowledge of the Bonaparte legend with you."

"On that we are in agreement. Bob, Susan go into that rowboat, not the canoe you might tip over. Push yourselves out into the creek and let the current take you out of sight. Bob, you can then get to the other bank and wait for me."

"No way Sherlock, I am not leaving you alone with Stockton."

"Shit Bob, he won't even know it's me not when he sees what he sees." Ron softly spoke into Bob's ear. "I know how to distract him from what he said in the bathroom." He had no choice but to let it be known that he heard something salacious. Taking Susan by the arm Bob led her into the rowboat and shoved off.

"Murat became agitated. "How could you know what took place in that bathroom? We were alone."

"So you thought, but I was in the stall and heard everything, but that's not important. Will you help us if we help you?"

"Yes, you have to trust me like Apollo did."

"But he's dead."

"That's true but not by my hand."

The swearing could still be heard over toward the bridge which they had been talking about as Stockton twisted his foot out of a protruding root which had tripped him. He stood, brushed himself off, shook his left leg and then put pressure on that foot. There was no appreciable pain. Cursing the root he began to move away from what appeared to be a mound but was actually the arch of the bridge. Had he fallen the in other direction he would have ended up in the same gully in which Murat hid. Mumbling something about finding a rowboat he looked about deciding how to get down the bluff to the creek to make his escape. Carolina had told him about the boat which Luigi and Pietro used to get to the estate.

"Number nine; where the hell…" He paused as two shadowy figures appeared ahead but down the incline. Realizing that there were stairs of some kind on which these two people were standing he headed that way though he didn't want to be seen until he could make sure what he was seeing were not some police but Missionary students or visitors. Ron was placing Murat in front of him so that he could see Stockton coming but the Professor could not tell it was Ron who Murat was with.

"Give me your hat. I need to conceal as much of me around my head just in case he might recognize me. Now kneel down like you know…"

"So you were in that bathroom and know about…"

"Sure, so you're a gigolo and had a thing for Apollo; lots of guys and women too like that Carolina Gianetti who had eyes for him. That's it. Can you see him yet?"

"No but I can hear him. He's swearing a blue streak. Hold on he's coming this way; what shall I do?"

"Pull down my pants just a little and don't touch my underwear or everything is off; do I make myself clear?"

"Trust me; your thing is the furthest thought from my mind right now. If Stockton did what the police think he did to Apollo then I'm up shit's creek anyway. This has to look real. I have to unbuckle and unzip you."

"No way in hell; I'll do it just look like you're enjoying me."

"Under different circumstances…oh hell I can see him clearly which means he can see us." Murat peeked around Ron's hip. "He's not moving; now what?"

"We improvise; just go along with what I do and respond to what I say like you're all upset."

"Okay, then what? He'll see you up close in a few seconds if he starts moving again."

"That's the whole point; I'm going to run away from you. But I won't go far just in case he isn't pleased with you. Now get ready, I'm going to push you down." There was no time to get ready; in a flash Ron shoved him over, "Asshole, you bit me. You can't even do it without teeth." Making a grand gesture of pulling up his pants he ran down the stairs and hid in the brush away from the boats making sure that only his back could be seen by Stockton.

Murat shouted after him. "Come back, I won't hurt you. I want you so bad." He crawled on the stairs but went upwards not down.

A deep voice shouted at him from the area at the top of the stairs. "Antoine, is that you?" Stockton precariously ran down a few steps until he stood over the still crawling Murat. "What the fuck is the matter with you? So you are queer as a three dollar bill." He bent down and took hold of Murat's collar pulling him up to his feet and looked into his hazel eyes.

Murat offered no resistance as he allowed Stockton to rant thus giving Ron time to conceal himself. He offered but a sickly smile and a shrug. "I almost had the punk talking about…"

"Spare me the details. I heard. You bit the kid. But that's not the issue here is it?"

Murat feigned ignorance. "I don't understand. That guy is a student here and knows all about the estate. I thought he could help me learn about the legend of Bonaparte when he lived here."

"Are you telling me that some Holy Joe needed to get off and you just happened to be here to do it?"

The improvised lurid scene was getting out of hand and Murat realized that he needed to get the focus on Point Breeze and not what he was doing in the woods with a missionary student.

He straightened his back bone, stood tall and pushed Stockton's hands off his collar. "Fuck you Richard; this was totally an accident. I was taking the boat up the creek like visitors would do in the days when Point Breeze was a showplace of gardens, a man-made lake and of course the Bonaparte mansion, both of them. My arms got tired so I beached the boat right by these steps and realized what I had seen back in that cabin on Birch Island in Lake Bonaparte New York. This is the very place where Joseph Bonaparte would come down. I needed to feel his presence so I began to climb up the steps and there this young guy was wanking off. He saw me and got all embarrassed, tucking his thing away. Well we got to talking and I told him that a man has needs, so does a woman for that matter but I focused on guys to see where it went and you saw where it went."

"Christ almighty Murat, is everything sexual with you?"

"No asshole, however in this case as with that poor Apollo fellow it worked. The young man opened up to me like a confessor or something like that and I comforted him."

"I get the picture. Spare me the details, I saw enough. Anyway I have problems of my own right now and need to get out of here quickly. I was looking for a boat with a number nine on it. But it doesn't matter; we can use your boat to get out of here."

"Mine?"

"Yes yours, the other one belongs to those thugs of Carolina's. Whichever one is handier will do. Now listen up and listen carefully because you're in this up to your eyeballs and don't' forget it."

"You sound like a criminal where's that high society snobby talk you usually impress people with?"

Stockton swung around grabbed hold of Murat, who was now shaking as he realized he had gone too far. "You piece of shit, do you want to end up like that guy on Lake Bonaparte?"

"Holy Christ, it was you who did it then. But why, he was already talking to me about the legend not sex stuff or were you jealous Professor Stockton?" He shoved Stockton who lost his balance and tripped down the few remaining stairs to the bank of the creek finally falling onto the side of the canoe.

Running down after him Murat made a sincere effort to catch him before the fall; he failed. He stooped down to help Stockton to his feet. The Head of the History Department looked up at him with distain but said nothing as he was brought to his feet and then he found words but swallowed them. He thought better of treating his colleague in an enterprise which was to make them rich in a manner which may get him to swing to the other side which was that of Carolina and Benton. Even though he had given every indication to them that he was only on the lamb because he couldn't afford the bad publicity for the University and was out to prove his innocence. But in his heart Stockton still had every intention to get to that legendary treasure before them. He rubbed his backside as that's what hit the tip of the canoe as he stumbled into it.

"I thought you said you came by boat."

"Canoe or boat, tomato or potato they're all the same to me. I had to paddle alone and it was easier with this thing."

Upstream in heavy brush and fallen trees Ron watched the confrontation and now the plan of getting Stockton off the estate and somewhere safe. He heard Stockton share that his car was left on a field and the cops would soon be there and be searching the grounds.

Carolina and Benton were continuing their plan to hold a couples retreat and thus be on the estate at the same time the excavation of the site of the first mansion was to take place. He leaned back and something poked him in his shoulder the one which had been shot. Muffling the gasp of twinges of pain he pulled back the branches and there sticking out of the brush was a metal bar. He dared not remove more and make noise so he watched Stockton and Murat get into boat number nine as they found it literally a few feet from where Ron was hiding. Once they were out onto the creek, he crawled out and ran to the canoe with the thought of following. As he got into the canoe out from the bank across the way came the rowboat with Bob and Susan.

"Ron, go tell Alessandro to meet us at the Bordentown Boat launch. Susan and I will follow that Professor guy and that asshole from Birch Island."

They didn't wait for an answer but each took an oar and began to row. Ron threw down the paddle and jumped out of the canoe and into the soft sandy mud of the creek's bank. He knew that time was of the essence and began his trek up the steps and out of the woods.

The van was clearly visible on the gravel roadway as he picked up pace and ran towards it. When he got to it, he found it to be empty but he did see a dark sedan which must have been the one Stockton referred to as being left on the grassy field. Deciding that it held no value, he walked toward the main entrance of the Missionary Building. An echoing voice which he recognized reached his ears. He knew it belonged to his sister. Stopping in his tracks he listened more intently and could hear several voices. They were coming from the rock formation behind a huge pool around which the rocks stretched thus creating an environment which was serene and very natural in appearance. Changing course he headed toward the glistening waters of the pool. Still he saw no people just heard voices. Climbing over the smaller rocks in front of the pool and walking through the garden planted between them he stood at the pool's edge and peered down into its aqua waters.

He was quietly listening for the voice while trying to identify the mythological scene created in the mosaic at the bottom of the pool.

"Ronnie, is that you? What are you doing here?"

Ron jolted back to reality and looked up. There stood his sister at the entrance to what could only be described as a cave. "Hey, what am I doing here? The question should be what are you doing here? You're supposed to be with Alessandro."

"And I am; come on inside it's a lot cooler in the cave. Alessandro is talking with some people who I think you'd want to speak with also."

If he could have run across the blue waters of the crystalline pool he would have. However his thoughts flashed back to that day when he was a student in the Abbey back in Wisconsin and how the Abbot had to jump in the lake to save him. They laughed later about how he wasn't like St. Peter who walked on water to get to the Lord. He thought better of it, though a refreshing dip was quite appealing, and instead ran around to his sister.

He gave her a hug and then a reprimand. "Now listen to me Sis; this is getting a bit rough and you need to be safe. I sent Susan with Bob back to the Crosswicks Inn because of what happened in those woods. We need to regroup and share what we know. Let's get Alessandro and get out of here."

Jan just stood there until her brother was done being the big brother. When he finished she simply told him to follow her and all would become quite clear.

"Clear as mud," was his response but he followed her. As his eyes adjusted from the fading yet bright sunlight he saw Alessandro standing over two big guys seated on a rock ledge.

"Holy shit, what the hell are they doing in America?"

"*Amico*, they are here for the same reason that we are. They have come to protect Cavelli's lover as she seeks the Bonaparte treasure."

"No shit Alessandro, Carolina is here in Bordentown too? Where is she? Isn't she still in bad shape after what happened on Capri?"

"That my friend was months ago. She recovered from the shot wound and seeks what we seek. Isn't that true guys?" he lifted the bowed head of Luigi and looked into his swollen eyes.

That's when Ron realized that the men were bound with their hands tied behind their backs and that there had obviously been a physical confrontation as Pietro looked worse for wear as well with dried blood on his face which had come from a head wound. It seemed that his sister had clunked him with a tire iron when they were getting rough with her boyfriend. The young Count of Pianore however could handle himself and soon got Luigi down and more amiable to answer his questions.

"We thought being out of sight would be best," added Jan. "So we brought them in here. Now what should we do with them Ronnie?"

"This is all too unbelievable but I think that we have to let them go. They are here like you said to find the jewels. That's not a crime. However now that they know…" he knelt down in front of the thugs and looked up into their frustrated faces, "that we are here too we can take precautions that they cannot be near us in our excavation project. Let's untie them."

"This we shall not forget Signori'."

"And you, Luigi, should have not gotten rough with my pal Alessandro. He was just protecting my sister as you obviously were supposed to do for Carolina who by the way doesn't seem to be here. Where is she?"

232

Pietro answered as Jan's silk accent scarf was untied by Alessandro. "She is meeting with the Superior General of this place." His hands now free, he turned Luigi so that he could unfasten Alessandro's belt which had bound his counterpart's hands. "And now you have no right to hold us against our will. We shall leave this place and hope never to meet you again."

He took hold of Luigi and pulled him off the ledge. They limped out of the cave into the late afternoon August day just as Carolina and Benton were exiting the Mission House entrance doors. With them stood Father Garcia and one of the students, one David Chan. They were shaking hands as Jan, Alessandro and Ron watched from the mouth of the cave in disbelief.

"This can't be happening. We have the rights to excavate the estate for whatever." Ron ran toward the priest who was a good distance from where they stood. Alessandro and Jan ran after him and catching up with him restrained him.

"Cool it Ronnie, you don't understand. The priest hasn't forgotten his commitment with us. They are here on the pretense of creating a couples retreat."

"What the F…. oh sorry Jan; I mean how can that be?"

"Watch your mouth brother as Dad would say and never mind how such language wouldn't be tolerated by Mom."

"Now is not a time for a lecture Jan. We need to figure out how to stop them from stealing whatever we find because there's no way in hell that they are here to conduct a couples' retreat."

"On that point we are all in agreement. So Ron, what's our next move?" Alessandro's question was not answered.

They stood on the lower rock border and watched the farewell when shouts were heard coming from the wooded area. Out from the woods came running two rather impressive looking young guys who could also give Luigi and Pietro a run for their money. One, speaking of giving one a run for their money, could easily challenge the deceased Apollo in looks and physique and the other was one of those tall, dark and handsome Latin types.

"Ah shit, it's Andreas and Dominic; what are they doing here. Bob was supposed to bring Susan to them and tell them what's been going on in those woods."

"Well that certainly doesn't sound like good news Ron."

"Let's go get them and get to the van."

"I think that you, Ron, should at least greet the Father as we'll all be here tomorrow for the excavation. We have to make it all look like a normal day for us. Jan can get our *amicos* and I'll get the van."

"Okay Alessandro, I'll go greet the priest but we are not leaving; not just yet. We are going back in those woods. I have something to show all of you. And bring a flashlight with you. I'll meet you at the edge of the woods."

While that jaunt toward the woods was taking place, Bob and Susan had docked the rowboat and watched Stockton and Murat as they got into a silver Mustang. They had no transportation but Susan had a pen in her purse slung over her back like Bob did with his satchel and he had some paper. They wrote down the license plate number.

"Why aren't they moving Bob?"

"You got me hanging. It looks like they are not very happy. Let's just stay here and wait for Andreas and Dominic to get back to the dock."

"We should have gone back to help Ron."

"No Susan, he wouldn't ever forgive me if I placed you in danger. Andreas and Dominic are strong dudes; they will be able to handle the boat and whatever they find better than me."

"Stop it Bob, you are a formidable guy and could easily take care of either of those two in that car."

Bob blushed at the compliment as Susan left him to watch while she went to find a phone and call the Inn to tell Captain Verdi that they had seen Professor Stockton. Unfortunately for her he had taken his new wife, Sophia out for a canoe ride on Crosswicks Creek. Running back from the rental office she found Bob crouched behind some dry docked boats with none other than the Captain and Sophia.

The Woods of Crosswicks Creek

Chapter Thirteen:
The Iron Gate

Ron had just crossed the gravel drive and walked toward the gray stone building which had none of the charm, beauty or artistic flairs often associated with Catholic Abbeys, Motherhouses and church buildings. It was strictly a functional structure. His attention was drawn to Father Garcia and the missionary student, David Chan waving at a black Cadillac slowly driving out from behind the building. He turned to check out the passengers whom he was quite certain was Carolina Gianetti, Luigi and Pietro but as to who the man with Carolina was when they were talking with the priest he had to only hazard a guess. The tinted windows made it impossible for him to discern who were in the back seat. Up front however, were the two he met in the cave.

At the edge of the woods checking out the cordoned off area where the excavation would begin the next day stood Ron's sister Jan, her beau, Alessandro, the Papal Guard Andreas Berne and Pettigrew's research assistant Dominic Fontana.

"Well there goes that hussy and to think how Susan and I were so sorry for her when we visited her in that hospital on Capri. Now she's hanging around with those two who are still loyal to Cavelli."

The young Count of Pianore wrapped his arms around her. "Easy *cara mia*, we'll get them soon enough. Your brother probably has it all figured out already."

"You're sweet, but she's a slippery one or have you forgotten so soon what happened after you saved her life on that balcony. Well let me remind you; she has a way with men if you get my meaning."

The reminder went virtually unnoticed because something else pierced his mind. "You did it again, this sweet term. I am not sweet; I am a man like the Warrior King David in Florence. You said it yourself." He called to Andreas and Dominic. "Tell her *amicos* that I am a true man and not sweet like…" He cut himself off realizing what he just inferred.

The Papal Guard dropped the arm he had hanging over Dominic's shoulder as they studied the placement of the flags for digging spots. He turned with a mixture of pity and fury in his eyes. Whoever and however he loved was not going to be defined by terms like "sweet." Dominic could feel the tension in him building and tried to hold onto his arm with the distraction of watching the Cadillac leaving. It didn't work.

"Exactly, what are you saying *amico*," the term of friend was not used sincerely but sarcastically. He stood within inches of Alessandro's face.

The young Count looked over his shoulder seeking help from Dominic who made the Sign of the Cross over himself and bowed his head. He was powerless to do anything not when this soldier lover of his had his manliness threatened. He glanced down at Jan with a silent plea to help him out. He got it.

She stretched out her arms pushing Alessandro away from her as well as Andreas, both of them could have crushed the gesture but neither attempted to do so. They stood like children being scolded in the Principal's office with heads bowed. "Now you two need to get a grip. Let me try to explain."

And she did with a story of the Space Center at Cape Canaveral in Florida and Houston Texas. Time and again the scientists and astronauts faced obstacles which made their rockets fail. The first thing they had to do was to admit that there was something wrong so they used a term, 'Houston we have a problem.'

238

It didn't cast blame on anyone as the cause of that problem. This enabled them to address the issue she told them and not attack each other, rather they banded together to solve the problem.

"So guys, let's just say it," then she called out, "Houston we have a problem."

The guys did not fully comprehend the analogy which Jan had made. However, they did, however, realize that they had a problem between them after almost two years of sacrificing for each other and bonding together to bring justice in often horrific circumstances. Not the least of these was to demonstrate that being gay did not mean you were any less of a man, or incapable of facing danger.

"*Si*, we do have a problem," Andreas pointed his index finger at Alessandro. "*Mi amico*, at least I have always thought him to be my friend." He lowered his hand and spoke softly. "Now I see that he thinks because Dominic and I are who we are, that we are 'sweet' not truly men because we do not make the love to women but to each other."

Tears welled up in the eyes of Alessandro. "But I don't think that; it just came out wrong. I was offended that Jan called me this sweetie term as if I was not a man and I do make the love to women…"

"You certainly do not my dear Count of Pianore."

"You see Andreas, Houston has another problem." He forced out a weak smile. "Jan I did not mean with you but with women in general before I met you." He reached out to her but she stood her ground to be a barrier between them. He dropped his arms like lead weights to his side. His broad chest heaved a heavy sigh.

Jan's heart was melting but she could not let herself do so. "Now listen to me *Signori* this problem is not one at all. Alessandro, are you not romantic when you snuggle me like on that pier on Lake Bonaparte when we watched the stars? And you Andreas, do you not feel your heart beat faster when you hold Dominic's hand and pull him close to you tenderly?

Both young men agreed that such reactions and gestures were made as she described. But both insisted that such acts did not make them less a man.

"Of course they don't because it's just a term of love and love makes us different. I was just trying to say that what Alessandro does to show me affection was romantic, tender and yes a sweet thing to do. He was confused by the use of what was supposed to be an endearing term. There is a language problem here as well you know. And you Andreas…you thought that he was calling you a sissy; you the brave soldier who guards the Vatican and protects the Pope."

"*Vero,* true," Andreas looked up to see the teary eyed Alessandro. "*Mi dispiacere amico.*"

"And I am sorry too my friend."

"And I will never use that term again…" began Jan.

"No Jan, now that I understand I want to be your sweetie but just yours."

"And I am already your sweetie," Dominic wrapped his arms around Andreas.

"So then we are all good here?" Jan asked with a twinkle in her eye.

"*Si!*"

"Well then let's have a group hug, come on be sweet," Jan laughed and they joined her in laughter and in the hug.

At the doors of the Mission House there was no talk of sweetness or love. It was all business as Ron introduced himself to Father Garcia and thanked him for housing him and his pal Bob. The priest was insistent that the pleasure was all his and that his friend Abbot Lawrence would have done the same for his people.

"And now young man shall we have some tea and talk about your time with Abbot Lawrence?"

"That would be lovely, perhaps another time Father. Right now my fellow team members are waiting for me. We'd like to see the area of the site where the excavation will take place tomorrow."

"Full of excitement aren't all of you, I'm sure. Well did you know that you'll be excavating at the site of the first mansion of Joseph Bonaparte….of course you do. But then there's the site of the second mansion which that Becket person tore down to build that Italian style villa mansion out along the main road. The English still had a grudge against the Bonaparte family. But I am gossiping. Perhaps one day you'll return and dig up something at the second mansion site."

"That's a for sure thing Father especially if we don't find anything at the first site." Ron turned to leave.

"One more thing, may I address you as Ron?"
"Of course Father, what is it?"

"Look way down the road on which you drove. You can hardly see it but you did pass it on the way up here. That house is original to the Point Breeze estate and built by a French American associate of Joseph Bonaparte."

"Right I think I was told about that. We hope to get to visit it."

241

"I'm sure we can arrange that but as I told that couple who just left, the interior is in bad shape and in need of repair. Locals refer to it as the Gardener's House. I do hope that Professor Pettigrew and all of you are successful tomorrow. If you need help with dirt removal or shifting soil, do tell him that several of our students would be anxious to help out."

"You are most kind. We'll be here for the night later this evening. Hope to see you then." Ron was about to run off but then paused. "Father, who was that couple anyway?

"Such nice people; the young woman so beautiful yet she was tender to her man. They want to create a Couples' Retreat to foster such love. Is that not a wonderful vocation?

"Right, keeping the fire of love burning is important but who are they?"

"They come from Italy just like you have. But only one of them is actually Italian. David here was the one who met them first. They were so in love weren't they? The priest turned to David who was standing behind him and pulled him forward. "Such a humble lad, now tell our guest about this couple."

"But Father, I only greeted them and escorted them to your office. I mean I really didn't talk to them."

"I see," the priest patted the shoulder of his student. "But David, when you arrived you were… Now how shall I say it? Ah yes, you were flushed with excitement. I thought that you had engaged in more than a greeting."

Now he had Ron's interest and he walked up to David who was around his age and looked into his eyes while noticing his glowing cheeks which sent out a message of embarrassment.

242

Father Garcia began to see what was going on. He suggested that perhaps he had placed too much on the young student by suggesting that a bond had been made between him and the couple. Ron looked over David's shoulder and winked at the priest. He got the message. Something else besides niceties had occurred.

Ron draped his arm over the student and guided him down the few steps leading to the entrance door. "So David, this lovely young woman as Father Garcia described, what did she say to you?"

"It wasn't what she said Sir; it was what she did while saying it."

"I'm the same age as you, please call me Ron. Oh, well what could be done in the greeting hall…" he stopped saying what he was about to say as he realized that they were talking about Carolina Gianetti the mistress of Niccolo Cavelli now in prison but a wealthy and influential tycoon before his downfall. "It's okay David, I think I know this woman, her name is Carolina Gianetti, am I correct?"

"Yes Sir, I mean Ron, that was the name she gave me as she bent over the desk and revealing her…I can't I'm a Missionary Brother and studying to become a priest, I cannot let this happen to me." He began to shudder in distress.

Father Garcia was about to come down to address the issue but Ron waved him off. He stepped back up to the doorway.

Ron wrapped his arms around the seminarian. "It's going to be okay David, trust me and allow me to tell you a story." He released him and suggested that they take a little walk away from his mentor. So they strolled toward the Rock formation. "I want to tell you a story David, a true story. About three years ago there was a young man who entered the Seminary to study for the priesthood just like you. In fact he was even younger than you. Well he had quite the time of adjustment what with the rules of the order and especially the Grand Silence. One day he had to collect his Latin Book at the gift shop and there distributing them was the most beautiful girl he had ever come into contact with.

She told him that he had no fashion sense and pulled off his shirt. He got so excited that…"

David's eyes were bulging out of his head.

"So you're beginning to understand what this excitement is, aren't you?"

"I…I think so, it's like when your man thing grows and you don't want it to."

"David, you're what twenty years old, I think we don't have to speak of our penis like we're in junior high school. In any case, he got an erection and ejaculated all over himself right in his clothes."

"Oh my Lord, Ron, I didn't do that, I just began to sweat and get hard that's all."

"You obviously have better control than this guy did. But that's not the point. He ran away and for over two years after that he could not be near her or speak of what happened except to his closest pal. And then one day he did get near to her. They were about to die as they were being held against their will in a dungeon like place. He told her that he loved her and then the weight of the world seemed to be lifted. He held her and kissed her and he reacted like you said you did but he was in love and it was okay. He no longer embarrassed himself. And the rest is history as they say. This year that guy and that girl are going to be married. So you see, as you study and take those vows of chastity in particular, you shall be tested. This woman, I know her and she has a way with men, luckily we have a couple of gay friends who don't react the same way as some of us do around her flirtations. Now look over there, see those people there, those are that guy's friends minus the one he loves and his best pal. Together we are quite the team but I am getting off point again."

"I got the point when you said what happened to you."

"Oh, so you know the story is about me?"

David smiled meekly and nodded affirmatively.

"Well then, let me end this by saying that your vocation will be tested a lot in these days of sexual revolution as they call it. Abbot Lawrence told me when I almost drowned that we must have faith almost as strong as to walk on water and that faith will guide us to a safe place. David, your reaction to this woman was courageous for you did not take advantage of what she was offering. One day you may find a true love, it may be with a woman or even a man or it may be for the Church you serve. Just go with the flow and let whatever will be happen."

"I get it Sir…Ron, thanks so much for the pep talk. I think if it happens based on how I reacted it will be with a woman but right now I hope it will be for the Church."

"Good man," Ron gave him a pat on the back and sent him back to his Mentor. "See you tomorrow Father." Waving good-bye he ran toward his friends.

David shouted, "See you and by the way the man's name is Charles Benton."

He came upon his sister and friends as they were having their group hug and wondering if Benton's presence in Switzerland had been directed by Carolina. "Whoa, what's this all about?"

The arms dropped and they separated immediately. Jan informed him that it was a long story, "but it's all fine and dandy now and they should get on with what was so important to him that they couldn't' wait to get Bob and Susan back with them. And let me tell you another thing Ronnie, she's going to be teed off big time that you treated her like some poor thing who needed to be protected and not able to help out here."

The guys nodded their heads in agreement though in their hearts they knew Ron loved Susan too much to risk her facing an accused killer. It was bad enough that his sister had actually faced Luigi and Pietro. And he told her just that. "It was foolish of you to confront them. You could have been really hurt."

"Get a life Ronnie, I had a tire iron in my hand and they had nothing."

"That's not the point and Alessandro you should have known better. On Capri those dudes carried guns."

The young Count could only stutter regret that he allowed his sweetie as he now felt comfortable in saying to be open to danger. "Ron, you know that I would die before anyone could harm your sister."

Placing his hand on Alessandro's shoulder he assured him that he knew that but things were getting too rough and they needed Malone and Verdi in the mix. "You all need to come to grips with the fact that not only is Stockton running around this town but he's with Murat who got me out of big trouble to be sure but we can't forget what he tried to do on Birch Island. Nor can we ignore that he is in cahoots with Stockton and Carolina and those thugs."

Once again an American term confused the guys. Alessandro turned to Jan and asked what this 'cahoots' was and did it mean that Murat and Stockton had a thing for each other and realizing what he said once again offered his apology to Andreas and Dominic.

"Listen *amico* you don't have to apologize over something like two guys having a thing any more than you do for you having a thing for Jan."

"This is not a good day for my English and my understanding of the love feeling." Alessandro took the hand of Dominic which sent a heartfelt message to everyone as they understood that when two Italian men held hands they had a relationship with deep meaning. "I am so very pleased that we are friends."

Dominic brought him into a hug and patted his back. "Me too, but now what is so important Ron that we cannot wait for the others?" He placed the hand of Alessandro into that of Jan as her big brother watched with approval.

"Right, enough of this mushy stuff; off we go. I need to show you something. If I'm right about what it is then we have a job to do without the good Father and certainly Carolina or Stockton learning about what I'm going to show you." Ron walked into the wooded area toward the stairs which led down to the creek. He was wishing that his Watson and his "sweetie" were with him. On the way he explained how Murat distracted Stockton from identifying him while he ran away and hid. "I guess I owe Murat something; the last thing I need is for Stockton to know that I was in that bathroom and heard his plot with Murat to cut out Carolina from the treasure find. And another thing, that guy Charles Benton who we almost crashed into back in Switzerland is part of the picture. He is with Carolina and those two goons."

The revelation of the extent of the connection of the Princeton Professor, Carolina, Benton and Murat had them thinking until they were almost down the stairs near the banks of the creek. Alessandro asked what Murat had done which allowed Ron to escape discovery.

There was dead silence as Ron avoided answering especially in front of his sister. Instead he pointed to the remaining canoe. "This is where Susan, Bob and I landed. When they escaped they took Murat's rowboat. That left the canoe which meant poor Murat had to think quickly and improvise a story. So he claimed it to be his otherwise Stockton would have known that besides the Missionary Student he thought he saw with Murat there were others who knew of his presence in Bordentown. So they left in the rowboat which was tied over here."

Ron showed them the deeper and bigger footprints. "These belong to Luigi and Pietro. Now just a few feet more in that clump of brush and debris I was hiding until Murat and Stockton shoved off to God knows where and that's when it happened."

"Ronnie, what happened?"

"Not much Sis, but it could be a big break for us in our search." He pulled back some of the brush and asked the guys to help him with some rather large dead tree branches. "Now here I was," Ron stepped into the brush to demonstrate his position. "After they left, I was relieved and leaned back and ouch I felt a pain in my bad shoulder."

He stepped to the side and pulled on an iron bar so that they could better see that it had a point. "This is part of a gate, see here," he pulled away more vines, asked for the flashlight and shined it on hinges and a cross bar. "I'm sure that if we dig further we will uncover what's left of a tunnel gate. The very section of the biography that Andreas and I were working to translate when Bob got all upset and Murat came into our cabin and tried to see what we were doing."

"Oh my Lord, Ron this is amazing," shouted Dominic as he kissed Ron on each cheek in the Italian fashion and then did the same to Andreas. "You have quite possibly found one of those tunnels which Bonaparte built from his house. We already know this from what we learned from the biography so far."

"And it's in a tunnel we are to find the legendary treasure?" asked Alessandro.

"Maybe," began Ron. "But it's not necessarily this one but who knows. Andreas you need to work with me on the Book as soon as we get back to the Inn. Tonight back in the Mission House Bob and I will put the pieces of our translations together and come up with a plan to find out if these are tunnel gates. Then we'll see if this is the tunnel Joseph Bonaparte used as a secret way to get out of his mansion."

"And if we find this to be true, then what?"

Ron stepped out of the brush and replaced it around the iron bar to conceal it once more. "Shit, some of these have thorns." He licked his finger. "I wonder would the Professor have gloves for each of us?"

Dominic assured him that everyone would be given gloves to begin the excavation. "*Gesu*, the excavation, how can we uncover what is here and still do what we came here to do?"

"And," Andreas added. "How do we keep this find a secret especially with Carolina running around the estate?"

"And what if this isn't a tunnel at all or if it's all caved in and there's nothing but dirt and a few bricks?"

Ron assured Andreas and his sister that their questions would have an answer and part of that answer would be in accepting Father Garcia's offer of Missionary students to help with the excavation.

As they walked up the steps and onto the open space where the first Bonaparte mansion stood the sun was in its descent. They picked up their pace and ran to the van never realizing that in the parking lot next to the Boat launch the very people he sent away to protect where hiding behind some old rotting boats with Captain Enrico Verdi of the Carabinieri of Italy and his wife Sophia. Susan was surprised to find the newlyweds there with Bob when she came back from the rental office.

"Wow that was fast Captain. I was just trying to reach you at the Inn. Do we have news for you; see those two in the car. That's Professor Richard Stockton and Antoine Murat."

"So Bob has informed me. I must contact Malone who is wasting his time searching that town of Princeton and then the local authorities. I have no authority to pick up this professor. But as for the Signore' Murat why would he be with such a person who is accused of murder? He seemed like a most amiable man when we met at the cabins."

"Well I think that it's all an act for Murat. He only seemed to be friendly. Remember how he steered me away from the guys' cabin so that he might get inside to spy on the work being done by Ron and Andreas."

"Work and what kind of work would that be, Bob? Are you not assistants to the Professor Pettigrew for the research on the estate of Joseph Bonaparte and was not the Signore' Murat writing a magazine article on that topic as well?"

The Captain's question suddenly made Bob feel the urgent need to clutch his satchel in which was the Book. He looked at Susan for help in answering the questions. She was at a loss for she and Jan were seated on the front porch of the guys' cabin and were totally unaware of what was taking place in the back and inside. Bob was in near panic mode, where the hell is Sherlock when I need him was the question repeating itself in his swirling thoughts. How should he speak and not talk about the Book and what it contained regarding the Bonaparte jewels.

"Of course Captain, Mr. Murat is a reporter and they often take ideas to create a story and that's what I think he was trying to do up on Lake Bonaparte. And don't forget he had ample time and means to get the Crossbow and kill poor Apollo though now of course it seems that Stockton did that so I guess that's not a legitimate conclusion."

"So it would seem Bob. Are you nervous, perhaps Sophia can give you an Aspirin or something which will calm your nerves?"

"That's nice of you, but I think I'm just worried about Jan and the other guys and Malone and the police not being here. What if those two decide to drive away, there's no way for us to catch them."

"That's a good point," noted Verdi. "So we must take action to stop them from leaving." He looked around and in seconds had an idea. "Bob, you look like a strong young man, do you think that you can carry one of these old boats upside down with me so that we may not be seen as our heads will be under it?"

"Sure, I think so, but what's the point of carrying a boat?"

"We shall fall in front of the car and prevent them from moving forward. By the time they can back up we shall pull them from the car for questioning." Verdi directed Bob to slip under the top boat on the pile. "Now lift just slightly so that I can get under the front end."

The boat teetered and swayed but Bob did not drop it. Verdi got under the bow and lifted; again they swayed and could not walk without toppling over. Susan and Sophia crawled under the middle portion and lifted up on the seat. It steadied the boat and lightened the load so that they could now walk but Verdi was not too pleased that his new wife and the *Signorina* were placed in such a potentially dangerous situation. Nevertheless they were moving and nearing the car.

"Now when we get in front of the car we shall tilt the boat towards the vehicle and let it drop to the pavement. Does everyone understand? Once we have dropped the boat you Sophia shall take Susan to safety away from the car, perhaps the rental office and call the local police. Bob and I shall try to hold Murat and Stockton in place by holding the doors so that they cannot get out of the car."

"What the hell is going on out there Richard?"

"How should I know? It looks like they're moving that piece of shit of a boat, probably to be picked up for the dump."

"Shit they are getting close, let's go help them or stop them."

Before Murat's suggestion was finished the four stood in the front of the car and tilted the boat. They lost balance in doing so and it fell on the hood of the car with a crash and then screams from those inside and outside of the car.

"Fuck this; get this thing in gear Antoine. We'll have to meet Carolina later."

Susan and Sophia were unhurt and ran to the rental office while the Captain and Bob picked themselves up off the pavement and ran to each side of the front doors. The engine finally roared and Murat stepped on the gas. The shattered remains of the wooden boat went flying in all directions. Bob and the Captain dove for the pavement and covered their heads with their hands. Susan and Sophia turned as they heard the engine and crashing sounds of wood splattering against metal. They screamed a warning for the guys to jump away which they had already done. Seconds later it was all over. The girls ran back to make sure the guys were not hurt. Covered in splinters of wood, they were not seriously injured except for their pride and some developing bruises.

Sophia cradled her new husband and picked off pieces of wood from his thick black hair. "So once again our honeymoon is destroyed my love, but it does not matter. You are not harmed; that's what matters."

Verdi kissed Sophia gently as his face hurt from the dive onto the pavement. As he did so Susan was picking off splinters from Bob's hair as well. "Now what shall we do? Ron will be so upset that you were almost killed by those jerks."

"It's okay Bob, the Signora Verdi and I were not harmed; that's what's important here."

"If you say so; we do have the license plate number, we'll get an APB out through the local police... ouch I think I'm sitting on a piece of wood and its sticking me right in the....well it hurts." Bob pulled a piece of the splintered boat out from under him.

Murat and Stockton sped out of the lot and into traffic almost hitting a black Cadillac going well above the speed limit. "Assholes," Murat yelled out the window as he screeched to a stop right in the middle of the street killing the engine in the process. "Shit, that was those two goons of Carolina driving."

"Well follow them before we get picked up by the police. We need to make a plan." Stockton jabbed him in the arm to emphasize the need to move.

Murat got the car started shifted into first gear and floored the gas pedal; the engine sputtered and died.

"What the fuck is the matter with you. Get out and let me do it. Murat jumped out and Stockton slid over behind the wheel. As he came around the car with pieces of wood still caught in its grill there came barreling down Prince Street a blue mini bus.

Alessandro and Jan were shouting in unison; "everybody, look ahead; it's Murat from the cabins, what should we do?"

Ron yelled for them to slow down and stop before they got too close. The young Count slammed on the brakes and threw everyone hither and thither, on the floor of the van and up and over the seat in front of them. Ron was hanging over his sister. "Hey, Alessandro I didn't mean quite that fast."

"*Mi dispiacere*, I'm sorry but I got excited. Now what do we do?" Jan looked into her brother's big dark eyes which were in her face. She pushed him back. "If that's Murat then that other guy has to be Stockton."

"Holy shit," Ron pulled on the handle and swung open the side door. "Okay, I'll run up there to see if they had an accident or something. Murat will recognize me and give me some bullshit story but in the meantime all you guys will encircle their car and stop them from leaving." He began to run ahead before anyone could answer.

Like the sheep they were when it came to obeying Ron in Sherlock mode they piled out of the van, except for Jan. She took over the steering wheel as she was to swing the van around Murat's car and block it. Murat froze at the passenger side window and yelled in that it was the kid from Birch Island, the one who has the Book. He fumbled with the door handle in a panic as Ron was closing in followed closely by three rather big dudes, Andreas, Dominic and Alessandro.

"I can't get the door open Stockton. He's getting close." He realized that the door was locked and as the window was only half open he could not crawl into the car through it. "Who the fuck locked the damn door?"

Those words no sooner left his lips than Bob and Captain Verdi ran out of the parking lot of the Boat Launch. Ron saw them and shouted that Stockton was in the silver Ford Mustang. Sirens could now be heard in the distance. Stockton screamed for Murat to run as he shifted into drive and sped off with Jan alone in the van on his tail. She had to cut him off or he'd leave her in the dust with that diesel powered mini bus-van. Stockton took a sharp left onto Park Street. The van was no match for the Mustang. Jan couldn't make the turn that quickly and stalled. She leaned over the wheel and pounded on it. Running at break neck speed past Murat now being held by Captain Verdi was Alessandro yelling for Jan to stop. She had done that but not by her own choice a block down from where Murat and Stockton had stalled outside of the boat launch parking lot.

The young Count of Pianore swung open the door and saw Jan slumped over the steering wheel. Tears were flowing like a waterfall as he called her name and prayed at the same time that the Lord make her alive.

254

255 | Arthur Cola

Jumping on the floorboard he reached in and enfolded her into his arms, trying to lift her out of the seat and to the ground. Her head rose, she too was crying but for an entirely different reason.

"*Cara mia*, you live, praise the Lord," he began to kiss her cheeks then her forehead, her eyes and then he came to her mouth. With the touch of a feather on silk he lightly kissed her. "I thought you were…"

"Well sweetie, I am not as you can see and everyone is looking at us," she was still crying as she spoke. "I lost him, he got away."

Cars were now lined up and down Prince Street gawking at the scene.

"And thank God for that; you could have been killed. He's an escaped murderer." He lifted her out of the van. "Let me get this thing started and out of the way of traffic. Walking her to the passenger side, she boarded onto her usual navigator seat as he ran around back to the driver's side. But before she entered, she had returned that final kiss on his lips. He ran around the van humming the tune of her Mom's favorite song, "That's Amore'" for he ran as if on clouds.

Captain Verdi was still holding Murat's arms as Ron and the other guys formed a circle around them. "Antoine Murat, I hold you for the police of Bordentown as an officer of Interpol and Captain of the Italian Carabinieri."

"You all don't understand. It's not what you think it is."

Ron got into his face reluctantly after all he had created the scene which enabled Ron to escape detection from Stockton. "Mr. Murat, you need to come clean, it will go easier on you."

"And what should I do, give you another blow job?"

Ron reeled back as the guys gasped and then became silent as the dawn over Crosswicks Creek. "You asshole, I'm trying to help you out. You were with an escaped suspect for murder."

"Right and I saved your life by sucking your dick."

Bob couldn't take it any longer. He ran up to Murat and tried to punch him in the face. "Sherlock would never allow such a thing; you don't know him like we do."

Dominic pulled him back before any real damage could be done.

Captain Verdi swung Murat around to face him. "You will stop such talk or I shall gag you here and now, police or not." He looked over to Ron. "Say nothing more to him. Whatever he speaks will be held against him." He called to Andreas to come and hold Murat while he removed his belt to tie his hands behind his back.

"Okay, I shall stop but not because of you but to keep Miss Liguri, your girlfriend I believe isn't she Ron? To be spared from the sordid details of what happened in those woods."

"Nothing happened, asshole and you know it."

Ron went up to Bob and gave him a hug. "Thanks pal."

Coming from outside of the circle and through the stopped traffic walked Susan and Sophia Verdi. "Enrico, we called the police." She ran to him as him tightened the leather belt around the wrists of Murat. "Thank you *cara mia,*" He held up his hand to signal that she should not embrace him. "I can see them coming. Just go back to the sidewalk with Susan *per favore.*" Then he smiled; one of those smoldering ones which melts the heart.

A squad car was escorting the van to the side of the street where Sophia and Susan stood in obedience to the Captain's directive. Jan and Alessandro swung open the doors and called to them to get in. The Captain's wife, Sophia, accepted the invitation but Susan stood frozen in place watching Ron being surrounded by the guys and embracing him in public but it was more than affection it was as if they formed a corral around him to prevent him from moving out of their circle.

She knew in her being that something awful had happened when the defiant Murat stood with hands tied yet snickering.

A second squad let out two officers one of which took over directing traffic and the other taking hold of Murat and guiding him and the guys to the sidewalk at the Boat Launch parking lot at the direction of the Captain who flashed his Interpol Badge. The guys made sure Ron could not break away from them as his eyes spoke volumes.

Verdi spoke very softly to Murat as Jan hung out the van window and his wife and Alessandro swung open the side door to better hear what was going on. "These nice officers will now take you to a place better suited for you given what you like to do with your fellow man." He turned to seek out his wife and there stood Andreas and Dominic right behind him. "I meant no harm to you; I hope that you understand this. I know all of you and because I do, I believe Ron would not do what Murat said they did in the forest. Not that you would do so either, I mean…"

"It's okay Captain; I think we understand that you meant that he would get a taste of his own medicine as they say in America." The Papal Guard placed his hand on the Captain's shoulder and leaned into him. "Go to your wife we shall take care of Ron. His only injury is that his manhood was attacked."

The Becket Mansion which replaced the second mansion of Joseph
Bonaparte.
As it looked before it burned down in 1983.

Chapter Fourteen:
A Murder Solved

As the sound of the siren faded and the flashing lights of the police car dimmed from view the guys opened their circle around Ron. He bolted out and ran to Susan tightly holding her in his rather sore arms from all the paddling and pulling of brush and tree branches off the Iron Gate. A slight August breeze swept over them as he began a litany of how sorry he was to have let her and Bob go into danger without him. Now he wished they would have stayed with the guys and his sister. This waterfall of guilt sweeping over him only got worse. He then thought about his sister alone in that van chasing Stockton and began cursing himself again for not planning better.

"Everyone depends on me like I was a real Sherlock Holmes, but I let them down. I let you down and sent you off into a deadly situation." His arms dropped to his side. His head bowed to cover the water building in his eyes as he thought of what could have happened. He began to shake. "Oh Jesus, Susan, you could have been killed and it would have been my fault."

Two smooth hands the nails on them painted a vibrant red touched his cheeks. "But I didn't, Bob and I are just fine."

She leaned into him and wrapped her arms around his neck as the guys, Jan and the Captain and his wife sighed. It was one of those sighs that one lets out without forethought when a beautiful thing is viewed. She looked up into those glistening eyes as his arms came back to hold her tightly. The breeze jostled her long crimson hair and mixed it in with his bushy almost black hair. None of that did they feel for their lips had touched and love was flowing through their bodies like an electrical charge. For that brief moment they were caught up in something which was not about "The Book" or murder or sexuality issues.

It all ended when Captain Verdi had to resume his role in law enforcement. He cleared his throat and in that baritone voice, which could even carry a tune he announced that the hour was getting late, the sun was setting. It was time to return to the Inn so that Bob and Ron could be brought to the Mission House where they were to be lodged he explained. He would have to retrieve his car so that he could question Murat in the Police Station after contacting Detective Malone.

Everyone piled in what the Americans called the van and the Europeans referred to as the mini-bus; in any case it was holding nine people. As they crammed themselves into the van, Bob pointed out that there was still a canoe which belonged to the Crosswicks Inn at the boat launch. It was the one which the Captain and Sophia had used for what was to be a romantic time on the waters of the creek. Ron cut off Alessandro and Andreas as he called out the canoe for him and Susan. He jumped out of the van and held out his hand for Susan.

"We'll see you back at the Inn; it's not far and we should be there shortly after you get back." The two of them ran off into the Boat Launch Parking lot.

"Enrico, look at them; they are in love, no?"

"*Si, cara mia, amore'* is in the air."

Alessandro turned to his navigator and his own love interest. "So your brother got the best of me with the boat." He paused, "But it's okay after what he just went through with that *Gavone* Murat and what he tried to do to your brother."

"What are you talking about Alessandro?"

"Oh nothing, just that Murat who presented himself to be a cultured man of letters and a reporter for the New Yorker is nothing more than a rude, uncultured and crude jackass."

"Wow, that bad huh; well don't worry when my brother gets over whatever has gotten to him he'll figure a way to get him and his partner in crime too." She snuggled up to him.

Paddling furiously on the creek Ron was splashing more water on him and Susan than back in the creek. It was as if he were lashing out at the water for having done something horrible to him. Susan was off in her timing with him as he just jerked the canoe forward down current. She pointed out that they were not far from the Inn and that the others would have to get to it using several streets whereas they had a straight shot to its backyard. He got the message and stopped paddling. She felt the canoe turning and began to compensate.

"I'm sorry, I was just so angry that I let this all get so out of hand. Just stop for a minute Susan we'll be all right. I'll straighten us out and then use my paddle as a rudder and let the current move us. Can you slip back and sit with me?"

Placing her paddle inside the canoe, she turned not with a smile but with a look of worry. "Ronnie, I feel like we're in that scene from the Sound of Music where Maria is paddling on the lake with those seven kids and…"

"We're not going to capsize, just scoot back to me; it'll be fine."

And indeed it was fine; for the first time since he proposed to her on the Isle of Capri in the Blue Grotto they were actually alone. With only a slight adjustment to their course now and then they floated down stream nestled next to each other with the handle of the paddle between them for obvious reasons else the canoe would turn sideways. Blissfully, they were enjoying the sound of a real babbling brook, the sun peeking through the trees lining the creek and serving as the border to the Delaware and Raritan State Park on the opposite side of where they had left from the boat launch. The brilliant reddish sky indicated that tomorrow would be another warm day.

"So you were saying Ronnie…what happened in that forest that has gotten you so upset?"

His immediately tensed up. She could feel it.

"That bad was it? You don't have to talk about it. It's not important for me to know now that I can see that you're not hurt."

"God, how I love you," he leaned over and kissed her. "Maybe later but for now I do want to talk about what's in those woods." And yet he couldn't help himself. "When I ran away from Stockton and Murat I hid in some bushes and found something which I think is really important to our quest."

Susan jumped a bit on the seat with excitement. The canoe tipped but steadied after they settled and sat quietly for a moment or two. "Sorry, but Sherlock found something important?"

"I was no Sherlock at that time trust me. I was a scared little rabbit. Anyway, while hiding I got stuck by a metal rod which wasn't a rod at all but part of an Iron Gate."

"And this is important why?"

"Right, I forgot that we didn't get a chance to explain what Andreas and I were translating in that cabin when Murat showed up." He went on to explain how Joseph Bonaparte had various tunnels dug from his house to different locations on the estate including the house he had built for his daughter (Zenaide) with his wife Julia Clary and her new husband (Charles Lucien Bonaparte), another one leading to the house of his mistress, Annette Savage and yet another to the Creek for an easy escape in case those seeking his demise actually got into the Mansion. After the fire destroyed the First Mansion those tunnels obviously collapsed or were filled in when the second Mansion was built he went on to say. "Anyway, I think I found the gateway to that escape tunnel."

Susan swung her arms around his neck, the paddle fell with a clunk and in an instant the canoe was floundering as they tried in vain to steady it. On the bank opposite the State Park side sat three people on some benches near several tied up canoes. They watched them approaching the Crosswicks Inn's backyard as it were when the mishap predicted just minutes before was about to take place. Professor Pettigrew, Professor Witherspoon and Detective Malone began to shout at them.

"Oh my word Andrew, aren't those your team members?"

"So it would seem Dorothy. Good God now what has Ron done?"

Susan was screaming, "We're going to tip over Ronnie; hold me or I'll drown."

"Don't panic, try to stand still and let the canoe float to shore," shouted Malone.

It was too late; over they went with a gigantic splash. Pettigrew ran to the Creekside with Malone at his side. Seconds later as they waded into the water to rescue them, up they popped. The creek was only three feet deep at that point.

"Ron De Cenza, what on earth were you thinking?"

"Don't be cross with him Professor Pettigrew. I just got excited and then this happened."

"Susan Liguri, you needn't protect your boyfriend. There's been no damage as I see that you two are just fine. Come up to the Inn and dry off."

"Where are the others?" asked Malone.

Coming down the Garden path between the azaleas and what was commonly called snowballs, came running the rest of Pettigrew's team.

"Oh my God Ronnie, Susan what happened to you?"

"Nothing Sis, we just tipped over the canoe. But that's not important Detective Malone is here, where is Captain Verdi?" He was taking off his Capri tee shirt and wringing it out. "We're kinda wet."

"No kidding, go inside and dry off; Susan is getting all hot and bothered seeing you like that," Jan whispered in his ear as he turned bright shades of red. "Come with me Susan, the guys can tell Detective Malone what just happened."

Ron unlike the girls had nowhere to go as he had no room at the Inn. He and Bob were to be transported back to the Mission House for the night. Bonnie and Steve were preparing dinner when they entered running to their room and Susan leaving a trail of puddles behind her.

"Could it be she fell in the creek?"

Steve smiled at his wife, "If she did, I'd say that boy Ron is also wet."

The ringing phone interrupted their laughter. "The Crosswicks Inn may I help you? Well yes he just arrived. In fact everyone in the Pettigrew party is here… yes of course I will get him." He placed the receiver down on the counter. "It's the police department asking for Captain Verdi."

The shirtless Ron stood on the path with Malone and Pettigrew facing him and the guys at his back. Dorothy Witherspoon and Sophia Verdi had the good sense to retrieve the maps for the excavation before they were blown into the creek. Pettigrew took off his tweed sport coat and placed it over Ron's shoulders.

"This should be fine until we find your suitcase and some dry clothes."

"I think my suitcase is still on the front porch…"

Steve's calling out to the Captain while running down the pathway to them stopped him from completing his sentence. "Captain Verdi, it's the Bordentown Police Department, they need to speak with you. It sounded urgent."

"*Scusi*, I need to get this. Malone, you should come with me. They will need to speak with you as well."

"The last time I got mixed up with these kids…oh well here we go again." Malone ran off with Verdi who was trying to give him a quick overview of what just happened on Prince Street by the Boat Launch.

Steve suggested that he take Ron and Bob to the service entrance at the rear of the B and B to avoid bringing water into the historic part of the Inn. Professor Witherspoon decided to present the excavation maps to those who remained. She was assigning jobs to each of the team members in total ignorance of what Ron had discovered in the woods.

When she got to Ron's name, it was Andreas who lied to her. "Professor Witherspoon, you needn't assign Ron or Bob a job; they have a special assignment already from Professor Pettigrew. They will have to come and go from the excavation site."

"Oh, I see, Andrew hadn't told me but then all this capsizing incident took place and…"

"And then they had to go get dried off," added Jan. "My brother, he's always in the wrong place but sometimes it's at the right time. Anyway, he and Bob are like brothers, they'll do their thing while we all do Pettigrew's thing."

"I don't understand the meaning of anything you just said…is it Miss De Cenza?"

Jan having just returned to the backyard smiled one of those half ass grins her brother was famous for. "Oh you'll understand soon enough Professor believe me. But for now I think our host had a great idea. Shouldn't we all freshen up before dinner?"

Witherspoon agreed though in taking the path to the front entrance she talked with Sophia about what happened at Princeton with the Crossbow being stolen and returned and probably being used in a murder up at Lake Bonaparte in upstate New York.

As they walked into the Inn, Antoine Murat was walking out of the Bordentown Police Station. His one phone call was to the Bordentown Inn. Carolina had sent Charles Benton to post a small bond. The only charge they could place on Murat was a misdemeanor of having oral sex in the woods with another adult male. His insults to Ron were not prosecutable and he could prove that he had no idea that Richard Stockton was wanted for the murder of Apollo Dimitri. Even what Ron heard in the bathroom could verify that fact. All of this was what the Sargent at the station was informing Verdi and Malone about in that phone call. The good news was that he was confined to the City of Bordentown and they knew he was staying at the Bordentown Inn pending further investigation.

The pressure on Carolina Gianetti was quite intense at this point. Stockton was somewhere out there but she didn't know where. She could not risk harboring a fugitive from justice and yet both, Benton and Murat, could have also had the time to kill the beautiful Apollo. So far only she realized that possibility. She would have to wait for Stockton to contact her. In the meantime now that Ron De Cenza and his friends knew of her presence she had to go on the offensive and that meant to get that Book. More importantly was getting those notes Murat saw in the Cabin about the possible location of Bonaparte's treasure. Murat would be given no time to recoup after his ordeal, he and Benton would have to get into the Mission House and into the rooms housing Ron and Bob. She knew that they would have the Book and the notes based on what Murat saw up at Lake Bonaparte.

Carolina was presenting her plan to Benton and Murat at the Bordentown Inn. At the same time in the Crosswicks Creek Room of Andreas and Dominic, Ron stood in the bathroom drying off and changing clothes. All the guys were sitting on the bed listening to Ron's story of what happened on the creek and poking each other. None of them thought of Ron as a romantic, even his Bride-to-be would agree on that point. After all wasn't it Dominic and Andreas who planned the moment of the proposal in the Blue Grotto for him?

"Shit, I forgot to bring in underwear. Bob, could you throw me a pair of underwear?

Bob looked at the guys and pulled a pair of tightie whities from Ron's suitcase but he also took out one of Alessandro's Italian style silk ones which emphasized the positives of the male anatomy. He still had them from when he had borrowed them back in Switzerland. "But Ronnie, I don't know which one. How frisky are you feeling?" The guys were muffling a roar of laughter.

Ron flew out of the bathroom wrapped in a bath towel. "Asshole, don't you think I've been through enough for one day." Instant silence followed. Was this going to become one of their famous brawls on the floor such as on Capri? "I should take the Italian ones because I'm staying with you tonight at the Mission House." He grabbed the Jockey briefs from Bob's hands and dropped the towel while pulling them up. "Have a good look because you're seeing what that asshole Murat never saw no matter what he said."

The guys all began to apologize at once; assuring him that they never meant to hurt him that they were just having a bit of fun after all that happened. Bob however slumped down on the edge of the bed holding the Italian silk briefs. He then threw them at Ron.

"You fucker, that's right fucker, you call me an asshole just like you did about Murat, me your best friend, your best man, your brother from another mother."

Ron pulled up his jeans and zipped. His jab hurt his pal in a way he never imagined. Calling each other 'asshole' was indeed their way to tease each other. It wasn't used in the same way about any of the other guys and certainly not when talking about Benton or Murat and their cohorts. It was their let us say special term of insult. Wringing the briefs in his hands he waved his hand for the guys on the bed to vacate it. They jumped up and stood at the bathroom door as he sat next to Bob.

"I'm sorry honest; I didn't mean it as a compliment of friendship for such a jerk. I meant it for real for him. Anyway, you called me the "F" word. Our Moms would be scandalized. And I think you went too far."

"I went too far. You asshole, I was just making a joke. Everyone knows how you hate to advertise your wares; that is until tonight."

There was a gasp from the guys. This could go two ways now. They could laugh or they could blow up in a fist fight.

Ron looked at Bob so forlorn and feeling rejected. "You called me an asshole."

"I know," a grin began to be formed. There was a sigh of relief coming from the guys watching the drama unfold.

"And they say we gays are drama queens," Dominic whispered into the ear of Andreas.

"So then does that mean I should change into these for tonight?"

"Shit no, I saw enough of you in high school to last a life time and tonight was too much."

"Santa Maria," Andreas yelled out. "You two had a gay fling in high school?"

Both Bob and Ron jumped to their feet as Ron threw the silk briefs at Andreas. "No, asshole, and we mean that with all our love not how we said it to Murat," Ron began. "At Oak Park High School guys had to swim in the nude in gym class."

"No girls were there, so don't think it was an orgy," Bob concluded.

"I see, I think," responded Andreas.

"So then, were your coaches gay?" asked Dominic.

"I don't think so. None of them ever tried anything with me or Bob."

"Or anyone we knew," added Bob. "They just sat at a table and handed us a towel as we came out of the shower room."

"*Madonna*," Alessandro exclaimed. "And they say that we Europeans with the nude beaches are progressive."

"Can we drop this now; my high school memories are being shot all to hell." Ron grabbed a souvenir tee shirt from his suitcase. This one was from Florence Italy with the Head of Michelangelo's David on it.

"Good, now Andreas, I hate to inform you but we're changing the sleeping arrangements for tonight. Bob and I need you at the Mission House. You'll bunk with us. Alessandro, you can stay with Dominic which leaves your room open for Malone."

"If that's what you think is best Ron, but are you angry with us because we suggested a gay fling in high school?"

"Ah, shit no man, it's just that I need you to translate passages in the Book and we both need you to help dig out the tunnel entrance that I think I found this afternoon."

Andreas hugged Dominic. "*Ciao bam*bino, I shall go with them. Miss me?"

"Always," he kissed him on each cheek in Italian style.

It was decided. After a quick dinner of pot roast Colonial American style with lots of veggies, so as not to insult their hosts, they all piled in the van to drop off Ron, Bob and Andreas at the Mission House. Everyone wanted to help with the digging but Ron squashed that idea saying that Malone, Verdi and Pettigrew would have too many questions and it may not prove to be anything at all.

The Main doors of the Mission House opened as they drove up. There stood David Chan who was about to lock up for the night for nightfall had indeed come. The chapel bells were ringing out the nine in the evening hour. The missionary student escorted them to their rooms in the retreat wing.

"Is there anything I can do for you before I leave," David asked.

Ron smiled. "Yes, we need flashlights for the excavation. Where can we get some?"

"I would think that your Professor Pettigrew has them with the equipment he arranged to have sent here. I'll show you the storage shed out back. Just lock it up when you get what you need."

As soon as David retired the three gathered in Bob's cell, for that's what they call sleeping rooms in Catholic Religious Houses. It was exactly like all the others, a twin bed, small dresser, a sink with a shelf and mirror above it and a small desk table with one chair. Ron and Andreas brought in their chairs. Bob took the Book and notes out of his satchel and spread them across the table. Ron paged through his notes to refresh what he and Andreas translated already which also caused the dream Ron had about the fire which burned down the first mansion of Joseph Bonaparte.

"Okay, it's time. We've got the idea of what happened. Now let's go prove that it did." Ron picked up the Book and placed it back in the satchel. "Bob, we'll take it with us, everything. Murat and Stockton and Carolina are out there and only God knows what they're planning."

What they were planning was to get into the Mission House grounds. Benton had been shopping at the local general store in Downtown Bordentown and returned to the Inn with bags of flashlights and small digging tools. They figured Pettigrew's team would be doing the heavy work and when they finished for the evening, they would come and check out the site. If they found anything then the plan was to wait until the excavation was concluded and steal anything of worth.

Carolina hoped that would be the Bonaparte Crown Jewels of Spain. She sent out Murat and Benton to the Point Breeze estate grounds. In the shadow of Clara Barton's historic schoolhouse Richard Stockton watched his colleagues leave the Inn about a half block away. When they drove off he walked along Farnsworth Avenue and slipped into the lobby.

With his satchel over his back, Bob also carried a burlap bag filled with flashlights. Ron and Andreas carried two shovels, a pick and smaller shovels and a rake. Down those granite steps toward the creek peacefully flowing they carefully treaded with one of those flashlights lighting their way. When they reached the creek's bank Ron stopped them about six feet from the end of the staircase. Taking the satchel from Bob he took out the only thing not related to the Book. It was a can of bug repellent which his Mom had brought from America to Italy for him, just in case they were not going to only explore in Switzerland as she put it.

"Okay, guys take off your shirts. We'll hang them on that branch in front of the Iron Gate and tie three flashlights with them to shine on where we'll be digging."

Off came Ron's Florence shirt, Andreas' Roma shirt with a Papal Guard on duty in St. Peter's Square and finally Bob's Mount Vesuvius erupting over ancient Pompeii. Ron created stage lights illuminating the area where he got poked by the iron bar. Then he sprayed his *amicos*.

"That should do it. My Mom said this should keep us from being eaten up alive when we're exploring. She should know that we're less than a thousand miles away from Oak Park Illinois."

First they began to tear out the dead brush, branches and vines to expose more of the Iron Gate. Than they picked at the rocks and dirt packed around it. Andreas used the pickaxe and the others shoveled out what fell off the mound against which the gate was embedded. What seemed an eternity of digging and shoveling in the August muggy night was only about an hour. The chapel bells were ringing out the time. It was Eleven in the evening.

"Oh my God, I think we hit something that's not dirt and stones. Hand me a flashlight."

Before handing the flashlight to Ron, Bob turned it on and shined it on the area where he said that he found something. Sure enough there were layers of brick forming a wall not just broken pieces impacted in dirt. They had the forethought to wear work gloves which they found in the tool shed and began to rub the brick wall which curved upwards in an arch over them. The bells were ringing and they were getting excited that they had found one of Bonaparte's tunnels. Was it just a piece of the tunnel, was the rest of it collapsed and filled in was not even considered. Rather they began to shovel harder to break through the century and one half old layer of dirt and debris.

The students and faculty of the Mission House were fast asleep but in the darkness there moved two shadowy figures towards that now unlocked tool shed. They crept into the shed and searched it in the darkness riffling through tools to find something to jimmy a lock on the Main House. A tool box was found and a screwdriver and hammer which Benton thought would work to pry open the back door. He lifted the tool box to bring into the moonlight outside but tripped on the only step leading into the shed and dropped the metal box. They froze as the crashing sound reverberated like an echo across the estate. All became quiet again. No lights were visible from their angle of view.

"For Christ's sake Benton why not just go ring the doorbell?"

"Shut the fuck up Murat; like you could do better. Help me find the hammer and screwdriver from this mess."

When they got the tools they thought necessary, the two made their way past the tree which Father Garcia had told Benton and Carolina earlier in the day as having been planted by Joseph Bonaparte. That's when Benton thought he saw a light in the woods. He took hold of Murat and turned him around telling him to look into the woods for a flashing light. They had no idea that it was three young men jumping around the opening of a tunnel.

The trio had broken through the layers of dirt and loose rock and found that the tunnel was not totally collapsed. Climbing through the hole they made, they crawled into the cave like tunnel. Despite having no clue if the tunnel was sound and firm, they made their way. Foot by foot, they moved forward, Ron in front and Andreas bringing up the rear. Each held a small shovel just in case there was a collapsed section ahead. What they had hoped to find was a clue of where the Crown Jewels were hidden. The house of Bonaparte was long gone so where did this tunnel lead to but to the foundation of that first house or so they thought.

The Midnight bells were now sounding as Murat told Benton that he too saw a light in the woods but that it suddenly was gone. They decided to abandon a break-in and check out the woods. They exchanged the hammer and screwdriver for two flashlights, turned off and walked in the bright Moonlight into the woods. What they didn't notice was David Chan standing at the back door which was their target in the first place. His room was on the other side of the building facing the woods. He too saw a light when the crashing noise disturbed his sleep. Dressed in slippers and white cotton pajamas he stepped outside and looked about. Though the flashlights were not turned on the moonlight was strong enough to create a visible silhouette. In only a few steps he came across the tool box and its contents strewn about the lawn outside of the shed.

It was clear to David that the two figures creeping across the excavation site were headed for the woods. Should he pursue them and do what or phone the police and possibly have them escape or do whatever they came to do while he did so; was the question he asked himself.

Inside the tunnel not a sound other than their crawling could be heard. The bricks forming the tunnel walls were damp and seeping water dribbled from some of them. So far they hadn't encountered any collapsed walls.

"Ron, how far do you think we've gone in?"

"I don't know Bob but I'd say each of us forms a five or six foot length on all fours so that's fifteen feet, I have been marking a brick every third time I moved from the previous mark. So in my estimation we have gone forty-five feet underground. Hold on guys; slowly come up next to me, I think we've hit another collapsed section."

The three shined their lights on the wall of dirt in front of them. They knelt in silence trying to figure out if it was just a small filled in section or the end of the road at what would have been the foundation of Bonaparte's house or just the bluff's soil. Bob began to get chilled.

"I'm cold; who would have thought in August it would be cool in here?"

"Ron shined his light on the Mickey Mouse watch on his wrist. "Holy shit; it's after Midnight guys. I think we should call it a night and finish up tomorrow. What do you say?"

"That seems reasonable to me." Andreas shined his light up and down the wall of dirt and shook as it came to something which was not dirt at the bottom. "Holy Mother of God, point your lights toward mine."

The beams illuminated the skeletal remains of a human. They were too long and straight to be that of an animal trapped when the tunnel collapsed. Besides there were pieces of deteriorated cloth and leather on parts of the remains, which consisted feet, legs, hips and part of the chest area, and still visible on the bones. The upper torso and head was still partially covered not by dirt but charred pieces of wood and broken brick.

"Oh shit Ron, we dug up someone's grave." Bob was making the Sign of the Cross over himself.

"I don't think so Bob. I think whoever this is got caught in the tunnel when it collapsed. Maybe if this really is the escape tunnel from the house as we suspected, he was returning to the secret entrance." Ron picked up one of the pieces of burnt wood and scorched brick.

"So what now; we can't just leave this poor thing here. We have to tell someone Ron."

"I know; one of us should go back to the Mission House and call the police." Ron held up the pieces. "If this is what I think it is, we have found the entrance to the Bonaparte Mansion's Library as I saw in my dream. And I think it may have collapsed when the house caught fire and burned down."

"Then the Book; it told us the truth. This is a Bonaparte tunnel and this might be someone from that first house."

"You're right Ron; don't touch anything else. I'll go back to the Mission House and call the police." Andreas turned to leave.

"Hold on one more second Andreas." Ron stooped over the remains and shined his light on a glittering metal of something just visible around the neck bone. "Look at this; it's gold, I think like a necklace of some kind."

"So then this could be a woman then."

"Maybe so Bob; or it could be a Chain with a Medal depicting a rank or service as was commonly worn in the time of Bonaparte." He brushed away some loose dirt around the neck; it revealed more of the chain and something else. There was a brick next to the skull of the person which was clearly crushed. "Oh shit, oh shit it can't be guys, it just can't be. My dream, the one where I was in the burning house in the secret room behind the library wall, in it I saw this man murdered. It was just like it was written in the Book of Bonaparte's life that we translated Andreas."

"Then this could be who Ron; not Captain Unzaga, Bonaparte's AIDE-DE-CORPS who was responsible for Joseph's safety?" Andreas stooped over the still brilliant gold necklace. "We still shouldn't touch anything Ron. I'll call the Crosswicks Inn and get the Professor here before we call the police. There's not much that they can do anyway. He's been dead since 1820."

"Yes, do that but know this; we do know who killed him. It was that spy Stanley Stonegate who passed himself off as a friend. He and that Russian woman were in league to destroy all things Bonaparte." He pulled out the Book and went to the marked section which was the cause of his dream. "It's written down right on this page in the margins in Latin no less."

At the outside of the tunnel Benton and Murat had found the flashlights fastened on the tree branch. Benton crawled through the hole of dirt. "It's a tunnel of some kind and I can hear voices and see faint lights."

Andreas stopped in his tracks. "Quiet you two; I can hear voices." The three huddled together keeping only one flashlight on and pointed to the dirt and brick floor.

Murat told Benton to get back outside that he had heard something in the brush. He was right. Down the stairs came David Chan and he easily saw the lights in the tree and the moving one being held by Murat.

"Hey there," called out David. "What's going on here?" He ran along the bank of the creek toward the lights in the tree.

Benton was crawling out of the hole when David appeared. Murat at first didn't know what to do or how to react to the young man in the pajamas. He began to back off as Benton got himself out and crawled away from the hole. He stood up and faced David.

"Listen kid, there's nothing going on here. We were just out having a bit of fun, if you know what I mean?"

"I do not know what you mean Sir and you will come with me to the Mission House and explain yourself to our Superior General, Father Garcia."

As this took place, Ron, Bob and Andreas made their way back to the entrance of the tunnel. Each few feet closer they could hear the voices more clearly.

"Hold on guys; I think that's the voice of David, the student who greeted us."

Benton who was at least four inches taller than the Seminarian came so close as the shadow of his beard could be noticed. "Now you listen to me young man. This could work out just fine if you go back to bed. We'll just be on our way and no harm will be done."

Murat slinked back behind the branch with the flashlights thus standing in darkness. He was patting the pocket of his jacket sagging with a heavy weight in it.

David stood his ground. "I'm not a little boy who you can order back to bed. Please follow me and we can end this amicably."

Ron crawled over to the hole through which they had entered the tunnel. "It is David and he's arguing with…shit, it's that Benton guy that we almost crashed into in Switzerland."

Andreas crawled next to Ron. "It's time for the soldier to do something." In an instant he was out and standing behind Benton motioning to David to step back and say nothing. "You there, what the hell are you doing?"

Benton swung around and recognized the Papal Guard. For a moment he said nothing but then he tried to continue his story of being in the woods seeking a good time. Andreas would not accept his fairy tale and told Benton to back off from the student. "Really, I think someone else today tried to use that story against my *amico* but it didn't work then and won't now. I know you and you're not into guys."

Murat, as this little confrontation was taking place, thought of just running away and leaving Benton to face Andreas alone. Then he thought of Carolina and her response to that so he again tapped on the pocket. He took from it the brick piece he had absentmindedly placed in it when he was hiding under the bridge listening to Carolina and Benton as they planned to cut out Stockton. He ducked under the branch and was now in the light. Ron crawled out of the tunnel telling Bob to keep the satchel safe no matter what happened.

He rushed Murat and tackled him at the ankles. Both went flying into the tree whose low hanging branch was holding the flashlights. The force jostled the branch and two of the flashlights fell out of the tee shirt holding it in place.

Benton reacted quickly and grabbed hold of David before Andreas could jump him. "Tell your friends to stop or say good-bye." He wrapped his arm around David's throat. The Missionary student struggled but to no avail.

Andreas in almost complete darkness save for ground light from the fallen flashlights and the one remaining in the tree tapped his crotch and stamped his foot then nodded to David. The message was received and he stomped on Benton's foot which startled the man so that he could turn and kick him between the legs. As he went down Andreas jumped on him and flattened him to the ground.

278

"Now you move asshole and it's going to be over for you."

Bob was now crawling out of the tunnel and being helped by David. Murat rolled across the ground with Ron on top of him. The brick he had held was dropped when Ron tackled him into the tree. He managed to get out from under Ron and as he tried to escape on all fours like a soldier in combat keeping low to the ground. He came across that brick. Quickly he grabbed it and turned just as Ron leaped onto him once again. The sole flashlight shined on the brick, Bob shouted and ran to push Ron away, David yelled and outran Bob as the hand with the brick came down to strike Ron. David pushed Ron aside and the blow hit him in the head. The Missionary Student screamed in pain. Stunned, he stiffened and fell into Bob's arms as he collapsed. Blood gushed from the side of his head.

Flames virtually flew out of Ron's eyes as he grabbed Murat and punched him in the face, then in the stomach and then in the face again. Murat had virtually no chance to hit back as one wild blow after another pummeled him. Bob shouted for him to stop, that the bastard wasn't worth the effort. Ron now had Murat held by the lapels of his hiking jacket shaking him. "You Son of a Bitch, if that kid dies you won't live to regret it."

Bob had never seen his pal in such a state. He cradled David who was moaning in pain. "Ron, please this guy needs help."

But Ron was deaf to Bob's words and the cry from Andreas to stop while he tried to restrain Benton with the belt from his jeans. Murat rattled but defiant looked in those flaming eyes of Ron. He tried to continue what he tried to imply to Captain Verdi and all the guys on Prince Street to further rattle him. "I give up. That naked beautiful chest of yours is so dirty and bloody but still it entices me. Let me comfort you."

Ron pushed him away. He was beginning to get himself in control. "You are a Son of a Bitch aren't you? It didn't work the first time with my friends and it won't work now."

Murat now pushed up against the trunk of the tree was planning his escape. Ron saw his eyes rapidly glancing to his right and left. He ran into him and rammed his arm onto his throat. "It's over asshole…sorry that's too good a term for you." He glanced back at Bob and smiled. He was returning to his Sherlock mode and to who he really was. Reaching up he grabbed hold of one of the tee shirts on the branch with his free hand. "Now this can go easy or it can get rough again. It's up to you."

It was over as the 2:00 a.m. bells rang out the hour. An aching Murat turned and let Ron tie his hands behind his back with the shirt. "Now sit and shut up." He pushed Murat to the ground, turned and went to help Bob taking the other tee shirt without a flashlight off the branch with him. "Turn this inside out to keep the dirt off the wound and press it on David's head." Then turning to Andreas he thanked him.

"Thanks *amico*, I needed that shout. Now if you could bring that jerk to that bastard on the ground and watch over them that would be great."

"I heard you almost call Murat an asshole and caught your smile. It's okay; he is a real asshole not like what we call each other." Bob had become Ron's shadow in the darkness.

"Shit Watson, stop being so nice to me. I can't take it. Let's get this kid back to the Mission House."

"I don't think it would be wise to move him. One of us should go and call an ambulance."

"Sounds good; I'll go if you two think you can handle the situation."

"I think Bob and I can take care of things here; you had best get this brave soul some help."

Off Ron ran to the stairs which was the scene which almost destroyed not only his reputation but his own image of who he was. After a slight pause and glance back at the light in the forest, he ran up the stairs and across the excavation site.

While the Mission House was being roused, Richard Stockton had entered the lobby of the Bordentown Inn. Seated in that lobby were Luigi and Pietro who recognized him and confronted him. They told him that he was jeopardizing the *Signorina* Carolina and the entire plan by being there. Stockton retorted that if she didn't help him he'd make sure that they never saw one penny of the Bonaparte treasure. They relented and had brought him up to the second floor. They also heard sirens screaming past the Inn as they entered the elevator but it meant nothing to them.

When the ambulance arrived it was not alone. Ron had also called the Crosswicks Inn and roused his friends, the Captain and Detective Malone who in turn alerted the Bordentown police. Thus a police car escorted the ambulance while the van driven by Alessandro as usual made its way on its own to Point Breeze estate. It was packed with not only Pettigrew and his team but also Malone, Verdi and Sophia and Professor Witherspoon, who, as it happened, was spending the night in Pettigrew's room so that she didn't have to disturb Susan and Jan or so the story went.

Alessandro pulled onto the grounds of the estate now the Divine Word Training Center as the bells rang out the 3:00 a.m. hour. They were met by several Missionary Students, Brothers and Priests who lined the roadway to guide them. They could see the flashing lights of the squad car and the ambulance which had driven onto the excavation site at the edge of the woods. He drove up to them.

Before anyone was allowed to exit the van, Malone made it quite clear that they were entering a crime scene. They were told to touch nothing and stay close together as there were so many of them. At the same time he did not want to prevent them from coming to the aid of their friends.

Landscape of Point Breeze with the First Mansion

Chapter Fifteen:
Discovery Amongst The Bones

The entourage made its way down the granite staircase or what remained of it. They slowly walked along the creek's bank toward a brightly lighted area in the woods which seemed to butt up against the wall of the bluff. Sophia Verdi held the arms of Jan and Susan reminding them that what they are about to see may be startling. She of course had no idea of what they saw in the ruins of Mellifont in Ireland; though she certainly was aware of what happened on Capri. She was, after all, there on her honeymoon when the murder took place. It was her way to keep things calm. Alessandro and Dominic walked directly behind Captain Verdi and Detective Malone while Professors Pettigrew and Witherspoon followed them.

"I should never have let them go without me."

"Really, so the research assistant thinks that he could have prevented this disaster."

"What are you saying Alessandro; just because I love a man that I cannot possibly help in a fight?"

The young Count of Pianore didn't know how to respond. He insisted that was not what he meant and yet in his heart he knew that is exactly what he was implying despite all that they had been through with the Vatican Murder, Mellifont mystery and the discovery of the Book on Capri. He became contrite and sullen as they came into view of a cluster of medics opening a stretcher. The area was floodlighted by spotlights powered by a generator which the fire department had brought in with the EMT's.

"Oh Christ Dominic, look at this; how could you or me have prevented this?" He turned to his *amico* and held out his hand. Dominic placed his into it. Alessandro pulled him into an embrace. "*Mi dispiacere,*" he had to apologize in their native tongue he thought.

"It's just that we're all on edge abut that damn Book, its clues, people out to steal it and hurt us in the process."

"*Va bene*, it's okay, I understand."

Malone and Verdi stopped and turned to face those following them. "Professors, you will see to the right what appears to be an opening in the mound of dirt. Ron has told me that it leads into a tunnel. That part of this scene is technically not a crime scene. You may enter it if you wish."

"Thank you Detective," Pettigrew responded, "but I think we need to see to the health and wellbeing of my team members caught up in this situation.

Witherspoon took his hand and gave it a squeeze. "I'm sure that they are fine Andrew, after all wasn't it Ron who called us?"

The shocked scream and muffling of it by Jan and Susan pierced through the scene before them as all heads briefly looked their way. They had seen the shirtless Ron and Andreas filthy with dirt and bloodied. Ignoring their own pain they were helping to lift what appeared to be a young man whose shirt had been removed by the medics as they worked on his vital signs. Two young men, dressed in what looked like pajamas of white cotton were helping the medics place the unconscious student onto the stretcher. At the head of it stood Father Garcia, who blessed David and traced the Sign of the Cross on his breast as his head wound prevented him from touching that area. The prayer having concluded, the medics lifted the stretcher with David's two friends, Sam Johnson and Daniel Rodriquez helping them to carry it. Rolling it would be impossible given the rocky terrain and stone stairs which they had to take to get to the ambulance.

Andreas and Ron with Bob at his side clutching his satchel stood in quiet reverence until David was taken away. Then they turned and grabbed hold of Benton and Murat still seated on the ground by the tree trunk with two Police Officers watching over them.

"Thank you officers," began Ron. "If you don't mind we'd like to have a word with these men."

They nodded their approval as Malone approached and signaled that it was all right to do so. The three, oblivious of their own wounds and bloody faces, chest and arms knelt before Benton and Murat. "It's over for you. Assholes that you are you can still get a break if you tell us why you were here and who else is part of this plan to do whatever."

Murat shot a glance at Benton to shut up. He would do the talking. "Suck my dick like you did on those stairs over there."

Ron didn't stir, he didn't lose his cool, he just smiled at Bob and then at Andreas at his side. Everyone could hear what was to be a quiet talk.

Susan grabbed hold of Jan's arm. "What's he saying Jan?"

"I don't know; it's just something to get my brother upset and in trouble." The she added, "as if he would hit him being handcuffed and restrained like he is."

Alessandro and Dominic however new exactly what Murat was trying to do. While Dominic got permission to approach Andreas, Alessandro made his way past the Professors and came up to the three women.

"Your brother was saved by that bastard Murat, cursed that he should be. But he didn't really want to save him; he wanted to be able to hold something over him, which would destroy his confidence and how he is viewed by others. Dominic could address that part better but let me just say that it was all an act to deflect Professor Stockton from seeing Ron who would then know that he was on to his scheme to steal the Book. He did nothing which should bring shame to him you do understand that don't you Susan?"

"Of course, let me get to him." She pushed her way through Verdi and Malone. "Ronnie, don't talk to them." She squeezed between he and Bob and that's when she saw how banged up he really was.

"Oh my God, Ronnie you're bleeding." She turned to seek out one of the medics but they were gone to the excavation site with the victim who was seriously wounded. She called out to Malone and Verdi to come and see what the brutes had done to Andreas and Ron. She pulled out a hanky from her purse and began to dab the blood over Ron's right eyebrow. "Here Dominic, I have a spare one you can use."

The tension eased as Susan and Dominic focused on Ron and Andreas. Malone ordered the officers to take the prisoners to the squad car but not to leave until he could speak with them. There would be no repeat of being able to get out on a bond before he even had a chance to question them. The officers picked each man up from the ground and stood them up. Ron stood in front of them.

"Murat, you are really a stupid ass and that's expressing it mildly. You could have been on our side and helped us uncover a historical legend but your greed got the better of you. And you Benton, you are so pissed at what happened to your ancestors that you joined forces with the likes of this guy and Carolina Gianetti."

Their eyes widened at the mention of her name.

"Of course I know about her but she won't get away with anything this night or any other."

The officers led them off as Malone had ordered them to bring back a First Aide kit and now was speaking with Bob and questioning him as to what happened. He quickly learned and then focused on the tunnel entrance. "It seems Professors Pettigrew and Witherspoon that Ron, Bob and Andreas have discovered a piece of history and a possible murder victim in the process."

"Okay Susan, I'm fine; we need to show Pettigrew what we found." He kissed the hand dabbing his face wounds. "I need to do this. Detective Malone hold on a minute. Captain follow us, we will show you exactly what happened here."

287 | Arthur Cola

The demonstration began with reassembling the flashlights on the branch, this time not with their tee shirts but with elastic bandages from the kit just brought back by Officer O'Meara. Then they showed them how they used the tools to dig around the Iron Gate until they created a hole which led them into an open space which turned out to be a tunnel. "I think we'll need to bring in a stretcher Sir, the skeleton at the end of this tunnel is that of a human and if I'm not mistaken, it is the Aide-De-Corps to King Joseph Bonaparte by the name of Captain Unzaga."

Malone, hardly the historian was nonetheless intrigued with the find. He was handed a flashlight by Bob and led to the entrance. "Sir, it's a tight squeeze at first but then it opens up and you can almost stand up straight for most of it."

The Captain stood ready to enter when he realized that his wife was missing. Sophia had gone after the officers when the talk of a stretcher began. She advised them to send back the medics with one as there was another victim in the tunnel. "I'll be right back Brandon."

He left Malone and sought after his wife, minutes later finding her talking with the officers taking the prisoners. She had joined Jan and Alessandro. They had decided that they could bring down the stretcher. While they were on the excavation site they spoke with Father Garcia and informed him of the other victim and as to who the victim might be. The priest called for some students and his faculty to fetch candles and clean linens. The deceased would be treated with all reverence and respect.

Running out of the woods, Captain Verdi called to his wife. "Sophia, there you are; you could have been hurt." He took her in his arms.

"Enrico please, not here. I am just fine; Alessandro and Jan would insure my safety. In any case we have the stretcher."

"So I see; so then I overreacted is that it?"

"No *cara mia*, it was very cute and sincere. I appreciate it even though it wasn't necessary." She kissed him on the cheek and took hold of his hand. Hand in hand they walked back into the woods. Jan and Alessandro took each end of the stretcher and followed them.

When they returned to the tunnel they found Malone, Pettigrew and Whiterspoon outside of it; everyone else was in the tunnel. They were forming a path for the Professors to follow holding flashlights to light their way. At the end of that now lighted path would be the skeletal remains which were found. Ron and Bob shone their lights on Captain Unzaga's bones.

Back at the tunnel entrance Jan entered first and Alessandro handed her the stretcher. She pulled it inside and he followed. Next went Professor Witherspoon followed by Pettigrew. Once inside they crawled to a wider space and opened the stretcher. Each of the four took hold of the handle. Malone pushed the generator nearer to the tunnel opening and then crawled through just as two missionary students, Sam and Daniel, appeared with linen altar cloths. They were followed by classmates holding candles. Captain Verdi and his wife accepted the linens and crawled into the tunnel. Should the tunnel be weak at any point such a number of people could easily cause a cave in. However all went smoothly.

Pettigrew and Witherspoon stood with bowed heads in awe of what they were seeing. The knelt down and examined the gold chain noticing that a medallion hung on it but was difficult to see given that the skeletal ribs covered most of it. "Ron, shine your light on this." Pettigrew pulled on the edge of the medallion and moved it out from under the remains. He flipped it over. "Dorothy, do you recognize this symbol?"

"I do Andrew; it's the Bonaparte Coat of Arms."

Pettigrew flipped it over. "And this shows what?"

She peered closely bending over but not touching it. "It's the rank of this person, I'm sure of it."

Ron couldn't resist. "Actually it shows the rank of Captain. This man is Captain Unzaga the Aide-De-Corps to Joseph Bonaparte. He was murdered on the January 3, 1820 during the fire which destroyed the first mansion."

"And what gives you such confidence that this is he, Mr. De Cenza?" Witherspoon asked not knowing the story of the Book found on Capri. Pettigrew had not shared that tale with her given what happened in the Pancake House and the subsequent chase from Princeton to Bordentown.

Ron smiled and nodded to Andreas and Bob. Andreas took the Book out of Bob's satchel and handed it to Ron. "This Professor is the autobiography of Joseph Bonaparte."

Andreas then read its title in French. "The memoires et correspondance Politique and Militaire du Roi Joseph."

Ron continued. "The three of us, Andreas, Bob and I, have translated a significant part of it as well as the handwritten notes in its margins which were made either by King Joseph or his secretary, one Louis Maillard his lifelong assistant since he was thirteen years old."

"Andrew, is this true, have they discovered something which may change history?"

"Dorothy, you have no idea what these young men and women have done even before I came to know them. They saved Michelangelo's Pieta from being stolen, they discovered how the Royal family of Italy was railroaded out of the country while saving the Italian government in the process, they found the Holy Grail of Ireland and then they solved a murder on Capri where they found that Book. In short, yes this is an impressive find which will impact how the world views the historical period of the Bonaparte Family."

"I do apologize for trivializing your abilities."

"Oh that's nothing Professor Witherspoon, wait until he demonstrates his Sherlock ability; but wait that's why we are standing here isn't it?"

"Cool it Watson, this is not a time for games."

"But Ron, the game is afoot isn't it?"

"Indeed pal but let us defer to our friend Professor Pettigrew and the archeological Professor. Professors, what should we do next?"

Bob answered before they could. "First don't you think we should say a prayer for the repose of Captain Unzaga's soul? You Ron, Andreas and I know why and how he died. He deserves to be honored. He fell in the line of duty serving his King, in exile or not Joseph Bonaparte was his King."

A chorus from all those gathered in that tunnel agreed. They decided that since Bob, shirtless or not, was the closest thing to a member of the clergy with them that he should lead the prayer. It began with everyone singing Holy God We Praise they Name, praying the Lord's Prayer and ending with Bob calling for the Angels to take the soul of Captain Unzaga to heaven.

The tone had been set. Pettigrew then instructed that one of the altar linens be placed over the canvas of the stretcher. The remains would be transferred on it and then covered with the other linen. The gold chain with its medallion of rank was then placed on top of the remains. Ron, Bob, Andreas, Alessandro, Dominic, and Captain Verdi acted as pall bearers one hand holding onto the stretcher bar and the other a flashlight. They were then led out of the tunnel by Jan, Sophia and Susan carrying candles which were brought to them by David's classmates. Malone exited the tunnel first finding Father Garcia and the students lining the path to the stairs and up the stairs to the excavation site; all were holding lighted candles. A procession was formed and followed the candle lighted path to the Chapel where the remains would be placed until arrangements could be made for a proper funeral. The bells sounding the hours were silenced as they rung the 5:00 a.m. hour and the single tolling of the bell of mourning replaced the hymn.

Detective Malone decided that given the hour everyone should get some rest. Father Garcia would arrange for a funeral and they would regroup after that to pursue Stockton and Carolina Gianetti. He had little confidence that Murat and Benton would be helpful in finding them. That opinion seemed quite probable as Stockton after his meeting with Carolina was to be hidden until they could regroup. Then they would join Murat and Benton to kidnap Ron if necessary in order to get the Book. That plan was to bite the dust later the next day.

Stockton had been taken to a camping site in the State Park. There they could keep tabs on the progress of Professor Pettigrew's excavation team. Little did they know that the flickering lights they would see across the creek and coming out of the woods that night was a procession with the remains of Captain Unzaga. Luigi was to camp with Stockton while Pietro was to return to the Bordentown Inn and protect Carolina. They would leave in the morning to meet up with the other two at the camp site.

The next morning Carolina was soaking in the tub and listening to the radio. She had called to Pietro. He hesitated at the door and asked what she needed. She told him that she needed him. The big man beamed at the prospect to have Cavelli's mistress but more so to have bragging rights over Luigi who fancied himself as a great Italian lover. He entered the bathroom to find her in the tub, her smooth left leg hanging out over the edge.

"It's going to be another warm day Pietro, you look like you need to relax and be refreshed."

With all his boasting he stood there not knowing what to do or how to react. She was after all his former boss' mistress but more than that she was now his boss as well.

She plunked her leg down in the tub causing it to splash out water. "Well, what are you waiting for; strip and get in here."

He slowly followed her order. After he hung his suit coat on the hook, he placed his shoulder holster with his gun over it. Then he kicked off his shoes. Her eyes twinkled with delight as he unbuttoned his shirt to reveal a chest filled with dark hair. She was becoming impatient as he hesitated after each button and was taking too long. She jumped out of the tub, the suds dripped from her body and his eyes froze on her breasts. She ran to him and ripped out the shirt and began to unbutton his pants, pulling them down and revealing his silk Italian style briefs.

"Are you as beautiful down there as was my Apollo?"

"Apollo, he was with the men; I make love with women."

"Ah so they say; but he was beautiful; every part of him…" she grabbed hold of his package. He could please a woman if he wanted to. Can you please me?"

The blood surged through his male member and he kissed her neck. It was at that moment that the ten in the morning news came on the air. They were announcing the capture of two men in the woods of the Point Breeze estate grounds. Carolina pushed Pietro away and told him to pick up his pants.

"Get dressed; do you not hear what they are saying?" She grabbed a towel, wrapped herself in it and stormed out of the bathroom as the names of the men captured were being announced.

Malone had deliberately released the news of the capture of Murat and Benton, both with family names familiar in the Bordentown area given the connection those families had with Joseph Bonaparte. The detective did so with the hope of forcing Stockton's hand. At that time he didn't realize that Carolina and Benton had been at the Mission House earlier the previous day.

The ten o'clock morning news was not heard by Malone or anyone else in the excavation team as they had hardly been asleep four hours when it was broadcasted. Thus in peaceful repose, as the poet wrote, they slumbered in blissful ignorance while running onto the camp site just across the Crosswicks Creek came Luigi with an armful of supplies from the grocery store.

"Stockton, get your ass up." He kicked him in that area of which he spoke.

The Professor was not use to being treated in such a fashion and told him to fuck off, it was early and Carolina wasn't coming until Noon. As for Luigi, no one had dared to speak to him in such a fashion and not expect a beating. He pulled Stockton out of his sleeping bag, his boxers almost coming off in the process and threw him to the ground. In colorful language he described Stockton as being born of a female dog and sucking not on her breast but on the dick of he who sired him. Standing in the morning sunlight in his plaid boxers, Stockton had nowhere to turn. Virtually naked, he had nothing to fight back with, except his words and one thing more. He pulled on his boxers and grabbed himself.

"So tell me hot shot, does this make you drool for a taste. Come, I'll forget that this ever happened, kneel before me and enjoy yourself." He smiled but his whole body was shaking with fear.

Luigi was enraged; he couldn't keep himself in control. He lunged for Stockton knocking him to the ground. He stood over him as if he was about to assault him as he unzipped his pants.

Sweat poured off Stockton's brow but he had no choice but to egg Luigi on. "So then you do like the men as you said Apollo did?"

It worked. He jumped away from Stockton and zipped up. Turning to run off and leave Stockton stranded he ran into Pietro. He had been running around the camp area searching for them. "Pietro, good...kill Stockton. We shall split his share of the treasure."

The confused Pietro didn't have time to respond.

Stepping out from behind a clump of trees was Carolina, dressed to kill in lime green Capri pants with a sheer matching top and wearing a white wide rimmed linen hat. "And what treasure would that be Luigi? The one we have yet to find or perhaps by some miracle you have found it for me already." She glanced at Stockton now pulling up the sleeping bag to cover himself. "Don't flatter yourself Professor; you are nothing like my Apollo or even my Niccolo from what I can see."

"This man is a lunatic. He threatened me and then attacked me."

She turned to Luigi and stroked his cheek. "And why are you so upset? Could it be that you have heard the news that Murat and Benton have been arrested?"

"So you heard too; is it true?"

"So it would seem. But that's not important right now. They won't talk. They'll think we will bail them out as before. And in that thought they would be wrong. We shall do as we planned and keep an eye on the excavation. Professor, go make yourself presentable; no one will have their way with you or harm you." Carolina took Luigi and Pietro by their arm and walked away from Stockton. "Now listen carefully; we need Stockton even now under these circumstances now that Benton and Murat are out of circulation. When we finally get that damn Book, he will be able to put all the pieces together concerning the Bonaparte jewels."

Now she had their interest. "*Si, Sigornina*, but what if the English Professor finds the jewels; the Book will be useless to us."

"True Pietro, but it will be our insurance policy so that they shall not be able get to the jewels before we can."

They stood at the edge of the Creek and looked over to the other side which was the grounds of the former Point Breeze estate. There was no activity but she could clearly see the generator still in the spot where Malone put it at the tunnel entrance. She knew something happened last night that got Benton and Murat arrested. In all probability it had something to do with that excavation site and the small bluff where the generator and light stand could be seen. She decided that it would be worthwhile to cross the creek and see what happened close up. However that decision created another problem which was that they had no boat. To keep Stockton away from Luigi, she sent him and Pietro to look for the camp grounds office to see if boat rentals were available. As they trotted off the feint sounds of bells could be heard coming from across the creek. She counted the chimes of the bell; it was eleven in the morning.

Malone checked his watch and noted the time as he and Verdi entered the Bordentown Police Station at the same time that Carolina was listening to the chimes. They were preparing to question Murat and Benton but separately; in fact their plan was to keep them apart so that they could not conjure up a story. To that end they were kept in separate cells on opposite ends of the holding area. Both locked up men had their chance to make their call. Benton called the Bordentown Inn and was informed that Carolina Gianetti had checked out around ten in the morning. He went ballistic mainly to give Murat the chance to hear the news that Carolina was gone. When he calmed down, Murat was brought to the Sargent's desk to make his call.

Murat's problem was now that Carolina seemed to be out of the picture, he had no one to call. He could not call the New Yorker Magazine and get one of their lawyers as he really wasn't a reporter for them. That was all a deception used at Lake Bonaparte so that he could meet Apollo and later the young people who were part of a research team on Birch Island. He decided to call Francois Parrot, owner of the cabins where they all stayed, up in Lake Bonaparte. Perhaps he could recommend a lawyer in Princeton as he went to the University there. In any case, that's where he and Benton would eventually be transferred as both were not in the clear about being the murderer of Apollo Dimitri. Even though Stockton was the prime suspect the others also had opportunity and as for the motive, it was clear that Murat had formed a relationship with Apollo.

As for Benton, he had one with Carolina who lusted for Apollo. It was a love triangle between Murat, Apollo and Carolina with Benton as her surrogate as he arrived in New York after the failure to steal the Book in Switzerland before she did.

Those same 11:00 a.m. bells were being heard in the Mission House. Father Garcia had delayed Morning Prayer several hours to 10:00 A.M. because of the events of the previous night which ran into the wee hours of the morning. The Brothers, Priests and summer resident Students had attended the service. Ron, Bob and Andreas were not expected to do so, given the circumstances of needing medical attention after the fight and subsequent apprehension of Benton and Murat. That service was held outdoors as in the chapel held the remains found in the tunnel. A Forensics team with the Medical Examiner was taking samples of the bone, and checking the skull and brick found next to it. That brick was still stained, almost 150 years later, with the victim's blood. Standing next to the M.E. like his shadow was Ron De Cenza. He was holding the gold chain and medallion found on the victim as if it was a holy relic such as they found in Ireland over a year ago.

Despite being beat up and exhausted he had a restless sleep. Once again that nightmare of that day on which the Bonaparte mansion was set on fire and destroyed flashed through his mind. Once again, he saw Captain Unzaga chasing after the so called Courier who was in league with a spy from Britain named Stanley Stonegate. And once again the flash of that scene as the mansion burned and the tunnel was collapsing was vividly imagined as that spy took one of the falling bricks and crushed the side of Unzaga's head. All of this he could see happening again as the coroner examined the remains found in the tunnel.

By the time the Noon hour was being announced by the bells and the chimes rang out the hymn of the Angelus, "Hail Holy Queen" the M.E. and his team, were finishing their examination and had taken their samples for analysis. The remains being so old it would be impossible to prove the identity of the person were it not for the few pieces of clothing, Chain of Office and what was found written in the Book on Joseph Bonaparte's life.

There was one thing more which was found but no one knew about it. When the bones were lifted out of the dirt and placed on the altar linen covering the stretcher canvas, Ron caught a glimpse of something that was not cloth, bone or golden chain. He had kicked the dirt gently and a leather pouch was revealed. Just before the procession began he slipped it into the side pocket of his Levis. What followed was so emotionally draining what with making sure the Missionary Student, David, would survive, the procession of the remains to the chapel and his own aches and pains from the fight that the pouch had become something which could wait.

Now in the chapel he began to feel guilty for not informing Malone or Verdi or anyone for that matter of what he had done with the pouch. Certainly Pettigrew and Witherspoon could have identified its age, maybe how it was made and so forth. As he prayed the Act of Contrition as a way to perhaps ease his guilt for not sharing the news, Doctor Kumar announced that the examination was concluded.

"Mr. De Cenza, you may inform Father Garcia that the planning of the funeral may commence. I shall contact Detective Malone, about the details of my findings as soon as I am able." He then directed his assistants to cover the remains and then gather their samples and materials.

Within five minutes, they were gone and Ron stood alone holding what could possibly be a priceless piece of history from the reign of King Joseph Bonaparte of Spain. He placed it back on the linen covering. He would leave it to Pettigrew and Witherspoon to determine its historical and actual value.

Taking the heavily worn and decaying pouch from his pocket he spoke to the bones. "Do you have something to say to us Captain Unzaga?" He pulled back the flap. The interior of the pouch was lined with another layer of material; it looked like fur of some kind.

And this lining protected what looked like a heavy duty paper, perhaps a letter, Ron was thinking. He reclosed the pouch. He could not bring himself to take out the paper. What if it disintegrated when he touched it, what if the air itself would cause it to crumble to nothing? He knew what he had to do. Off he ran through the chapel but not outside rather he took the side entrance and entered the hallway which led to the Retreat wing. He would rouse his pals Andreas and Bob, share the news of his finding and then call Professor Pettigrew to come to the Mission House as quickly as he could with Professor Witherspoon.

He pounded on Bob's door and then the door of Andreas' room and back again to Bob's room. The door opened and two blue eyes peeked out. "Shit Ron, what's wrong with you. We didn't get to bed until six in the morning."

"I can't keep it to myself any longer, let me in."

Bob swung open the door just as Andreas poked his head out of his room. "Ron is that you? What time is it?"

"It's already Noon. Come over to Bob's room, it's important."

"Right now; can I get dressed?" He stepped into the hallway in his underwear of a more traditional kind which the Papal Guard soldiers wore. It reminded Ron of one of his classes when he studied Religions of the World. Those undergarments were either designed by Michelangelo when he created the Swiss Guard uniform or copied from the Mormons.

"You're covered just come over." Ron entered Bob's room. "Oh shit, you're still wearing those sheep and clouds PJ's your Mom bought you three years ago when we entered the Abbey's Latin School?"

"So what's it to you; they have plenty of wear left in them."

"You're twenty-one years old not eight that's what."

"Go to hell. Don't look if it bothers you and another thing…"

Andreas entered the room and began to laugh.
"Well you can both just go to hell together as if that thing you're wearing is not laughable."

"*Amico*, it's just that after all we've been through to see such funny clothes brings on amusement. Ron don't you agree? It is not an insult, we still love you." He ran to Bob and gave him a bear hug.

"Yeah okay, I get it. I love you too…"

"Am I included in that pal?" Ron stood with his arms outstretched. Andreas released Bob.

"Yes, you too," he gave Ron a slight embrace. "Now let's just drop the subject shall we? So what's so important that we couldn't sleep?"

Ron pulled Bob's desk to the middle of the room. The bright noon sun shone through the window and he didn't want it to directly hit the pouch. "Just this," he pulled out the pouch and laid it on the desk.

"It looks old, like something our great great grandfather might have for a wallet."

"Watson, that's it. This must be Captain Unzaga's wallet."

"Holy shit, are you saying that…"

"Yes that's what I'm saying. I found it in the dirt under his bones."

"Madonna, can this be? Ron is there something in it?"

"Actually there is, but I couldn't make myself take it out without having the Professors here to do it properly."

"I think that is wise," noted Andreas.

"But is it something Sherlock would do?" asked Bob.

Ron plopped himself down onto the wooden desk chair, leaned his chin onto his hands and began to study the brownish leather wallet. "Listen pal, Sherlock Holmes wasn't real."

"I know that but what he did and who his character was…well that is real just like us. And think about it, he was a detective but also a scientist of sorts always examining things and finding clues to come to his conclusion."

Ron looked up from the leather pouch. "I know, but we're talking about a dead guy's wallet and not just any old dead guy. He was the Aide-de-Corps to Joseph Bonaparte kind of his protector."

"Exactly Ron, and wouldn't he want you to know what he carried in that wallet? It might be something which leads us to the Crown Jewels."

Andreas was getting concerned that Ron was being talked into examining the wallet. "You're right *amicos*; this may have something in it or it may just be 19th century money after all it's a wallet. Listen, the bells are ringing. Holy *Madonna*, it's one o'clock. The Professor will be here with our *amicos* any minute."

Ron jumped up from the chair. "You're right and you two need to get dressed *pronto*. We'll do this with the Professor." He had returned to his commitment which he made in the chapel.

Bob was unbuttoning his PJ top and insisting that they need to have lunch before anything else. "We need our strength for the dig and this too."

"Food, really; we are about to prove that a century and a half old legend may be true and all you can think about is your stomach."

The retort he got was a pitiful look on his pal's face as he wiggled his stomach. He then pounded on it as if it was an empty drum. That got both he and Andreas in stitches. "Gross, okay, okay we'll have lunch but first go shower. I'll greet everyone and fill them in on what we have here."

Andreas made for the door but Bob took hold of Ron's shoulders and looked into his eyes, "You will do no such thing until we eat, got that."

"Right, we'll talk about it at lunch, how's that?"

A broad grin crossed Bob's face as he finally felt that Watson had finally gotten his way. He joined an amused Andreas at the door and off they went to the shower room. Standing alone and staring at the wallet Ron moved toward the desk. His hand shook as he went to pull open the flap thus abandoning his commitment to wait for Professor Pettigrew. His conscience was telling him that he was betraying his pals. His investigative instincts were telling him that he was about to uncover a historical treasure and his scientific brain again brought him back to the possibility that his hand and even the air in the room may harm whatever was in the wallet. Science won out. He grabbed a fresh hand towel wrapped it around the wallet and went to look for a pair of gloves like the ones Dr. Kamar and his team had used when examining the remains. He headed for the Chapel with the hope that they had left some behind.

The house of Louis Maillard, Secretary to Joseph Bonaparte,
commonly called the Gardener's House.
Point Breeze Estate Grounds, Bordentown New Jersey

Chapter Sixteen:
The Final Clue

When Ron ran into the Chapel, he found it filling up with the summer resident Missionary Students being led by Father Garcia and the faculty. They were entering the pews on what the priest called the Blessed Mother side of the Chapel. While this was taking place in walked Professors Pettigrew and Witherspoon and his friends through the front doors which faced the Hammond Rock formation and gardens. They all stood in the back of the Chapel waiting for Father Garcia to tell them what they should do. Ron didn't wait. He slipped in back of them and took hold of Susan's arm turning her to face him and placed a kiss on her cheek.

"Good morning...I mean afternoon."

"Ronnie De Cenza, we're in church. What's gotten into you?"

"Shh, nothing except that I think we found something which will help prove the legend of Bonaparte's treasure."

"No kidding..." he planted a kiss on her lips to keep her from shouting.

His sister put an end to it. "Ronnie, stop that; what's going on?"

The others gathered around the two wondering the same thing. Dominic in particular asked where Andreas was. Ron told him that he and Bob were taking their showers and that he should go get them. Then he asked what was going on; why was everyone being brought to the chapel. "I was just here a couple of hours ago with the Medical Examiner and no one else was around."

Coming up to them, were Father Garcia flanked by Pettigrew and Witherspoon. "Perhaps, I might be able to shed some light on the matter," the priest began.

He explained that Dr. Kamar had called him to give permission for the funeral. Ron felt instantly guilty of not fulfilling his duty. He got so caught up with the wallet that he forgot that informing the Superior General was his job. He stood with a bowed head holding the wallet wrapped in the towel as the priest continued. By the time he concluded they knew that the local undertaker had brought a burial vault to hold the simple wooden casket, also delivered some twenty minutes ago, in the burial plot. They also learned that the funeral Mass would be in the evening so that as the sun was setting the remains of Captain Unzaga would be lowered into the ground. This would give the excavation team a chance to do their work during the day the priest suggested. He then excused himself and returned to his students to lead them in the afternoon prayer. They would talk further at lunch which was to follow.

As soon as Father Garcia left, everyone including the two Professors swarmed around Ron who was now backed up against the side door. It opened and he fell into Andreas and Bob with Dominic behind them. He tightened his grip on the towel wrapped Wallet which drew attention to it as he brought it up to his chest. Pushing the three behind him back into the hallway, the others followed.

Professor Pettigrew felt that he had to do something after all it was his Excavation project which the priest mentioned. He couldn't take his eyes off the towel as he spoke. "Let's all calm down here. Last night was a rather frightening and harrowing one. The Mission House almost lost one of their own. Only the quick action of Ron, Andreas and Bob saved him from being killed. I have been informed that today he rests comfortably in the hospital and should be back this evening."

The news was well received, yet at the same time they knew Pettigrew wanted to say more and have questions answered. They were correct.

The Professor went on to say that the excavation would take place despite the find in the tunnel and the tunnel itself. It was his hope that more would be learned about the destroying of the first mansion.

"However, before we do that, perhaps Ron would like to explain what he's holding so firmly in his hands."

Susan poked Ron in the ribs lightly and urged him to share any news he had. The young man was slipping into Sherlock mode and Bob could see it. His mind filled with a view of what they found last night. The finding of the gold chain with medallion, the remains of Captain Unzaga and the tunnel itself was all because of what was discovered in the Book and the notes in the margins of its pages. It was his duty to follow through with what he now knew and continue the investigation with examining what he held. He suggested that everyone come to Bob's room as that's where the Book was and he felt confident that it would be needed.

Sophia who was with the Professors since Captain Verdi went with Malone to the Police Station asked if she should call her husband. Everyone agreed that he and Malone should get back to Breeze Point as soon as possible. Antoine Murat and Charles Benton could stew in their separate cells for a bit longer. Professor Witherspoon said that she would go with Mrs. Verdi so that she could contact the University and insure that the gallery with the Crossbow was on lock down and that the Princeton Police be informed that Stockton was still on the loose but others were captured.

As the two women sought out the office and the others made their way into the Retreat Wing the hymn of "Oh Most Holy One" could be heard from the Chapel. As they walked through the doorway leading into the wing two men were coming out of one of the cells.

"Hey you, what's going on?" yelled Ron.

The two men looked for a way out, found none except another door to the next room from which they had come out. They ran into it, locking the door behind them, they then went to the window.

Bob was hysterical as the room they entered was his and he thought he recognized who they were. He was shouting that it was the two guys from Capri who they fought. "It's Luigi and Pietro, I'm sure of it."

There was no time to question the identity and how they were in America. They had to react quickly. Ron pointed out that the only way out was the hallway or the window in the room. He began to shout orders, "Andreas and Dominic go to that next room, Bob and I will take my room, Professor, you, my sister and Susan take the back door at the end of the hall. Make sure that they don't double back. No way that they'll come out here but they may head for the woods. We'll have to jump out of the windows but so will they.

Luigi and Pietro found that they were in Bob's room though they didn't know it. They only recognized the satchel which Carolina told them held the Book. Pietro opened the window as Luigi grabbed the satchel and pulled the strap over his neck. One then the other jumped from the first floor window and tumbled onto the grass beneath it. As they rolled and then lifted themselves up, the guys were shouting at them as they jumped from the other windows creating a waterfall of humans crashing onto the lawn. Ron had given the towel wrapped Wallet to Pettigrew telling him it was the key to what they found last night as he sent him off with Susan and Jan. They were running around the back end of the building as the guys were in hot pursuit. The thieves were in a panic as they realized the woods through which the creek flowed and where their rowboat was tied downstream was on the other side of the building.

Seeing the rock formation with the cave they ran towards it. They thought that they could hide there or between the rocks. It wasn't until they got to them and saw the turquoise blue water of the pool with the mosaic bottom that they remembered that it was all a decoration. The cave was just a passageway from the pool to the backside of the mountain of rocks. It was where Alessandro had bound them after being captured. They nonetheless headed for it. They would hide on the backside, climb up the rocks. When their pursuers couldn't see them and gave up, they would circumvent the backside to the road. Then they would run across the excavation site into the woods and down the bluff to their boat.

As the girls ran after the guys toward the rocks, Pettigrew tightly holding the item in the towel yelled that he would go fetch the women in the office. Alessandro and Dominic were well ahead of Ron and Andreas given they were still hurting from the fight with Murat and Benton the previous night which was actually pre-dawn hours of the current day. And then there came Bob, who hated running. Such abhorrence of running went back to his being in the same gym class with Ron. It was in their Freshman year in college. He never finished running the mile course. But he was plugging along nonetheless when the girls caught up to him.

"Bob, what's wrong with Professor Pettigrew, asked Susan. "He's holding onto that towel like it held the Crown Jewels of Spain that we're trying to find."

He paused to take a deep breath. "It's a long story and now's not the time to tell it. But it's important that he guard it with his life; next to the Book it's invaluable." He began to run again.

He needn't have worried about Pettigrew; he understood its importance if not its contents. Witherspoon and Sophia came running out of the main entrance doors which faced the Rock Formation and saw everyone yelling and running toward the rocks. They could hear the cursing and shouting all the way at the front of the Mission House. The building was actually a long two story building with a back wing which housed the Retreat Center. That wing was reserved for those who came to pray and meditate in a peaceful environment. It was damn lucky that none were scheduled on that hot third week of August.

From their vantage point they could only see the guys, Susan and Jan. Until Sophia thought she saw something crawling on the huge rock backdrop of the pool. She began to scream which only served to stop everyone in their stride. "The rocks look up at the rocks."

The words were still being understood when Luigi jumped off the rocks directly above Alessandro crashing both of them onto the garden area and rolling toward the pool. Even though the young Count of Pianore was a big guy, Jan's description of him as being a living Michelangelo's David was not far off; the impact threw him for a loop. Dominic was the closest to him and lunged for Luigi. He was one of those tall, dark and handsome Latins but hardly a fighter. Soon all three were rolling over each other as Ron and Andreas entered the fray and pulled Luigi off of their *amicos.*

As they did that, Pietro jumped down from the rocks taking out both Ron and Andreas who were thrown off balance and rolled into the pool. Bob was at the pool's edge by then and sought to help them by jumping in but all that did was create more confusion as now Alessandro and Dominic were fighting both Pietro and Luigi. Quickly the girls fished out Bob while Ron and Andreas crawled up onto the lip of the pool. Before they realized what was happening, Dominic came flying over their heads and luckily into the cool waters of the pool and not the cement trim which bordered it. As Andreas dove back in to get him; Ron was up and running to help Alessandro who now was holding off two huge guys. Bob was coming around the end of the pool with the girls who now held small rocks in their hands. As soon as they had a clear shot which wouldn't harm Alessandro, they would be used.

Carolina's goons felt the situation may now get out of control for them. Luigi shouted to Pietro to follow him. One last punch into Alessandro's face sent him flying backwards tripping over Bob and causing both of them to take a plunge into the pool.

309 | Arthur Cola

The hiking boots which Alessandro was wearing didn't help him to stay afloat. But Bob's built in inner tube did and he pulled the young Count to the side of the pool.

Cutting through the fake cave, Luigi and Pietro ran behind the rock formation to the outer edge of the estate and back toward the road. In the middle of that road stood Professor Andrew Pettigrew, Sophia Verdi and Professor Dorothy Witherspoon all waving their hands frantically in the air. They were shouting at a dark sedan coming down the road from the front entrance. The protectors of Carolina ran behind them and onto the excavation site as the sedan screeched to a halt. Pettigrew handed off the towel wrapped item to Witherspoon and gave chase. The archeologist stood in awe that the man from Oxford was such a virile man and a courageous one as well. She tucked the towel into her purse and followed Sophia to greet the two men jumping out of the unmarked police car.

"Enrico, there was a fight; two big men hurt the boys."

Verdi said nothing but kissed her on the cheek. "Malone, I know those men. They got off when we arrested them with their boss Niccolo Cavelli on Capri. I'll be damned if they'll get off again." He began to run after Pettigrew shouting for him to wait up. The Oxford man did not and ran into the woods.

Malone shouted that he'd follow as soon as he radioed for help. Within a minute he was running towards the woods as well.

"My Enrico, he goes to save your man for he knows that those two who did that to our boys are evil." She pointed to the pool area where Jan and Susan were now trying to deal with the aftermath of the fight. Each of the boys they had stretched out on the side of the pool. They took off their boots and gym shoes and had them soak their feet in the water. Why they had no idea but it seemed to calm them. Ron was first to sit up and demand the return of his shoes.

"Those assholes won't get away with this again. This isn't going to be Capri all over again," he looked at Susan, "Pretty please with sugar on top."

The rumble of snickering could be heard from the other guys but not from Alessandro. Jan was dabbing his bloody hands and face with one of the towels she took from a stack unnoticed in the corner of the cave. They were made available for swimmers to use when visiting the Mission House at Point Breeze. Every one of the guys was soaked to the skin though the August heat made that condition rather comfortable in a soggy sort of way. There was, however, no time for anyone to even think about changing into dry clothes not with Luigi and Pietro on the loose. None of them were aware of what was going on across the road until Sophia and Witherspoon showed up with the news and the towel wrapped item.

Sophia couldn't control her emotions. Tears were flowing as she tried to tend to their wounds. She was a professional nurse and checked for bone breakage, and lacerations which needed attention. She called them her and Enrico's boys and girls and shared the story with Witherspoon of how they had saved them on Capri. Ron was tying up his sneakers when she came to him red eyed and weeping as she insisted that he be checked out before he ran off to more danger.

"Signora Verdi, you are most kind but time is of the essence. I need to go help them." Off he ran leaving Susan and Sophia weeping at such foolish courage. As he was leaving, he told Professor Witherspoon to have everyone go back to the Retreat Center and guard the item in the towel and this." He stooped behind a decorative pile of rocks in the garden and pulled out Bob's satchel.

Bob who was more water logged than injured couldn't believe his eyes. "You saved it, but how…you look like a piece of shit stepped on how did you do it?" he embraced his Sherlock, his best pal and took the satchel but only briefly. "Watson is coming with you." He handed the satchel to Jan. Together Sherlock and Watson ran off across the road and into the excavation site.

There they found Father Garcia with his faculty and the few students at the Mission House during summer forming a straight line at the border of the woods.

"You boys be careful, we will make sure no one comes out of those woods onto the grounds without running into us." As the priest spoke the bells rang out the 4:00 p.m. hour.

The song of the bells filtered through the forest. Luigi and Pietro heard them as they pushed the boat off the bank and jumped into it, Pettigrew heard it as he reached the bottom of the Bonaparte steps and Malone and Verdi heard them as they reached the top of the steps. They yelled to Pettigrew to wait for their back up. The Professor chose not to hear them and ran for the boat just as Luigi pulled Pietro into the boat. He took a flying leap from a boulder jutting out into the creek and crashed into Pietro knocking them both off the boat and into the creek. Luigi was trying to hit Pettigrew with the oar when Malone and Verdi arrived at the shore of the creek. They demanded that they give it up and told them the police would soon be on the other side of the creek. There was nowhere for them to go.

The creek was only about four feet deep at that point. Pietro and Pettigrew were dragging themselves up and out of the water while swinging at each other. Captain Verdi waded into the creek and went after Pietro. He and Pettigrew grabbed hold of each arm and soon had him on land. Malone cuffed him and entered the creek to help Verdi who was being hit with an oar as he grabbed hold of the rim of the boat. Verdi managed to grab the oar; it was a choice between losing his balance and falling into the creek and into Verdi hands or let go of the oar. Luigi chose to let go of the oar, the instant release of pressure flung Verdi backwards into the creek. With only one oar left, Luigi was now trying to use the oar as a paddle and get downstream.

"Professor, keep an eye on this guy," Malone then splashed through the slow current of the creek. He tore off his jacket and shirt and threw them onto the shore as he began to swim rather than try to walk in the muck at the bottom of the creek. Verdi had already followed suit when they first arrived at the creek. Both were now swimming toward the rowboat being used like a canoe but not very well. The current though not particularly strong still made their effort a bit challenging as the boat was being carried faster downstream where it would converge with the Delaware River and if Luigi got that far, he could easily get away.

By the time Bob and Ron got down the stone steps, the boat was downstream well ahead of the two policemen who were swimming after it. "Bob, I can cut him off. You go help the Professor with that asshole."

"No way, we do this together as a team, Sherlock and Watson finishing the game. Besides the Professor needs his moment of glory holding that jerk."

Having a moment of glory was an understatement. Pettigrew was in Pietro's face grilling him as to why he was stealing the satchel all the while not once mentioning the Book inside it.

"Come on Watson," they ran downstream faster than the current was carrying the boat and the swimming policemen. They were now ahead of the boat as they came across a tree growing out of the bank and leaning over the creek. Ron climbed up onto the overhanging branch. His plan was to jump onto the boat as it floated by knocking Luigi out of it. Bob would then hold him long enough so that Malone and Verdi could catch up and get him in custody.

Inch by inch he made his way onto the bent tree's branch. The plan was working until Luigi noticed the shirtless and once again shoeless lad crouched over the branch. The current was pushing the boat right towards the tree. Up went the oar and when he got close enough he swung it at the branch knocking it. It threw Ron off balance and he hung desperately holding on as his feet were swinging just over the water. He managed to pull himself up onto the branch. Again Luigi swung and this time the boat was closer. Ron tried to grab hold of the flat paddle shape end of the oar. He missed and almost fell off the branch but not toward the boat. Balancing himself again, the screech of Luigi's cursing rang in his ears. It was all about what he'd do to him. He swung the oar again and this time Ron caught hold of it and the tug of war began as it had between Verdi and Luigi. This time however Ron studied the grizzly face and just about read his thoughts. He let go when Luigi gave a tug to pull him off. The oar went flying backwards toward Verdi and Malone and Luigi lost his balance. The boat was rocking furiously as Luigi's huge body tried to find footing. Bob waded into the creek in an effort to catch the rocking boat; it distracted Luigi and that opened a moment of opportunity for Ron.

In an instant his slender body flew like a flying squirrel and fell onto Luigi's back as he turned to curse Bob. Both he and Ron fell out of the boat and into the waters of the creek. Ron had him in a neck hold in the four foot deep water just long enough for Verdi and Malone to catch up and take hold of him. "Wow, that guy was like hitting a brick wall," was all he could say to them.

"Gesu, Ron that was a foolish thing to do. This man, he is double your size."

"Yeah, I get it Captain but he was like Goliath in the Bible story not worried about scrawny ole me until he got hit by a flying object which in this case was me." Ron tried to laugh but he hurt too much and winced instead, grinning at Captain Verdi. "I only did what Sherlock would have done in desperation."

The current began to push Ron over; the Captain took hold of him. "Put your arm around me."

Bob was beside himself thinking that his pal was really hurt bad. He managed to pull the boat ashore and grab the oar which caused the collision of the two bodies in the first place. "Captain is he all right?"

Verdi helped Ron to sit on the mud packed bank leaning against the trunk of the bent tree. "Take care of your *amico*, I must help the Detective Malone."

Bob knelt in front of his Sherlock. "Look Ron, I saved your shoes." He turned them over to pour out the water with a laugh.

"Thanks Watson, it looks like we got both of them. Now all we have to do is find out if Carolina is behind all of this." He tried to put on his shoes. "Owe, Can you help me pal? I'm a little stiff; that guy was solid cement not flesh."

"Sure, what you need is a nice hot shower to loosen you up and maybe then Susan can apply first aide or something." He shot him a mischievous smile.

With his arm around Bob for a bit of help to get moving and stay standing, they walked past Malone and Verdi restraining Luigi seated on the ground. The goon looked up at them, "This is not over."

Malone took hold of his head and turned it to face him. "It is for you," and he read him his rights.

They walked toward Pettigrew to check on how he was doing with Pietro. Ron was saying that Luigi was right that it wasn't over; Carolina was still out there though now with no thugs or colleagues.

"Except for one," Bob noted.

"Very astute Watson; where the hell is Professor Richard Stockton?"

The question was a good one. Across the Creek watching some of what happened on the Creek was Stockton looking through binoculars which were focused on Ron and Bob going up the stone steps. "Fuck me; those punks got the best of Luigi and Pietro." He looked around for Carolina shouting, "Did you hear me? That English guy is holding Pietro and that Detective Malone must have Luigi because those punks are alive and well."

Carolina was casually walking back from the parking lot as he was ranting. "Will you quiet down; the whole camp site can hear you and probably those policemen across that damn Creek."

Stockton couldn't get himself under control. He ran to her and grabbed her by the shoulders and shook her. "Don't you fucking understand? I killed for you and this grand plan of yours to become rich and now it's all gone. Luigi and Pietro are in police custody, so are Murat and Benton; the satchel with the Book is with those punks and so is the secret about the Bonaparte treasure."

"Take your hands off of me," she slapped his face more to shock him back into control than anything else. "Now you listen to me. All is not lost. We know where the Book is. Now we'll try to get Murat and Benton out of jail. Then we'll get back to that Mission House and we will just wait and watch especially those two who fancy themselves as Sherlock Holmes and Dr. Watson, such arrogance."

Walking very carefully up those uneven steps, Ron suddenly stopped and held his hand over Bob's mouth. He softly spoke. "Someone's shouting Bob and it's coming from the other side of the Creek. Shit, he just said that he killed someone."

Bob's little blue eyes suddenly widened. He tried to talk.

"It's gone, maybe the Professor heard it," he removed his hand from Bob's mouth.

"Ron was it a voice of a man or woman because I didn't hear anything; my ears are still filled with water."

"It was a man's voice but it's all quiet now." Ron called down to Pettigrew but not too loudly. He asked if he could hear someone from across the Creek. His tone was low. He understood that if he could hear someone from across the creek so could whoever was there hear him. As he did so, Malone and Verdi reached the stairs holding Luigi by his arms.

Malone left Luigi with Verdi and went to take custody of Pietro. "Professor, I'll take over, why don't you go help the boys it seems that Ron needs you? He's pretty banged up from catching that one."

Pettigrew thanked Malone. As he stood up he was head butted by Pietro in the back. He crashed into Malone and the two of them fell down the embankment into the creek. Pietro made for the steps as Bob and Ron ran up the few remaining ones. His balance wasn't great but Pietro even with his hands tied behind his back was formidable. Verdi threw Luigi to the ground and ran to help Malone and the Professor and then made for the steps.

Pietro had already run out of the woods and onto the excavation site. When Verdi emerged from the woods, there stood Ron and Bob perfectly safe and Pietro being held by the injured David's friends Sam and Daniel. The rest of the Mission House students and faculty had formed an arc behind them just in case. The brief excitement was over. Father Garcia walked up to Verdi.

"Captain, I believe this gentleman belongs to you." He turned to his students. "You may release him to the Captain now."

The chapel bells were ringing out the 5:00 p.m. hour and the sun was in descent when sirens could also be heard coming onto the Mission House grounds once called Point Breeze. The flashing lights of the squad car could now be seen coming down the gravel road. It wouldn't be long before the officers took Pietro. In that short time Malone who had stayed with Luigi made his way up the stairs and out of the woods with his prisoner in tow.

Ron was thanking Father Garcia and everyone for their help and begged to be excused so that he and his pal could get ready for the Funeral service. "We're still having the service aren't we Father?"

316

"Of course my Son, but it will be at 7:00 p.m. a bit later so that…well so that this situation can be taken care of and everyone can have something to eat. Please invite your friends to come to the refectory, the women too are welcome. We are not a cloistered order."

By 5:30 p.m. Ron and Bob were in the shower room letting the hot water pour over their bodies. They did so in silence which Bob broke.

"So what are you thinking Ron?"

"Huh, oh yeah…well nothing much just had a sudden flashback to our time in the Abbey in Latin School."

"Shit, who would have thought you'd think of that? Now I'm half expecting a fake Brother Michael to appear and trying to grab your junk."

"What the hell Bob; you really know how to blow up a moment. I was thinking of how we solved our first murder not about being with a bunch of naked guys in the shower and certainly not about that asshole. That's where I first met Susan…"

"And that's a good memory? Bob looked at Ron; he was still looking up into the shower head. "You do remember what happened don't you?"

"Stop it, not now when we're naked. And yes I vividly remember but now it's almost funny in a weird sort of way. I'm okay being near her and holding her and you know everything."

Bob stepped out of the shower and wrapped himself in a towel. "Who would have thought that love would bring that pecker of yours under control." He laughed and ran to the other side of the room by the wash basins.

Ron didn't even swear at him or make a comment because what was said was true. Every time Susan got near him he got an erection that wouldn't quit; but now that he expressed his love it was all under control. He grabbed his towel to dry off. It was not an easy thing to do as every part of his body was still aching. He changed the subject by getting back into Sherlock mode. "Witty as all this is Watson we need to focus on what comes next."

"And what would that be boys?" Professor Pettigrew appeared at the shower room doorway with a towel wrapped around him and dry clothes in his hand. He hung the clothes and towel on a hook and stepped into the shower area.

With their backs to him the guys slipped on their underwear and tried to answer his question. It was not an easy thing to do because they couldn't get the vision of the Professor being naked with a woman in Dublin. She tried to seduce him when they were on their research holiday which ended up with murder and a discovery as well not unlike what was happening at Point Breeze. Ron shook the thought off and got to the next step of a developing plan. It wasn't as if Pettigrew was some old codger like in the Sherlock Holmes classic movies with villains smoking a pipe with long gray hair and a beard to match.

Dorothy Witherspoon had quite the catch with him. He was a handsome man in his late thirties with a beard closely cropped which made him look distinguished rather than aged. He was well put together for a classically educated British subject of Her Majesty, the Queen. It stood to reason that the deception of the seduction was not such a challenge for that woman in Ireland.

"Professor, before we go to dinner there's one little thing we three need to do."

Pettigrew continued to dry off but had a twinkle in his eye. "Ron, I'm not into threesomes."

The shock in the eyes of Ron and Bob was priceless. They thought of Professor Pettigrew as always being so prim and proper; never implying something sexual in nature. All they could do was pull on their pants to send the signal that what was being suggested had nothing to do with threesomes or otherwise.

Pettigrew pulled up his Jockeys and began grin at them as he paused and then put on his pants. "So did I shock you two?"

"That would be an understatement Sir."

He laughed and patted them on their bare backs and squeezed their necks. "Well then it served its purpose. Things were getting a bit rough and tumble out there in the woods. I thought we needed some fun."

"Professor, you may not realize this, but Ron here doesn't see sexuality things as funny. He has an issue you see but it's under control now that he's in love with Susan and we have gay *amicos*."

"Wow Bob that is quite the mouthful if you pardon my term. But now the fun is over however; those two poor excuses for gentlemen are in custody and the excavation must continue after the funeral of course. So then Sherlock and Watson what is your plan for I'm sure that you have one."

Ron pulled over his head yet another souvenir tee-shirt this one depicting Michelangelo's Sistine Chapel painting of God giving life to Adam. The image showed only the two hands about to touch. "If my best pal is finished with discussing my shortcomings," he shot Bob one of his famous scowls, "I would like to discuss the plan but first who has the wallet wrapped in the towel?"

"Why Dorothy…I mean Professor Witherspoon does. Why is that important and what wallet?"

The bells were announcing the 6:00 p.m. hour. Everyone was heading down to the refectory for dinner after which would be the funeral for Captain Unzaga. It was important to Ron that whatever was in that wallet be examined before the funeral. He was sure that its contents would have a message of some sort and that message would be the last thing Unzaga would deliver some hundred and fifty years later.

"Professor, would you please ask your girlfriend for the towel and meet me in Bob's room speaking of which, where is the satchel with the Book?"

Bob replied that he had given it to his sister, Jan.

"Sherlock and Watson what is now afoot? That is what you refer to yourselves as isn't it?" The Professor still filled with adrenaline flowing was rather enjoying this adventure as he saw it.

Sherlock and Watson fully dressed looked with amusement at the Oxford guy. "And by the way you don't have to keep calling her Professor Witherspoon. We all know that you have a thing going between you."

"Is that so; am I that obvious?"

"I'm afraid so but you certainly are handling it better than I did with Susan." Ron grinned. "But now to the plan gentlemen; like I said, first the Professor gets the towel, then Bob you'll run to the refectory to get the satchel from my sister. And don't dilly dally and try to eat dinner; we need to get this done before the funeral."

"Asshole, I am weak from hunger but okay just a tidbit and the satchel and back to where?"

"Come back to my room and tell all the others to come as well, when they have finished eating. By then I hope the Professor will be able to identify the contents."

Pettigrew left immediately and ran down the hall to the main part of the building where the dining area was located. Bob stayed.

"So, what will you be doing until then?"

"Shit Bob, can you just drop the inquisition? I'm going to take a leak what with the pool, creek and even this shower I think my bladder's going to explode. Happy now?"

"There's more to it but I'll drop it and go." Off Bob went leaving Ron walking to the urinal.

The hallways were strangely quiet after everything that happened. Ron felt quite alone and isolated as he entered his room quite in shambles what with moving the desk from the window and pushing things around so that they could climb out of the window. But the bed was there and quite inviting. He slowly lowered himself onto it and rolled over, his head spinning and throbbing. The quiet and lying flat seemed to help. He didn't feel nearly as dizzy and could think about what would come next should the passage from the Book, he and Andreas just translated, proved to be what he thought it to be.

It was a good fifteen minutes before the creaking of his bedroom door followed with Bob's head popping through startled him. "Are you okay? I brought the satchel and something else." He slipped into the room with Pettigrew right behind him holding the towel. "Mrs. Verdi gave me a bottle of aspirin; she said that from what I told her that you may have a concussion or if not a bad bump on the head causing the headache."

"Christ Bob, oh sorry Professor, but did you have to tell everyone?"

"What, like you're some kind of super hero who can't get hurt? You fought with those jerks last night, and today you were involved in two fights; it's okay that you feel like shit and need a pain reliever. It's not like she's giving you morphine. Anyway only Mrs. Verdi and now the Professor know anything. I didn't even tell Susan or your sister and will have hell to pay about that I can tell you."

Ron pulled himself up to a seating position, his legs dangling off the side of the bed. "Okay already, I'm sorry; I should have known that Watson would know what to do. Hand me the aspirin. I suppose you didn't bring a glass of water."

"Asshole no, I didn't; but there's a glass on your sink." Bob filed the glass and brought it and two pills to Ron. Then he and the Professor pulled the desk over to the bed. "Now what's the plan?" He plopped the satchel on top of the desk and took out the Book and a notepad.

The Professor placed the towel next to the Book. Ron began to unwrap it revealing the worn and damaged wallet. He explained that there was something in it that looked like paper. If it was his hope that it would connect with what was in the passage of the Book. He opened the Book to a marked place which talked about the Crown Jewels of Spain and how the jewels were sold to buy the property and build the first and second house of Joseph Bonaparte. All was in code which he and Andreas had cracked.

"By the way where is Andreas? This may be written in French. I thought everyone would be here."

Bob told him that he didn't tell everyone to come because he thought him to be sick and needing some rest.

"Oh my God, you are a Watson, my Watson; but I really need him and the others but it can wait. Let's see if this paper says anything at all."

"Good thought Ron as Unzaga was from Spain and if this has a message it is probably written in Spanish."

"Then Professor, let's get it out and find out. Bob can go get the others as soon as we know what we're dealing with." He explained that he tried to find examination gloves because he feared the touch of a human hand may harm the paper after all the time which had passed. The Professor agreed but at the same time pointing out that there were now another two choices.

One was to wait and get the proper materials thus delaying what might help with the finding of the jewels. Second was taking the risk and sharing it with everyone at the funeral to honor Captain Unzaga.

They ultimately chose the latter and pulled back the flap of the wallet. Pettigrew then carefully using his handkerchief pulled out the paper. It was a heavy duty linen threaded paper. Bob grabbed hold of Ron's arm as the Professor unfolded it. It was not a letter but it was a written passage of some kind. It also was written in Latin. Thus Ron and Bob if they could decipher the writing would be able to translate it. Bob picked up the notepad and rummaged in the satchel for a pen.

"Okay Ron, go for it. I'll write down what you say."

The Professor, of course, being a Historian and Researcher of the Classical, Medieval and Renaissance periods was well versed in Latin as well. If Ron got stuck, he would be able to help discern the meaning. It didn't take long. The writing was from Joseph Bonaparte telling Unzaga that Maillard and he were changing the hiding place for the Jewels given the current political upheaval in France, the offering of the Throne of Mexico to him (which he later rejected) and suspected British activity spying on him. That latter part seemed to indicate that he was aware of a spy in the Bordentown community but not who it was. The Book on Joseph Bonaparte's life would confirm that it was Stanley Stonegate the murderer of the missing Captain Unzaga who most thought perished in the fire of the First Mansion.

Bob's hand shook as he wrote everything down. "Holy shit Ron, we've just solved a hundred and fifty year old murder."

The Professor congratulated them and leaned over the paper to continue reading it with Ron. A knock on the door stopped them. Pettigrew opened the door and found his girlfriend and Pettigrew's team in the hallway. "Well do come in; it's a bit small but Ron wanted you all here."

Susan ran to Ron and felt his head. "Thank God, it's cool. Mrs. Verdi you were right, just a headache from all the excitement." She kissed him on the cheek. "So what's so important now, Sherlock?"

"Oh not too much," began Bob, "just that we have proved that Captain Unzaga was murdered and who did it."

The cheers, hoots and hollers for Andreas, Ron and Bob were deafening but since there was no one else about it didn't matter or so they thought. Who would have dreamed that Carolina and Stockton would dare enter the estate grounds after what had just taken place. But they had as no one knew their car or that they were even in the State Park across the Crosswicks Creek. When police arrived to search the Park, they were gone. They stashed the car off the main road which ran in front of the estate and came onto the grounds from the back of the Rock Formation which ended the estate property.

Carolina waited in the cave while Stockton crept across the road to the rooms with open windows. He could hear the chatter from one of those rooms. He heard about the Unzaga murder and was now listening to Ron telling his friends about the final passage of the note from the wallet. It was strange that here Stockton was working with Carolina once again when each of them had plotted against each other in the hope of getting bigger shares of the jewels when they were found. And yet that is exactly what was taking place. He lurked behind a Cedar bush anxiously waiting to hear more of what was found. He knew that there was more because of the cheering and yelling.

Quiet returned and all waited for the next part of the message from the wallet. Ron continued to slowly translate with the Professor adding an interpretation here and there. The result was that it appeared that Captain Unzaga on the day of the fire had transferred the jewels to another location per Joseph Bonaparte's direction. When he was returning, he encountered the spies in the hidden chamber behind the library wall and at the end of the tunnel to the creek.

"That is clearly stated in the Book which was written well after these events," Ron noted. "The exact location however is only alluded to in the Book but it's as plain as day written on this paper."

Stockton couldn't believe what he was hearing. He was really about to learn the location of the Bonaparte Treasure long said to be a legend despite proof that jewels were sold to buy the Point Breeze property in Bordertown as well as the Lake Bonaparte site. He wanted to call Carolina over to hear as well but dared not leave and certainly not call out. Already lights were being erected at the burial site at the front end of the estate. The bells were ringing out the 7:00 p.m. hour. Everyone in Ron's room heard them along with Stockton who made no connection to them, but Ron did. He looked at his Mickey Mouse watch.

"Hey, it's Seven o'clock; we need to go. We'll finish this at the grave of Captain Unzaga. Professor, please return the paper into the wallet." It was done and placed, with the Book, into Bob's satchel; he then placed it on his back as usual.

Gold Table Ware belonging to King Joseph Bonaparte
Courtesy of Mr. Peter Tucci

Chapter Seventeen:
Secret of the Gardener's House

Two officers held open the front doors of the Bordentown Police
Station on Farnsworth Ave. as Malone and Verdi pulled up in front of
it. A squad car followed and those officers took the prisoners out of
their back seat. Handcuffed Luigi and Pietro were led up the steps into
the station where Captain Verdi saw Francois Parrot talking with the
Sargent at the duty desk. He alerted Malone that he was the owner of
the cabins up at Lake Bonaparte. Then he called out to Parrot who
greeted them warmly. After a quick explanation of what was taking
place, the prisoners were brought to the Booking desk where Parrot
learned of their charges.

"Sargent these prisoners, Luigi Tonnelli and Pietro Giuliano are
charged with assault, attempted theft, resisting arrest, and aggravated
battery. They are to be held in separate cells." The charges were not
brought forth by either Malone or Verdi. They were out of their
district. It was done by the arresting Bordentown police officers who
came to the former Point Breeze Estate. After they were led away
there was time for them to speak with Parrot.

They found out that Antoine Murat had called him seeking his help to
get legal representation. "Naturally, I couldn't imagine why a reporter
for the New Yorker was arrested when he had been so well received
up at Lake Bonaparte especially by those young people who you
Captain Verdi were quite chummy with as well."

Captain Verdi was feeling rather uncomfortable that he had been
duped by Murat but admitted to Parrot that he had. Malone too,
admitted that he had swallowed his story of writing an article on
Joseph Bonaparte's time at the Lake Bonaparte area. Both suggested
that he talk with Murat but as for them they had to return to the
Mission House at Point Breeze for a funeral.

When they explained that the funeral was for a man found in a secret tunnel and identified as Joseph Bonaparte's Aide-De-Corps one Captain Unzaga, the descendant of Bonaparte's cook of the same name asked if he could accompany them and pay his respects to one who had a relationship with his family. The New York Detective and the Captain of the Carabinieri welcomed his to do so. Murat would have to wait for his return if there would be one after what he was hearing.

Another sad part of this unfolding drama was that both the Murat and Benton families had intricate ties to Joseph Bonaparte back in the day. Back at the estate, Stockton ran back to the cave where Carolina waited. He was able to confirm that the De Cenza boy had found the remains of a dead body which was connected to Bonaparte.

She was unimpressed. But when he talked about the relocation of the Bonaparte treasure her eyes lighted up and she embraced him. "Don't get any ideas; this thing we have is all about the jewels and nothing more."

"I concur completely, besides I am a Princeton Professor, I don't think you'd fit it."

"Really, and they accept murderers do they? You see I did listen to your rants back at the camp site."

"I shall deny everything."

"Ah but one day you will have to as I shall see to it if we do not find the treasure."

"Then let us not waste any more time. The one they call Sherlock, Ron De Cenza said that he would reveal the secret of the treasure's hiding place at the burial of this Unzaga person after the funeral service."

Carolina was concerned about hanging around the grounds for such a long period of time. At the same time the lure of the jewels was too much for her. She had lost the posh life style when her lover Niccolo Cavelli was imprisoned. Now she felt compelled to finally get her desires fulfilled.

The funeral was getting a late start which was the result of the fight and capture of Luigi and Pietro followed by Ron's translation of the message found in the wallet of Captain Unzaga. When Pettigrew and Witherspoon finally led them into the chapel, the students and faculty were already in their pews, including David Chan. He had just been brought back from the hospital so that he could be with his classmates for the funeral of the man whose remains he enabled to be found by confronting Murat and Benton at the tunnel.

The remains of Captain Unzaga had been placed in a simple wooden coffin and draped in the Flag of Spain which had been sent to Bordentown by the Spanish Consulate in Philadelphia. On top was laid his gold chain of office. Professors Pettigrew and Witherspoon had told Father Garcia that it was not only valuable as a historic item but also because of its precious metal and goldsmith work. The priest however told them that it belonged not to the Seminary but to the Unzaga family and as there was none to those who found it. That would be Ron, Bob and Andreas who had no idea that they were to be entrusted with it as yet.

The organ began to play and the Mass began with Mozart's Laudete Dominum. After the final blessing and incensing of the coffin, the student choir began to sing "The Lord is my Shepherd." Ron, Bob, Andreas, Dominic, Alessandro and Pettigrew acted as Pall Bearers and carried the coffin out of the chapel and across the excavation site along the gravel road to what would be the final resting place.

At the front of the estate stood a building, which was original to the Point Breeze estate. It was commonly referred to as the Gardener's House particularly since those days when the Hammond Family and then the Divine Word Missionaries took over Point Breeze.

Ron, Bob and Andreas and soon all who attended the burial would soon learn that it wasn't always the Gardener's House. In the beginning it was the home of Louis Maillard. He was the private secretary to Joseph Bonaparte and was with him until Joseph died in Florence Italy in 1844 and buried in Santa Croce Church in that city. Later Napoleon III, Emperor of France, had his Uncle's body moved and buried at the Cathedrale Saint-Louis-des-Invalides in Paris near his brother, Napoleon Bonaparte's tomb. The burial of Captain Unzaga would not be on that grand scale. It would be in a small garden at the rear of this Gardener's House. Little did they know, until that night that the burial would be near a house which he visited many times.

The flag draped coffin was placed over the opening of the grave. Father Garcia asked everyone to join hands and pray the Lord's prayer. He then told the story of Jesus when he told his followers that he was the Way, the truth and the Life and that whosoever believed in Him should have eternal life. Father then took the Gold Chain of Office and held it as Holy Water was sprinkled by each of the Pall Bearers, who then removed the Flag, folded it and gave it to Francois Parrot as a descendant of those who went into exile with the fleeing King of Spain. It was over. The women placed a flower on the wooden coffin and it was lowered into the burial vault by the local Funeral Director.

But no one left. They all stood in silence waiting to hear something from Ron. But his mind was back on Capri when they first found the Book on the Life of Joseph Bonaparte. Flashes of all that happened which brought him and his friends to this moment in time exploded in his mind. The fire in the first mansion, the crushing of Captain Unzaga's head, the tunnel and the secret chamber, Bonaparte's rejection of the throne of Mexico, Maillard's hiding of jewels and then going back to recover them in Switzerland, all of these scenes from the Book swirled so as to make him dizzy. He staggered in place and wobbled. Bob saw it, so did Susan and all surrounding the grave. His pal and his gal went to stand at each side of him holding his arms.

The time had come to prove the legend to be true or expose it as just a game put on the margins of the Book. But why; was it to lure people for decades to spread the tale of the Crown Jewels of Spain and their disappearance.

Francois Parrot the only one there with a connection to Joseph Bonaparte's life in America stood in wonder as to what had happened to bring about such a response of reverence and respect for a murder victim of a hundred and fifty years ago. He held the flag next to his heart. But there was another who had a connection to the King of Spain in exile. Carolina Savage Gianetti crept with Stockton to the cracked pillar with a partial hanging gate dangling from it. It bordered the main road thus making it easy for them to literally walk away into darkness if things went the wrong way for them. Until then, they too waited to hear what Ron De Cenza had found and fought for particularly these last few days.

Susan squeezed his hand and Bob spoke into his ear, "You can do this Sherlock."

A nod signified that Ron had heard Bob and felt the touch of Susan's hand. He was now ready so were Detective Brandon Malone and Captain Enrico Verdi. The two policemen moved ever so quietly out of the circle, from the darkness outside of the gates officers appeared each holding onto one of four prisoners. Carolina and Stockton stood right in their path. Hearing the crunching of stones they turned to flee and ran right into Malone and Verdi; it was over for them. In a quick minute they were handcuffed and brought along with Murat, Benton, Luigi and Pietro to the gravesite. While the shock of seeing them was expressed; it soon faded. Malone and Verdi nodded and smiled at Ron.

It was all well planned and Ron was in on it. They were convinced that if those captured and those who sought to steal the Book were to hear what Ron found out, one of them would break. So this elaborate time of silence and not sharing the last part of the message found in the wallet was staged to lure the only two still on the loose to stay nearby.

"We're ready Ron any time you are." Malone crossed his fingers and held them up for Ron and Verdi in particular to see.

"Yes Sir," and he began the tale of the Book found on Capri. He shared all those scenes which had flashed through his brain earlier that evening right up to the last part of the message found in the Wallet. Then he stopped the story telling. The four accused and the two suspects began to squirm in place. Stockton even shouted that he was the Head of the History Department at Princeton University and how dare the Bordentown police hold him for no reason. During his tirade, Ron suddenly made a connection. It was the voice he had heard after the fight in the waters of Crosswicks Creek. He was sure of it. Proving it would be another matter so he started up the story again. This time he focused on what happened up at Lake Bonaparte and what he heard in the Men's room between Murat and Stockton. All of the details of how Murat became enamored with Apollo would be presented. This included using sex to get information from Apollo about where Bonaparte may have hidden his treasure in one of the caves surrounding Lake Bonaparte.

Murat began to shout that he did not kill Apollo, that he only took the pouch he hung around his neck to see if the map of the cave was in it.

"Yes Antoine Murat, you didn't want Apollo dead, because you had fallen in love with him. But you couldn't admit that especially to Charles Benton or Carolina Gianetti. You worked for them while at the same time you worked for Richard Stockton secretly to find the treasure before Carolina could and cheat her out of her share."

Carolina began enraged. "You scum," she kicked Stockton who was standing next to her. "I financed this whole operation and you betrayed me."

"Ah betrayal *Signorina* Carolina they all did to each other as well. Charles Benton you too were working both sides, Stockton and Carolina. You only wanted revenge on the Bonaparte family because you thought history slighted your family all these years.

It was you in the Roman ruins in Switzerland who tried to steal what we found there, nothing but a coin and a sarcastic note but that didn't stop you. You spied on my friends and me in our hotel room with a listening device."

Benton denied everything but Carolina told her story of how she met him in Switzerland and set him on the tail of Pettigrew and his research team. She was not about to go down alone. Then she turned on Stockton again. "You bastard, you set up all of this to betray me and steal what is rightfully mine. It was my man, my lover Niccolo Cavelli who paid for the search for Bonaparte's treasure. It was his right hand man before the betrayal who found it with Lorenzo Medino in Florence. And it was you Ron De Cenza who stole it from the hotel room on Capri. That Book belongs to me."

There was a bit of truth in what Carolina said but Ron clarified one point. Yes he did find the Book in the murder victim's room. But the Book was stolen from a vender in Florence in the first place. "So it belonged to no one since that vender was murdered by Lorenzo's partner, the lover of Apollo, Stefano Rinaldi, now in prison in Italy. So Ron kept the Book to help Professor Andrew Pettigrew set a piece of history straight on behalf of King Joseph Bonaparte. Oddly, it was an Englishman who brought down the Bonaparte family and it's one along with some Italians, Americans and a Swiss man who will prove the legend of the Crown Jewels of Spain gone missing to be true."

Jan held the hand of Alessandro tightly. "Gosh, isn't my brother great when he gets on a roll like this?"

Andreas and Dominic squeezed their hands and took hold of the hands of Susan and Jan on either side of them while Jan held the hand of Alessandro. Susan and Bob were standing on either side of Ron but they couldn't take his hand after all he's an Italian American and needed them to express points in his story telling.

"So then who killed Apollo Dimitri on Lake Bonaparte? You Charles Benton came to America before Carolina arrived, did she send you to find Apollo and kill him for what he knew? And you Antoine Murat, we already know that you lied about being a New Yorker Magazine reporter. You did try to take our translations of the Book from our cabin and you were on Birch Island before we arrived and had ample time to kill Apollo with whom you've admitted to having fallen in love. But did you kill him? But then there is the question of the Crossbow being the Murder weapon. Who could have easy access to it and get it returned after its deadly use?" Ron pointed to Stockton.

"How dare you, I told Murat that I didn't do it. You must have heard it in the bathroom where you said you were hiding in the Library."

"I did hear it and I also heard Murat not believing it."

"You, you are the murderer of my beautiful Apollo," screamed Carolina. "You told me at the camp site this very day how you killed for me. I would never have killed that gorgeous man even if I couldn't have him all to myself. I would share him before that would happen."

It was over. Malone ordered all of those in cuffs to be brought to the police station for further questioning. Ron however asked for a favor. He wanted them to witness what he was about to prove, to see what they killed for and what they betrayed each other for.

So began the final piece of the story with Ron explaining how the House behind them often called the Gardener's House was first and foremost built for Louis Maillard, the Secretary to Joseph Bonaparte. As with Joseph's daughter and the escape tunnel where they found Captain Unzaga, a tunnel was created. Maillard would be able to come to the Mansion quickly as needed but still have a place of his own. It was finished shortly before the fire destroying the first mansion in 1820. Captain Unzaga had just finished transferring the jewels to their new home where Joseph Bonaparte's most trusted friend and colleague could keep an eye on them.

Ron pulled the pouch out of Bob's satchel and handed it to Bob to hold as he took out the Book which caused all that happened on Capri and now in Bordentown New Jersey.

"The final paragraph of what is written on the note in that Wallet which belonged to the man whom we just buried and this page in the Book on Joseph Bonaparte's life verify several things. First, that there were jewels. Second that they were taken from Spain when Joseph had to flee, and Three, that they were hidden first in the hidden chamber of the First Mansion and then moved to a cellar which led to another secret tunnel from the House of Louis Maillard to the First Mansion and altered to reach the Second Mansion. That Second Mansion was eventually destroyed by another anti-Bonaparte family named Becket and with it the tunnel and all reference to where the remaining jewels were hidden."

Ron turned to leave the gravesite. "If everyone would please follow me into the Gardener's House; Please be careful as it is in grave disrepair."

The police officers distributed flashlights and all followed Ron. Father Garcia was quite correct in saying that the house was not taken care of for over a century. But they managed to get Malone and Verdi with the prisoners, Sophia Verdi, Pettigrew, Witherspoon, Father Garcia, and the *amicos*, Ron, Bob, Susan, Jan, Alessandro, Andreas and Dominic and Francois Parrot into what most would call a basement or cellar.

There they found digging tools. Ron showed them the wall which was the target. "Behind this wall should be something like a storm cellar which connected to a tunnel which was deliberately collapsed when the second mansion was torn down. That's when Maillard's House actually became the Gardener's House." Ron lifted a large pickaxe, "so who would like to strike the first blow? Father Garcia this house is on our order's property would you like to do it?"

"Most generous of you my son, however I shall defer to one with a bit more...shall I say power."

With that description, Ron had only two choices and since Andreas helped to translate the Book to find the clues to this site it seemed appropriate for him to be the first. He handed him the pickaxe.

"Here goes *amicos,* stand back." He swung the tool high above his head and crashed it against the wall, the plaster surface crumbled with the blow. He was urged to take a few more swings. Ron and Bob shoveled out the pieces of plaster which turned out to be a façade over brick. Alessandro began to help the Papal Guard chip away at that plaster surface and knock out the bricks. It turned out that they were not foundation stones but simply a concealing wall. The bricks fell out of place as everyone but those in custody took a turn. A gaping hole was revealed, Ron crawled through it. Asking for a flashlight he shined it about the small cellar and found himself in what he called a wine cellar.

"There're shelves in here with actual bottles of wine on them." He began to hand some of the bottles out of the opening.

Witherspoon and Pettigrew examined the labels still visible on some of them. It pictured the Bonaparte coat of arms. It appeared they said that Joseph made his own wine at some point on the estate. Two of the bottles still had visible dates on them, one was 1820 and another was 1830.

Andreas climbed through the hole and Ron asked Bob to bring more flashlights. The cellar appeared to be ten foot by twelve foot. They soon saw that the wall opposite the opening was not a wall at all but a collapsed heap of rock, brick and dirt. It obviously was where the destroyed tunnel had begun to the second mansion. When Becket tore down that second mansion, he ordered the tunnels to be filled in, those that they found. The tunnel which Ron found by the creek was part of the first mansion's tunnel system and was obviously not totally destroyed.

"It must have been the Becket family who bricked up the foundation wall and plastered it when they turned the Maillard House into the Gardener's House," Ron concluded and Pettigrew agreed.

All the *amicos* had now entered the cellar including Jan and Susan. The few bottles which were still intact where handed out to the Professors, Parrot and Sophia. Malone and Verdi could off little help given that they had to keep watch over their prisoners. With each bottle that was handed out, Carolina, Stockton and the others became more disappointed. It appeared to them that the secret room was nothing more than a wine cellar.

"Well that's it for the wine bottles," Jan called out as she handed out the last of them. There were twelve intact bottles in all. "So now what Ron?"

Ron was now shining his light in between the shelving units looking for some kind of hidden door or even a safe. There were only two walls which had shelves as whatever was on the back wall from where they entered would have been destroyed when the tunnel caved in.

"We need to move these shelves to get a good look at what's behind them."

The guys got right on it and began to pull on the one covering the left wall as they faced the debris of the tunnel entrance. Some of the wood began to crack and crumble as they dragged the unit away from the wall. It turned out that it was not attached to the wall and for Ron that was a good sign. He called for everyone to shine their light on the wall. The rounded beams hit the wall in various spots like when a movie studio had a premier and shined spotlights into the air. One of those beams hit something that looked like a piece of metal stuck on the bricks.

Bob began to shout; the beam of his flashlight shook as he jumped up and down. All the other light beams converged on where Bob was shining his flashlight. "Oh my God, Ron we've found a door, oh Lord, we found something." He dropped his light and hugged Ron.

Everyone was cheering and hugging and no one knew what they had found as yet. Susan kissed Ron and Jan kissed Alessandro and Andreas kissed Dominic then they all swarmed over Bob not to leave him out and embraced him one by one.

"The Book did not lie," shouted Dominic sticking his head out of the opening to tell the others of what they had found. "Even if there is nothing behind the door, it proves that there once was."

Carolina fell to the ground stunned with what she was hearing. In her scenario she should have been the one who was discovering the secret room of Joseph Bonaparte. Her partners in crime ignored her depression and focused on what would come next. They too however were thinking of what could have been. They began to curse each other.

Dominic was now asking if there was a crowbar or flat head screwdriver amongst the tools. Pettigrew handed him a screwdriver. Bringing it to Ron he noted that this was the moment of truth. "All that happened on Capri, In Switzerland, on Lake Maggiore and Lake Bonaparte has brought us here Ron."

"Right, who would have thought that in Bordentown New Jersey the former King of Spain, Naples and Sicily would settle down and just maybe leave a trinket or two for history to admire." Ron began to pry the edge of the metal door rusted but intact. It didn't take much; it swung open. "Bob shine the light in here." He reached in, "Holy shit, I mean I can't believe it. There's something in here, I can feel it and I can see it." He reached in and began to tug on a metal chest; inch by inch he slid it to the edge of the open door. Clearly it was made of iron, dark and unadorned.

"Here goes everyone; I'm bringing it out into the 20th Century." He lifted it out; it had weight. The lights were shining all over it and in his eyes as well but he could see that it wasn't just a plain iron chest. On top there were letters spelling out ROI JOSEPH which was French for King Joseph.

Andreas read the words in French. "ROI JOSEPH," he beamed a smile. "This has to belong to Joseph Bonaparte."

Ron handed the box to Bob to hold. It had a flat top and not the usual curved top that a chest usually had. There was a latch on the front but no lock. Using the screwdriver again he pried it open, lifting the lid which was hinged on the back side. Everyone stepped closer and the light intensified so much so that an explosion of color and brilliance seemed to burst out of the chest. There was no doubt; something was in that box and it had color and brilliance. Ron slowly felt around what were loose gem stones, rings, brooches and one thing more. He pulled up a gold chain encrusted with precious gems and when he had it totally out of the chest, it had a large medallion hanging from it. In his mind flashed the portrait of Joseph Bonaparte as King of Spain. Unlike the golden chain found with Captain Unzaga, this one was quite intricate. The chain held gold symbols of his reign; there were castle towers, soldier helmets, royal lions and the hanging medallion was really two. The top was a Crown out of which hung a Gold Star embedded with a precious stone which appeared to be a large diamond which the gold surrounding it gave a yellow tint. The chain itself was really a double chain. The top portion consisted of squares of gold separated by a precious stone. Attached at the bottom of it was the chain which consisted of the symbols of his reign and authority. It most definitely was the Coronation chain and emblem in that portrait he called to mind.

Ron lifted it up so that everyone could have a good look. "So what do you say guys, shall we get out of here before it collapses on us?" He placed the Chain of the Sovereign back into the chest. "Okay Bob hand it out to Professor Pettigrew. We'll check out the contents in better conditions."

The chest was handed out and one by one they all crawled out of the wine cellar. Pettigrew was cradling the chest in his arms like a child as Stockton, Carolina, Murat and Benton literally wept over what could have been and Luigi and Pietro fumed that they were caught up in Carolina's plan and got nothing but a future prison sentence for their efforts.

Malone called for officers to come down and take the prisoners away. Once again Ron asked him to wait but one minute more. He opened the chest as Pettigrew held it. "This may sound cruel but I think we should show them the contents of the chest."

Malone agreed. The top was lifted again and Ron pulled out the Sovereign's Chain. Sophia held onto Verdi's arm, Dorothy Witherspoon did the same to Pettigrew and soon everyone except those in cuffs were embracing and congratulating each other on solving the legend of the Bonaparte Treasure.

As the prisoners were led away, Ron brought the chain before Father Garcia. "Father, it's your call; we found this on your property."

"No son, this is not part of our property. It belongs to History and probably the Nation of Spain if what you said is accurate."

Ron turned to the Professors who after all sponsored the expedition to Point Breeze in the first place. "And what do you say Professors?"

Pettigrew who was still holding the chest agreed with Father Garcia's point of view. "This chain in particular belongs to the Royal Family of Spain. It is part of their history. We shall examine the other pieces to discern if they are personal pieces of Joseph Bonaparte, part of his reign as King of Naples and Sicily then present them to the appropriate museum to display for posterity."

The resounding applause from everyone gathered demonstrated agreement with the man from Oxford.

As they filed out of the house of Louis Maillard, once again they stopped at the now filled in grave of Captain Unzaga. Ron felt the need to report that what he was charged to protect and save has been found and will be preserved for generations to come. "And that gift Sir, may include living members of the Bonaparte family, and descendants of those who came to America with King Joseph Bonaparte. Francois Parrot who had silently been watching the events unfold had a tear trickling down his cheek.

Behind them on Route 662 several squad cars with flashing lights rode off with four weeping and two cursing prisoners. Father Garcia invited everyone to the refectory for some refreshments and to better view the contents of the Bonaparte Chest. A procession of sorts led by the priest and Professor Pettigrew holding the chest made their way across the excavation site which would be tended to on another day.

The seven *amicos* held back for a moment as Ron asked. "So who's up for a trip to Portugal?"

"Portugal," exclaimed the others in unison.

"Why sure, that's where the King of Spain lives while Generalisimo Franco rules Spain."

"Well then, it's to Portugal then to present the King with a piece of Spanish History," Dominic ecstatic about another adventure announced.

"Hold on boys, there's one more thing before we go off on any adventure. There's a thing called a wedding," Susan grabbed hold of Ron's arm. He leaned over and kissed her on the lips in front of everyone.

"So guys first we go to Oak Park Illinois for a little celebration and then we go to Portugal." Ron wrapped his arm around Susan.

"Ah let's make that two celebrations," added Jan. "It's going to be a double wedding."

Alessandro lifted Jan into his arms and not to be outdone Ron did the same with Susan twirling her around as Bob jumped out of the way clutching his satchel with the Book and the Wallet.

And from the heavens above Joseph Bonaparte finally welcomed Captain Unzaga.

****

Joseph Bonaparte as King of Spain

Acknowledgements:

Special thanks to the following for their invaluable support and help for the plot development of the story of Murder on Capri and Book Six of the De Cenza Murder Mysteries, "Murder at Point Breeze."

France's Legion of Honor Recipient Peter Tucci of Philadelphia: Trustee of the Bordentown Historical Society of New Jersey

The Bordentown Historical Society of New Jersey: Co-Presidents Steve Lederman and Bonnie Goldman and Vice-President Doug Kiovsky

D and R Greenway Land Trust: Princeton NJ, Linda Mead and Nancy Faherty

Columbus Citizens Foundation of New York City

Italian American Museum of New York City

The Joe Piscopo Show/ AM970 The Answer, New York City

National Italian American Foundation, Washington, D.C.

The Italian Community Center, Milwaukee Wisconsin

Casa Italia, Chicago, Illinois

The Joint Civic Committee of Italian Americans, Chicago, Illinois

References:

Delaware River Heritage Trail

Shannon Selin: Imagining the Bounds of History

Lake Bonaparte: New York State Dept. of Environmental Conservation

The New York Times: From Waterloo to New Jersey, a Glimpse of Joseph Bonaparte's Life in Exile by Eve M. Kahn.

Wikipedia.com

Princeton University: pr.princeton.edu

"The Vatican on the Delaware" by James Frascella, June 2012

The Books of Arthur Cola

Available at
Feedaread.com/arthurcola, ARPress.com/arthurcola,
amazon.com/arthurcola, austinmacauley.com/arthurcola,
barnesandnoble.com/arthurcola

Fantasy Books:
Papa and the Gingerbread Man

A children's fantasy tale of a Grandfather who seeks to catch the
Gingerbread Man for his grandchildren's school Christmas Party.

Fantasy Books: Celtic Folklore and Legends
Papa and the Leprechaun King
The Shamrock Crown

The Colonna Family's adventure to Ireland brings them face to face
with the current King of the Leprechauns and into the realm of King
Arthur and his Knights of the Round Table.

Supernatural Thrillers: **Ring of the Magi Series**
The Stone Cutter Genius
 The Brooch

A professor and his two teen sons are told of the Legend of the Ring of
the Magi said to hold supernatural powers which protected the Medici
Family rulers of Tuscany in Italy. They soon find themselves on a
quest to find the long lost ring.

Biography: **Il Divino Michelangelo**

A slightly fictionalized life of the Renaissance artist Michelangelo as
told by the artist from his deathbed as he reflects on his life to find
love and perfect it in his art and sculpting.

Murder at Point Breeze

Holiday Tales: **Stolen Christmas**

A young Hispanic boy tries to save his Church from demolition on the day after Christmas with the help of his teen sister and her secret boyfriend from an Italian-American family. In the process they become involved with a white bearded stranger who helps them confront the Diamond Development Corporation to save the Church in this David vs Goliath tale with a Romeo and Juliet sub-plot.

Historical Fiction: **The Doonagore Theft Trilogy**
The adventures of two lads and a lass as they struggle to leave Ireland during the famine era and travel to Pre-Civil War America in 1848.

Journey of Three Pure Hearts: James, Aengus and Meghan travel to New York City aboard the ship, the Cushla Macree.

Pure and Tarnished Hearts: James, Aengus and Meghan arrive in New York City to find civil strife and challenges as they pursue the American dream on the way to Philadelphia where they are joined by other immigrants and form the "Celtic Warriors" singing group.

Torn and United Hearts: The singing group called "Celtic Warriors" which has become a 19th Century sensation becomes involved with helping a runaway slave and in helping him assist the Underground Railroad as well.

Age 16+ Crime Adventures: **The De Cenza Murder Mysteries**
Set in the 1960's this series follows the lives of Ron De Cenza and his best pal, Bob Wentz as they are joined by Susan Liguri in solving crimes of murder and mysteries.

Murder in the Abbey: The only son of an Italian-American family announces that he wants to become a priest much to their horror. He is sent to a Latin School at a remote Abbey in Wisconsin along with his best pal. Once there, he finds himself to be ogled by one of the Monks, saving the life of another Monk, having his vocation tested by a girl in the gift shop and becoming the prime suspect in a murder.

Murder at the World's Fair: Ron De Cenza, Bob Wentz and the seminarians of the Abbey School are sent to New York City to act as guides for the Vatican Pavillion where Michelangelo's Pieta will be on display. Susan Liguri and her mother are also going to set up the Papal gift shop. They become involved with a traumatized artist who is being hunted by a mob boss who seeks to pull off the heist of the century.

Murder in the Vatican:
Ron and Bob are sent to the Apostolic College in Rome. They witness a violent attack on the banks of the Tiber River and are drawn into political intrigue, murder and theft of Vatican treasures along with Susan and Ron's sister Jan who have come to Rome to study at the University.

Murder in Mellifont:
Ron, Bob, Susan and Jan are joined by their friends from Italy and Professor Pettigrew of Oxford University on a research expedition during which love blossoms and which takes them to the Medieval ruins of Mellifont Abbey where they witness the murder of a Woman in Black who dies in the arms of Ron De Cenza.

Murder on Capri:
Seven friends begin a holiday on the romantic Isle of Capri which becomes a nightmare when Ron De Cenza, Bob Wentz and Susan Liguri discover the naked body of a dead man in the famous Blue Grotto which leads them to a discovery about the legend of Joseph Bonaparte, once the King of Naples and King of Spain and brother to Napoleon.

Murder at Point Breeze:
Ron De Cenza and his friends continue their quest to solve the mystery of the Joseph Bonaparte legend by leaving Switzerland and going to Lake Bonaparte New York and Point Breeze estate in Bordentown New Jersey to seek the truth of the hidden treasure of Joseph Bonaparte only to find bodies instead.

Author's Statement
Bringing to life fictional and historical characters and using actual historical events and eras, as well as inventing scenarios for them to breathe life into the tale, has been my joy. I hope that readers of my work will detect that spark of love which binds the stories together and the joy in which I present them.

Joseph Bonaparte outside his mansion in Bordentown, c1820

CPSIA information can be obtained
at www.ICGtesting.com
Printed in the USA
BVHW050237261022
650294BV00001B/6